TALLAHATCHIE
TIMEBOMB

AND OTHER STORIES

David Lister

Tallahatchie Timebomb

And Other Stories

★★Corps du Chien Books ★★

Stories first published separately in Great Britain in 2010 on Kindle by
the Author
First Anthology published in 2016

God Damn a Potato
Copyright © David Lister 1993

Tallahatchie Timebomb & The Shepherd
Copyright © David Lister 2009

Corps du Chien Books
36 Mandeville Road
Potters Bar
EN6 5LQ
UK

Main cover image by Author
© David Lister
Cover Design by Cover Creator

ISBN 978-0-992904586

Contents

For

Veronica Kelly
First Guardian of Worldwide Listerature

Tallahatchie
Timebomb

Part One: From a Privileged Viewpoint

The Loose Photograph & Some Letters

Subject: Bobby Lee McDonald
Title (written in ballpoint pen on the reverse): Last picture of Bobby
Lee. Dressed up for Church, June 1ˢᵗ, 1958.
Description: A colour portrait, 3 x 5 inches, seventeen-year-old
Bobby Lee is wearing his Sunday suit. His hands are in his pockets
and he smiles widely while leaning up against a white 1950 Chevrolet
sedan.

***

Colin wasn't a McAllister. Neither was the murdered young
man whose body was thrown off that bridge, but who's to
gainsay the lyrics of the old song? Shall we stick with the
misnomers and preserve the privacy of decent people, or
shall we name names? Perhaps a compromise, but at the
same time let's put paid to the long held belief that Billy Joe
McAllister jumped off the Tallahatchie Bridge.

Colin (who we'll say was a McDonald and not a
McAllister) discovered that he was first cousins with Billy
Joe (who we'll call Bobby Lee – nudge, nudge, wink, wink),
on a Sunday afternoon a fortnight after his father's funeral.
He had not attended the funeral for three reasons: Colin
and his mother had been estranged from Sam McDonald
and they were far from close; secondly, Sam was buried in
Oxford, Mississippi while Colin lived in a north London
suburb, and perhaps most salient of all, neither Colin nor
his mother Rose had any idea Sam had died until the
package came.

It arrived in a Jiffy Bag and comprised an album, a few
pieces of correspondence, and one smaller padded
envelope of which Colin was not initially made aware. It
had been addressed to Rose but Colin collected it from the
Post Office and paid the VAT and handling fee with as

11

much politeness and alacrity as he could muster for what he saw as legalised theft.

'Here's a nice picture of your cousin, Bobby Lee,' Rose said. 'Such a good looking young man.' She sighed sadly while staring into the space above the TV as if his ghost might be standing there. 'I never told you, dear, but he was almost definitely the inspiration for that song about Billy Joe McAllister jumping off the Tallahatchie Bridge.'

'You're joking,' Colin said and then, incredulity smudging the edges, 'You *are* joking, aren't you Mum?' Colin knew he had a cousin who had died young and he'd even seen photos, but it was that connection with the song of which he had been completely oblivious.

Rose held a steady eye. She was plainly not joking.

'Blimey, Mum! That's crazy. It's just an old song.'

It wasn't crazy. And it was a lot more than just a song. Colin was staggered as certainty hit him between the eyes although he couldn't tell who'd thrown it. He was excited, appalled and intrigued at the same time: excited by his connection to someone almost famous, albeit fictional as far as the world was concerned; appalled that his cousin had committed suicide and intrigued that there might actually be an explanation for his actions that were not given in the song.

'You always told me Bobby Lee had died in a drowning accident, nothing about him jumping.'

Rose took the knitted tea-cosy off the pot and poured a steaming mug for her son. 'Well, dear, we were hardly going to go into details when you were a little boy, and the subject hasn't cropped up since … Lewis.'

The pain was as brief as it was intense; Colin covered it up well. 'Mother, I'm 42-years-old. I've been grown up for a long time.'

'Nevertheless …'

'And Bobby Lee would have been … what?' Colin added Bobby Lee's seventeen years to his own age and took off two. He had been two when Bobby Lee died and had the shadow of a memory of meeting him 'He'd be 56 or 57 if he'd not drowned, or jumped. What a waste.'

'He was a March baby, so he would have been 57.'

'Does anyone know why he did it?'

If anyone was likely to have a clue it was Aunt Hettie. She was still alive but unfortunately the families had lost touch. For several years after Rose and Sam divorced, Rose and Hettie kept up the Christmas card exchange but even that died out in the end.

Rose took a sip of her tea and rearranged the newspapers on the footstool. 'There was a girl. You have to understand, things were very different in those days, here in England let alone in the Mississippi Delta. We had our suspicions, but ...' She lifted an envelope from between the pages of the book that was her current bedtime reading. 'If this letter is to be believed, Bobby Lee didn't jump at all.'

'God, he got her pregnant? It wasn't a ... Jesus Christ it wasn't a *baby* they threw off the bridge, was it?'

'Don't be ridiculous! And please don't take the Lord's name in vain.'

Colin swallowed and took the rebuke like a little boy until the instant of shame mutated into indignation. He didn't show it.

'If Beth was pregnant when Bobby Lee jumped, she certainly wasn't far enough gone to show, and she had the good grace to leave town before anybody's suspicions could be confirmed. As for what they threw off the bridge, I've always suspected it was an engagement ring. It was an old southern tradition at the time. If you broke off an engagement, you threw the ring into a river.'

Colin pictured the scene. 'It all adds up. Miss Beth ...?'

'Beth Monroe.'

'She breaks off the engagement, Bobby Lee is heartbroken, and he jumps.'

'And you a professional researcher. You should be ashamed of yourself, settling for an explanation before you've examined the evidence.'

'I was merely –'

Rose interrupted by holding out the letter in its faded and worn out envelope, flapping it impatiently.

Colin took it and looked at the stamp. It was a five cents stamp executed in shades of green and it showed a backwoodsman cradling a Brown Bess flintlock in his arms; Colin thought the postmark would be discernable with the help of a magnifying glass. He sang under his breath. *'Davy ... Davy Crockett. King of the wild frontier.'*

'What are you blithering on about now?' Rose said leaning forward and cupping a hand to her ear.

'The stamp's Davy Crockett. It reminded me of the song, that's all.'

'Well never mind that, and no need to shout. Just open the letter and see what it says.'

Colin slipped the letter out. It was worn thin and felt so frail to the touch that he wondered if it would fall apart. He'd handled medieval documents with more body than this.

Carefully unfolding the letter, he read.

'December 5th, 1967

Dear Mr McDonald,

It's getting on for ten years since Bobby Lee jumped off of the new bridge and now the bridge is showing rust in places. A lot of water, and a lot of time has slipped under it and wouldn't you think that a body's sad memories would wash clean or at least fade some? Not mine, sir, because for all them years I have been keeping something inside of me and it don't heal, just festers and hurts me now just as bad as it ever did, maybe even worse for the longer goes by the more of a damned coward I feel for keeping quiet.

I sat here now for a whole half of an hour and the words are not coming easy. They are not easy to write and I believe they will be less easy for you to read, Bobby Lee being yours and all and none of my own, but I must come out with it, plain and simple. Some days before Bobby Lee was found in the water a ways downstream from the bridge, I saw something truly awful and what I saw places me in the position where I can say with sure certainty there's no truth in the damned lie that he jumped. That young man was dead before he came within sniffing distance of the Tallahatchie River.

Now certain people have passed on I have at last got enough brave about me to tell what I saw, but with certain other people still walking the green earth and sucking wind, my brave is not so great that I can put everything in a letter. To mention names in a letter might be the ruin of me.

You know where I live, Mr McDonald, or if you don't you can easy find out. If you give a damn and love the truth more than any comfort lies may bring, come see me any time and we will talk. If you would rather we left those muddy waters a settling, then pass me by and my story will accompany me to my grave even though the weight of it is hard to endure and Bobby Lee's ghost won't leave me be not for a moment.

I hope you will choose to hear me not least of all because Bobby Lee won't lie quiet until the truth be out. He was a fine young man and would have grown up to be somebody but that was all stole away from him and for these past years I have been without the courage to speak. Now I'm ready.

Yours most truly,

Harrison Bardwell.'

Colin folded the letter with even more care than he'd opened it and slid it reverently back inside the envelope. 'Jesus,' he said, quietly and without realising it.

'I knew it!' Rose forgot to admonish her son for another infringement of her religious sensibilities. 'You and your ridiculous Caesarion Complex. Am I right in assuming your interest has been peaked?'

Of course she was right. Bobby Lee McDonald ticked all the boxes: he had died in his teenage years – always sad but never the deciding factor; there was a mystery surrounding his death, and most important of all, there was now evidence that his death involved a cover-up of some kind. And on this occasion there was room for a brand new never-been-seen-before box that came in ready-checked: Bobby Lee McDonald was Colin's own blood.

Colin's wife referred to it as DBS – Dead Boy Syndrome – but it was Colin himself who coined the phrase Caesarion Complex. He had an interest in young men: dead young men; specifically young men whose potential had been ripped away in mysterious circumstances, or those involving unfair process. Accidental deaths and murders were bad and always drew Colin's sympathy, but there would never be an end to that kind of untimely demise. To really grab Colin's attention the death had to involve historical cover-up, unfair execution, or murder for the sake of dynastic self-preservation. Julius Caesar's seventeen-year-old son by Cleopatra fit the mould exactly, hence Colin adopted the boy's nickname when casting around for a tongue-in-cheek title for his self-acknowledged interest.

When Colin was young he liked to speculate about the changes in history that would spring from the survival of his subjects and often wrote short stories about them. Later he turned from fiction to research; now he almost had enough for a decent-sized book that would include chapters on Tutankhamen, Emperor Hadrian's friend Antinous, Arthur of Brittany, the two Princes in the Tower, Thomas Aikenhead, several young men who had been shot at dawn for leaving the trenches during the First World War and a handful of others who collectively spanned the years between ancient history and almost up to present day.

Early in their marriage Miranda had speculated as to her husband's obsession and they had argued. It was an unusual *interest* and far from an *obsession*. Yes, he researched each

16

case thoroughly. Of course he was single-minded and left no stone unturned, but for all that he did not see it as deserving of the dark appellation 'obsession', nor did her misnomer – DBS – come anywhere close to an accurate label.

Colin's argument had walls of granite, but its foundations rested in sand. Colin new exactly why he had a Caesarion Complex. It came of too much empathy, and a dark secret that, like Harrison Bardwell's knowledge of Bobby Lee's death, was probably doomed to go to the grave without ever seeing the light of day.

'Who's Harrison Bardwell?' Colin asked after surfacing from a sea of turbulent thoughts.

'Back in the land of the living, are we dear? I thought for one moment we were having a *petit mal*.'

'Mother!' A warning across the bows: 'Harrison Bardwell?'

'Haven't the foggiest, dear. We didn't live with your cousin's family, just visited occasionally, so I have few memories of their neighbours and acquaintances. Our home was in Hattiesburg and Bobby Lee lived slap-bang in the middle of the Delta. It's a wonder the boy didn't have webbed feet.'

Colin lifted the album and sniffed, taking in the musty odour of ages past. He rested the book on his lap and turned the pages carefully. The pages were black and thick but nonetheless fragile, and each photo was attached by sticky-backed corner brackets, some of which had fallen away. Most of the photos were family snaps and not that interesting and anyway, he'd seen copies of them before. Only seven in addition to the loose one of Bobby Lee in his Sunday suit were new to him, and he meant to study them in detail, if Mother would let him take the album home for a few days. On first sight, each new photograph contained a potential clue, either in the image or the appended title, and taken together they gave a snapshot history of Bobby Lee's short life.

'Was this all that came?' Colin asked, suddenly wondering why an old photo album had cost so much in import fees. 'Just the album?'

'Well, there was a letter from the executor of your father's will, and something a little more personal, which knowing you, I think it is safe to say you will cherish out of all proportion to its true value.'

Colin felt the same thrill that he remembered having as a boy at Christmas time in the years before Lewis was killed, the same thrill he still had on rare occasions when his research uncovered a fact that confirmed a theory. He felt the corners of his mouth turn up.

'Hold in your enthusiasm for a moment and read the executor's letter first.'

It was from a gentleman named Brewster Roebuck. It was short and to the point. Sam McDonald had appointed him as executor and asked him to send his son and ex-wife a small token, there being precious little in the way of large tokens or anything of any real value that he wasn't obliged to leave to his second wife. There were, apparently, no half-siblings for Colin to discover, or at least none were mentioned in the letter, but it did bear one other feature of particular interest and that was the address shown top right: Mr Roebuck's home was at Choctaw Ridge and so that, if nothing else, was a link to the old song.

Rose judged perfectly, and handed over the little padded envelope at the precise moment when Colin had finished reading Mr Roebuck's business-like letter.

Colin took the envelope tingling with anticipation. Rose had already used the letter-opener so the flap was slit. He squeezed the sides and the envelope opened like a mouth. Inside was a fold of paper and something shiny. He tipped the shiny object into his palm. It was a ring, on a dirty piece of string, at once recognisable as Masonic from the engraved compass, square and quadrant design containing the little letter G at the centre. The initials P and H flanked the symbol. It was a simple 10mm flat band of gold with the engraved symbol, crude if not unclear. Colin turned it over and checked the inner surface for any marks. There were none, not even hallmarks. He began to pick at the knot so he could remove the string but Rose quickly interjected.

'You might want to read the note before you discard the string.'

Colin set the ring down in the centre of the open album and fished out the note. It was handwritten in fountain pen on the back of a flyer advertising gardening services. The address for the gardener was in Oxford, Mississippi, the city where Sam had died. The florid hand was at odds with the informal message.

Hi there Rose,

Colin might like to have this ring. I had it from Hettie on Bobby Lee's passing. She said to give it to Colin when he was old enough to appreciate it but I guess it slipped my mind all these years. It was around Bobby Lee's neck the day he was dragged out of the river. Too big for any of his fingers I guess. Hettie was at a loss as to where he got it but wanted Colin to have something of his. I doubt it is worth a whole lot but it was Bobby Lee's and I have a feeling Colin would appreciate something of his cousin's. I'll always remember that day Bobby Lee dandled Colin on his knee and you said that you had a feeling they would grow up close. Maybe you should tell Colin about Bobby Lee jumping if you haven't already.

With some happy and some sad memories of old times, best regards,

Sam.'

Colin's eyes stung and his nose tingled but he got a hold of himself. At first he thought the emotion came from realising, for the first time, that his father knew something important about him, or that a cold tendril reached out for

19

him from that dark place of shame and terror, but it was neither. Rather, he felt an immediate connection to his cousin through the ring, and an intimacy with his death. Perhaps the brown stain on the string was dried mud from the Tallahatchie River. For an instant it was as if Colin felt his cousin's ghost-like presence and it called out for him to discover the truth. Never before had he had such a tangible link with one of his research subjects, and there wasn't the faintest doubt, Bobby Lee was now such a subject.

'So Colin, when should Miranda expect you to go swanning off to the good old Delta then?'

Colin shrugged. 'It's a possibility, but there's a lot of groundwork to do first.' He spoke without taking his eyes off the ring and his words forced themselves out through a jumble of thoughts that were rushing to parade and lining up for inspection: death certificate, coroners report, local newspaper stories, contact addresses for potential witnesses. 'Can I borrow the album for a couple of days?'

'You may.' Rose emphasised the last word, grammar being another of her precious children for whom she would invariably rush to the defence. Colin had long ago given up the notion that his mother would ever treat him as an adult. 'Keep it if you like.'

Colin drove the short distance home with the album filling the passenger seat with as much presence as a living person. He even spoke to it a couple of times, asking what secrets were hidden behind the images within. Arriving home to an empty house – Miranda was still at work, the children at school – he kicked off his shoes and changed out of his work suit and put the kettle on. His usual routine for a new subject was to take a new hardback notebook, write his subject's name on the front page and then jot down a list of the initial steps necessary to further his research. This time, he had an album to examine, but even before that there was something else.

Colin took Bobby Lee's ring from his pocket and carefully unpicked the knot. He put the string into his trinket box to share space with his Granddad Grayson's war medals, his father's US Army Military Intelligence collar pins and small collection of other treasures. And then he tried Bobby Lee's ring on various fingers until it slid over the knuckle of his right ring-finger where it was a perfect fit. A tingle shot up his whole arm as he slid it home and he smiled, knowing that he would never voluntarily remove it again.

Settling down at his study desk with his tea on the floor beside him and the keyboard pushed back to make room for the album, he slowly opened it, a gesture that signified the very beginning of a new adventure. This wasn't going to be research confined to dusty archives and clinical cyberspace, although that is how he would spend the early days: he anticipated travel and meeting new people and conducting interviews. He did not anticipate deliberate obstruction, threats and personal danger but even if he had, such was his determination to find the truth, he would have steamed ahead regardless. He had his own dark secret to consider, and with every new subject came the hope that his past would make sense. The young men he studied had all died young, gone forever like his big brother Lewis. When Lewis had died something in Colin died too; sometimes he felt as if he were an empty shell who went through the motions of life, just as dead as his elder brother. He was rapidly approaching middle age, and he wanted to live, and perhaps Bobby Lee would teach him how. If he could only bring old secrets to the light of day, maybe, just maybe, his own secret would wither and die.

He took a deep breath, adjusted his glasses and looked down at the first photo. 'Okay Bobby Lee McDonald, what can you tell me?'

The Album

Photo # 1

Subject: Sam McDonald and Joe Paolini
Title: Big Ben and the English Parliament buildings, 1944.
Description: A colour shot. Sam and Joe wear the uniforms of enlisted men in the US Army. They stand on a bridge against a background of the Houses of Parliament.

***

No sooner had the shutter fallen than the distant pulsating drone of a doodlebug stamped its imperative upon a hot, summer afternoon. Some people crossing Westminster Bridge stopped and peered downstream, trying to spot the mechanical invader; others feigned indifference and carried on, life as usual and Sam McDonald brought a hand to his temple and pressed hard. Damned V-bombs had the same effect on him as an impending thunderstorm in the Delta; they made his head ache.

Joe Paolini took off his forage cap and with one fist planted pugnaciously on his hip dared the bomb, if it had the guts, to try blow him off the bridge. He was an impulse away from shaking his free fist and if that bomb had come within striking distance he would have ripped out its gyroscope with his teeth. Joe reminded Sam a lot of his brother Nate: usually as nice as pie but with one mother of a temper if a person hit the right spot.

Master-Sergeant Bill Hendon handed Sam's camera back and suggested it was time to be heading for home.

'There it is!' Joe cried pointing at a dot in the distance. The engine noise was out of all proportion to its size. 'Kraut bastards!'

'Time to saddle-up, guys,' Hendon said. 'We'll be a whole lot safer on the underground system.'

Sam turned to follow Hendon when the doodlebug's engine cut. Everyone froze and waited to see where it would fall and all with one shared thought. *Let it be somewhere else.* Birds stopped singing and the Thames no longer flowed below. The bomb was a menacing black bird now, pot-bellied and stubby winged; a fearsome silhouette, plummeting from the sky of brilliant blue. It soon dipped below the battered wounded skyline, and then came the crump followed by the minuscule trembling of the bridge underfoot. Sam heard, or imagined he heard, the distant, clattering tumble of masonry. He wondered if children were dying, and thanked the Good Lord that his little nephew Bobby Lee was safe at home in Greenwood.

An elderly man in a cloth cap looked back over his shoulder and then continued pushing his bike. 'Unusual for them to come over in daylight,' he said. 'Somewhere off the Waterloo Road I should say,' he carried on addressing Sam in what Sam supposed to be a cockney accent.

'You don't say?' Sam knew there had been a Battle of Waterloo but had no idea where the Waterloo Road might be.

'Yes,' continued the man as if they were old acquaintances. 'Probably not a lot further down than Baylis if you want my opinion.'

'Too close for comfort, sir, wherever it might have landed.'

The Brit took one last look over his shoulder before mounting up and riding off without another word, a stranger once again.

'Move it, guys!' Hendon called. 'I didn't hear the all-clear yet, so there's like to be more of them.'

The three soldiers crossed back to the south bank and made their way to the tube station against a tide of pedestrians. Fifteen more minutes and the tube station was in sight. A fire engine swept around the entrance, bell ringing and elderly tin-helmeted firemen hanging on for dear life. Sam noticed the truck was speeding down Baylis Road towards a plume of black smoke.

'Looks like the old guy was right on the button,' Sam said, but Joe and Hendon were already crowding the tube station entrance, so Sam ran to catch up.

'Lower Marsh got hit,' the uniformed lift operator said, raising his eyebrows and shaking his head. 'Lucky it's not a market day. God knows how many it would have copped for.'

The locals present clucked in agreement.

'Was it bad?' Sam asked, directing his eyes up and in the general direction of the detonation.

'A terrace of houses flattened according to the last bloke I took down. No word on casualties but there's bound to be a few.'

Sam nodded sympathetically as the lift reached base. Joe Paolini repeated *Kraut bastards* under his breath as if it were a private litany.

They found seats in the first train but when they changed lines it was standing room only. Sam, Joe and the master-sergeant exchanged barrack-room gossip until Sam spotted a young lady sitting half-way down the aisle. She had her back to the window and was reading a paperback. And she was the most beautiful girl Sam had ever seen. From that moment on, Joe and Hendon might well have continued their conversation without him, or they might have shut up and concentrated on reading the advertisements; Sam really couldn't have said.

'Hey Sam,' Hendon said swatting his shoulder with a forage cap. 'You deaf? We're rolling in to our stop!'

'He ain't deaf, Sarge,' Joe said. 'More like smitten.'

Sam caught his colleagues exchanging a knowing look, and then Joe nudged him with his elbow. 'Not due back at base until supper time,' Joe said, and he winked. Joe and Master-Sergeant Hendon and a whole regiment of other people got off, and suddenly the seat opposite the young lady was free. Sam didn't remember crossing the distance along the aisle, nor did he quite recall sitting down. He would even be hard-pressed to say how long he sat gazing across the aisle, waiting for this vision in a summer dress and veiled hat to look up from her book.

And then when she did, Sam was too discombobulated to do more that smile, like a goofy teenager. The girl smiled back and then returned to her book with, Sam felt sure, the hint of a blush. Next time he'd be ready for her with a line so dazzling she could not ignore him.

'Like a stick of gum, Ma'am?' Sam asked when the girl next cast a nervous eye towards him. *Of all the dern fool things to say!*

'Oh, yes please,' she said smiling shyly while she drew the fine black netting from her face.

'I'll save it for later.' She took the gum and put it into her purse.

And then Sam sat smiling, his head as empty as a cotton gin in June, and waited in vain for his muse.

'That's a nice badge,' the young lady said pointing to his collar. 'A sword in a … flower?'

'I don't rightly know what it's supposed to be ma'am,' Sam said fingering the corps pin. 'It's the emblem for Military Intelligence,' he said feeling he had a dearth of any kind of intelligence right now, military or otherwise.

'Rose, please. Call me Rose,' the young lady said and laughed lightly. Sam thought it sounded like the chiming of tiny bells.

He introduced himself and they leant forwards over the aisle of no-man's-land to shake hands.

'That's a real pretty name, Rose, for a real pretty lady.' *Oh jeez, man, that is so corny.* Sam could feel the heat spread up from under his collar and wondered if his ears were the beacons they seemed to be. In all his 23 years he had never said anything so outrageously embarrassing.

'Military Intelligence? That must be exciting.'

Phew! Off the hook! 'Well ma'am … Rose … it sounds a mite more impressive than it deserves to be. I'm just a driver is all.' He thought it too early to mention he often drove secretive looking men dressed in suits who worked for the Office of Strategic Services. He asked no questions.

They spoke about the weather, about missing Mom's pecan pie or how the Red Sox were doing.

Sam and Rose chatted about every subject under the sun and before he knew it Rose was rising and getting ready to say goodbye. 'Parson's Green,' she said. 'My stop. It's been lovely …'

'Rose, you have to let me walk you home.'

'Oh no, I wouldn't dream of it … unless you're sure.'

Sam was sure.

They made it to Rose's house through scurrying ARP wardens, ambulances, more fire trucks and at least two more doodlebugs landing close enough to shake the earth and raise the dust. Today they were being nothing if not persistent.

Rose insisted Sam stayed for a cup of tea and to meet her parents, and Mr and Mrs Grayson were ever so thankful that he had taken the trouble to escort their daughter home through one of the nastiest raids of recent weeks. 'Almost as bad as the blitz,' Albert Grayson had said.

By the time Sam left for base he was as full of carrot-cake as the ration-cards would allow and overflowing with coffee made from roasted dandelion tubers. More importantly he was well-in with the Grayson family and had a date to see Rose again. He stood on the platform at Parson's Green and studied the map for the best route back to base. Pulling out his pack of gum he smiled.

'Thank you, Mr Wrigley. That's one I owe you.'

Photo # 2

Subject: Rose Grayson
Title: Rose sings during an air raid.
Description: Black and white portrait. Eighteen-year-old Rose looks older with the makeup. She holds a pose as she delivers the lines of a song. She is in evening dress and sports elbow-length white gloves.

***

The soldiers cheered and wolf-whistled as they passed the photo around and Sam made futile snatches at it as it was passed from hand to hand. He only managed to secure it when the Chevy 3-ton truck hit a monster bump and his colleagues were too busy rearranging themselves on the bench seats to keep a grip on it.

Joe Paolini cussed the driver who wondered if Joe could do any better driving through town in the blackout when the only lights visible were up in the sky and shooting out the back of V-Ones.

'Let me see that, Sam,' Master-Sergeant Hendon said, more of an order than a request. 'Don't worry. I won't let the wolves get it.'

The boys put up a round of hoots and mock-protests and Joe roughed up Sam's hair.

'You say you're engaged to get married to this fine looking woman?'

Sam had no time to answer before a bomb landed a few hundred yards up the road. The whole truck rocked and the driver threw on the anchors while letting out the cry 'Shit!' in a two-syllable expletive that gave away his southern roots.

'We need to get out of this,' Hendon shouted. 'Anyone have any ideas?'

'Well,' Sam retrieved the picture of his intended for the second time in two minutes. 'I know a place we can go, if they'll let us in.'

'Keep it to yourself, why don't you,' Joe called from the back end.

'We're a couple of blocks away from Mornington Crescent. There's a lift down to the deep shelter, and I might just have us a ticket to get down there.'

'What are you waiting for McDonald? Get your ass up front and tell the driver which way to go.'

***

Fifty-year-old Albert Grayson had his face made up to look like he was an octogenarian. He wore a wing-collar and bow tie and held his left eye tight to stop the monocle falling out.

He hurried down the long tunnel with its sides sectioned off and curtained to give people a little privacy and smiled affably and all the people who recognised him from the show and called out greetings. At last, he came to the few feet of tunnel that was his little space in the air raid shelter, deep under the streets of Camden.

He wrapped at the curtain. 'Are you decent, Rose?'

'Yes, Dad. Come on in.' Rose drew the curtain aside. 'Oh, whatever is the matter?' she asked, and stopped applying her lipstick.

'Don hasn't turned up yet and he's due on in five minutes. We'll have to reshuffle the bill, put your monologue up next and then if you can do your number with *The Sunrays* ...'

'I haven't got time,' Rose said as she grabbed the compact-mirror and had at it with the powder puff.

'Of course you have. You look fine, now leave all that and get your skates on.'

'Can't you put *Those Cockney Kids* up first?'

'Little Micky's not here either,' Albert said as he grabbed Rose's arm and half dragged her back up the tunnel. Rose's high-heels echoed before her like a herald and people stick their heads out of curtains and cheered.

They got to the intersection where the theatre had been rigged up and the players were gathered, but before Albert could begin directions the Station Master collared him.

'Albert Grayson?' the portly man in the blue uniform asked.

Albert confirmed his identity.

'There's a truckload of GIs up on the station level. One says he knows you and can they come down here? I says to him the deep shelter's only for those what's been bombed out and he says he knows and they won't be stopping just visiting.'

'Sam McDonald?'

'That's him!'

Albert said it was fine for them to visit and then organised some extra programmes for them. 'Let Sam in on the nod, but charge the others a shilling a head,' he told the admissions boy.

'Slight change in the order of the bill,' Albert called to the assembled players,' and then he began to reorganise.

They were only a few minutes late when the admissions boy – who was now the curtain boy and chief lighting technician – pulled the string and revealed the players to whistles, cheers, good-natured banter and much applause.

Albert Grayson held up his hands and the crowd settled down. '*The Admirable Creightons* would like to welcome you all to their Grand Variety Concert.'

The crowd were off again, with as much gusto as if they were at the London Palladium, and now they were joined by fifteen US soldiers who added their enthusiasm as they squeezed in to the back seats.

Rose started with her *Baby Bill* monologue and instead of the usual polite applause she received a standing ovation, with Sam McDonald first up on his feet and all his friends following. Their infectious if a little raucous bravos could hardly be ignored, so the resident house tried to drown them out, not wishing to be outdone by a bunch of yanks. It was the best reception Rose had ever had, and as the evening progressed, one to be repeated often and each time with more volume.

Fred, the light baritone, was well received for his repertoire and the comedy sketch went down a treat. Albert's ventriloquist turn and his *Talking String* act on the one-string fiddle brought the house down – which is exactly what you need in an air raid shelter. By the end of the evening, the ears of players and audience alike were buzzing and the mood was exaggeratedly high. While the bombs had fallen above, everybody had a good time and for a little while, everyone forgot about the war.

The Sunrays closed the night with a stirring rendition of *God Save the King* and everyone stood to attention, even the American's who each held a hand over his heart and thought of a different red-white-and-blue.

'You were wonderful, Hon,' Sam said and he gathered Rose up into an embrace. 'And Mr Grayson, you made that phono-fiddle sound just like my Uncle Howie, a whining and a moaning like his life depended on it.'

'Just a bit of fun,' Albert insisted, never one who knew how to take a compliment.

The American boys stayed for tea, which was rustled up from somewhere, and they supplied biscuits, sugar, jam and various items that were on ration but that didn't seem to affect the GIs, and it was getting on for bedtime by the time they left. Rose and Sam had no time to be alone together.

Then while Sam and Albert spoke about the state of the war, Joe Paolini chatted with Rose about when she and Sam would wed and what they would do after the war.

'Go back to live on Sam's ranch in Mississippi, you say?'

'Yes, Joe. It all sounds so lovely, I can hardly wait. Sam says once we settle we can send for Mum and Dad and there's enough land to build them a little place next door.'

Joe frowned slightly. 'Don't have many ranches in the Delta.'

Rose rolled her eyes. 'Farm, ranch. I get mixed up.'

Joe smiled again, not wishing to burst Rose's bubble.

Later, when all the goodbyes had been said, Joe sidled up to Sam as the lift was ascending. 'Reckon the first thing you should do, Sam, is tell that little lady the difference between a planter and a tenant-farmer, else she's going to be one disappointed wife the moment she sets eyes on your place. A shack and an old hog don't make a ranch nor hardly even a farm.'

Photo # 3

Subject: Nate, Sam and Bobby Lee McDonald
Title (written in white ink on the black album folio): BR helping Papa and Uncle Sam. Itta Bena, Mississippi, spring 1947.
Description: Black and white 3x3 inch snapshot of Nate and Sam McDonald working under the hood of a 1935 Ford Pickup while five-year-old Bobby Lee holds up a wrench.

***

Nate stood up straight, stretched the kink out of his back and mopped his brow with a brilliant white hanky.

'If you have quit fooling with that camera, woman, maybe you could make yourself useful and bring us something cool to drink.'

Hettie McDonald took the rebuke to heart and hurried into the house without a word. As she prepared a pitcher of lemonade she recalled the trouble one of her earlier shots had caused. Bobby Lee and that sweet little Negro boy playing at the edge of the creek and both as naked as jaybirds: now who could take offence at that, the encapsulation of childhood innocence? Mr Jackson for one, the man who developed the film: he came to the house in his Sunday suit with a face like he was bringing news of a death. Thank goodness he was an acquaintance of Nate's and on friendly terms, otherwise the scandal would have spread all through town and the consequences might have been upside of dire. It was times like this Hettie longed for her childhood home in Nantucket and wished she never come south. The nudity didn't rile Jackson a tad, but a white boy playing with a "Nigro" gave him a severe case of sour stomach that could not be tolerated.

Nate wrote off the lack of proper decorum by blaming it on Hettie's Quaker ways. Jackson left happy, just as soon as the offending photo and the negative had been destroyed. He'd raised his hat and called her ma'am but he couldn't hide the contempt in his eyes.

Hettie slammed the pitcher down and some lemonade slopped out onto the kitchen table. That extra spoonful of

31

sugar, she tipped right back into the bowl; he could have his drink sour, to fit his mood, and serves him right!

Dabbing the jug on her apron, she put on a smile and headed back to the men and as she did she whispered to herself. 'From now on I'm going to develop my own film, Mr High-and-Mighty-Jackson!'

***

Bobby Lee hated it when Papa was mean to Mama and now he felt sulky. He didn't want to help Papa and Uncle Sam any more and he dropped the wrench onto the grass. He was cleverer than Papa knew because Papa thought he didn't understand his subtle cruelties, but he did. Wasn't it always the way of adults to underestimate the understanding of little children?

'Pick up that wrench, Bobby Lee.'

Bobby Lee glowered. And he rocked his weight from one foot to another; weighing left, Papa will spank me; weighing right, Papa will let it ride.

'Won't,' Bobby Lee said and his bottom lip stuck out all of its own without him telling it to. He watched Papa from under lowered eyelids. He couldn't outrun Papa if he came to tan his hide, but he would have to try. It was one of the rules.

Papa came towards him, slowly, not overly angry looking. He bent down and picked up the wrench. For a moment Bobby Lee thought Papa was going to hit him with it and he reasoned how that would surely hurt a fearsome lot.

But Papa didn't hit him, with the wrench or anything else. 'Well, I reckon you've grown a little tired. Thank you for helping me up until now. Best you scoot out of the sun and get cool.'

Bobby Lee smiled. The sulks fled and he couldn't remember why he had them in the first place. He turned and ran for the house reaching the screen door just as Mama came out with the tray of drinks. Papa and Uncle Sam exchanged words and set to laughing and Mama told him to go inside and she'd fix him his own glass of lemonade.

She was back inside soon and stirred a spoonful of sugar into Bobby Lee's drink and told him to sit up at the table to drink it and that he could draw if he liked. He said he would and she found the crayons and some paper, but when it was spread out over the table he found he didn't really want to draw.

He gulped his drink and it seemed to come out again all through his skin. It was a hot day and the grasshoppers sounded straight through the walls and his head hurt a bit. Not real pain, but a kind of insistent pressure that made him feel listless. While Mama took a broom to the pump house, Bobby Lee found a cool spot under Mamma and Papa's bed and he crawled under feeling bored, but more tired than bored and after a moment or two of playing Itsy-Bitsy Spider with his fingers he lay quiet and fell asleep.

He would never know the trouble that nap would cause. The neighbours came out to help look for him and the Negroes from the farm next door but nobody could find Bobby Lee. Mama was panicking and Papa stopped saying he'd turn up in a moment and old Uncle Abe waded out into the lake and swirled around the muddy water with a hoe but still nobody could find Bobby Lee. They called in the sheriff while he slept on in dreamless oblivion until he found himself being gently shaken away.

'Why there you are, Bobby Lee,' Deputy Sheriff Davidson said. Bobby Lee wondered if he was dreaming because he couldn't think of a reason for the deputy being in his parent's bedroom, and then Mama dragged him out crying and hugging him and Papa sat heavily on the bed and shook his head and then everyone was laughing, and without knowing why, Bobby Lee felt he was the centre of it all.

Papa stood up and took his hand and he saw it in Papa's eyes that he loved him. Papa led him out and the yard was full of folks who cheered and clapped, and Papa thanked them for there neighbourliness and apologised for putting

33

them out. And there over by the gate were Lucien's folks and neighbours and Papa looked at them and nodded. Abe Harris, Lucien's Grandpa, he nodded back and then they began to melt away as if the sun had caught them out.

'Hello Mr Harris!' Bobby Lee called out. Abe looked up but did not reply or even act as if he'd heard. His head dropped and he shuffled away all the more quickly, and some of the white folk chuckled and Mrs Jackson frowned as if Bobby Lee had made a rude noise in Church.

'Can I go play with Lucien, Papa?'

Papa's gripped tightened and it hurt. 'Not right now, son. It's been a long day and Mama will be fixing supper soon. Time to wash up.'

Maybe it was something to do with all those folks who were called out to help look for him. Maybe Mr Harris was cross with him, because he was never given permission to play with Lucien again. But Lucien was his friend and the only other boy anywhere near who was close to his own age, so Bobby Lee learnt how to be deceitful and although he knew it was a sin to tell lies, he found ways of meeting up with Lucien and their friendship grew and was a secret between the two of them, because just as much as it seemed Papa didn't want him to see Lucien, Grandpa Abe didn't want Lucien seeing Bobby Lee.

Most of the time grown ups got their own way, but in this instant, the children were the victors.

Photo # 4

Subject: Tom Pike, Beth Monroe and Bobby Lee McDonald
Title (written in ballpoint pen on the lower border under each child respectively): Mickey, Froggy and Buckwheat (Characters from a series of children's movies).
Description: The three children, Tom about ten or eleven and the others a little younger, stand in front of a small picture house. There is a poster for the movie "Broken Arrow" on a stand-frame. The boys are both grinning while Beth does not look amused.

'Oh come on now, Beth. You have surely forgotten how to smile, girl. Cheer up some for the next shot,' Chris Monroe said as he wound the film on a frame.

Tom and Bobby Lee exchanged looks and fell to laughing. Beth stamped her foot.

'I should like to see you smile, sir, with a big ole slimy frog making itself at home inside of *your* shirt!'

That was it. If a person had thought the boys were laughing before, they now learnt what laughing really was. Tom fell in a heap on the sidewalk and Bobby Lee doubled up. Chris too, he cracked up so much there was no way on earth he could hold that Box Brownie straight, not even for a second. He tried anyway and looked down into the viewfinder, just in time to see his sister stomp out of shot to the right. He let the shutter fall on a giggling heap of boy instead.

'Come back here, Beth! We were only funning,'

'Yeah!' called Bobby Lee. 'Come back … Froggy!'

And they were at it again.

'Well you can laugh some Bobby Lee,' Tom said after he'd managed to straighten up. 'But if you're Buckwheat that makes you a nigger, and I think I'd rather have a frog dropped down my back.'

'Your turn next then Tom,' Chris said. At almost fifteen he was nominally in charge of the little group and he knew how to spot when funning was heading towards trouble.

Tom and Bobby Lee dusted themselves down and somehow gained a little more composure.

'So what makes me Buckwheat?' Bobby Lee said as he fell into step beside Tom who in turn shouldered up to Chris. Beth was a way down Lexington Street now and Chris stepped up the pace wanting to catch up with her and talk her down before she could hit Papa with a raft full of tales.

'Aside of your sunburn and your big white teeth, didn't you once say your only friend when you was small was a nigger?' Tom asked. 'Reckon that's good enough to make you count as Buckwheat, and anyway, I look more like Mickey, so there's an end to it.'

'If my Pa hears you saying nigger he'll surely make you walk home,' Chris said. 'It ain't polite talk and if Carrollton to north Greenwood don't bring up a passel of blisters than *you're* the boy of colour, Tom Pike.'

'I still say it's Bobby Lee.'

'Are you saying I *look* like Buckwheat?' Bobby Lee said sounding mad but still grinning across his face. That smile would have got him out of many a scrape if he'd been the kind of boy to get in them, which he wasn't.

'The subject is closed,' Chris said. 'Now see up ahead? It looks to me like Beth is telling on us and Mr Frog.'

'Yes, cut it out Bobby Lee,' Tom said. 'Mr Monroe's truck is up the road a piece, so how about changing the record?'

Bobby Lee rolled his eyes from the cheek of it realising as he did that it probably make him look even more like Buckwheat. 'O'tay!' he said grinning.

Bobby Lee McDonald and the other two children shared the truck-bed while Chris sat up front with his papa as befit a boy who was so nearly a man. Just then he leaned out of the cab with a wide grin for those in third-class and waggled a cigarette between his first and second fingers which signalled to the whole world that Mr Monroe considered him close enough to a man as made no difference. He brought the cigarette to his lips and drew in a lungful before dipping back inside the cab. Bobby Lee suddenly wished he had chosen a *Bit-O-Honey* from the candy store instead of a liquorice pipe as he now felt rather silly sucking on it and pretending to be all grown up.

'If Mama finds out Papa's allowing Chris to smoke, she'll have a thing or two to say.' Beth seemed to have found a new bee for her bonnet and had apparently forgotten about the frog incident, which made for happier relations. Tom was asleep with a rolled-up cotton-sack for a pillow and when Beth settled with her back to the cab and her eye on the horizon, Bobby Lee stretched out on the truck-bed, watched the clouds above and let his thoughts wander off with his conscious mind trailing behind a pace or two. His thoughts led him back to Itta Bena and to Lucien Harris, a boy who was good enough to be his best and only friend back then, but who now appeared to be from a lesser race who settled somewhere behind real people and a few steps ahead of a mule or a dog. Not for the first time in his nine years of life, Bobby Lee wondered if life was quite fair.

Mr Monroe dropped Bobby Lee off at the sawmill up on Choctaw Ridge and he minded to say thank you and Mr Monroe said that it was okay and be careful not to get lost again. Bobby Lee grinned and Mr Monroe rolled his eyes and shook his head. Bobby Lee had a reputation to uphold: he was apt to getting lost, he had a dubious choice in friends and what's more they all said he hadn't got a lick of sense. So long as it stopped them asking too many questions, it was a reputation Bobby Lee liked to maintain.

'Well, hello Bobby Zee,' Hettie McDonald said. 'Did you have a good time?' Hettie hugged her son and kissed the top of his head.

'Buzzard's a smart bird,' Bobby Lee said with an exaggerated drawl; a very good impersonation for a boy not yet ten.

'Oh, you lucky boy!' Hettie said. 'You saw a James Stewart movie, didn't you? I so love Jimmy Stewart.'

'Sure did, Mama, *and* an old *Our Gang* re-run.' He dropped the imitation. 'The main movie had the Indians as the good guys. It was neat.'

'"Neat" indeed, you little beatnik.' Mama chuckled. 'Still, your Granny Starbuck would have liked it that the Indians were shown in a good light.'

'And your Grandpa McDonald would have hated it,' Papa said gruffly.

Hettie and Bobby Lee jumped, neither having heard Nate McDonald approaching. Six-two or not, he could move like

37

a cat when he wanted to. The emerging subject of Bobby Lee's Indian heritage was immediately closed – dead before it spread its wings.

'I hope you minded your manners, Bobby Lee. It was kind and neighbourly of Mr Monroe to take you along.'

'Yes, sir. I was a good boy.'

'Glad to hear it. You had a good day son?'

'Yes, sir. The movie was great and we got candy too.' As soon as the words were out of his mouth, he knew they were the wrong ones. Papa's lips tightened, like giving the candy was some kind of an insult. 'Just a tiny piece,' Bobby Lee added. 'A taste really.'

'Hope it hasn't spoiled your appetite,' Nate said. 'Either way you'll sit at the table tonight until every last piece is cleared off of your plate.'

Nate McDonald was gone just as quick as he'd appeared and Bobby Lee relaxed.

'Your papa's been very busy at the mill today. He gets a little grumpy when he's tired, but don't let him worry you. He told me earlier he was glad you'd got away for a day of fun. The noise of those saws spinning all day is sure to rattle your nerves.'

The wooded land up behind Nate's sawmill was known locally as Choctaw Ridge because that was the name of the mill. And the sawmill was so named because Grandpa McDonald moved to the Delta from the hills about a hundred years ago as far as Bobby Lee could tell, and named it after the place he just left. It was no more than coincidence that Hettie's mother had been a Choctaw Indian and it was not a fact that Nate McDonald liked to talk about. Hettie saw no reason to be coy about it though until Nate pointed out how Bobby Lee would fare at school if his friends found out he was a quarter redskin.

Photo # 5

Subject: Bobby Lee and Nate McDonald

Title: Greenwood, 1953. Bobby Lee with his almost new Shelby Flyer.
Description: Black and white shot, matt finish. Twelve-year-old Bobby Lee in short-sleeved check shirt and slicked down hair proudly sits in the saddle of a bicycle. Nate stands behind in white shirt and wide-brimmed Fedora a hand resting on Bobby Lee's shoulder.

***

Clouds were gathering but threatened nothing immediate. The sun still beat down on the dusty sawmill yard and Bobby Lee ground his back teeth until they were likely to sheer, but he would not cry. He took the photo between the thumbs and index fingers of each hand and was about to rip, him on one half and that mean sonofabitch on the other. But no, it would be a useless gesture. Mama was sure to have copies. And anyway, if ever there came a time when he hated his father any less than at this moment, he would use the photo to stoke it up. He slipped the shot in his back pants pocket and looked once more at the mangled heap of metal that used to be his beloved bike, deliberately run over by his father in a log truck. The only explanation: *I told you to stay clear of Itta Bena* which more or less translated into *I told you to stay clear of that nigger bastard you used to call friend.*

Used to? Ha! If you new the half of it, Papa. If he was ever found there again, Father promised to take a belt and lather out every last drop of ornery injun buck blood he had in him. So what if it was just a quarter, it was a quarter too much. Forewarned was fore-armed, and Bobby Lee decided he would just have to be more careful not to be seen when he went visiting. He was fifteen years old, and he wasn't about to let that bigoted bully push him around … if he could avoid it.

Papa told Bobby Lee to sweep up the iron and rubber mess of it all and tote it back side of the mill and throw it in the lean-to with the other scraps of metal. Papa could go have congress with a wild hog far as Bobby Lee was concerned. He headed off towards the main road and made

39

a show of stomping until it got uncomfortable and then boiled up inside as the walk took a site longer than the ride used to.

The air was so hot it melted and coated Bobby Lee all over making made him boil all the more. The air pressed in and made Bobby Lee his own, personal prison and the grasshoppers laughed at him so that he was fit to squish the first one came anywhere near. And outside of the heavy air was the sorriest county in all of Mississippi and Mississippi the feeblest excuse for a state and the only one that hadn't even ratified the 13th Amendment and outside of that … Bobby Lee stopped a while to consider what exactly lay beyond. It had to be better than here anyhow, sure did. Outside of Mississippi was the rest of the world.

He set to walking again and taking off his limp shirt he tied the damp arms round his middle. If only he could shuck off the oppression he felt as easily as the shirt. Reaching the road he turned south towards Greenwood, the little wooden church where the coloured folk worshipped a ways up the road behind him. He had no set idea for a destination but somewhere in his mind he figured he'd get as far as the new bridge, claim a rail near the middle and spit in the Tallahatchie River – maybe piss in it if nobody was coming. Hell, the way he felt he'd as soon drop his fruit-of-the-loom and dump in it, although quite why he blamed it all on the river he couldn't say. He was hurt and he wanted to hurt back.

Bobby Lee McDonald didn't get as far as the Tallahatchie Bridge.

He'd pretty much forgotten about his bicycle. By now it was little more than the straw that Papa had set on the camel's back, and his thoughts were clogged up with more important, more painful issues. He plodded on like he'd had a blow-out on the highway of life with no chance of a spare tyre. But at least the stand of trees that marked the drive up to the Monroe place offered a little shade. Bobby Lee was on his own in the world with his legs on automatic and his mind playing a Sonny Boy Williamson harp lick, so

Beth Monroe's voice about made him leap out of his cotton socks.

Bobby Lee hadn't seen much of Beth lately and he noticed at once that one or two things were different about her. And perhaps she had noticed the same about him.

'Well I declare, what a thing to see walking down the Money Road. Mr Bobby Lee McDonald, and ain't you all slicked up, bare-chested and looking fine like an oiled Egyptian slave?'

For a moment Bobby Lee thought Beth was talking about the plantation near Itta Bena and that he looked like a coloured boy, but then she mentioned Claudette Colbert and images of pyramids came to him … only he couldn't quite rid himself of the urge to look down at Beth's newly formed pyramids. Had it been so long since they'd last met?

'My eyes are up here, Bobby Lee McDonald,' Beth giggled. She leaned on the gate that separated her from her Egyptian slave boy. Bobby Lee was drawn to her, into the shade of the trees so that his sweat-drenched torso suddenly felt chill. It was a feeling of an entirely different kind he experienced when Beth reached out with the back of her fingers and mopped at a run of sweat that followed the line of his breast bone. From where the sensation and delicious thrill of pleasure seated itself she might just as well have reached down and squeezed between his legs.

Bobby Lee actually yelped and jumped back, like he'd just leaned into an electrified fence wire. He forgot about his bike. He forgot about his troubles. Harp licks flew out of his mind and he didn't recall ever having a feud with the child-killing waters of the Tallahatchie River. In that moment all he knew was that someday, maybe soon or maybe not, he would have to lie naked with Beth Monroe or die.

'Beth Monroe …'

'That's my name,' Beth said after a moment's silence.

Bobby Lee was tongue-tied, but determined to get in with something before Beth chided him for gawping. He snapped shut his mouth, and then fell back on his old standard as he let the smile spread slowly across his face. He thought maybe he'd got away with it.

'And where are you walking, sir, on such a hot and sticky afternoon, only I wouldn't stray too far as it's like to thunder.'

'Well, I was just going to spit in the river some, Beth Monroe. I do it when I get angry and Papa has seen to it that I'm angry as angry can be and that's a plain fact.'

Beth hopped deftly over the gate and held down the front of her skirt so the draught wouldn't lift it. 'My Daddy has a way of doing that too. I'll walk with you Bobby Lee, least if you don't have an objection.'

Hardly ever failed, that smile. 'Fine by me, Miss Monroe, but maybe you should think of something else apart from spitting.'

Beth Monroe laughed and Bobby Lee thought that was the finest sound in all the world.

'If I do spit there is only Daddy to blame,' Beth said and then stepped out towards the river and Greenwood beyond. Bobby Lee asked just how Mr Monroe had got Beth's goat, but she was not in the mood for elaboration.

The new bridge was actually called the Ashwood but some folks referred to it as the Tallahatchie to differentiate it from the other Greenwood bridges that actually spanned the Yazoo. The Tallahatchie River itself died a silent and unnoticeable death a little over a mile to the north-east – downstream – where the Yalobusha muscled in from the north. From there the converged rivers both lost their names and the waters flowed on as the Yazoo.

Bobby Lee leaned over the rail on the upriver side of the bridge. The metal was hot and came near to making his sweat sizzle. He hawked up and let fly and Beth squealed and declared that he was the most disgusting boy she had ever had the misfortune to know, and then she let fly with her own spit and they both laughed. Beth was not so proficient at the fine art of spitting as her young Egyptian slave boy, and Bobby Lee was obliged to wipe a little spittle off of her chin with the back of his finger. From the look in her eyes, he wondered if his innocent touch had the same effect as hers earlier on, albeit that she didn't exactly have all the required equipment for it to register in quite the same way. It crossed his mind that he was pretty ignorant of women's bodies but that he was good and ready to start learning.

Bobby Lee had now completely forgotten that he was supposed to be angry, and Beth Monroe showed no more signs of it than he did.

They didn't stay long. The clouds had covered over and there were a few rumbles. More than that, Beth didn't have permission to be off her daddy's land and he would certainly have a thing or two to say if she was seen walking with a shirtless boy. It would be bad to be caught out by Mr Monroe, but worse if they were seen by Beth's brother Chris. It was a well known fact that Chris Monroe was wildly protective of his little sister, a fact corroborated in town by at least one broken nose. Tom Pike let everyone know he'd run into a door, but most people weren't that easily fooled.

Bobby Lee put his shirt on and spent a while tucking it in at the front, entirely more time than was necessary just to tuck the shirt in, but good and necessary for the other adjustments he had to make for his own comfort and Beth's peace of mind.

They parted at the gate to Beth's property but not before Bobby Lee tried to give Beth a peck on the cheek. She dodged it and asked what in Heaven's name he thought he was doing. He blushed, and smiled at the same time, and that smile did its magic once again, so Beth Monroe said that maybe someday in the future but certainly not today.

The temperature dropped and Bobby Lee was half-way up the mill track when the first fat rain drops came and all the way along when the heavens opened. He took in a lungful of the newly washed air and found he no longer hated his father, and that as he was here he might just as well clear up the mortal remains of his old friend.

'Carrying all that metal, mind you don't get lightning struck.' Jake had come out of nowhere, so it seemed, and he started to help Bobby Lee with the pieces of bike. Pure white hair showed below his cap and his face was deeply creased but he wasn't yet 40 years of age. They said Korea was to blame and that might have been so. It was definitely responsible for his gammy leg. 'Seeing that log-truck roll over this here bike I was like to died, thinking you was still on it and next your broke up legs would be poking out from underneath.'

Bobby Lee laughed. 'He ain't that mean, Jake. But maybe you shouldn't help, thanks all the same. He's sure to be watching from the office or the house, and he told me to clear up so I'd better tend to it myself.'

Jake Washington straightened his back and stretched out the creaks. 'Standing here just watching while you work kind of don't set right, know what I mean.' Jake winked, and then checked over his shoulder.

'Get inside Jake. No sense the both of us getting soaked.'

Jake limped after Bobby Lee and picked up the pieces he dropped; a screw, a piece of the chain guard and a bent-up spoke. 'Just as soon tag along talk some, if it's all the same to you, Sergeant Joe. You still following that show?'

'Sure am, Jake. Every week I get to visit Tom Pike and his TV.'

'All we wants is the facts, ma'am.'

'The story you are about to see is true, only the names have been changed to protect the innocent,' Bobby Lee said in his best Joe Friday impersonation. 'This here bicycle was murdered, and the killer is a known suspect.'

Jake threw the scraps on the pile, then slapped his knees and chuckled. 'Maybe we should pre-serve the scene of the crime and call in the coroner.'

'Or a mechanic, Jake Washington.'

A few moments later Bobby Lee was running through the deluge towards the house. *Rain like a mule pissing on a flat rock* was Jake's way of saying it. He was soaked to the skin but he didn't care. Most all he could think about was Beth

Monroe and how he was going to find an excuse to see her again. He kicked his shoes off on the porch and Nate opened the door.

'Get in here, son, and get out of them wet things,' he said, stepping aside to avoid contact with his soggy boy. 'Take them off here and don't be traipsing the wet all through the house.'

Bobby Lee stripped to his shorts peeling of his shirt, socks and pants like sloughing an old damp skin. He was about to slip-slop into his bedroom when Papa grabbed his shoulder.

'I saw you clear up the bike, Bobby Lee. It's a man, and not a boy who can accept his punishment and make amends. I'm proud of you, son. Now go get dry.'

Bobby Lee dried off in his bedroom and put on clean things all the time thinking what a strange mix of a man his father was. What conventions, what rules made an otherwise kindly man so mean? Maybe it was something to do with the climate or the inertia of history.

In the meantime the fierce had died out of the rain and it came gentler, allowing Papa to scoot over to the office without getting too wet. Mama was in her dark room so in effect Bobby Lee had the rest of the house to himself.

He stood in the middle of the living room and pondered on the best position for a TV, come the day Papa ever gave in and bought one, and then he noticed the photographs on the desk. Mama and papa on their wedding day; the photo seemingly required by law, of a naked Bobby Lee, aged six months, laying on a sheepskin rug, and another of Papa looking proud in his Ranger uniform with the actual little blue lozenge of material from his uniform jacket stuck to the frame. Bobby Lee wondered if it was memories from the war made him moody. He'd fought on D-Day and he'd heard his Uncle Sam say as how he broke a German soldier's neck with his bare hands. Bobby Lee could believe it.

Bobby Lee picked up the frame containing his baby-picture and thought it was high time this shot was removed from public view. It wasn't hard to imagine how embarrassed he'd feel if he brought Beth Monroe home for dinner and she was confronted with his little baby butt. And then he wondered if the Monroe household sported such a picture of Beth, which in turn made him think of 16-year-old Beth without any clothes on. His imagination worked overtime and his body stood ready for a duty that would be a long time coming if it ever came at all.

Bobby Lee was suddenly and urgently presented with some personal matters that needed addressing, and he decided that the time had come for him to get a lock for his bedroom door.

Photo # 6

Subject: Bobby Lee
Title: BL the flying fish.
Description: Black and white full plate. Bobby Lee wears cut-downs and is caught mid air having just let go of a swing-rope over Roebuck Lake.

***

Bobby Lee came out dripping and loping like the monster from the black lagoon and the only thing that saved Lucien Harris from being taken hard and low was that he was carrying Hettie McDonald's camera.

'Your turn Lucien, get up on that rope and let me take a picture of you.'

'You the craziest boy. Do you want to get your friend swinging in the trees, blood on the leaves and blood at the root? 'Cause that'll happen if the good white folk get any inkling that this nigger sonofabitch is leading one of their'n astray. Then they'll take a picture or two and maybe even sell them as postcards.'

Bobby Lee flopped to the grassy ground at Lucien's feet, water streaming from his body. 'Hand over the camera

Lucien and don't be fretting. My Mama prints her own pictures these days and she knows we're friends and don't mind none. She won't let Papa nor anyone but me see it.' Lucien sat down next to his friend.

'T'aint worth the risk, Bobby Lee. You'd surely get the skin whupped off your skinny ass and I'd get pistol-whipped at best or accused of touching your itsy white tail and strung up at worst.'

'Now you know I ain't itsy it that department.'

'Hell no. If I have to pick me a best pal he's sure got to be hung right even if he ain't shaded right.'

'Why thank you, Mr Harris, but now I fear you're just zaggerating in the other direction and on behalf of your whole race.'

'Shoot, now you're calling me mister. You obviously mean me harm, sure do, anyone hears you mistering me. Anyways, Bobby Lee, shouldn't you ought to take a picture or two of the wildlife, like you're supposed to? Even your mama will think it a mite strange if you go out hunting critters and come back with only coloured boy.'

'Mama knows exactly what I'm at. It's only Papa I have to be careful with. Sides I got plenty of wildlife shots already and he don't know one from t'other. If he asks I'll show him shots I already got. And you talk of risk, well every time we come here we risk getting ass-bit by a cottonmouth, and it don't stop us having fun. So are you going to get your carcase up that rope and let me take a picture?'

Lucien rolled his eyes and stood. 'Yessir master boss. I's going and no two ways.'

The old slave-act: that was too much for Bobby Lee; with the camera safe on the ground he took Lucien hard and low, like he had a mind to earlier, and they rolled on the ground wrestling and fighting, which is what all healthy red-blooded boys do when they love each other.

Bobby Lee and Lucien had a spot by the lake that lay back a bit and was heavy with Cypress trees, shrubs and Tupelo gums dipping their feet in at the water's edge. They

47

were mostly safe from prying eyes, such as those of that bullying pain in the ass Dewey Hopwood and his sidekicks, and they usually came by the lake at times when prying eyes were not so prevalent. They also had a stock of viable excuses should anyone spy them together.

The fight ended a draw and left both boys hot enough for another dip. They swam for a while, in their secret little cove, and then clambered out and sprawled on the ground.

'Be good if you could just come on up to the mill and set down for supper with us,' Bobby Lee said.

'Uh-huh, reckon it would and the same if you and yours could come visit me and Abe, but ain't gonna happen.'

Bobby Lee sat up and skimmed a stone off the lake, each skip hop and splash taking his mind a little further into the future. 'Well, maybe one day it will. Me and Beth will get married and have kids. You and Becky Anne will too and on Sundays we'll take turns whose place to eat, both families all together.'

Lucien pulled on his shirt. 'That'll be round the time we all sprout wings and get good at playing the plucking-harp. You just dreaming Bobby Lee.'

It would soon be time to part. Lucien was only a couple of miles from home but Bobby Lee had three times the distance to cover and then there was a ride to catch. Tom Pike's daddy had business at Fort Loring and had agreed to let Bobby Lee have a ride if he could be there in time, because he was sure not hanging around. Miss the ride and the walk would not be pleasant.

'Maybe you and me should hop a ride on a northbound freight, Lucien, and go to Chicago or maybe Nantucket.'

'And leave your pretty lady behind? How are things with you and Beth Monroe? Any rocking and rolling?'

'A little maybe. Sure not as much as I'd like. How bout you and Becky Anne?'

'As much as you could handle and then some, poor lonesome white boy.'

Bobby Lee slapped Lucien's thigh and then called him a lucky dog. 'Well then, you, me, Becky Anne and Beth. We'll all ship out somewheres the nineteen-fifties has actually reached.'

Lucien heaved such a sigh, and then after a few moments another one. 'You know Bobby Lee, I read one time about how Mr Hitler had all the Jewish folks wear yellow stars tacked on their shirts. Well my yellow star is stitched on all over my face, and there ain't no unpicking it come the end of the war.'

Now Bobby Lee heaved off a sigh. 'You reckon the world's always been crazy, Lucien Harris?'

'Pretty much. One crazy ends another kind starts up. Hey but without crazy we'd never have found the blues.'

Done philosophising the boys sat up and Lucien took a harp out of the Prince Albert can he had in a sack and blew a fine lick he said he'd heard up at Money a few weeks back. Bobby Lee fished in his pants pocket for his and tried to lay down a back rhythm. Failing miserably he left it to Lucien.

For some reason the sound was more lonesome and mournful than usual and when he was done Lucien looked fit to cry.

'Time's coming when we might not be able to be friends no mo,' Lucien said as they pulled on their clothes. 'So throw me that ole can, there's something I want you to have.'

Bobby Lee wrung out his cut-downs. 'What's going to stop us being friends?'

'You know good and well. Now, throw me the can.'

Lucien caught it and looked at the worn out picture of Albert and the chipped red paint before popping the lid. 'It was my Granddaddy's and I want you to have it Bobby Lee, I surely do.'

It was a brass ring ... maybe even gold and Bobby Lee hardly knew what to say, but he knew he wasn't going to insult Lucien by refusing to take it.

'Lucien Harris, I never had such a treasure before,' Bobby Lee said while trying the ring on, one finger after another.'

'My Granddaddy was fat as a tub of lard and then some with fingers like corndogs. Used to wear it on his pinky. Here,' Lucien said, handing Bobby Lee a piece of string. 'Tote it round your neck until you grow some.'

Bobby Lee let Lucien tie the ring round his neck and then lifted it to admire a while.

'If a time comes when you ever forget that a white boy and a coloured boy could be friends, promise me you'll just look at that there ring and remember us.'

'Such a time as that won't come, Lucien, but it sure is good to have something like this as a keepsake. Thank you. Now you promise me something?'

'Try me.'

Bobby Lee took out his mouth organ and held it up. 'Promise me you'll never go anywhere without your harp.'

'That's easy. Consider it a promise, but it's one you have to keep too.'

Bobby Lee promised.

There was a beat of time, like something was passing, coming to an end, then Lucien told Bobby Lee to pick up the camera. 'Shoot me setting on a log. Point, snap, in the can.' For better or worse, Lucien Harris was soon inside that little box, smiling and preserved on celluloid.

The boys shook hands, lingered a little before the release, and then turned each in their own direction. No goodbyes were said. Their next meeting was already planned and if there were to be changes they could write, their letters following a well planned route. The French Resistance had nothing on Lucien and Bobby Lee when it came down to surreptitious communication.

Bobby Lee caught his ride at Fort Loring and most of the way home he pressed at the heavy weight of gold under his shirt. How many boys could say they were blessed with such a friendship? He'd show Mama the ring, and Beth – perhaps – but Papa would never set eyes upon it. When he was sure Mr Pike wasn't paying him any mind, he slipped the ring out from between his second and third shirt buttons and studied the design. Curious, he thought and tried to fit a name to the initials … P, G and H. He slipped it back under his shirt and wondered if there was something he could give Lucien in return.

He'd ask Lucien about those initials next time they met up, he thought, not knowing there never would be a next time.

Photo # 7

Subject: Bobby Lee, Lewis and Colin McDonald
Title: "Choctaw Ridge", Greenwood, 1957. BL gets to know little cousins, Lewis and Colin.
Description: Bobby Lee sits on the porch steps and smiles for the camera while sitting Colin on his knee. The baby had apparently been sick and there is a white stain on the lower leg of his jeans. Lewis plays with a toy dumper-truck.

***

Bad news travels fast is what they all say, but still Hettie McDonald was worried. The buzz saws threw their dusty cry into the air through the walls of the mill. It drifted over with blunted teeth and mixed in with the sounds of cicadas and grasshoppers. Nate was up at the office, Jake Washington was sweeping sawdust from the mill yard and the boys were busy hauling timber, but where was Bobby Lee? His bed hadn't been slept in.

Hettie set the folding table on the porch from where she could watch the track down to the road and she looked often, shading her eyes from the bright yellow light that bounced off the ground. The sky seemed awfully big today and so very bright. In the distance a car drove north along Money Road and threw up a cloud of dust. It was a little early for the almost daily spectacle of a funeral cortège – one of the coloured folk making their final journey from Greenwood to lay down their burden down by the riverside

51

at Little Zion – and they didn't throw up nearly so much dust.

Looking down to the black page of her photo album Hettie saw a blue and green image of the fence she just been watching over. She blinked to rid her eyes of the encumbrance, and then dipped her pen into the pot of white ink. She wrote *BL gets to know little cousins, Lewis and Colin,* and then blew gently to help it dry.

Jake was a tiny figure, close to the back of the mill, but he caught sight of Hettie and raised his hat. Hettie waved back and smiled, though she felt sure he was too far away to see her expression. She knew Jake posted letters for Bobby Lee and on occasion brought him one, but they would have to be more careful. Last evening she had seen Jake handing one over and if she had seen, why it wasn't past chance that Nate might and that was sure to bring awkward questions. Nate liked Jake a mite more than he like other Negroes on account of his service record, but that wouldn't much modify his anger if he ever found out Jake was a key element in his son's continued contact with Lucien Harris.

Where *was* Bobby Lee? Only two days ago she had found him in his room sobbing his heart out. Young love didn't always work out – hardly ever in fact. She knew there was no point in asking what the matter was; boys didn't communicate when they were feeling vulnerable and no amount of coaxing or bullying would make them. It was in their evolution and Darwin or Freud might have an explanation but Hettie didn't, she only knew it was a fact. She just sat on the edge of Bobby Lee's bed and stroked his hair a little, and when the tears had died down, she left him to his privacy.

Later, while she peeled the vegetables for dinner, Bobby Lee told her in simple, not-to-be-repeated sentences that he had proposed to Beth Monroe and she had turned him down because her daddy would never approve.

Her loss, Bobby Lee. And anyway, seventeen is perhaps a little too young to be thinking about marriage.

Where was that boy? With Lucien? Maybe that sweet boy was helping Bobby Lee cope with his sorrows. A few cans of beer, a smoke maybe or a shoulder to cry on. Or was he with Beth, leaving the boy behind and becoming a man? She hoped not. She wasn't at all sure how Nate would handle a scandal. Actually, she knew precisely how he'd handle it, and it frightened her. She refused to imagine how Mr Monroe would react but figured he wasn't so uncivilised as to take up a shotgun.

The white ink on the black cartridge paper was dry now and another picture secured for her old age, when she would take up her albums and smile or laugh or cry at the memories they brought. She ran a finger over the shot of Sam McDonald and his family. Rose sure was pretty and Hettie had liked her a lot. She found she could speak of matters that weren't usually acceptable, such as her son's friendship with a coloured boy. Being from England, Rose had trouble with the local status quo and told her a story of her first week in Hattiesburg. A heavily pregnant Negro lady had been coming along the sidewalk towards her, two heavy shopping bags and a little boy at her feet. Rose had stepped aside to let her by and Sam had exploded. *You don't step off the sidewalk for no goddamned nigger!* And Sam soon to become a church pastor! Rose had been frightened and couldn't reconcile the facts. She thought a friendship between the boys was sweet and boded well for the future, and her Englishness made her blind to the dangers in it for the pair of them. Hettie had trusted Rose enough to show her the picture of Lucien sitting on a log beside Roebuck Lake, and then hid it again as if it was something shameful.

Hettie closed her album and patted the cover and then took up her diary. *June 3rd, 1958* she wrote, and then *Where oh where has my baby boy taken himself? He didn't come home last night.*

She looked up from the page to check the track once again. Another car threw up a cloud. Still not a funeral, but somehow the cloud oppressed Hettie like the pall of death. At such a distance it looked like a dung beetle overdosed on caffeine and she was about to return to the page when she noticed the tail-cloud diminish and almost settle to nothing. The car slowed almost to a stop and then turned up the mill track. She dropped her pen: the car was coming for her.

When the car was close enough for her to notice that it was liveried up in Sheriff's Department markings, Hettie's bottom lip and chin began to tremble. *Please no. Please no. Please Lord, no.* Hettie knew the Sheriff was here to break her heart.

The car pulled up by the office and Gary Stroud got out slowly, and then he took off his hat. Sheriff Stroud *never* took off his hat, and by that simple gesture Hettie McDonald knew all the light had gone from her world.

***

'Morning, Gary, come in take the load off,' Nate McDonald said rising from his office chair to greet the unexpected guest.

Before Sheriff Stroud had time to close the door behind him, a shrill and pitiful scream of anguish burst through from the house and shocked into action Nate pushed by to go to his wife, the Sheriff close on his heels.

Little Brewster Roebuck had been wading by the muddy banks of the Tallahatchie much later than his mama approved, checking his trotlines for catfish. His daddy had told him it wasn't the best place but for a nine-year-old Brewster had quite a mind of his own. He saw Bobby Lee jump and he must have come down awkward and hit his head on a floating log. Brewster ran as fast as his little legs would carry him. A call was put in and a deputy had gone by but it was too dark to do much more than shine a torch around, from the bridge, from the banks.

Brewster knew it was Bobby Lee who'd jumped, but it was only confirmed when the poor boy's water-sodden corpse was dragged out of the river several days later.

Hettie formally identified her son and her grief mutated into withdrawal and silence.

Hettie was numb after her initial burst of grief. Nate McDonald had to be medicated and he used *Jim Beam* as his sedative of choice.

It was pretty much an open and shut case but nevertheless Hettie felt it was all a little rushed. And while the grief sat like a dark spot inside her, anger flamed and gave her something to cling to. She became fierce and implacable and determined, as if the flames were fanned by shame that she had not stood up for Bobby Lee in life; she certainly stood up for him in death and with the intercession of Jake Washington and the kindly understanding of the preacher, she arranged for her son to be buried next to the spot where it was said laid the mortal remains of a famous blues man.

What Hettie achieved in the face of close-to-rabid opposition from her own people was no mean feat. Bobby Lee became the only white boy to be buried at that little church a ways up the road, and until she moved away Hettie just about the only white visitor to the unmarked grave. There was no headstone and no grave to tend, as such, but every year on the anniversary of Bobby Lee's death, flowers were placed on the spot and nobody quite knew who brought them. Most said it was his mama, but she had moved all the way back to Nantucket and as the years passed and the flowers kept coming, folks owned that the little old lady would be too frail to travel.

Those yearly offerings to Bobby Lee became a mystery to the churchgoers and Jake Washington once set out to see if he could discover the person who wouldn't forget, but he fell asleep and when he woke the flowers had been placed and the flower-bringer still a mystery. It got so folks guessed it was the way things were meant to be and nobody tried to find out who that steadfast and loyal person might be.

It was years later, Jake was up back of Choctaw Ridge mill – it had been sold on in the mid-sixties when Nate

McDonald died – and he saw Beth Monroe picking wild flowers. Jake couldn't rightly describe Beth Monroe's features. He had never looked at her direct when up close. It was a thing he just couldn't do, look directly into a white woman's face, and he didn't look now, but they were on the same path and he couldn't very well avoid her. He found himself looking at the flowers she was carrying. Nothing fancy, just little blooms you could find this time of the year, the kind a barefoot boy picks for his mama: blue day flowers, red Indian Pinks, white May Apple and Bigroot Morning Glory and a splash of other colours, Butterfly Milkweed, Beauty Berry.

'Morning Miss Monroe,' Jake said keeping his eyes on the blooms.

'Good morning Jake Washington, and you know very well it's Mrs Thomas these days.'

'Uh-huh. Forgot. Don't see you round here much since you married Brother Thomas,' he said, and then it dawned. It was June 3rd. 'Flowers for Bobby Lee, Mrs Thomas?'

There came no answer, and Jake looked up although it went against the grain and saw Beth's cheeks colour up and tears spring to her eyes.

'He was just the sweetest boy,' she said.

Jake owned that he had liked Bobby Lee a great deal and thought him the only white boy who could blow a decent lick out of a harp and then he saw something climbing up a fence post: Butterfly Pea, purple flowered and proud. Jake picked a few and asked Beth Taylor could she maybe lay down some flowers for him.

'I'll surely take the flowers, thank you Jake.' She took the blooms, smiled sadly, and went on her way.

And so the mystery was solved, or so Jake believed, and his own favourite theory was shattered. He'd always hoped the flowers were from that boy from just this side of Itta Bena, the one who Bobby Lee and those few folks in on the secret had been obliged to keep quiet about. It was nice, he supposed, that Bobby Lee's old flame was laying the flowers, but there was something more special about a

56

friendship between boys that lasted past the grave. Oh well, life's what it is and rarely as the heart may wish. Work to be done. No time to stand and dream.

Part Two: One Man's Account

Case File

Document # 1
The Newspaper Clipping

Publication: *The Greenwood*
Date: *Friday, June 13th, 1958*

Headline: *Bobby Lee Death was Tragic Accident*
Report: *The coroner's court returned a verdict of accidental death today in respect of 17-year-old Bobby Lee McDonald whose body was recovered from the Yazoo River last Friday. Bobby Lee, son of Nathan and Hettie McDonald of the Choctaw Ridge Sawmill Company, Greenwood, was seen to jump off Ashwood Bridge at a little after sun-down on Tuesday June 3rd by nine-year-old Brewster Roebuck who was on the bank of the Tallahatchie River tending to some fishing lines. "I seen him go under but he didn't come back up again." Brewster raised the alarm but Bobby Lee was not found until three days later and over a mile downstream, his neck broken and dressed only in shorts. Sheriff Stroud opined that Bobby Lee had been affected by the stifling weather of late. "It had been a sticky and uncomfortably hot night. We found his clothes on the bridge and it seems reasonable that he took the notion to cool off with a swim. Like to be, he dove in and hit some floating driftwood." The Sheriff took the opportunity to warn young folks against jumping off of bridges, even comparatively low ones like the Ashwood. The coroner stated that naturally, the thoughts and prayers of the people of Greenwood were with the McDonalds at this sad time.*

***

Do you remember the story? It was a long time ago, but then you may have had cause to give it some attention. That aside, I'm sorry I'm a little late but grateful you're here. Best I begin.

It didn't kill me so I suppose it made me stronger. Yes, definitely stronger, and happier. I am Colin McDonald, the wild-west sheriff with the white hat and the silver badge. Better still, I am a different kind of lawman from further north with a scarlet jacket and a pre-war scout-hat. As I write it is 2011 and I survived to tell the story, and what's more, I got my man, just like the Canadian Mounted Policeman. I tracked down a killer and solved a forty-year-old murder. And it all started thirteen years ago with a colour photo of my seventeen-year-old cousin, Bobby Lee McDonald. Billy Joe McAlister? Perhaps, but whether or not his story inspired the song, I have added a new verse and I like to think it's not half bad for a man who is neither a song-writer nor a poet. I'll leave that for you to judge. Be gentle or scathing as the mood takes you, for I am immune. Slings and arrows bounce off. Compliments barely touch my ego. It takes a lot these days to wipe the smile from my face and the smile in my heart is ingrained, immutable and pervasive. You'll call me a bastard. People died, and still I smile but in the end I hope you will understand.

I came through the cleansing fire; a lot of useless material was burnt away, but there were others who did not fare so well. Some were scorched and some perished in the inferno, and for that I bear a share of the blame, but what's done is done. I really don't lose a lot of sleep over it and when I do dream about those days, I usually wake up with a grin and a warm glow.

Even the crucible of memory has to be fired up with a single match; time to light the blue touch-paper, but let's not stand back. I'll return to the first spark which was that fateful photograph.

Isn't it scary? I'm dressed in baggy bib-topped pants with my diaper showing at the legs. Bobby Lee sports his girl-killer smile and has me on his knee with all the confidence of a new father. He is dressed in jeans and a shirt. He wears sneakers very like those Converses that kids are so fond of these days. His dark hair is full but well-trimmed, a little above collar-length. If he let his shirt-tails hang loose instead of tucking them in he would not look that out of place if he walked down the High Street today, and yet the shutter fell and captured the image over half-a-century ago. Half-a-century should be ancient. Half-a-century should be a different world where all fashions are ridiculously outmoded by today's standard. In reality, half-a-century ago is the genesis of The Beatles, and what's worse, I remember it. I remember that day in the photo. I have vague recollections of Bobby Lee and the minor, everyday event that was captured by Aunt Hettie's camera, and I think that is why I was so determined to get to the truth: my cousin, a boy whose death may or may not have inspired a famous song, a person whom I had met and remembered meeting, was a victim of murder. Add my Caesarion Complex to all that, and resistance was pretty much futile.

I'm over the psychological challenge, by the way. No more Caesarion Complex for me. It did not survive the crucible. But then how could it? I always knew that if I could put the history books right for just one of those young men, if I could solve just one mystery or uncover one truth, my unusual compulsion would evaporate. To Caesarion, Arthur of Brittany, Alexei Romanov, Manfred von Loewenstern, Peter Fechter and all the others: thank you. You all helped shield me against a personal tragedy until I was strong enough to face up to it. Because of you I am able to add Lewis McDonald, the brother I think of every day, to the ranks of those to whom I say, rest in peace. I can love the memory of you Lewis, without being torn apart by guilt. But what about the injustice of it all? This story ends in serious injustice, but you know, I'm living with it and as I said, I hardly lose any sleep. I hope you will feel the same.

That's quite enough of a scrape with melancholy for one day, so on with the investigation. I am a cheerful person, thanks mainly to the mission I began thirteen years ago. Death put in an appearance or two but he always came in grinning and who can feel downbeat in the face of such hilarity? Life might just be the joke that Death finds so amusing, and I have learnt to see it in the same way. Apart from anything else, it does wonders for my blood pressure. I went for my annual check-up last week and the doctor assured me I had the blood pressure of a pregnant school girl. He said it with a smile, so I took that as being pretty good.

You might suspect I began the investigation by returning to the lyrics of Bobbie Gentry's ballad, *Ode to Billy Joe*. Not so. The link between my cousin Bobby Lee and Miss Gentry's Billy Joe was little more than a family rumour. It certainly wasn't a sound foundation on which to build a case, despite the fact that Bobbie Gentry spent some of her childhood in Greenwood, Mississippi. Nor did I pay more than passing interest to the Herman Raucher film of the same name, although I enjoyed it and I have to say Bobby Lee had a striking resemblance to Robby Benson, the actor who took the title role. In my mind Bobby Lee and Robby Benson might just as well be the same person; if memories of Bobby Lee are lacking, Robby steps in and fills the gap, but in no real sense was my research influenced by the song or the film. I started with the documents to hand and called in some favours from a stateside acquaintance to secure some primary source evidence. I also wrote to Aunt Hettie in Nantucket at the last address we had for her.

I had the photo album, of course, and the letter from my father. Then there was the letter from Harrison Bardwell that raised suspicions in the first place, and another one from Dad's executor, Brewster Roebuck. Not bad for a start, and even better when the first thick envelope arrived from my American contact with several documents, one bearing a surprising link.

Link: I love that word. It is a particular favourite of many researchers; such a solid, friendly and encouraging word. It is the hand that grips yours when you are about to go under, and it drags you up and makes room for you in the lifeboat. You're not quite saved yet, but you have the means to carry on.

The envelope contained a copy of the Leflore County coroner's report on Bobby Lee's death, a newspaper clipping from *The Greenwood* and some notes my friend had drawn up to show which avenues she had explored, the results of her exploration and suggestions for how I might proceed. There was one name that immediately drew my attention. It jumped up and down waving its arms at me: look at me, look at me. Unless "Brewster Roebuck" was the Mississippi equivalent of "John Smith", the executor for Dad's last will and testament was one and the same as the small boy who was the sole witness to Bobby Lee's disastrous leapt from the bridge. Now wouldn't you think he might have mentioned something about it in his letter? I was going to have to tread lightly lest my questions be seen as accusations.

I don't want to give the impression that I was so financially secure I could drop everything and apply myself single-mindedly to solving the case of my cousin's demise. I had a mortgage to pay and a family to support, and so everything pertaining to Bobby Lee had to be done in my own time, at least in the early stages. That I secured a little funding some time down the line is a sore point between me and a certain commissioning editor. The poor man never did get his prime-time drama-documentary *The Truth behind the Ode*. I supplied everything he needed, but the proposal didn't make it past company solicitors: too many people liable to be hurt, or should I say, too much risk of litigation.

Nowadays much of my research could have been completed by use of the web and the internet. We're only going back thirteen years and both were well proven and improving exponentially, but they still were not quite ubiquitous in their reach and we still relied on paper records and writing. Given that the cyber-world had some catch-up to do, and that I had to keep up the day-job, it probably isn't surprising that it took me several years to get to the bottom of the mystery of my cousin's death in all its esoteric detail. There were also a number of violent encounters along the way and if you really want to look I can show you the scars to prove it.

Before the violence, there were the snubs, or at least, turns of circumstance that I took as snubs. At the same time that I posted off my letter to Yvonne, my stateside contact, I sent another to Brewster Roebuck. My letter included words of gratitude for taking on my uncle's will as executor, and then some general enquiries. For example, who was Harrison Bardwell, and might there be a contact address for him? I mentioned Harrison's letter to Dad but didn't go into any details and kept to myself all hints of the suspicions it raised. I received no reply.

With the package from Yvonne I had a further lead involving Brewster Roebuck. I let a few weeks pass and carried on such research as I could. The World Wide Web led me to several Harrison Bardwells, but I was soon able to establish that none of them had anything at all to do with the man who had "seen something truly awful" in respect of Bobby Lee's death.

I also got a letter from Aunt Hettie, or rather, on behalf of Aunt Hettie. It came from one of her cousins, Zak Starbuck, who explained that Hettie found it difficult to write these days as she was so afflicted with rheumatoid arthritis. He had no news to pass on but said Hettie would be very keen to be kept abreast of my research. That was a huge relief. I had feared she would be hurt by me delving into the past.

Several weeks passed and I was pretty much absorbed in my work. In that time I learnt much about Japanese history in general and kamikaze pilots in particular. I wrote up my findings wondering what would be omitted for the sake of a good story. As a researcher you must resign yourself to the fact that much of your research will be squeezed into a story that has already been written and that dramatic effect will trump truth any day of the week. In the case of the kamikaze documentary, the director was particularly blatant. It gave the story a nice air of mystery if the particular squad of kamikaze pilots in question flew off, never to reach their targets or to be heard of again, and so that is how the film ended, despite the fact that the fate of the flight was well known and fully documented. Oh well, I got paid. Trouble is I got credited too and I hated to think that historians would consider me a history-prostitute. On the other hand, I found out early in my career that it does not pay, metaphorically or literally, to tell a director where he or she is going wrong; if they want blaring sirens in situations where cops actually make a silent approach, that's their concern. Rack up the drama, death to realism. Ah but I am a clever little researcher, and over the years I have discovered a trick or two that helps to preserve the truth … sometimes. Don't appeal to a director's sense of truth; rather tell him the scene is a little too formulaic, somewhat passé or done-to-death. That'll get him thinking where an appeal to truth falls on deaf ears. Unfortunately I had no chance in securing a historically accurate ending for the kamikaze docu-drama.

It was November, 1998. On the same evening that I submitted my report on the kamikaze, or *tokkotai* as they are more correctly called, I wrote a second letter to Mr Brewster Roebuck. This time I was a little more direct. I asked him if he was the same Brewster Roebuck as mentioned in newspaper clipping and the coroner's report, and if so I would love to talk to him about it, if the memories were not too painful. I cited my family ties with Bobby Lee McDonald, a boy of whom I had clear memories, and wrote that I wanted closure that he might be able to supply. I had no idea that the closure I really craved would come as a by-product of my investigations.

I had a reply within a fortnight. Bearing in mind the distances and the diverse postal services involved such a speedy reply must have represented reply by return. The contents of Brewster's letter were surprising to say the least, but before I could act on them other news came from his side of the Pond which destroyed the last vestiges of religious faith that still clung to my heart. At that time I believed my cousin Bobby Lee McDonald had been murdered. There was some considerable doubt. With Matthew Shepard, there was no doubt at all, and his murder affected me greatly and out of all proportion. Remember, I still had a dose of the old Caesarion Complex back then. Cometh the hour, cometh the trigger; Matt's fate and its aftermath together formed the trigger that launched me into atheism.

Of course, I had heard about the murder on the news broadcasts, but somehow I missed the sickening aftermath. That November evening I'd started using the internet to look up flights to Mississippi but I'd drifted past that into the realm of browsing. I can't remember exactly what I typed into the search engine, but I know I was feeding my Complex. I was just about to hit the shut-down button when a photograph began to form on the monitor, line by painfully slow line. Remember dial-up? It was taking forever and I was overdue a cup of tea. Reaching out to hit that button a block of pixels suddenly formed the words "God Hates …" on what appeared to be a placard. I was intrigued to find out the meaning of this oxymoron. What could God possibly hate, as opposed to having some loving reservation about? It turned out that the bearer of the placard, a spiteful-looking and wizened up old duffer wearing a baseball cap, was advertising the view that God hated fags. *Good on you God! I'm sure that if you join the anti-smoking campaign you will save as many lives as the ones you've lost through your stubborn refusal to sanction the use of condoms.*

If the tobacco barons had made the same erroneous interpretation as I, they would have been in like lightning to put matters right. What a shame the greater part of Christianity did not do the same when one of their crazy sects disrupted a young man's funeral with such a hateful spectacle. "God Hates Fags", "Fag Burn in Hell" and other such sweet sentiments were blazoned on placards being toted with self-righteous venom by people who probably lacked the spare brain-capacity to be called deluded on account of it being stuffed full of bigotry.

Matt was a young student who had been befriended by two louts who lured him to the countryside outside of Laramie, Wyoming where they dropped all pretence of friendship, tied him to a buck-rail fence and smashed his skull in with the barrel of a pistol. When the police found him, still tied to the fence, his face was a mass of drying blood, except for the two white paths that showed the tracks of his tears. Matthew Shepard died several days later without ever regaining consciousness. He was murdered simply for being gay.

I can remember the spit-flecking fury that built up in me as I read the story. The murder was awful enough, but the reaction of those so-called Christians with their placards dripping hate took it to another dimension. I was not so naïve as to believe these people were in any way representative of true Christianity, but where were the true Christians? Where was the condemnation for the hate-mongers? By their lack of vociferous and unambiguous condemnation for this sickening behaviour, they condemned themselves. That was how I saw it, anyway. Kind of still do.

It's a very personal thing, but if Christianity was born on a cross at Calvary, for me it died on a cross in Wyoming.

Since Matt I have held and hold to this day the strongest of beliefs, that all religion is a lie. Sometimes it is a benign lie, but a lie nevertheless, and in that my belief has a direct link to Matt's death, I guess that makes me a Shepardian, or as we will see later, a Shepherd. If I were to wear a silver cross, it would be a cross in saltire (to represent the upright frame of a buck-rail fence) bedecked with tangles of twine, and it would stand for all that is good in humanity and all that is moral and all that is perfectly achievable without the taint of religion.

Please excuse me, but I cannot recall those days without reliving the passion. Watch me now as I climb from my soapbox and kick it away. I will do my best not to jump onto it again.

I researched the subject of Matthew Shepard in as much depth as the web of the day would allow, and I wondered if I should include him in my book of murdered young men, but as horrible as it was, Matt's murder lacked the state cover-up dimension.

It was time to move on. It was time to arrange some leave for private research and book the flights. Brewster Roebuck's letter did not say much, but it did imply there were discoveries to be made about Bobby Lee and that those discoveries were best not committed to writing. The letter also included an invitation to visit Brewster at his home on Choctaw Ridge.

Document # 2
Letter from Brewster Roebuck

Choctaw Ridge
Wednesday, November 25th, 1998

Dear Colin,

I received your letter, and the previous one. Thank you, and I should have replied to the earlier one.

I feel we should speak face to face. I am not comfortable committing my views and concerns to the written word.

In spite of our age difference, I knew Bobby Lee reasonably well and our families were on friendly terms. I believe I recollect us meeting one time, you and me. You were just beginning to talk and I, being an eight or nine year old with a little kid's sense of humour, tried to teach you to say "son-of-a- bitch". I got caught and Daddy tanned my hide.

Why not come visit? If you've a mind to, bring Miranda and the kids for you would all be welcome to stay at Choctaw Ridge.

We have several spare rooms now our kids have flown the coop, all except the youngest, that is.

I will leave it to you and append contact details. If the idea appeals, call and we will make arrangements.

I would wish you happy Thanksgiving, but I understand it is not a holiday you folks recognise.

Yours truly,
[signed] *Brewster Roebuck*

***

It wasn't until February that I could get the time off, and then only for a week and only for myself. It was work. It was Miranda. It was fitting in with Brewster Roebuck's schedule. Having dual nationality and a US passport helped but for a man who detests flying I can't say it made the journey any easier. I had to fly a lot, and even a little more than I anticipated. I went from London to Houston, Texas. From there I reached Greenwood Municipal Airport via Atlanta and Memphis. Relief on touching my feet to solid ground at Greenwood was short lived: Brewster met me, as promised, and yes he certainly took me the rest of the way to his home in Pontotoc County but he hadn't explained he was a pilot, and the last leg of the journey was by Piper Seminole, a twin-engined affair with just enough room for the pilot and three passengers, or as it transpired, the pilot, Brewster's 17-year-old co-pilot son, and one very nervous passenger who had already had enough flying to last a year.

I could not believe how tiny and close things were in that cabin, but luckily I was in one of the back seats, so I just hunkered down and listened while Josh Roebuck read through the pre-flights and Brewster checked them off.

'Fuel selectors, on,' Josh said. It sounded like a good idea to me.

'Check,' Brewster said.

'Carb heat, off.'

Hadn't a clue; off or on or stuck on sideways would have been fine by me, but it all sounded very professional and efficient and I was happy to let father and youngest son get on with it.

The flight lasted just under half-an-hour and was, to my surprise, quite relaxing and less stressful than flying in a liner. Perhaps I only trust pilots when I can see them. It was good to eavesdrop on the informal banter between Roebucks senior and junior and it indicated a strong bond. I was included and given a guided tour but the only landmark I now recall was heralded by Josh singing.

'Hello Mudder, hello Fa'der …' his voice warbled over the headset.

'Here we are in … Camp Granada,' Brewster added and then dipped a wing so I could get a better look at Lake Granada however many zillion feet below. I much preferred straight-and-level, and I think something must have conveyed that to Brew, because he was a perfect gentleman for the rest of the flight.

We came into land at a little airstrip with 29 painted on one end, and the very last leg of the trip, from the strip to Brewster's home was by crew-cab pickup truck. We swung by the local high school to pick up Josh's friend for a sleep-over. Cal was a young man whose skin was just a shade or two lighter than the black sports top he wore. It had "Warriors" blazoned across the chest and the number 23 and "Wheatley" on the back. Cal Wheatley and Josh Roebuck both played in their high school basketball team and I was to learn that Cal 'drills a mean trey-ball', although I was never made a party as to what in the world that might mean. These two young men were clearly best of friends, and I found it encouraging that race-relations had so improved over the years. What's that saying? One swallow doesn't make a summer? Still, I knew, or I thought I did, that such a friendship would be totally impossible in the Mississippi of the nineteen-fifties.

The boys bailed out as soon as Brew stepped on the parking brake. They had hoops to shoot and there was no time to waste. The Roebuck homestead was a generously proportioned timber house with a porch, a picket fence and a swimming pool. It was set back from the road and secluded by its own stand of trees. Well maintained and comfortably appointed, Brewster's property suggested he was doing pretty well in the crop-dusting business. He owned the business, the Piper aircraft we'd travelled in and another two planes purpose-designed as crop-dusters. I was to learn on the journey that his daughter, May, piloted a duster, his eldest son Steve worked a cotton farm near Greenwood and young Josh was pinning his hopes on getting a place at Ole Miss, as they called the University of Mississippi.

'If I had my way he'd go out of State, maybe an Ivy League for the good Lord knows he has the brains but where from, that's the mystery.'

Holly told him not to be obtuse as it was a well known fact the brains of the family came from her side. Brew pretended not to know the meaning of the word obtuse and Holly rolled her eyes. The family dynamics made for a very welcoming atmosphere and I felt at home almost at once.

The décor was light and modern with seating placed to optimise conversation. There was, of course, a TV but it was not in a dominant position. If I had expected a frontier-look to the place, well I wasn't disappointed but the masculine, cowboy paraphernalia was restricted to Brew's study. It was in the study, just the two of us, and over large mugs of coffee that we first touched on the reason for my visit.

As soon as we crossed the line from convivial, general conversation into quasi-official interview, my nerves began to show. I dropped my papers and the family photo album hit the boarded floor hard, seriously creasing a corner of the cover. I could almost hear Mother chiding me for my clumsiness. I felt a fool picking up the strewn papers and even more so when Brew stooped to assist and we banged heads. We managed to laugh about it, but it was somewhat forced. I wondered if Brew was nervous too, and that soon proved to be the case.

Brewster Roebuck was a tall, wiry gentleman just short of his fiftieth birthday. He very much put me in mind of John Wayne: unfailingly polite he was also direct, and there was no doubting he was not a man to cross. Fumbling and embarrassment over, I found the copy of Harrison Bardwell's letter and handed it over.

'Well, here's the critter that started the whole thing off,' he said. He looked at the paper without reading and then laid it almost reverently on his desk. 'I already read it, Colin. It was among your father's effects. Just another old letter and nothing marked out as special or kept in a safe place. It might easily have ended up on the fire like a lot of the other stuff did, but I decided to include it in the package I sent your mother. It seemed mighty important to me, and dragged up memories that had sunk out of sight under more years than I care to remember.'

I wanted to confirm that Brew had witnessed my cousin jumping off the bridge all those years ago. I wanted to question him as to the accuracy of the newspaper report, but it was too soon; it would all sound too much like an accusation, so instead I asked who he thought it might have been whose death prompted Harrison Bardwell to write to my father, and more to the point, who was it still alive at the time of writing that he feared.

There were two people who died early in 1967 that Brew had in mind. There was my Uncle Nate – who of course, I knew about – and then there was Gary Stroud. 'My guess is that old Sheriff Stroud knew a mite more than he was telling.'

And then the question at the front of my mind was answered without me having to voice it. There were details about that fateful evening in June 1958 that young Brewster Roebuck was encouraged to keep quiet about. Of course, it was getting dark, and your eyes can play tricks, but Brew had been pretty sure Bobby Lee was fully dressed when he jumped, and yet his clothes had been found up on the

71

bridge. And his face was bloody but again the Sheriff convinced him that shadows can make you see things that aren't really so. Then there was the earlier splash. A catfish, the Sheriff said. And sure enough Brewster Roebuck knew the rumours that the king of all catfish lived in the shade of the Tallahatchie Bridge. Hadn't he been trying to catch him for six solid weeks?

'Stroud told me I had to speak about only those things I knew for a fact. He said that's how the law worked and there was no room for maybe or what if. I was sure I saw Bobby Lee jump of that bridge, or at least I thought I was. The mind has such a way of filling in the gaps. I saw him plummet through the air and hit the water. I didn't actually see him jump, and the commotion that made me look up in the first place might easily have been a struggle or someone pushing him maybe.'

'There was a commotion?'

'Maybe, what if … nothing I was allowed to comment on. There were voices too, or one voice at least. Like "Nooooo" or as Stroud convinced me "Geronimo!" Yes I know, makes me sound impressionable and stupid.'

Brewster had been nine years old. Of course he was impressionable, especially when the impressions were being supplied by the sheriff. But he was far from stupid. I reassured him and he seemed to appreciate it.

'There're just two more things. I didn't even mention it to Stroud at the time, but I had the impression Bobby Lee was unconscious when he dropped. It's something I couldn't explain at the time, but his body just didn't have the right balance to it. He fell like a sack of potatoes, not like a man jumping. And lastly – and here's something that didn't register until weeks later – there'd been another witness.'

'Harrison Bardwell?'

'I'm pretty sure of it. I was in town with Daddy getting gas when there came an almighty crunching of gears. It put me in mind that I'd heard that sound before, on the night Bobby Lee jumped. That sound made me jump right enough, and Daddy laughed. He told me Harrison Bardwell had a real old truck and he had to double-clutch or risk crashing the gears. Reckon he crashed more often than not. It wasn't until then I recalled and it was way too late to tell anyone about it. The case was all over and Bobby Lee laid to rest.'

When Brew had been sorting through Father's effects he came upon the letter from Harrison, and all the memories came back. He figured it wasn't his place to go stirring, but included the letter in the package just in case the family were minded to look for the truth.

I made notes and asked Brew to recall his steps on the day in question. He'd been on the south bank of the river checking his fishing lines when he heard an almighty splash and then the commotion up on the bridge a little closer to the opposite bank than the halfway line. He looked up, saw Bobby Lee fall and then ran up to cross the bridge. It was then he heard a truck and the crashing of gears. He ran all the way home, five minutes at top sprint, and his mother put in a call to the Sheriff's Department. It was the day after they found Bobby Lee's body washed all the way down to the Yazoo River that Sheriff Stroud convinced Brewster that the truth of the matter amounted to no more than seeing Bobby Lee jump and not come up again. Anything else was unimportant, and in any case only amounted to a little boy with a big imagination. Bobby Lee McDonald went swimming when he shouldn't have. Bobby Lee paid the price.

Sitting in Brew's warm study that evening nearly 80 miles from the scene of the crime, for that was what I was now convinced it was, it was clear to us both that Harrison Bardwell had seen something and that Sheriff Gary Stroud had possibly helped to cover it up.

'Harrison Bardwell …?' I asked.

'He died two years back. I know, it's a bitch, isn't it?'

True that! But I was a professional researcher. I was used to the enticing come-on that led to nowhere or to a dead-end. I was also experienced enough not to give in at the first, or second or third hurdle. Sometimes the next piece of the puzzle came from the most unexpected quarter. This time it was as a result of my innate clumsiness.

My room had en suite although it was a little too pink for my liking. It had been May's room before she got married and moved up the road to Pontotoc. It was clean, comfortable and fully appointed and had a TV and computer terminal which Brew told me to make use of if I had the need. I decided to write up the day's notes, and back then I still did that with a pen in a hard-backed notebook. But first I need a dose of Bobby Lee's smile. I wanted to go to bed with an image from his happier days and not the awful spectre of his bloody face plunging into the cool muddy waters that would carry him, lifeless, downstream.

I opened the album to the page that held the joyful shot of Bobby Lee suspended in mid-air between swing-rope and water, and noticed another photo peeping out at the corner. Hidden behind the swimming-hole shot, and jarred into view when I'd dropped the album, was the photo of a young black lad of about eighteen or nineteen. He was sitting on a log, dressed in cut-down trousers. The integral date on the lower border matched the date on the swimming-hole shot of Bobby Lee, so it didn't take Sherlock to surmise the boy was a friend of my cousin's. Brew didn't remember ever seeing the boy before, but he recalled rumours – a scandal back in those days – that Bobby Lee had a black friend who had gone missing around the same time as the incident at the bridge.

The first splash? Brew and I considered the possibility, but without a name to go on it was another dead-end. As we ate breakfast next morning, the pieces started coming together and I jumped to a few conclusions. Some might call it unprofessional. I call it speculation and that morning I wondered if Bobby Lee's unconventional friendship had been the cause of his death, and possibly that of his black friend too. When Josh and Cal came down for their breakfast I was glad that times had changed. I was later to learn that times had not changed as much as I hoped.

With such a tight schedule my planning had to be good. That first day I was happy to put up with another flight. Brew flew us back to Greenwood Municipal where his eldest son Steve met us in his truck. We were due to see the bridge where it all started and I had an appointment at the archives where I hoped to learn more from the coroner's case file. But first there was an unplanned excursion. Steve thought I might like to see where they had filmed the 1970's movie, *Ode to Billy Joe*. The bridge they had used was gone now. It had been old when they made the film and already out of use, but most surprising of all, it didn't even span the Tallahatchie River. The film-star bridge crossed the Yazoo River several miles south of Greenwood.

'I only know about it because it crossed over to the old Roebuck Road,' Steve said as we looked out across the Yazoo at the place where the bridge had been.

'You have a road named after you?'

Steve didn't think the Roebucks whose name was commemorated were the same branch of the family.

The actual bridge where it had all started was a pretty plain affair to the north of Greenwood. Steve's farm was north of the bridge and it was here that several more pieces fell into place. Steve was a credit to his father. He had turned a profit during some bad cotton years and was one of the first to use Roundup-Ready which, as I understand it, is a seed that has been modified to grow cotton plants that have high resistance to weed-killer. He'd also gone into business with a friend and together they owned a cotton-picker, module builder and boll buggy, an essential trio of machines needed at harvest time that they hired out. Steve had a wife and young family, and once again I was made to feel welcome.

Steve told me that the farm used to be owned by the Monroe family and that Beth Monroe had been Bobby Lee's sweetheart. 'Old Jake Washington tells how he ran into her a few years back,' Steve told me over lunch, 'and found out that she still puts flowers on Bobby Lee's grave to mark the anniversary of his passing.'

Beth was still alive! That was a lead I would have to follow, except nobody knew where she lived. Her brother Chris had a place up in Tupelo and Steve was sure he had the address somewhere, so all was not lost. Of more immediate excitement though, was that Jake Washington was even now working on the module builder. He was a very old man now but liked to potter about, and Steve was happy to find him work: cleaning, oiling, that kind of thing.

'What's more, from your point of view, Colin, is that he used to work for your Uncle Nate up at the old mill.'

The mill was no longer there. All that was left was a concrete floor and the remains of what looked like it could have once been a tool shed. The area was no longer known as Choctaw Ridge; that name faded over the years that followed the departure of the McDonalds. Nate died and Hettie moved back to Nantucket.

Jake had to be eighty if he was a day and he walked with a stick. When Steve told him who I was he put down his oil can and hugged me tight, as if I was a long-lost son. We talked a little about Bobby Lee and he wondered if it wasn't a little far along the road to be looking back. I had to keep an eye on the time as I had an appointment to visit the archives, but just on the off-chance, I showed him the photo of the black boy sitting on a log by a lake.

Jake took the photo and smiled widely and tears came to his eyes. 'Went that self-same day as Bobby Lee, sure did. Nobody saw him no more. Name was Lucien Harris. He was the son of old Abe who died long time back.'

'Lucien and Bobby Lee, were they friends?' I asked.

'Powerful friends,' Jake said. 'None better, but your uncle didn't like it none. Bobby Lee didn't rub it in his daddy's face but he didn't quit seeing Lucien neither. From little babies, right up to the end, powerful friends, best of friends.'

More food for my theory: Bobby Lee's death was connected with his friendship. 'Do you think Bobby Lee and Lucien died on the same night?'

Jake breathed deeply and picked up the oil can. 'I surely suspect it, but spent a whole heap of time hoping otherwise. Used to think it was Lucien kept placing them flowers until I ran into Miss Beth long time back.'

Before we parted Jake asked if it might be possible there was a spare copy of Lucien's picture. I promised to send him one.

Next stop, the archive. Steve ran me into town and once again we crossed Bobby Lee's bridge. As we crossed I imagined the scene and saw him falling. It was an image that would haunt me with almost the same regularity as the one of Lewis, dying under the wheel of that truck.

Document # 3
Statement from Deputy Sheriff Dale Davidson

On the evening of Tuesday, June 3rd, 1958 at 7.45pm I was on patrol on Money Road, Leflore County, about midway between Greenwood and Money when I had occasion to issue a citation for dangerous driving. At that time I heard my call-sign on the patrol car radio and was directed to Ashwood Bridge to answer a report of a youth falling in the Tallahatchie River. I abandoned the citation and drove with all due haste to the location where I arrived at sundown and I met with persons I know to be Mr and Mrs Cary Roebuck and their small son Brewster who had witnessed the fall. I noticed a pile of clothes on the west sidewalk about midway along the bridge. I later collected the clothing which was a pair of blue jeans, an undershirt, a plaid cotton shirt, shoes and socks. I thought I saw some blood on the road nearby but I later attended the scene and found a smashed tomato ketchup bottle together with a small

77

amount of other garbage that suggested a discarded take-away meal. As soon as I had the story from Master Roebuck I searched the area of the river below the bridge using my flashlight. I also searched each bank downstream for a distance of some hundreds of yards except where the banks were not accessible. I would say my search was a thorough as possible given that night was drawing on. I do not recall being told the youth concerned was believed to be Bobby Lee McDonald. With no other leads I abandoned the search at 9.15pm. Being on night shift I was not involved in the operation of the following days.

***

Apart from the detail of Bobby Lee's injuries, there was little of interest in the coroner's case file and nothing that I hadn't already read in the various newspaper clippings, except for the mention of blood at the scene. Deputy Davidson thought he saw blood, and later it had magically transmuted into ketchup. Then there was the mention of a citation for dangerous driving. Which way had that perpetrator of a traffic misdemeanour been travelling? Were they hot-tailing it away from the scene of the crime? What a pity Deputy Davidson hadn't been more thorough and mentioned names. Local archives were in pretty good order, but there wasn't a chance there would be any trace of a partially issued traffic citation forty years after the event. As I said earlier, no piece of information is ever too small to interest a professional researcher.

When we had landed back in Pontotoc County and motored to Brew's home on Choctaw Ridge, I showed Brew the copy I'd made of the deputy's statement and mentioned my frustration at the lack of names.

'Dale's a good friend of mine,' Brew said. 'He has the memory of an elephant. He's a good man and I'm pretty certain he'd be happy to answer a question or two about that night.'

Somebody who hadn't actually died? We'd have to see about his memory but I didn't hold out too much hope. Occasionally I lacked sufficient hope; it buffered me against disappointment. This time, any realistic hope I might have harboured was surpassed. Not only did the retired deputy remember who had barely escaped a fine, but the lucky culprit, Dewey Hopwood, turned out to be a neighbour of Brew's. Before our visit with Dale ended I asked about the blood, and why he had mentioned it once it had turned out to be red sauce.

'I was pretty sure it was blood when I first saw it and that's what I wrote up in my notes. But next evening Sheriff Stroud called up on the radio for a meet at the scene. He showed me the broken ketchup bottle and the French fries and half a hamburger bun, but you know it didn't look like it was in exactly the same place to me. But Stroud talked to me like I was a fool and made me re-write my statement. He tried to make me rewrite it one more time on account I mentioned the blood at all but I squared up and told him it was my statement and I wasn't about to do it again.' It was quite clear there was no love lost between the retired deputy and his former boss.

I have to go a little out of sequence, but it keeps the story tight. I didn't get to meet Dewey Hopwood until my last full day in Mississippi. He graciously came into the office at the airstrip and we spoke over coffee. It wasn't a huge room and it was pretty crammed. Brew shared the office with his secretary-slash-office manager, Iris Dunlop.

In his late fifties Dewey made a decent living selling top-of-the-range ovens. He had taken an active part in local projects and now the business ran at various outlets under area managers, he could pursue his interests in local government. He had no recollection of meeting Deputy Dale Davidson on the night of Bobby Lee's death, or rather he had no recollection of that particular encounter as there had been so many.

'I was a bit of a loose canon as a kid. Got into a lot of scrapes, but I saw the error of my ways before it was too late.' He pushed a hand through slicked black hair, a little too black for a man his age. Too lean as well, a little skeletal in fact with steel grey eyes.

Dewey admitted that he and Bobby Lee had no time for each other, and on one occasion had actually come to blows. 'I don't rightly recall what it was about, but I do remember being surprised at how much of a punch he packed for a quiet kid.' Dewey fingered his nose as if remembering the pain. 'That would have been, oh about a month or so before he was pulled out of the river. I was pretty upset about that. Made me feel mean and kind of guilty that we had been on bad terms and now here he was dead.'

I mentally punched the air for Bobby Lee's well aimed strike. There was something I didn't like about Dewey in spite of his pleasant demeanour and I couldn't help wondering if he remembered exactly why they had fought, and if that reason had been to do with the skin-colour of Bobby Lee's best friend. Was I looking into the face of a killer? It didn't seem likely. Dewey Hopwood gave me his card and said to call anytime if I had more questions. Was Dewey on my list of suspects? Yes he was, right along with Gary Stroud, but experience told me the obvious suspect wasn't always the true culprit. Only two days before I had added another to my list: Chris Monroe.

Steve Roebuck had found Chris's address and phone number in Tupelo and I'd made a call. Chris sounded pleasant enough on the phone but different altogether when we met. He was abrupt to the point of rudeness, couldn't understand why I was rooting through the dirt and wondered why I couldn't let dead dogs lie. Overweight, bordering on obese, he grew so red in the face at one point I thought he might have a stroke. He seemed to relish in telling me that although Bobby Lee had been a nice enough kid, he grew up to be a shit, always sniffing round his sister. And no I certainly could not have his sister's address and just leave decent people the Hell alone!

We met in a diner and I was feeling more than a little self-conscious with all the fuss he was making in public. It was almost as if he was playing to the gallery. I asked, quietly, why he had agreed to meet with me in the first place. I had apparently caught him unawares, and if he'd had time to think about it, he would not have agreed to any kind of a meeting anywhere, anyhow. Having made himself perfectly clear, he stormed out and left me to pick up the tab. It did not qualify as my best day of the trip.

The trip ended all too quickly but in spite of Chris Monroe's best efforts, my abiding impression was a positive one and it had to do with Brew's youngest son and his best friend. Josh and Cal spent a lot of time together, and by the end of the week they had lost their awe of the Englishman and loosened up. I was able to observe the signs of the closeness of their relationship and I found it refreshing.

That last day, they came in from shooting hoops, both in their basketball uniforms. Both well over six-foot, I would have felt intimidated but for the fact I'd seen more fat on a pair of oven-ready chips. If they both grew out in proportion to growing up, they would each be a force to be reckoned with one day. Josh prepared some cold drinks, by way of snapping the ring-pulls, and both boys joined me in the living room. He had certainly loosened up in my presence, no longer calling me "sir" in that peculiarly American way that is rather disconcerting to Brits not used to such niceties from teenagers. And Cal was getting there too, though I believe I detected a certain reluctance to completely trust the guy with the funny accent. Now they asked about my research and I told them it was going well, and I asked about their sport.

Josh told me he was a power forward. Cal was a little more hesitant saying he liked back court and front court positions equally.

'He's more of a tweener than anything else,' Josh said and Cal's last ounce of reserve was broken. He skelped Josh upside the head and Josh responded with a similar attack.

'You call me tweener, your little white twink ass lined up 'tween all those black ones come shower time, you're the tweener, boy!'

'Pretty easy target to aim for, bro,' Josh said wiggling his rear.

'"Pretty" and "easy", true on both counts,' Cal said and smacked it hard; Josh yelped and they set to wrestling. But not for long.

'Yard for rough-housing, inside for peace and quiet,' Brew said, his outline filling the doorframe, his tone making the floorboards tremble. Both boys apologised. Both boys called him sir. Both boys scooted out into the yard wearing expression of suitable contrition. The moment they had disappeared Brew's hard look melted into a smile and he shook his head. 'Kids!'

If I regret one thing about the whole affair it would be that the boys were dragged into the nastiness that followed. I would give anything to have saved them the pain. But all that was to come. My first trip was over and I left with the knowledge that Sheriff Stroud had covered up certain aspects of Bobby Lee's death, that Bobby Lee was dead before he hit the water just as Harrison Bardwell's letter said, and that someone, for some reason had killed him. There wasn't nearly enough to put before the police, but I was getting there, although it has to be said, at that stage I was still on a quest for the truth. Police and courts were the furthest thing from my mind. And culprits? I was convinced there was a crime involved, but as to suspects, the chances were they had all died long ago. So the threatening letter was a bit of an own goal.

Just after the plane had achieved cruising height I was approached by a stewardess and asked if I was Mr Colin McDonald. I affirmed and she gave me a letter. No, she didn't know who had handed it in for delivery. She was just passing it on as requested by ground crew.

The letter wasn't signed. It expressed the sentiment that I should enjoy my journey home and never bother to visit Mississippi ever again. Nobody, it appeared, wanted me there. I was not welcome and I had no right to delve into a past that was long gone and buried. My first thought was that the letter must have been penned, with use of a ruler to disguise the handwriting, by Chris Monroe. The tone of the letter was identical to his spittle-chucking indignation.

They might as well have waved a red rag at me. I spent the rest of the trip veritably pawing at the ground. I was planning my return before the first touch-down. Back home I phoned Brew. If anything, he was even angrier than I. 'I've never been intimidated into changing my mind but one time, and then I was a nine-year-old little boy.'

Document # 4
Report of the Medical Examiner

Deceased: Bobby Lee McDonald

Details of Recovery: *As reported by Sheriff's Dept, from close to east bank of Yazoo River just downstream from the confluence of the Yalobusha & Tallahatchie Rivers at dawn on Friday, June 6th, 1958.*

Date of Examination: Monday, June 9th, 1958

Report: *The body is that of the deceased (above) identified by Mrs Hettie McDonald (mother of deceased). Clothing at time of recovery, underpants only. Other clothing reportedly found on west sidewalk of Ashwood Bridge a little north of halfway point.*

The body presents as that of a young adult Caucasian male (16 to 20 years) approximate height 6 foot and one inch, estimated life-weight 155 lbs. Excepting facial/spinal trauma as listed below, the overall condition is good and intact although there is tissue maceration from immersion in water. There is some distension of the abdomen due to build-up of post mortem gases. Tissues and internal gas levels suggest immersion for three to five days. The external auditory canals and nasal passages are compacted with mud. There are also traces of blood in the nasal passages commensurate with the injuries detailed below.

There are facial injuries as follows:

1. Dislocation of the left condylar process;

2. Crack to base of mandible;

3. Depression of right zygomaticofacial formen;

4. Displacement of middle and inferior nasal concha and broken perpendicular plate.

5. Dislocation of $3^{rd}/4^{th}$ cervical vertebrae with associated severing of spinal cord.

6. There is soft tissue damage to the face commensurate with the underlying bony injuries listed above.

7. There are contusions and abrasions to the tissues lying over the first and second proximal phalanges of the right hand. The underlying bones are intact.

8. There are numerous very minor abrasions, lacerations and incisions scattered about the epidermis commensurate with wildlife activity.

Further to above I examined the body for evidence of foul play. There are no signs of injuries associated with binding of wrists or of any defensive injury. The genitals are normal showing no sign of injury or recent sexual activity. The anus shows no injury or any sign of sexual activity.

Toxicology is negative.

Gut contents unremarkable.

Brain, spinal cord, heart, liver and lungs normal except as at 5 above. No sign of congenital conditions or acute or chronic dysfunction.

There was no water in the lungs.

Cause of Death: *Broken neck as at 5 above.*

Conclusion: *Injuries are consistent with either a heavy blow to the face with a blunt instrument or a fall onto the face from a height of 10 to 15 feet. Given the statement of witness (Master Brewster Roebuck), the scene examination report by Sheriff*

Stroud and details of recovery, the injuries suggest the deceased dove into the Tallahatchie River from Ashwood Bridge and struck a floating object causing injury shown at 5 leading to instantaneous death. This likely cause is supported by a lack of water in the lungs.

***

I found it difficult to settle back to the day job. Try as I might to concentrate on any given task in hand, Bobby Lee would insinuate himself into my thoughts and I would drift. At Kew in the National Archive I remember looking for a soldier's records and Bobby Lee muscled in and led me on another path to his death while I peered left and right down all the side turnings looking for clues. Who else might I interview? Where could I write for more documentation? Another time I was being briefed by a TV producer. He was working on a programme about fishing boats, which made me think water, which led me to the Tallahatchie River and Bobby Lee floating face down. Bobby Lee's was the last face I saw at night, drifting in my mind, and Bobby Lee woke me up each morning. In dreams I would see him beaten by Chris Monroe, thrown over the guardrail by Sheriff Stroud, surrounded by the Clan and derided for being a "nigger-lover". I knew I had to get back to Mississippi soon and get amongst it. That letter I read on the flight from Greenwood did nothing at all to warn me off, and everything to fire my determination to get to the truth. It proved to me that there were people out there who knew the truth and couldn't abide for it to surface.

And then there were obstacles at home. Mrs McDonald didn't like it that so much of my time was spent speculating about Bobby Lee, nor that Josh Roebuck and I were in regular email contact – initiated by him I hasten to add. It wasn't natural, according to Miranda's view of the world, that a boy the same age as my own daughter should be interesting in talking to an old man. I on the other hand, have never felt so old that I believe there is nothing I can learn from the younger generation. As to my research, Miranda was absolutely adamant: we were not rich and could not afford to drop everything so I could chase shadows. Consequently there was no way I could even think of carrying on my investigation until next year. One trip a year was all I could afford if we were still to have a holiday trip, and that was that – except it wasn't.

I had two lucky breaks at the beginning of April, 1999. One was a letter from Brew with an exciting enclosure, but first let's talk about the real ace. As Bobby Lee was always on my mind it wasn't unnatural that he should creep into my conversation. Cutting straight to the chase, this led to a commission. I was actually hired to research the mystery of the kid who jumped off the Tallahatchie Bridge by a man in the film business who saw the opportunity to produce a docu-drama about the whole affair. Now I was going to get paid to track down Bobby Lee's true story and any trips I made would be work and not vacation and on expenses. Miranda couldn't possibly object, only of course she did, but that's another story.

Back to Brew's letter, the second package I'd had from him full of goodies. At this rate I'd have to start paying him. It was good to hear news of Choctaw Ridge and the Roebuck family and I was flattered that Josh was enjoying our continuing email correspondence, but the other letters were the gems. One was from Chris Monroe, who was just about the last person on Earth I thought would ever take the time to write to me unless it was another threatening letter, which it most decidedly was not.

Chris apologised for the attitude he had shown and told me he had been having a bad time. He said he had no right to block access to his sister Beth, as she had told him in no uncertain terms when Chris had spoken to her of our meeting.

The other letter was from Beth Thomas, nee Monroe: Bobby Lee's sweetheart. I could hardly contain my excitement; I was so sure she would have more pieces to the puzzle, maybe even the key – four corners and all the straight edges!

I wrote to Beth immediately. I wrote an old-style pen-and-paper letter because she had not included an email address. Back then it was entirely possible she didn't have an email address; they were not quite as ubiquitous as they are nowadays, but if only she had, I might have been able to solve the mystery a little more quickly. I booked a trip for July, but had I received her second letter sooner, I would have booked it for the beginning of June.

Document # 5
Letter from Elizabeth Thomas

[ADDRESS REDACTED]
Vicksburg, Mississippi
June 24th, 1999

Dear Colin,

Your letter stirred up such feelings, some happy some sad. Of course I remember you as a very small boy and I remember Bobby Lee's English aunt, your mother. Bobby Lee was so proud of his English relatives and spoke of you often.

As to us meeting, I do not think it is a good idea. My husband Philip is a good Christian man who has done right by me and our son Jeremy and I fear your enquiries might hurt him in a way he doesn't deserve.

Let me just say that Bobby Lee McDonald was my first love. He was the sweetest and kindest boy and I wanted to die when he was so tragically taken. To learn that he might not have taken his own life, which had always been my personal belief despite the coroner's finding of accidental death, and that he might have been deliberately harmed opens old wounds, and yet please do not feel guilty as I am glad to know because the truth, no matter how painful, might help to lay old ghosts.

87

You might ask why I thought Bobby Lee ended his own life. Let me just say this. We were both very young, excited by life and love and open to all the temptations youth and vigor have to offer. The tree of knowledge stood between us and so yes, I plucked, I ate, and a few days later my paradise was lost.

But not entirely: please look carefully at the enclosed picture of my son Jeremy. It was taken in 1976, when he was 17-years-old. I do not think I will need to say more, except that the day before Bobby Lee went missing we met. Sweet, kind Bobby Lee made a proposal of marriage, and I turned him down. Daddy would never allow such a thing and I was too young to consider defying him. Of course, neither of us knew we had started a new life. We leaned over the rail on that bridge over the river that would soon take his life and one by one we threw in the flowers that he had brought me. Bobby Lee cried as did I, and then we parted for the last time. I never saw him again. I have carried a measure of guilt all these years and so you will see how I am as keen as you to know the truth of it.

Philip is not so much of a fool that he cannot see Bobby Lee in the son he has raised and loved. He has never so much as mentioned it and so we cannot meet and you should not write again. I owe Philip that. I have told you everything I know and I hope it will help you find the truth. If there is a conclusion to your investigation I know Brewster Roebuck will find a way of passing it to me.

Finally, there is something you said in your letter that puzzles me. Yes, there will always be a part of me that will never stop loving Bobby Lee, and yes every June 3rd I make my pilgrimage back to the Delta and pick some fresh flowers for him, but I do not lay them on his grave. If you have been to Little Zion you will know there isn't a headstone for him and nowhere to place flowers with any certainty that they are anywhere near Bobby Lee's remains. No, if flowers are laid each year as you say, there is someone else who remembers Bobby Lee. As to my offerings, I

88

drop them off of the Tallahatchie Bridge just like we did that last time we met. I cry and I say a prayer and I move on, until the next year.

Jeremy has grown into a fine man. He served in the Gulf rising to the rank of Major and now he works with the wildlife conservation services. So you see all that Bobby Lee was is not lost entirely. I know you will respect my wishes and that all I have said concerning the connection between my son and Bobby Lee will be held in the strictest of confidence.

With kind wishes,
Yours
[Signed: Beth]

***

I looked at the photograph of Jeremy Thomas. I might just as well have been looking at one of Bobby Lee. My cousin had fathered a child, but it wasn't a fact that was about to add to my list of suspects. Bobby Lee died before anyone knew Beth was pregnant. Was it possible someone suspected they had made love? It was circumstantial, but the case against Chris Monroe had just advanced a step, and now his father was peeking over the page too.

But just who was the person who placed flowers for Bobby Lee every year if it wasn't Beth? I had already made the mental note and now wrote it into my notebook: be at Bobby Lee's grave on the 3rd of June, 2000 – almost a year ahead. I would track down this mysteriously loyal person I had missed by a matter of two short weeks. I wondered if Lucien Harris was still alive: another avenue of enquiry.

I made arrangements, placed bookings, planned the next stage of my investigation and swapped a few more emails with Josh. He was edging towards a revelation and when it came there was no surprise. Josh and Cal were more than just good friends. I was the first person he had told and it was important to him that I knew. He hadn't told his father yet and I had the feeling he was using me as a kind of testing ground. I took a great deal of time over the reply. It was important to get it right. I told Josh that for all it was worth I supported him and that he should be safe and careful. I mentioned Matt Shepard little knowing that because of me and my stubborn refusal to have done with the past Josh was destined for a similar fate.

This time I stayed with Steve Roebuck and his family, right there in the centre of things, a few hundred yards from where Bobby Lee was killed. Furthermore I had the services of a research intern in the shape of Josh Roebuck. He'd asked if he could tag along, help out in any way he could, and I was happy for the company. I had a lot of miles to cover in the next few weeks and I found driving on the wrong side of the road a real chore.

My first couple of day in Mississippi though were not in the Delta but back on Choctaw Ridge with Roebuck senior. I spent an enjoyable time with a man who I had come to think of as a good friend. It appeared I had made an impression too, for when Brew's friend Dale Davidson, former Deputy Sheriff, heard I was back in town he insisted on meeting up.

The evening had cooled sufficiently to be able to risk the outdoors where the air conditioning couldn't reach. I was a fool in planning my trip for July and found it hard coping with the heat during the day, but the evening was tolerable. Crickets laid down a nice background track for noisier beasts and birds and the four of us – me, Brew, Holly and Dale – sat in rockers sipping mint-flavoured drinks. Mercy me and I do declare, I was beginning to feel like a good old boy. Where was the whiskey and rye? On a more serious note, I have always had an ear for accents and soon picked them up, a fact that was often reflected in my writing.

We conversed about everything and nothing, just enjoying each other's company, when Dale conjectured that he considered me a level-headed guy and asked if I was a cautious kind of a man.

I recognised some terminology immediately and smiled. 'It's the ring, isn't it?' I said holding up my right hand and wiggling the finger that bore a band of gold that wasn't a wedding ring. 'I'm not a Freemason Dale. This ring was Bobby Lee's. It was on him when they pulled him out of the river.'

Dale chuckled and gave a fat wink and asked if he could see it a bit closer. 'Well now, if I'd had on my glasses I could've told it wasn't your ring.'

'From the initials?'

'That's right. The G in the middle of the compasses stands for God. Now see here, the PH stands for Prince Hall, and he was a boy back in the eighteenth century who started a lodge for black fellows. This here's a black Freemason's ring. And you say it was Bobby Lee's?'

Snick, snap, push it down all smoothly: another piece had just fallen into place. I now felt sure the ring had been given to Bobby Lee by his friend Lucien Harris. I thought of Josh and Cal, and although theirs was an entirely different kind of relationship, I was impatient to tell them about my cousin and his best friend.

But Dale had more. One of the reasons he was keen for another meeting was that he had done a lot of thinking since the last time and some rooting around in his attic.

'Took me a while,' he said. 'Found it eventually.' He handed me a slim buff-coloured reporter's notebook stamped with the spread-eagle seal of the Leflore County Sheriff's Department. 'I should have given it in when it was filled up, but notebooks had a way of going missing just when you needed them, so I kept all mine.' He told me I should turn to page 43.

Document # 6
Extract from Notebook of Deputy Davidson
(Original written in pencil)

June 3ʳᵈ – 7.35pm. Mon. Rd. 1 mile
N LZ Bap. ✝
1955 Imp Newport convert. green white
top. Licence [REDACTED]. Drv
Dewey HOPWOOD. F/pas Ralph
WEBSTER. Speed ex & dang.
Ticket F000736

***

It roughly translated that Dewey Hopwood had been driving like a fool and that he was going to be written up for it. But then the call came over the radio and Dale had rushed off to deal with the bridge incident. I knew all that, but now there was another name. Maybe Ralph Webster had seen something. Unfortunately neither Brew nor Dale knew where Ralph might be these days. I could always ask Dewey Hopwood, but that would be my last choice. Better I find him independently of his old friend.

Those mint-flavoured drinks had a kick to them and Dale had one too many. Dale told me to hang on to the notebook for a while. 'Might he'p you get to the bottom of all this.' He leaned forward in his rocker. 'I was always one to write up a lot of notes. I learnt it from an old deputy who took me under his wing when I was a greenhorn.' Dale hiccupped and excused himself with a smile. 'I reckon your uncle features in my notebooks more then a couple of times.'

'Dale Davidson! Now you are the limit!' Holly chided and Dale held up his hands in apology.

'As a complainant is all I'm saying, pardon me, Colin. I don't mean to imply he was in my books as a suspect. Nobody more upstanding than your old Uncle Nate.'

I assured Dale that I had taken no offence.

'There was this one time I recall he found a stray boy sleeping back of the mill – a runaway. He ...' Dale's smile froze in memory, and then faded. 'Well, times have changed, thank the good Lord. Let's just say no runaway was like to settle on his land for a second time.'

I understood by now that "boy" generally meant black man, irrespective of age and I knew that Dale's unfinished sentence had but one meaning: Nathan McDonald was a fine and upstanding man of his time, which did not preclude handing out summary justice to those of the oppressed race whenever the need took him. I shuddered to recall old photos I had seen, snapped in the nineteen-thirties, of smiling crowds in their Sunday best surrounding the swinging corpse of the victim of a lynching. Were these all fine and upstanding members of the community? You can bet your life on it.

Dale's daughter came to drive him home. He reminded me to be sure to have a good look through his notebook. 'No telling what you might find,' he said, with a look that told me he knew exactly what I might find.

Holly took her leave saying that she wanted an early night. Brew and I stayed a while listening to the music of the night and watching the stars peep through the canopy of Brew's private stand of woodland. We discussed the next day's travelling arrangement. Once again Brew was going to fly me and Josh into the Delta. Steve would meet us and drive us through town and out to the farm. It was all set, all planned like a military operation. All I lacked was a gun. What a shame that in the days to come, that was one piece of equipment that might have come in handy.

'I hear as how Josh has told you something … something kind of personal about himself.'

My stomach contracted. It can't be a good feeling when a son chooses to confide in a virtual stranger about something so important before he broaches the subject with his own father. 'Yes, I guess it's easier to talk across the divide of the ocean sometimes, especially if you're unsure of the reaction you might get.'

Brew looked up into the night. 'As I hear it, your reaction was nothing short of a tonic for Josh. He told me … "came out", as they say … a little while after he read your email.'

Suddenly the crickets sounded a lot louder, and their song particularly interesting. At least it filled a long silence. I couldn't stand it any longer. 'And … you're okay with it.'

Brew laughed. 'I knew since he was thirteen years old. Why is it that kids think their parents go through life with their heads stuck up their asses?'

'I guess, because most of us do,' I said, not without a little guilt. 'That and the fact that kids are so secretive these days.'

'There is that, I suppose.' Brew stood and stretched his back. 'I can't say it's something I'd have chosen for my youngest kid, and it makes me worry some, but it doesn't make me love him any less. And I truly thank you for seeing him through a rough patch.'

Out of one rough patch and straight towards another: I wonder if Brew would have thanked me if he knew what was coming.

Josh had already proved his worth. In the same email that I told him I'd be happy to have him along as my intern. I set him some tasks and he'd already come up trumps. Through his older brother Steve via old Jake Washington he'd traced people in Itta Bena who remembered Lucien Harris, and what's more they seemed keen to talk. Secondly he had found an address for Harrison Bardwell's widow.

On my first day back in the Delta Josh drove me from Steve's farm to Itta Bena, via the bridge (a replacement for the one that had been used in the film) and along the banks of Roebuck Lake.

Rebecca Taylor had been a school teacher at West Tally High. She'd recently retired though she didn't look nearly old enough to have run the course of a teaching career. Tall, slender and with strikingly fine features I could imagine her causing quite a stir among the young men in her classes.

We met at her house, a small neat building near the centre of town. Being Lucien's old flame, she remembered him well and spent a lot of time smiling at the photo of him sitting on the log.

'Just like he was before he disappeared,' she said. 'I wonder if this is the last picture that was taken of him.'

I could tell the image meant a lot to her, and I promised to send her a copy. That old shot was becoming very popular.

Unfortunately Rebecca couldn't provide us with any leads, but she spoke a lot about her family and how they missed Lucien, and of Lucien as a boy. His friendship with Bobby Lee was a matter of considerable concern for the Harris family. 'Back in those days it most certainly did not bode well for any black person to be on friendly terms with whites. Such relationships never ended well.'

Without meaning to, I looked over and caught Josh's eye. He looked down and blushed. Maybe I spoke out of turn, but I told Rebecca that Josh's best friend was black and that had to be encouraging for the future. We all agreed that there was a way to go yet.

Later Josh and I bought take-outs and ate by an old wartime field-gun set on the green. We should have stayed inside the diner; in moments my shirt was wet through and I wondered how anybody could get used to the heat. We discussed the next move and I assigned Josh another task. The following day I'd planned to spend at the archives, so while I was grubbing round in the dust of ancient paper, I wondered if Josh could trace Ralph Webster, one of the two boys Deputy Dale Davidson had pulled over that night of Bobby Lee's death.

It was early afternoon, heading east along Roebuck Road back to Steve's farm, when we had our own brush with death. With the lake on the driver's side and open fields spreading far to the right, the sky appeared unnaturally big and blue. The sun beat down so that there was a heat haze rising off the road ahead. I was thankful for the efficiency of air conditioning and for the fact that I didn't have to drive. I settled back in the seat and closed my eyes when Josh noticed something up ahead.

'What the …?' Josh was gripping the wheel.

'Is he on our side of the road?'

'Sure looks that way.'

Split seconds passed and there was no doubt. There was a truck, a big truck, not a little pick-up like ours, converging with us on our side of the road. Josh blasted the horn and turned on the headlights. The truck then moved centre-road leaving no room for us to pass on either side, or no time to brake. Josh opted to stay on the proper side and steered for the gap. The nearside tyres overlapped the edge of the road and the two vehicles passed at a converging speed of about 80 miles an hour, our offsides within inches of each other.

Our nearside tyres threw up dirt and debris and put us off balance. We slewed and Josh corrected, slewed the other way and Josh corrected again. Eventually we came to a halt sideways across the road in time to see the other driver give us the finger, a red-shirted arm stretched out of the cab.

'Crazy fucking asshole!' Josh shouted at the top of his lungs. I'd never heard him swear before. He jumped out the pick-up and glared at the receding truck as if he could blow it up with laser eyes.

I joined him and slapped his shoulder. 'Well done, Josh. That was a great bit of driving. I know I wouldn't have been able to get out of that one.'

'What's with him? Was he trying to kill us?'

I assured Josh that, just in case he hadn't already noticed, the world was full of fools and that no doubt we were just in the wrong place and the wrong time. Looking back and in light of things that were to come, I'm not so sure.

Back at the farm Josh spilled it all out to big brother Steve. We all concluded that there wasn't a lot of point in calling the police about it, but the subject wouldn't go away and it held centre stage around the dining table that night at dinner. I never tasted black-eyed peas before. Dishes were passed and we all helped ourselves generously.

'Pass the biscuits, please,' Steve said, and one of his daughters duly obliged. I wondered how different this domestic scene was from the one in Bobbie Gentry's song just about the time news of Billy Joe came in, and whether that was all a facsimile of the occasion when the Monroe family first heard about my cousin, Bobby Lee.

Before I went to sleep that night I sat up in bed going through Dale's old notebook, and found my next lead.

Document # 7
More Extracts from Notebook of Deputy Davidson

> *Jan 23rd – 9.45pm. F.Lor g/pump. 1955 Imp Newport convert. green white top. Licence [REDACTED]. Drv Dewey HOPWOOD. F/pas Ralph WEBSTER. B/pas Bo SIMPSON. Loit. Moved on.*

> *... Mar 6th. Meet Offcr HOWARD Greenville PD. Susp disorder in town 3 nights back. Dewey HOPWOOD, Ralph WEBSTER, Bo SIMPSON.*

> *... Mar 21st. Backup assist Greenville PD. Main. Fight.Dewey HOPWOOD, Bo SIMPSON & R. WEBSTER*

***

The notebook was stuffed full of entries, but I got used to scanning the pencilled notes for that little gang of three: always together those three, except for the night of the incident. Now I'd give Josh another name to trace: Bo Simpson.

That night I had a nightmare. It had been a while but big brother Lewis was back, always in the clothes I'd last seen him wearing, always 12 years old. I was driving the big truck down the middle of the Roebuck Road, except instead of bearing down on Josh in his pick-up, I was aiming for Lewis McDonald on his pedal cycle. He tried to get out of the way. He looked me in the eyes, and screamed, and died under my wheels, and I yelled and woke up. I was in a sweat despite the air con. Once again I killed my brother in a dream, just as I had killed him in real life. It crossed my mind that without Lewis's loss, I would never have developed my Caesarion Complex, I might not have even become a researcher and it was doubtful I would be here now trying to find out what really happened to my cousin.

The next few days marked a turning point. There was a person, or people, as keen at keeping the truth hidden as I was at rooting it out.

My day at the archives was almost entirely unsuccessful, but Josh proved to be a man of gold once again. He traced Ralph Webster by the simple expedient of going through the phone book and calling up several R. Websters before he reached the right one. He showed particular initiative by booking us an appointment. He had no such similar luck in tracing Bo Simpson though. My partial success was to trace an article which spoke of the unidentified body of a young black man being found in the Yazoo River in July 1958. We would never know for sure, or at least I thought we never would, if it was the body of Lucien Harris.

The following day I met with Harrison Bardwell's widow, Margie. Of course she remembered the incident. Harrison had been very upset by the news. He'd even got a visit from Sheriff Stroud a day or so after Bobby Lee jumped.

Call me insensitive, but the truth now meant more to me that people's feelings. I showed her a copy of the letter her husband had written to my father.

She was a grand old lady, Marge Bardwell, who put me in mind of the stereotypical southern matriarch. She let the letter drop into her lap, and told me how it must explain why they received a visit from Sam McDonald and why he and Harrison had locked themselves away in the study to talk. Now, that particular revelation hit me right between the eyes.

As a researcher you learn not to assume. You speculate, you ponder and you formulate possible explanations, but you do not make assumptions. After Brew told me there were no more papers of interest among my father's effects and that his wife had no previous knowledge of the letter Harrison Bardwell had sent, I assumed his widow would have nothing of interest to add. Now I discovered my father had indeed met up with Harrison. I knew I had to speak with my father's second wife, if only to eliminate the possibility of new information. But that was a meeting to come later. Next on the list, thanks to Josh, was Ralph Webster.

Ralph lived in a little town west of Greenwood. He hadn't moved a long way in his life, either in terms of distance or personal growth. He'd muddled through, taken such work as he could find and raised a family as best he could on his meagre income. Now he lived alone, the family all gone: wife left, children moved on. He was far from healthy and was in the advanced stages of emphysema. Sitting in a chair most of the day with his oxygen tank nearby he appeared to be waiting for death and was glad to have a few callers before that final appointment came along. Old Death wouldn't be long in coming, going by Ralph's deeply lined and yellow-skinned face. He was skeletally thin and broke off conversation often to let the oxygen do its work.

I kept my powder dry. I didn't tell Ralph about Harrison Bardwell's letter or the inconsistencies between Brewster's account to Sheriff Stroud and what actually ended up in his statement. I told him who I was and how my cousin's death had always played on my mind. I wanted closure, as they say these days, and so I was revisiting every place and everyone who were remotely connected to that day.

He told me he had been out driving with Dewey Hopwood and Bo Simpson, much like he always did when work was done. They sure were a tribe, he mused. I asked him about the others, and did he keep in touch with them. No, Dewey drifted up to the hills a little while after the incident and Bo just dipped out of the scene. Despite his frailty, Ralph's mind was as bright as a pin, and he clearly recalled being stopped by the deputy.

'Deputy Davidson sure had it in for us,' Ralph chuckled. 'But he could never make anything stick. He'd write up a citation and Dewey's Uncle Gary would come along and make it go away.'

Oh wow! What a gem. I tried to keep the excitement from my voice. 'His Uncle Gary? You mean, Sheriff Gary Stroud?'

'Sure do,' Ralph wheezed. He chuckled some more and the mirth changed quickly to a bout of coughing. It took him a while to recover and Josh brought a glass of water in from the kitchenette. 'That night we near barged old Dale straight off the road. He came after us with his sireen blaring and his lights a-flashing and he was good and mad. "Now, don't be wasting your time, Dale," Dewey said. "You know this ain't going nowhere" he said but Deputy Davidson wasn't keen to listen. That is until a call came in on his radio. Something about a kid falling off the bridge. Later we all knew just what that call was about.'

There was nothing else Ralph could say about the 3rd of June, 1958 but he was happy to keep talking. He didn't get many visitors and he was keen to oil his vocal cords while he had the chance. He reckoned Dewey and Gary Stroud were fruit from the same tree. They both had a mean streak and they both had a powerful hatred of black people. Stroud had once run a "boy" in because he didn't raise his hat to a white lady. Ralph's smile only faded when he notice Josh and I did not share his enthusiasm for the event.

Although his information was interesting I wasn't sorry to leave his squalid little apartment. Nevertheless I thanked him politely and gave him my card, writing my temporary mobile number on the back. We'd had to park some distance away from Ralph's home and on the walk back to the parking lot we discussed the inconsistency in Ralph's story. He'd just told us that on the night he was stopped by Deputy Davidson, he had been with Dewey Hopwood and Bo Simpson. According to Dale's notebook, Simpson wasn't there.

We got back to the pick-up and such niceties were irrelevant. We stood and stared, and then I heard Josh swear for the second time. Things had suddenly got frighteningly serious.

Document # 8
A4 sheet with Four Photographs printed thereon

The photos show a red 1997 Nissan King Cab Hardbody 4x4. All four tyres are flat and there is graffiti sprayed extensively over the paintwork. A close-up of the bonnet shows the words "Go Home Brit!" in white paint. Another on the door shows the initials KKK. The opposite door shows a stick picture of a man hanging.

***

The local police were not very interested in my story about a possible crime of forty-odd years ago. The officer attending was little impressed by my theory that if there was someone willing to go to these lengths then there were still people with something to hide. I got a little angry. It is not a good idea to get angry with a police officer.

'See here, Mr McDonald.' He stabbed his finger towards my face as if it were a loaded service pistol. I shut up instantly. '*That* I am going to do something about,' he said redirecting his loaded finger towards the KKK somebody had sprayed onto the pick-up door. 'That royally pisses me off and it's not just because I'm black. If I catch who did that, they are going to be mighty sorry. But forgive me if I can't get over-excited about something that *might* have happened a dozen years before I was born. Surprising as it may seem, that was not my watch!'

He went on to say the perpetrator might have a point. I should forget the dim and distant past and stop upsetting people.

It took us the rest of the day to arrange recovery for the pick-up. The tyres hadn't just been let down, they were slashed. I paid for new tyres, wouldn't dream of allowing Steve to pick up the tab. It was good of him to lend me the vehicle without him ending up seriously out of pocket.

An expensive day, all told, and one full of surprises; a few more pieces to the puzzle, but no place for them to fit. Until, that is, my mobile rang. It was Ralph Webster and his indignation and excitement was clear through all the wheezing. He'd had more visitors after we left, and these visitors had threatened him.

'Nobody going to threaten me and get away with it,' he said with all the conviction of a man who has nothing to lose but his pride. 'Thing is Mr McDonald, I wasn't exactly free with the truth when we met earlier. There's stuff I need to tell you, get off my chest. Do you think you can drop by again tomorrow morning?'

We dropped by, brand new tyres, bodywork a little stained and muzzy but the white-painted words all obliterated. But we were too late. Ralph Webster was dead. We arrived in time to see a filled body-bag being wheeled out of the apartment on a gurney. There had been a fire. Just a small one but with all that oxygen around … No suspicious circumstances, so it seemed. He was a very sick man, his neighbour told us, and like to go at any time. Well, I'd hold judgement until the coroner's report came out.

I got another call on the way back to Steve's and a coroner's report appeared almost redundant. I made Josh pull over so I could record it in my notebook while my memory was fresh.

Document # 9
Transcript of Call Received Friday, 9th July, 1999 at 11.10am

Caller (Male Voice): Mr Colin McDonald?

Colin: Speaking.

Caller: Why good morning to you, Mr McDonald. I hear you've been having a lot a bad luck just lately.

Colin: I beg your pardon? Who is this?

Caller: Nearly run off the road, a nasty run-in with vandals and now poor Mr Webster.

Colin: What do you know about these things? Who are you?

Caller: Who I am don't matter. What matters is you quit stirring up dirt NOW and you pack your bags and go home. You've been warned before and you won't be warned again.

Colin: Are you threatening me?

Caller: (Laughs). Well, they say you can tell an Englishman but you can't tell him much. However I do believe you might just be the exception to the rule. Pretty quick on the uptake, but just so there's no confusion, quit now or people will get hurt.

Call terminated by caller.

***

We called it in to the police. They were not a lot of help, and by the following day I was leaving the Delta. What do you think of that? You don't blame me? You think I am a coward? Are you wondering why you invited me over to tell a story where the hero is a gutless wimp who chickens out when the chips are down? Well, what I say to that is don't make assumptions. I made that mistake once and now I was putting it right. I said I was leaving the Delta, not that I was leaving Mississippi.

It was a long drive to Oxford and the landscape was very different: cooler, a little shadier, more trees. I was visiting Jenny McDonald, and wondering how she would feel meeting her husband's son by his previous wife. Jenny had certainly sounded welcoming on the phone, but she wondered if we could meet elsewhere than at her home.

She called me back once she had made some arrangements and supplied me with an address and rough directions. It was right in the middle of town.

Of course before I'd decided to continue with my investigations, now that we had absolute proof of the obstacles we might encounter, there was a discussion between me and the people likely to be affected by any nastiness aimed at me. The Roebucks stood with me, shoulder to shoulder. This was personal now, and as much their investigation as it was mine. Josh protested when I told him it made sense to end his internship, but there was no way I was going to put him in any danger ... I thought. Reluctantly Josh saw sense but made me promise I'd let him help with anything computer-based, anything he could do remotely and from his home in Pontotoc County.

It was all agreed. Being almost on the way, Josh shared the long drive with me and I dropped him off at Choctaw Ridge, and then pointed north. I was looking forward to meeting my father's wife.

I stopped outside the address on Jackson Avenue West, surprised to see that it was a company of lawyers. It passed through my mind that Jenny McDonald was going to have me served with some kind of injunction or restraining order. I took a piece of paper from my pocket and checked, and double checked, the address. It was 11.15am and at 11.30am I was supposed to meet Jenny here. Steeling myself, I went in.

The receptionist told me I was expected, so at least I had the right location. She showed me straight into the office of Jason Seven Elks, co-owner of the company, who greeted me like an old friend. Shorter than average, Jason was a little overweight. He had a rounded face and black hair and was dressed in a dark suit with a button-down shirt and one of those cowboy string-ties. He told me he was expecting Jenny any moment and meanwhile, would I like a coffee. He asked about my business in Mississippi and I gave him the cut-down version of the story keeping details to the minimum and outlining my work, in general terms, as a researcher. We agreed that our lives had been made so much easier by the advent of the World Wide Web.

'Makes my job a whole lot easier and sure saves on the shoe-leather,' Jason said patting his terminal affectionately.

'I dare say that is reflected in lower fees to your clients,' I said and winked.

Jason laughed. 'Hell no! The day this heap of chips can stand up in front of a judge and advocate, well then I might think about it.'

Jenny arrived on time and the introductions were made. I didn't know the etiquette for a meeting with your deceased father's wife, so we shook hands and exchanged pecks on the cheek. I was surprised at how similar Jenny was to Mother. I guess Dad went for a type.

There was little time for small talk and I felt nervous, wondering exactly why we had to meet in a lawyer's office, but the answer was soon revealed. Dad had lodged some correspondence with his lawyer, and it was to be kept, seal unbroken, until such time as a direct member of his family made any enquiries about the death of his nephew, Bobby Lee McDonald, or Jenny died, whichever came sooner. If Jenny had died the correspondence were to be opened by the lawyer, read, and then passed on to such officials or authorities as he saw fit. If, as was the case, a direct member of the family made the required enquiry, the scenario that was about to unfold was to be set up.

I took the package and my fingers tingled as if it was plugged into the mains. Emotions tumbled through me, of many kinds and all mixed up but there was anger among them. I had spent a lot of time, a considerable amount of cash and put people to a lot of trouble that would have all been unnecessary had my father told me the true story about my cousin, for I felt sure that's what the envelope contained.

I broke the seal, which was date-stamped March 1968, and withdrew the contents. There were three envelopes each containing a single piece of paper. The first was a hand-written copy of Harrison Bardwell's initial letter to

105

Father. Father had signed and dated it as a genuine copy. The second was a letter *To Whom It May Concern* outlining details of receiving the letter, making contact with Harrison and the visit that took place between them. It told how Sam had persuaded Harrison Bardwell to write down everything he saw that night. The third was the account of Bobby Lee's death as given by Harrison.

'Are you okay there, Mr McDonald? Can I fix you something? A brandy maybe?'

My hands were trembling, but I told Jason I was okay, and I read about the killing of Bobby Lee.

Document # 10
Testament of Harrison Bardwell
Concerning the Death of Bobby Lee McDonald

It was Tuesday, June 3rd. I'd had some business up at Money and I was heading back home. The headlights on my truck were like to be dim and so I was in a rush trying to get home before dark. As I got to the new bridge, that is Ashwood Bridge over the Tallahatchie just north of Greenwood as some call the Tallahatchie Bridge, it was close to sundown and the shadows were long. I saw a commotion up ahead near the middle of the bridge like some kids fighting and when I got close I saw it was Dewey Hopwood and his no good sidekicks whose names I disremember and they were beating up on Bobby Lee who I knew from business up at the sawmill on Choctaw Ridge. I got closer and saw he was all over in the face with blood and he looked like he was dead. He was stripped to his drawers and then Dewey just upped and tipped him in the river.

Now those boys were mean. They had a reputation and everyone knew the Sheriff was soft on Dewey on account of their kinship. And here I was just seen them murder someone. I put my foot down and raced for home and most all of that time kept my eyes on the mirror. Soon as I got home I called it in that I'd

*seen a kid fall in the river, but I was not surprised when a few
days later Bobby Lee was drug out dead. But by then I had
already had a visit from Sheriff Stroud.*

*He told me Dewey had seen me when they had been up on the
bridge having some fun with Bobby Lee. Turns out they were all
daring each other to jump off the bridge and that tragically
Bobby Lee had jumped in once too often and drowned. That's
what all the evidence showed and anything I seen that suggested
anything different was just plain wrong. My truck was a pile of
junk and the folks knew my lights didn't work and so best I
just keep quiet if I knew what was good for me.*

*And I did until I wrote to Bobby Lee's Uncle Sam, has
daddy having died last spring and what's more important,
Sheriff Stroud has now died too and Dewey Hopwood and his
goons have moved God knows where.*

*This is all I have to say and I am just sorry I never had the
guts to say it many years ago.*

Signed: Harrison Bardwell.

***

I don't know who was more shocked, Jenny or I. Father
had been particularly foresighted even if he, like Harrison
Bardwell, lacked the courage to make the true facts of
Bobby Lee's death known. Not only had he lodged the
papers with his lawyer, but he had paid up-front for a one
hour consultation for whoever started the ball rolling by
enquiring about the death.

It didn't take me long to tell Jason of my research and
findings to date. I told him that Dewey Hopwood was alive
and well and living in Pontotoc County and of course, I
handed over Harrison's testimony for him to read. I wanted
to know if what we had was enough to screw that bastard
Hopwood down.

'I'm sorry to have to tell you, but no way in a million
years,' Jason said laying the paper down. 'All we have is the

uncorroborated and un-sworn testimony of a dead man and a few other pieces of circumstantial evidence. Now, we certainly have enough to make an allegation to the police, but I doubt they will do a whole lot about it. Even if they run Hopwood in for questioning all he has to do is cite the Fifth or simply tell another story and there is nowhere near enough to bring charges. We don't even know exactly what Harrison thinks he saw. It's a non-starter whichever way you look at it.'

'But what about the threats I've been getting? And then there's the damage to Steve's car. Surely there's a pretty good bet that's all the handiwork of Mr Hopwood too?'

Bottom line, without a living witness, we were stuffed. We didn't have motive and the evidence was ambiguous. We lacked the events that led to Bobby Lee being flung off the bridge, if that was indeed what had happened. Jason also warned me to be very careful who I told about the day's revelations. I didn't want to provide Dewey Hopwood with enough material for litigation. It was ironic that if I dropped his name in the wrong place, he had a better chance of suing my arse off than I ever would at bringing him to justice.

Lunch around Brewster Roebuck's table that afternoon was a sombre affair. Brewster, Holly and Josh had the whole story from me, and I knew I could trust them to keep quiet about their murderous neighbour.

Brew shook his head, his eyes dark and brooding. 'I tell you I'm sitting here and my ass in knitting button-holes –'

'Brewster Roebuck!' Holly chided. 'In front of guests, mind your mouth!'

'That a murdering son-of-a-bitch can get away with it all these years and still he'll get away with it.'

I had a lot of thinking to do. Most of my things were back at Steve's place and anyway I wanted to be as far away as possible from Dewey Hopwood. Strangely I needed to be back in the Delta. I was happy that Josh insisted on coming with me. Brew had business in town the next day and he'd be able to fly his youngest back home.

As always I was happy to leave the driving to Josh. We made Steve's place by early evening and once again I went through the story. I settled to writing some letters to those I thought might be interested. I was not so arrogant as to ignore Jason Seven Elk's professional advice and I was careful to keep names out, but I called Rebecca by phone and wrote to Aunt Hettie via her cousin Zak Starbuck. I gave them as much information as I could.

Next morning Josh told me I'd spent so much time up to my middle in archive papers that I was missing the real beauty of the Delta. He suggested we took a walk and sensing that he really meant there was something he had on his mind, I went along with the idea. We'd start by exploring the old sawmill and see if we could turn up a few ghosts.

It was hot, but there was no rush so we kept at a slow pace. Where the path from Steve's house met the road there was a stand of trees where we rested in the shade for a while. At the gate we could turn left and take a walk to that fateful bridge or right and head on up to the overgrown path that led to the ruins of my Uncle Nate's sawmill.

There wasn't much left of the mill, and nature had taken over. The dust was just dust, and not sawdust. Of the house there was nothing left at all, and the mill itself was represented by nothing more than a concrete floor all weeded over and almost indiscernible. Just visible through the weeds was the large circular impression of the underlying saw-blade and at one side of the base, a box-like structure that had probably once been a tool shed.

Josh and I drew apart, each to conduct our own exploration of a time gone by. I kicked at the weeds over the circular saw and Josh grubbed about at the far side.

'God dawg! Hey, Colin. Come look over here,' He was rooting around by the old tool shed.

I joined him and examined his find. It was the mangled and rusted remains of an old bicycle and at once I saw Lewis's mangled body messed up with those pieces of bike, and within a heartbeat I was crying. I knelt and fingered the twisted and decaying spokes and wondered whose bike it had been.

'Colin,' Josh said gently. He reached out and squeezed my arm. It wasn't right: Josh was of the generation to need comfort, not provide it. 'I think I know what it is,' he said. 'I think I've know from the start. The underlying sadness …'

Josh told me he had chosen to come out to me because he sensed I would understand, and why would I understand? Because I too was gay. Josh tapped the side of his head. 'See, I'm fitted with gaydar!'

From sobbing I went to the verge of laughing. I pointed out that Josh would have to recalibrate his "gaydar" because he had got it completely wrong. 'But there is a kind of coming out for me to do, and as you did me the honour of trusting me, I'm going to do the same with you.' I then told Josh how I had killed my big brother Lewis.

Lewis had been twelve years old. I was just ten. We had argued. He did what he always did when we argued and shoved me. I went down onto my behind, no injury but to my pride. He laughed and went inside. I loosened the nut on the front wheel of his bike. He went for a ride that afternoon. The wheel came off. He was run over by a lorry. I'd killed Lewis just as much as Hopwood had killed Bobby Lee, and I'd evaded justice for almost as long.

'You're the first person I've ever told.' It was as if a weight had lifted from my shoulders.

I shaded my eyes from the bright yellow light that bounced off the ground and looked down the tack that led to the road. The sky seemed awfully big and so very bright. In the distance a car drove north along and threw up a cloud of dust and I had the most powerful feeling of *déjà vu*.

'I can see how you feel bad Colin, but you have to realise, you didn't kill your brother.'

His words didn't match the heavy mood that was settling, like the dust from the back of that car down there. Too light to make an impression as the car slowed down.

110

Josh's mobile rang and he answered.

The car slowed almost to a stop and then turned up the disused track that led right up to where we were standing. Somehow I knew that car was coming for me. I felt scared and excited, and I wondered if Dewey Hopwood was coming to put me out of the way for good.

'That was Steve on the cell. He says some visitors called forward asking if they could see you.' Josh folded his handset and pocketed it. 'He directed them up here, and it looks to me like they are about to arrive.'

The sedan drew up and an arm waved from the driver's side. Two people got out, Rebecca Taylor and a man I didn't recognise.

'Hi, Mrs Taylor,' Josh called. 'Good to see you again.'

Rebecca smiled and strode purposefully towards me. 'I understand you know what happened to Bobby Lee,' she said cutting straight to the chase. 'But there are certain legal complications that need to be overcome. Is that right?'

I assured her that she had hit the nail on the head.

'Then I wonder if my friend might be able to help.'

Now the gentleman stepped forward. 'I believe I may just qualify as a living witness,' he said and put his hand out. We shook. 'My name is Lucien Harris.'

Ever felt like you were shaking hands with a ghost? I had convinced myself that Lucien had died on the same day as Bobby Lee and here he was, as large as life.

'Oh my!' Lucien said. 'You're wearing the ring.'

I raised my hand so he could see it better. 'You gave this to Bobby Lee, didn't you?'

'I did, on the last occasion we ever met.'

My assumptions were falling like flies, but as it turned out, one of them was right on the button. The incident on the bridge, Bobby Lee's death, the whole thing sprang from hatred and bigotry, and once Lucien's story was out, I couldn't help but feel proud on my cousin.

Bobby Lee had been feeling depressed since Beth had turned down his proposal of marriage. Lucien figured he could do with some company and they arranged, through the usual channels, to meet on the Money Road between the bridge and the sawmill track. The trouble began when Dewey Hopwood and his friends came along first. It started with abuse and name calling and foul references to a "nigger's" sexual practices. When Lucien lost his temper and spoke back, they jumped him, threw a cotton sack over his head and bound his hands behind his back. They whooped it up and made as if they were going to lynch him.

'I say we throw him in the river,' one of Dewey's friends said.

'Say, that's not a bad idea,' Dewey said. 'I hear they threw some other nigger in the river upstream of here a year or two back. Maybe you can say Hi!'

'We got us our nigger. Let's go find a gin fan and some barbed wire and we got ourselves the whole damned lynching kit.'

'Yeah! I reckon this river is good and ready for more nigger-meat.'

Lucien then heard all hell broke loose. He could hear fighting and yelling and recognised Bobby Lee's voice among all the rest. It was clear to him Bobby Lee had come along as arranged and was wading in on Dewey and his friends, but Lucien was blind and bound and could do anything to help. He was pushed to the ground and writhed and twisted trying to free himself of the cotton sack but it was no good. His heart sank when he realised Bobby Lee had been overcome.

'You no good lousy nigger-loving sonofabitch!' Dewey called. 'You wanna see what happens when you interfere. Here! Take the nigger up the roads a-piece and clip him. There a shovel in my trunk so you can bury the stinking bastard.'

There came more yelling and screaming, more commotion; Lucien was dragged to his feet and then along the road until he was tied up to a fence post. Someone moved in close. He could smell their beery breath through the weave of the sack.

'I didn't aim to do no killing tonight, boy. So you just keep quiet and if you hear anyone coming, just act dead.'

The pistol shot, so close and loud, made Lucien wet himself. It was a minute of two before he realised he was unhurt and alone. Lucien struggled and this time he managed to free his hands. He pulled the sack off his head. It was dark. There was still a commotion going on half way across the bridge and Lucien ran to see if there was anything he could do to help. A truck came along from the direction of Money and Lucien tried to flag it down. He guessed they didn't see him, a black boy in the dark and it with such poor headlights, so he had to jump out of the way, but he followed in its wake just in time to see Dewey Hopwood heaving Bobby Lee's virtually naked, limp body into the river.

'Bobby Lee was dead,' Lucien said. 'And I knew I'd be dead within a day of me reporting what I'd seen. I'd be dead and Dewey Hopwood would be free to carry on just as he liked. That's how it was them days. No way that a black boy could testify against a white and live to tell the tale. Catch a white man red-handed and any white jury would let him off. Look at the case of Emmett Till. Dewey was going to tie me to a cotton gin fan with barbed wire just like they did to that poor child and they would stay just as free as Emmett's killers.'

Lucien decided to run away. He said goodbye to his family, told them they should say he hadn't been seen and nobody knew where he was, and he headed north where he made a life for himself in Chicago. He'd kept in touch with his family and visited the Delta occasionally but the time had never come when he felt safe telling what he knew, until now.

It was a shame that Josh had an appointment to keep as he would have so loved to hear the stories of Lucien and Bobby Lee when they were boys. Josh had to meet with his father at the airport, but I fully intended to pass along these wonderful tales just as soon as we next met. How was I to know that Dewey Hopwood had other ideas?

Phone calls were placed and arrangements made. Lucien Harris agreed to come with me next day to the law firm in Oxford where he would make a sworn testimony. Jason would then advise us of how best to proceed. It couldn't come soon enough for me. I was paranoid that somehow our one living witness would be converted to a dead one.

It was at the end of another tiring day. Lucien had gone home to Itta Bena where Rebecca, his one-time girlfriend was going to put him up, and I was exhausted from all the travelling and excitement. We had also made another important discovery concerning the threats I'd received.

Brewster Roebuck's office manager, Iris Dunlop, was a former girlfriend of Dewey Hopwood's. It transpired that Brew had made the majority of calls concerning our investigations from his office and Iris had simply passed the information on. He was able to work out our location and call in favours from several friends to make our lives difficult. Brew had his suspicions once he had put his mind to the problem, and being no mastermind criminal, she had folded at the first confrontation, but that confrontation followed the next frightening sequence of events.

I was about to say goodnight when the call came in on the landline. Steve answered, light and friendly. He sat up, suddenly concerned and we were all infected by the tension. He made the standard replies and noises people do when they hear the worst kind of news. He made his dad promise to keep us in the loop and asked if there was anything he could do. And then he hung up and made eye contact with each of us in turn, his wife, his eldest daughter (the smaller children had already been put to bed), and me.

'Josh and Cal headed out to Shannon for a night out. They were jumped.'

Carolyn gasped. Little Fiona's eyes went big and round and it looked like she would cry. I felt my insides contract.

'Cal's been roughed up pretty bad. He's in hospital, but they took Josh and nobody knows –' Steve's voice caught as the enormity of the situation slammed into him.

'He's been kidnapped?' Carolyn said grasping for her husband. 'You're saying he's been kidnapped?'

I felt sick. Steve must have read my mind because he told me it was nothing to do with the investigation. All the signs were that Cal and Josh had been attacked because someone had labelled them as gay. It tuned out all the signs were wrong. We discovered the truth a little while later.

We dropped everything and we were heading west within half-an-hour. Shannon was about 20 miles on the other side of Choctaw Ridge but we broke a few traffic laws and pulled into the hospital a little over three hours later.

Brew was there already. There were police and a couple of Lee County deputies. There was even a reporter and mention of the FBI. Kidnapping was a federal offence.

Cal Wheatley was propped up in bed, conscious but with his face a mass of bruises and swellings. He was angry about what had happened to him and frightened for Josh, and his mood swings displayed both extremes. I was in the room when a detective asked Cal if he was sure the attack wasn't racially motivated.

'Are you kidding? It was brothers who beat me and took Josh. It was because they thought we were gay.'

'And are you?'

'Does that really matter a whole lot, one way or the other?' Brew said. I swear the detective trembled a little.

'Not at this stage, sir, but if we catch them it might mean a longer jail term if a homophobic element is proved.'

'Hell yes, I'm gay,' Cal said. 'They didn't beat me because I'm black. They beat me because I'm gay. They were quoting Bible as they kicked my face. Religion would do well to keep the Hell out of people's pants.'

Brew's deep, calm voice capped the rising tension in the room. 'Cal, now you know I am a believer, and I want you to realise that the true word has bypassed the ears of the sons-of-bitches who did this. Right now it's important to answers this man's questions, one more time, and see if we can find out what's happened to Josh.'

Cal nodded. 'Yes, sir,' he managed before he started to cry.

I have no idea how Brew managed to keep a lid on his emotions. It was more than I could do a little while later.

Brew and I had stepped out for a few minutes to take in the cooler evening air when my mobile rang.

Document # 11
Transcript of Call Received Tuesday, 13ᵗʰ July, 1999 at 10.52pm

Colin McDonald (CM): Hello.

Caller: Hello, Mr McDonald. You still here?

CM: What do you want?

Caller: Why so tetchy? It almost sounds like you don't want to hear from me.

CM: I haven't got the time for this.

Caller: No of course not. How insensitive of me. You're at the hospital, aren't you?

CM: How do you know that?

Caller: Well you have to understand, I know a lot of things. Like for example, those two skinny-assed faggots, the nigger and the nigger-lover, they think they've been rolled on account of their sick perversions. But you and I know different, don't we, Colin?

CM: What have you done with Josh?

Caller: The Roebuck kid? Well, we had to rough up the nigger a little, but that was too good for the white kid, too easy. Whites should know better. You should have quit when you was told Colin, because all this could have been avoided.

CM: [Little above a whisper]. What have you done with Josh?

Caller: I'm sorry Colin, but Josh had to die. No other way, and it's all your fault.

CM: [Silence, 25 seconds]

Caller: Are you still there, Colin.

CM: [Silence, 30 seconds]

Caller: Oh Coooolin! I know you can hear me. I can hear you breathing.

CM: Yes Dewey Hopwood, I'm still here, but not for long. I'm coming for you Hopwood, you sick shit and when I get you …

Caller: [Terminates call]

***

The kidnapping and the call, they were Hopwood's downfall. He didn't know we'd fingered him as Bobby Lee's killer. He had no idea and so he thought he was still in a safe place from where to pull the strings. He was home and safe, until he arranged the attack on Cal and Josh. And that last call to me sealed his fate, but I feared it was all too late for Josh.

Things moved really quickly after I received that call. Brew and I ran back inside and I reported it to the detective. I may have sounded calm and collected when I told Dewey Hopwood I was coming for him, but now I was racked with guilt and I found it hard to hold it all together. The Tallahatchie River, a boy killer? No, I was the real killer. I'd killed Lewis and now I had as good as killed Josh. It was all coming on top. I wasn't made for this kind of pressure, but if Brew could remain as calm as he did, I could at least give it my best shot.

Within an hour of placing his odious call to me, Dewey Hopwood was arrested by a pair of deputies from the Pontotoc County Sheriff's Department and an FBI agent. They found him packing some bags for a quick getaway. Not fast enough, and where did he think he was running to anyway? If Harrison Bardwell and Lucien Harris didn't provide enough evidence against him, there were telephone connection records and computer examinations to help but at the time we couldn't have cared less. Josh was missing,

117

probably dead, and Dewey Hopwood wasn't talking. He had the best lawyers, and he was saying nothing. I would have given anything to suspend human rights in respect of Hopwood and torture the truth out of him.

The next two days were horrible and still rate as the worst in my life, excepting only the morning of the third day. There was nothing to do but wait, and although it was further away from the scene of Cal's beating and Josh's kidnapping, the Roebucks gathered at Steve's house. We moped, tried to comfort and encourage each other, and jumped out of our skins every time the telephone rang. In all this I was treated as one of the family. My pain and fear was never made to feel any less than Steve's or Holly's or Brews. For the duration, I was an honorary Roebuck.

It was on the morning of the third day when things got worse. The Roebucks needed to get in supplies and decided to stick together on their shopping trip into Greenwood. I stayed behind and pottered. By mid-morning I was feeling antsy so I took a muesli bar and a bottle of water and walked up to the ruins of the old mill once again feeling the need to be close to Bobby Lee's ghost. I gravitated straight to the remains of that bike Josh had discovered a few days before. The pieces of spoke, the bits of chain and the perished rubber no longer had a hold on me. This wasn't Lewis's bike.

I crouched down a touched the pieces, remembering what Josh had said. It was an accident. I hadn't killed Josh, but then it was possible Dewey Hopwood hadn't meant to kill Bobby Lee. I had only wanted to hurt Lewis; maybe Dewey wanted to hurt Bobby Lee. For both of us things just got out of control, went too far.

It was hot. I took a gulp of water and decided to head back to the house. I'd just reached the road when the call-signal sounded on my mobile. I took the phone out and looked at it, scared to answer for fear of what I might hear. I considered hitting the cancel button, but at the last moment I flipped it open and said hello.

'The kid's body, it's in the woods between the river and the churchyard at Little Zion. I'm sorry man, it wasn't me did it. I wasn't even there.'

The caller hung up; no time for me to ask questions, but no real need. I could almost see the church from here. It was a little more than a mile north and I ran all the way. How sick for the killers to leave the boy's body so close to his brother's home. If that wasn't an insight into the workings of the killer's mind, then what was?

The visions that went through my head were mostly of Josh in various states of bloody decay interspersed with shots of me being bushwhacked by a gang of Hopwood's cronies: I knew the whole thing could be a set-up, but I kept running anyway, and my mind was so far from working properly that I didn't even try to call the police.

I'd visited the graveyard before to look at the bare patch of grass that covered Bobby Lee's bones. There were few headstones, not even many markers, but Bobby Lee lay a few yards to the left of the tiny black stone marker that showed the burial place of the great Robert Johnson. That's where I headed, just in case the sick bastards had laid Josh out over the bones of a previous victim of Dewey fucking Hopwood.

There were cars parked on the track leading to the church: a reception committee, perhaps? I ran past and onto the grounds. I was out of breath. My shirt was soaked through and I drew the attention of several men who were gathered around Johnson's simple stone. They turned towards me as one, and I thought my ticket was up until one of them spoke.

'Are you okay, mister?'

'Josh, my ... nephew. Kidnapped. They said he was in the woods... there.' Nephew? I had neither the time nor the breath for long explanations.

'That poor white child who's been in the newspaper this week?'

I affirmed and headed for the woods and one of the men shouted for the others to spread out and help me look.

I don't know how long I spent quartering that strip of wood between the open grass of the churchyard and the muddy banks of the river, but the caller hadn't been lying. At first I thought his body was a bundle of rags or a sack propped up against a tree, but as my eyes adapted to the deep shadow I realised it was what was left of Josh. He was slumped to one side and it looked like his hands were tied up behind the trunk. He was gagged and blindfolded, and there was dried blood in his hair and on his face. I was close to vomiting, and all I could think about was Matt Shepherd. Not a lot of difference between a buck-rail fence and a tree when you were left all alone to die.

I stumbled closer over the roots and tangled undergrowth and knelt by poor Josh. 'I'm so sorry. I'm so sorry,' I managed through sobs. Brew and Holly, this would destroy them. I began to think ridiculous thoughts that had to do with me finding a way to kill Hopwood. I reached out and ran my fingers through Josh's matted hair. He was warm, and my fingers were coated in blood. Fresh blood. And then he moved and made a small animal sound through the material of his gag.

'Josh!'

He responded; a horrible sound of desperation and hope all muffled and pitiful.

'It's me, Colin. You're going to be alright.'

I yelled for help and within moments the others were around us. One of the men had a Swiss Army knife and while I picked at the knot on the blindfold he cut at the wrist-binding.

'Good Heavens above, the poor child. Who would do such a thing?' the man with the knife said under his breath as he sawed at the rope.

Freed from his bindings and with the blindfold and gag lying on the dirt, I helped Josh to water telling him to sip slowly. He revived with surprising speed and from a cursory examination he appeared free from major injury. We helped him into the safety of the church. While the others administered first aid, found him clean clothes and saw to his comforts as best they were able, I called Brew.

'Hi, Brewster. It's Colin. I'm with Josh. He's shaken up a little, but he's going to be alright.'

The sounds I heard on the line, well let's just say I knew that Brew had allowed free rein to his emotions at last.

I briefly filled him in of the details. With an unsteady voice he thanked me and told me he'd be sure to let Cal Wheatley know straight away.

The men from the churchyard drove us back to Steve's and we arrived at the same time as the Roebucks. A little later the police came and a detective gave me merry Hell for single-handedly destroying the crime scene and getting Josh into clean clothes. Forensics, she told me, would now be severely compromised. Brew told her to stick her forensics where the sun don't shine (Ma'am) and think a little on her priorities.

My last few days in Mississippi were taken up by police interviews and statements and enjoying what little time was left with the Roebucks. I signed a paper to the effect that I would return to the State to give evidence at the trial of Dewey Hopwood, and then it was time to leave.

I never did have to give evidence. The District Attorney no doubt entered into a phase of plea-bargaining. Hopwood escaped kidnap charges but copped to conspiracy to assault Cal Wheatley and Josh Roebuck. The men who had been paid to beat Cal and kidnap Josh were never traced and nor was the man who told me where to find Josh. Hopwood was never charged with murdering my cousin Bobby Lee either, but he admitted to manslaughter. That was a big surprise to everyone; lawyers for the State warned us that the evidence was probably insufficient for a conviction, so maybe Dewey Hopwood wasn't so clever after all.

And that, as they say, is pretty much that. So, I apologise if the story does not end with deadly confrontations, car chases and last minute rescues by the FBI, the Sheriff's Department and the 7th Cavalry. And yet, hold on a minute,

121

because the story is *not* over, especially not the part that concerns you.

As I flew out of Mississippi, the mystery of my cousin's death had been solved and all due credit to me, I was the catalyst that led to the discovery of the truth. Hopwood would soon be facing charges and a couple of years down the line he would be sentenced to twenty-five years imprisonment. He would be a very old man before he breathed free air again and I sincerely hope he would die behind bars. I had discovered the truth about one of my dead boys and set the record straight so I should have beaten my Dead Boy Syndrome, my Caesarion Complex, and made my peace with Lewis. But it wasn't so, and then, there was another mystery.

It had been a rare and wonderful privilege to meet and talk with Lucien Harris on that day he came to the farm. I had loved hearing about his friendship with Bobby Lee: their stolen meetings; their long discussions about how they would put the world to rights. Theirs was a friendship that laughed at boundaries and flourished in the face of opposition, but it didn't quite outlive death in the way I believed it had. As soon as I realised Lucien was still alive, and the proof was that he stood in front of me and introduced himself, I believed another mystery had been solved.

'I think it speaks volumes about your friendship that even now, forty years on, you come back each year to put flowers on Bobby Lee's grave,' I'd said.

Lucien looked at me sideways. 'Someone does that? What a beautiful thing, but it isn't me.'

It would be another two years before that last mystery was solved, and it would provide that very last piece of the puzzle that changed my life.

The Scrapbook

Scrap # 1
A Newspaper Clipping

Publication: *The Greenwood*
Date: *Tuesday, June 4th, 2002*

Headline: *Man Sentenced for Homicide 44 Years after Killing*
Report: *It is good to learn that justice does not have a best-by date. Pontotoc County man, Dewey Hopwood (62), was sentence yesterday at the U.S. District Court in Oxford to serve a period of imprisonment for 15 years for the manslaughter of Bobby Lee McDonald (17), 44 years after cruelly pistol-whipping him to semi-consciousness and throwing him off the Ashwood Bridge near Greenwood. Hopwood was also sentenced to serve 5 years for his part in each of two serious assaults, the sentences to run consecutively...*

***

Life got back to something like normal. New commissions came in and I set to work. Miranda was pleased with the result of my research and probably surprised that I had achieved something I had set out to do, and Claire made us all proud by winning a place in a Cambridge college. And I made a successful effort in keeping anyone from suspecting that Lewis still gave me nightmares and that sometimes guilt still overcame me. In that respect, nothing had changed.

In the summer of 2002 Josh and Cal visited and stayed with us for a few days; part of their "doing Europe" trip and I discussed a project with them. For some time I had been working on an idea. It had to do with Matt Shepard, and Cal and Josh. It had to do with you and me and Miranda and Claire. It had to do with every one of us, and it came to me while I stood by Cal's hospital bed. We beat one kind of bigotry and another brand springs up to take its place.

Call it pie in the sky, call it naïve in the extreme but I wanted to start a movement with a non-religious, spiritual foundation that stood for equality for all, bar none. I wanted to offer a philanthropic and spiritual alternative to other groups that defined membership and therefore had an element of exclusion. Membership would be dependent on accepting an all-embracing creed, and would have nothing to do with who you were, what colour your skin was, how you worshiped or how you loved.

'You want to invent a new religion?' Cal asked. 'I have nothing to do next Monday. I'll start a new religion in the morning and then do something difficult in the afternoon!'

The three of us had a good laugh about that, but joking aside, they *got* me; they saw what I was trying to do. Together we came up with the basic idea for the Fellowship of Shepherds. And so I wrote my book, part parable and part pattern for the accepting life, and I managed to interest a publisher. You know what, it didn't do too badly either and even made the Amazon top one-hundred for a couple of weeks. Now the Fellowship of Shepherds is catching the imagination. There are Shepherds everywhere.

Scrap # 2
Extract from "The Shepherd" by Colin McDonald

The Shepherd's Creed

All people deserve and are worthy of respect, compassion and equality. This is the one immutable truth, and I will do whatever is reasonable and within my power to realise this truth by my actions, words and behaviour, especially where respect, compassion and equality are lacking.

***

But even that did not lay my ghosts. Fellowship business kept me busy but it didn't make me sleep any easier. No, my ghosts were to be blasted from left-field in a way I could never have predicted if I lived to be a thousand.

I had been in correspondence with Lucien Harris; letters at first and then emails. We had decided that we'd try and find out who had been leaving flowers on Bobby Lee's grave all these long years, and I planned a trip for June 2003. We were going to sit around the churchyard at Little Zion from just after dawn until the mystery person came along with the flowers, and then we'd have him … or her. The flights were booked and the tickets secured, and then I thought I would let Aunt Hettie know how things were going. A week after posting my letter, I had an email from Aunt Hettie's cousin Zak Starbuck.

They say the answer is almost always right under your nose, and that was the way of it this time. Ask yourself, of all the people in the story, who was most likely to leave flowers on the anniversary of Bobby Lee's death, every year without fail? His mother of course!

Zak told me there was no big mystery and that since she had grown too frail it was Zak himself who had taken on the task and every year he laid the flowers on behalf of Hettie. I don't know why, but the truth was a bit of a let-down; a mystery that was really no mystery at all. If only I had known what was coming …

I replied to Zak saying it was a shame I hadn't known earlier as all the flights and arrangements were made and too late to cancel. His next message suggested we stick to our plans. It would be kind of neat to meet up and he would appreciate some company on what had always been quite a lonely and sombre occasion.

Fast forward a couple of months to Tuesday the 3rd of June, 2003. It's a little after eleven. I am standing close to Bobby Lee's grave admiring the fine new memorial that has been put in place for Robert Johnson. It is strewn with offerings: flowers, some in pots, some cut; mouth organs in various stages of rusting away, even some beer bottles. I am waiting to meet Lucien Harris again and Zak Starbuck for the first time. I had suggested we meet somewhere else and make our pilgrimage to Bobby Lee together, but Zak preferred to meet at the grave.

All at once I was compelled to visit the place where I'd found Josh, but I had just got in among the trees when I heard tyres on gravel and I wondered if it was Lucien or Zak. I made my way back to Bobby Lee's grave and heard another car. Meanwhile I guessed it was the driver of the first who walked slowly toward me from the direction of the road. He was taller than me; slim and a few years older, he had grey hair and a well-trimmed grey beard and moustache. There were flowers in the crook of his left arm. He was neatly dressed in a sports jacket and open-necked button-down. He quickened his pace and smiled widely reaching out his arm to shake hands.

'Well, look at you all grown up. Old even,' he said as his eyes flicked over my greying hair. His smile was so warm I didn't take offence.

'We've met before?'

The man said we had and asked if I could guess when and where. I said no and he said try harder, look further back. He smiled again and I knew that smile from somewhere.

'Cousin,' he said. 'Last time we met I do believe you yakked up all over my best blue jeans.'

I have never had the misfortune to pass out or faint, but I came close right then. All at once I recognised the smile from that loose photo. 'Bobby Lee?'

The smile faded a little and his eyes took on a look of acute sadness. 'Bobby Lee died a long time ago. People call me Zak these days, and have done for the best part of half-a-century.'

I had so many questions to ask. There was so much unexplained, so much I had to know, but it would all have to wait. While we had been talking, Lucien Harris had come up beside us, and he had heard Zak's last words. He held one trembling hand over his chin and his eyes were filled with tears. 'I thought you were dead, Bobby Lee. How can this be?'

Zak caught his breath. 'And until a little while ago, I thought the same about you, Lucien Harris.'

I was a mere observer from then on, watching as two old friends stared at each other across the years, wondering each if the other was a ghost about to blow away on the breeze.

Lucien fumbled in his trouser pocket and then held up a mouth organ. He smiled and nodded. His gesture broke the awkwardness and then Zak brought a mouth organ from his pocket too. I knew I was witnessing something that alluded to their past, but I was never to find out what. I wish I had thought to ask.

Zak then took out his wallet and showed Lucien a photo. 'Lucien Starbuck,' he said. 'My firstborn.'

Lucien had one to show of Bobby Lee Harris, his second child and first son.

It was right about then that I knew I was an intruder and so I quietly withdrew to the car. I'd like to think they hugged. I feel sure they must have cried a little, but whatever passed between them was for them alone and anything else I add would just be speculation.

It turned out that nobody saw exactly what they thought they had on that night exactly forty-five years before. From Zak's point of view, it happened like this: Zak – Bobby Lee as was, had come along the road to keep his appointment with Lucien and arrived at the meeting place in time to see Dewey Hopwood, Ralph Webster and Bo Simpson rough-handling his friend. They had put a sack over his head but he knew Lucien's voice well enough. The red mist came down and he steamed in to help, only to be quickly overpowered. They ripped his shirt and Bo stole the ring Lucien had given him, the one he wore on a string round his neck.

Dewey flew into a blind rage and told Bobby Lee he needed to learn a lesson and see what happened to niggers when nigger-lovers interfered. Ralph Webster then dragged Lucien away at Dewey's command and shot him, at least that was how it appeared to Bobby Lee, and Bo Simpson must have seen it the same way because he got very scared and started to protest.

Bobby Lee lost all his fight. He'd been badly beaten and now his friend had been murdered. Dewey said they were going to have to kill Bobby Lee too because he was a witness. Both Ralph and Bo protested. Dewey grabbed Bobby Lee but Bo dragged him off shouting for him to leave off. There was a scuffle. Bo Simpson punched Dewey but Dewey snatched Ralph's pistol. Bo managed to kick it out of Dewey's hand but he came back at Bo with the flat of a shovel and hit him hard in the face. Bo went down hard, his head striking the side of the bridge and Dewey hit him again with the shovel. He looked like he was dead; his neck was at an impossible angle, and now Dewey began to panic. Ralph just looked stunned and confused.

At gunpoint Dewey made Bobby Lee strip to his shorts. They'd make it look like a swimming accident, he said. Dewey ordered Bobby Lee to kneel in front of him and all he could see was Bo's blood on the pavement. That was the last Bobby Lee remembered until he hit the water. The cold rush revived him and he managed to get to the bank. He looked up in time to see Dewey hurling Bo Simpson over the railings.

Bobby Lee swam to him. It was obvious he was dead, and his face was all mashed up. In that moment, Bobby Lee saw how the future would unfold. He got Bo's body to the bank and managed to strip off his shirt, pants, socks and shoes and then pushed him into the current. Bobby Lee pulled the wet clothes on and made for home avoiding the road. He decided he was leaving this feeble excuse for a State with its feeble people and Bo Simpson was going to help. They'd find Bo and think it was him, Bobby Lee. No one would miss Bo. He'd drifted into the county and people would believe he drifted out again, and in one respect wasn't that just the plain truth?

Bobby Lee hid in the woods for a night going over his plan which amounted to little more than getting out of Mississippi. Mama thought he was a ghost when she saw him but quickly realised the Sheriff had been mistaken. Bobby Lee wasn't dead after all. When she heard the story and realised the danger her son was in, she gave him her blessings. If she could help in any way she would. First she helped by giving him the fare to Nantucket and the address of relatives who were sure to take him in. She helped again three days later when she identified Bo Simpson as her son. They were almost the same height and weight and had similar colouring, and what the river had done to the poor boy in just three days was about as much as a person could stomach. She wasn't expected to look at him long and nobody questioned her word.

All this came out as the three of us sat in Zak's hire car, but I remember the first thing I said when he and Lucien joined me. 'You do realise Dewey Hopwood is serving twenty-five years for your manslaughter.'

Far from looking guilty, Zak smiled. 'I heard that, and I must say it appeals to my sense of humour.'

Lucien chuckled but whether at Zak's words or the shock on my face, I couldn't tell.

'See Colin, in a very real way, Dewey *did* kill Bobby Lee that night. You might see a little injustice in the situation, but I won't be losing any sleep.'

'Me neither,' Lucien said. 'And remember, he really did kill Bo Simpson and seeing as how there's no chance getting justice for Bo, I think it's all kind of worked out for the best.'

I looked over in the direction of the grave that until a short while ago I believed was Bobby Lee's. 'Is that why you bring the flowers every year? You feel a little guilty that Bo's bones are where everyone thinks yours … Bobby Lee's are?'

'Not guilt, Colin. It's gratitude. When the chips were down, Bo Simpson tried to help me, and in the end he helped give me a new life. God knows there was nothing to keep me in Mississippi.'

It turned out that Hettie was a shrewd lady too. She'd anticipated there might be problems regarding identification a few years down the road, so she arranged to have Bo's body buried in a place where there were rarely any grave markers. The situation had never arisen, but if it had, nobody would know precisely where Bo – Bobby Lee – was buried so nobody could dig him up.

The Roebucks had once again offered their hospitality and the plan was, after our time by the graveside, we would be welcome at the farm for refreshments, but before we went there was a promise to be made. Only three people outside of Nantucket knew that Zak Starbuck had once been Bobby Lee McDonald and all three of us were sitting in the same car. Zak wanted to keep it that way and so Lucien and I gave our word.

'Before we head on down the road,' I said, 'why go with the name Zak Starbuck?'

The answer was simple. Officially, Bobby Lee had never been Bobby Lee: his birth certificate had him down as Robert Zak McDonald. When he was very small Hettie used to call him Bobby Zee but Nate thought it sounded stupid, so he mutated it to Bobby Lee (after his favourite Civil War general) and it stayed like that until June 3rd, 1958. As for the surname, well Starbuck was Aunt Hettie's maiden name, so it was a natural choice. Zak had his last name changed all legally and above board and thereafter chose to be known by his official middle name. As I said, simple really.

There was another surprise to come, and it would prove to be life-changing for me. The Roebucks sensitively withdrew and left us in privacy to talk old times and family, and then the subject came around to my brother Lewis. Cousin Zak was only the second person I had ever opened up to on the subject of my part in Lewis's death.

'Is that how you think it happened?' Zak said. 'Because that sure doesn't match the way I heard it.'

I was never told the full story, and so I filled in the gaps with obvious causes and over the years that mix of fact and invention solidified into an idol calling itself the truth. For most of my life I had lived in the shadow of that idol until that afternoon when Zak took a sledge hammer and reduced it to dust.

I slept well that night. I never have trouble sleeping these days and the Caesarion Complex is a thing of the past. Zak told me how it really happened and when I got back to England a few days later, the chief source of his information, or rather, an electronic copy of it was waiting for me.

Scrap # 3
Scan of Letter from Sam McDonald to his sister-in-law Hettie McDonald

March, 1969

Dear Hettie,

Thank you so much for those kind words you wrote us about Lewis. It is strange you said there was no way you could really know how we felt, seeing as how you lost Bobby Lee in such sad circumstances, but I guess you mean on account of just what a young boy Lewis was. Is there really any difference though, 12 or 17 they were both just boys and I guess they will always stay boys in our hearts and in our memories.

My memories of Lewis that last day include fixing his bike and him handing me the wrench. I still have that wrench but I never use it, funny how every day objects can acquire a measure of special. Lewis found a loose nut on his front wheel and we fixed it together. Later he was pestering to get to the post box before the mail man collected but I made him finish his chores and then I waved him off. Seems he was in so much of a rush to post his letter in time for the afternoon collection, he propped his bike against a hedge and ran out over the road without looking.

There is some comfort in that it was all so quick he wouldn't have even seen it coming.

We are thankful we have little Colin, but he has taken it so badly, we wonder if he will ever be the same.

Once again, despite the circumstances, it was real good to hear from you again. It is a shame we have lost touch a little since Nate's passing.

With best wishes from me and Rose,
[Signed] Sam.

***

I don't know if I could have kept a new identity a secret from my own father as Zak had done, but reading between the lines they were not close. Such was his fear in those early days, and his anger with anything to do with Mississippi, that he didn't want anything to threaten his new life. There was nothing to tie him down. Beth had spurned him, he had no idea she was carrying his child and he thought Lucien was dead. As to the baby, well that was one part of the story I knew and Zak didn't, and I never did tell him about Jeremy Thomas, his son and my first cousin once removed. What good would it have done?

Now I'm finished. I kept the secret so the truth can do no harm and I haven't told a soul. Not until you, but you can keep a secret, can't you? And anyway, who would believe a word of it? Let's keep it between us. You can't keep a good researcher from plugging away until he catches all the loose ends and it took me a while but here I am. You should know, Mrs Simpson, that every year someone puts flowers on Bo's grave, just like someone does on yours. Mr Simpson? Another child you never lost? Well, at your lost son's resting place it's become something of a Starbuck family tradition to lay those flowers, and it's a time for me to meet with Zak and catch up on family news.

It only remains to put that old song right, and here's my best effort. Yes I know; you don't have to tell me. It's not very good, is it? Never mind; so long as I tack it on every time I hear the song, I feel I've done my bit.

Scrap # 4
Unofficial Additional Verse to Bobbie Gentry's
"Ode to Billy Joe"

Half a lifetime went by but it's never too late for the truth.
And it's a fact a boy died never passing his youth,
But no one saw it like it really happened that night
And it took more than forty years just to get it right.
Now I'm walking my old haunts up on Choctaw Ridge.
Truth is they threw me off of the Tallahatchie Bridge.

The Shepherd

Modern Morality & Secular Spirituality
A Work in Perpetual Progress

by
Colin McDonald

The Shepherd

Are you a Shepherd?

The Shepherd's Creed
All people deserve and are worthy of respect, compassion and equality. This is the one immutable truth, and I will do whatever is reasonable and within my power to realise this truth by my words and behaviour, especially where respect, compassion and equality are lacking.

Introduction

Have you got time for a short story and a little conversation? Good, because here we have a few thoughts for anyone who is interested in the thinking behind the Shepherd's Creed. That's you, for one. Maybe you are the only one, but even one more Shepherd in the world is something to smile about. A little Shepherding goes a long, long way.

Following this introduction you will find a story and then some musings on what it means to be a Shepherd. The aim: to open up a discourse that leads to an increase in happiness and so far as is possible, a reduction in hatred. The means to achieve this, or at least move towards it, is to offer a focus and a point of reference to all people for whom the Shepherd's Creed rings true, be they religious or atheist.

So then, we'll polish that off by breakfast and then find something difficult to do? Perhaps not, but you will see from the following pages that the aim is quite simple in execution. I hope by the end of it you will be able to answer the opening question with the reply "Yes, I am a Shepherd" for Fellowship is open to all, and what is more, it doesn't cost a penny.

The Fellowship of Shepherds is not a religion or a cult. It is not a charity and does not collect or solicit funds in any way. Membership is not exclusive, being open to every human being on the planet who will commit, without reservation, to the Shepherd's Creed. A little more detail before moving on:

Part One: The Shepherd

This is a short story that introduces the ethos of a shepherd as he relates it to a disparate group of travellers. They are overtaken by inclement weather and isolated from the rest of the world by a mysterious mist or fog. They are a captive audience, but you are not. If you are not into stories, you may bypass this part altogether. In fact, the same applies to the whole book: pick and choose, dip in or discard; treat the whole thing as the opening gambit of an evolving dialogue.

Part Two: Considerations and Controversies

This is the part that looks deeper into the preceding tale (which you may skip if you didn't read the story) and then goes on to discuss certain themes and beliefs that tend to divide us. There is also a chapter on what it means to be a Shepherd and how Fellowship can work for the good of its members and for the world at large.

This is a pocket-sized book. It encompasses subjects such as faith and belief, spirituality and morality but it does so in broad brush-strokes. To go into detail would take many volumes, but detail is unnecessary here, for we look at the subjects with one question in mind: how does all this apply to a Shepherd?

Ready? Let's get started then.

PART ONE

The Shepherd

I

The warrior awoke, chilled and uncomfortable but relieved that the raging storm had spent its fury. Dawn crept in timidly, still quivering from the thunderous excesses of the night. The warrior sat up, rubbed his eyes and looked about him to discover that the world stretched no further than the span of his arms. The air was thick with mist and the sun made its presence known by no more than a patch of ill-defined fuzz a shade lighter than its surroundings.

There is the east, thought the warrior. *I must walk in the other direction.* Rising, he gathered together his pack from the lee of the boulder that had provided him with shelter, but cast about as he may, he could not a lay hand to his weapons. No matter: his page must have taken them, perhaps to keep them from the rain.

The warrior called out for his page, but the air was too overburdened with mist to carry his words and they fell, dulled and blunted. He called out again, and again his words were swallowed up. There was no echo, and no other sound. No bird sang out to welcome this dawn. The usual hustle and bustle that always accompanied the birth of a new day was absent, and not even the breeze that shifted and swirled the mist into unnatural shapes came to his ears. It was as if the air had encased him like a tomb, and suddenly the warrior became certain that his surroundings were not of this world. When did such a thick and impenetrable mist ever follow on the heels of a storm?

The warrior became afraid, and wondered if he had crossed into the land of the dead. But he had not been in battle before the storm came. He had merely been on the road between the town and the city, in his own land, far from enemies, and in a place unknown for cut-throats or bandits. The storm had come, sudden and fierce, and he

139

had found the boulder that protected him from the driving rain. The gale raged in his ears until he crouched by the rock, and then he heard only the noise of the rain. At last, wrapped against the elements, he slept. And then he awoke, to a changed world.

The warrior held his hands before him and moved his fingers. He touched them to his face and felt their warmth. And then he laughed. *What nonsense! Of course I am not dead.* It was inconceivable to him that a man as famous as he should die at the roadside before he had come to full power.

The warrior decided he must find the road, and then head west. In an hour, maybe two, he would surely be sitting by a warm hearth and laughing and talking with others about the strange turn of weather.

He could not find the road, although he was careful to quarter the land around the boulder, and then he lost the boulder and though it was only a thing of stone he was troubled, for it had been an anchor to the world he knew. The ground under foot became uniformly devoid of any feature of rock or shrub or tree. Once again the thought hovered: had he died and come early to the road we must all travel?

For a long time the warrior cast about. An hour may have passed, or the entire morning. The warrior could not tell because time passed in the measure of heartbeats and he had lost count of them. Even the fuzz of light that he had thought was the sun had been subsumed by a uniform blanket of white. For another stretch of three thousand heartbeats the warrior walked and called out, and then at last he found something and seized upon it as if it were gold when it was no more than a simple wooden staff with a cross-piece attached at one end for a handle. That it was fashioned by human hands in this inhuman landscape gave the warrior comfort far in excess of its true worth. It was proof that he was not alone.

The spark of joy was quickly extinguished. At last, he heard a sound pierce through the air, but it was the distant howl of a wolf, now faint and woolly-edged, now sharp and chilling to the heart. Wolves rarely attacked man, but then mist rarely followed a storm, and the warrior held the staff before him like a weapon and was more afraid than he had ever been, even before battle.

'Come and get me then, Wolf!' he cried. 'I am ready for you!'

The howling ceased, abruptly, and the warrior had second thoughts about the wisdom in calling out a challenge, but at least he had dispelled fear.

Silence.

'Are you lurking? Show your snout and I shall brain you with this stick!'

There came another sound, high like the howling of wolves and yet no howl at all; intermittent and staccato, a small sound that wished itself still smaller. The warrior relaxed a little a cocked an ear. Surely he was hearing the bitter weeping of a child. 'Hail there! Do you hear me?'

There was no reply, and so the warrior advanced slowly towards the sound until he could make out a shape in the mist. So close now that he hadn't the slightest doubt the shape was of a crying child, he quickened his pace.

In fact it was not a child, but a young woman of sixteen, perhaps seventeen summers, and she sat on the ground with her robes pulled close in a futile effort to keep out her fears. When she saw the warrior she threw up her arms to him and she wept as he embraced her, too upset to hear his comforting words.

'Is it just us two, alone in the world?' the warrior said, speaking into her long dark hair. Her looks were plain and her clothes were of poor quality but he held her close, enjoying the warmth of another human person. For the time being, neither rank nor class nor beauty was of any relevance.

'I have seen no other, sir. You are the first to come by. I thought the wolves should have me, for sure.'

'If they come near, they shall feel this across their backs.'

'Oh, sir! You have found my walking-staff.'

The young woman had a club foot and could not stand for long or walk at all without the aid of her staff, but the warrior was loath to return it, representing as it did, his one and only weapon. Instead he offered to carry her upon his back, and so they set forth, into the mist once more, and did their best to keep a straight path. They spoke while they walked and the warrior learnt that, like himself, the young woman had been on the great-road between the town and the city when the storm came and that she was separated from her companions and slept on the bare earth.

The young woman recognised the warrior as a man of much fame. When they took one of their many rests, she told him that she had seen him once at a feast in the town and she had heard the songs that were sung about his deeds and even knew the words of one of the most popular.

They did not like to take long when they rested, for it was when they stopped that the sound of the wolves returned, and it seemed that each time they rested the wolves grew closer.

'I am heartily sick of this unnatural mist,' the warrior said. 'It leaches all colours and sucks at my soul. I feel I am turning into mist myself.'

The young woman did not answer but gasped as if in fright. She tightened her grip around the warrior's neck and gripped his sides with her knees.

'What is it?' he asked, a second before the cause of the young woman's fear became obvious. He gently lowered her from his back and turned to face the monster.

Looming dark and shadow-like in the mist was the shape of a foul beast of Hell. It stood as tall again as a man and its head bore great spiralling horns. It was a terrible creature from the stories of bards, a thing that would be at home in a man's worst nightmares. Slowly it turned its massive head towards the warrior and the young woman, and then it made a noise, deep and resonant, something between a cough and a bark.

'I think it senses us,' the young woman whispered.

The warrior was unable to move. How did one prepare for the attack of a monster from legends? *You pray*, came the answer from the warrior's thoughts. *And you prepare to die.*

And then a gust of wind shifted the mist and for the first time since waking, the warrior saw further than a few paces ahead. The wind spiralled and eddied about the beast, and for an instant it was revealed as it really was: nothing but a hoary old ram sitting on top of a pillar of rock.

The warrior and the young woman began to laugh at the same time.

'See what the mist does?' the warrior said. 'It makes us like children, to be frightened of shadows and false images.'

The ram coughed again, but this time instead of instilling fear in the travellers it added to their relief and hilarity. It was short lived. The ram sprang to its feet, alert to approaching danger. It stamped, snorted and leapt from the rocky pillar almost bowling the warrior over in its panic. There came in its wake the sound of wolves.

No howling this time, but the short barks and yips of a pack setting up an attack, signalling each to the others. There were armies in the east whose generals borrowed the tactics of the wolf. First their calls came from ahead, and then from the flanks. A husky yelp to the right was answered by a yelp from the left, and then the sounds of claws on rock. From behind came a guttural growl, and then silence.

'They're all around us, sir. What shall we do?'

The warrior bent low and pick up a large stone. 'We must do all that we can and hope that it is sufficient. Take this and hurl it with all your might if a wolf should attack while I am kept busy elsewhere. I must make do with your walking-staff.'

The mist moved. A dark area passed in front of them, came close enough for the air to take on the fetid stench of wolf. Another shape moved in and the warrior let out a mighty battle cry and feinted at the air with the staff. The dark shape receded but another rushed in. A great snarling

143

head with yellow fangs barred and dripping with frothy saliva burst out of the mist as if it had torn through hanging silks. The warrior aimed a blow at it, but with a speed and savagery that is denied to humans, the wolf snatched the staff and wrenched it from the warrior's hands.

The young woman threw her rock with all the strength she had, and just as the wolf lunged with ripping jaws towards the warrior's throat, the stone bounced off its snout with a resounding crack. Pain reduced it to a yelping pup and it retreated into the white shadows.

The warrior tried to retrieve the staff and the young woman her stone, but neither could set sight on their objective, and the dark shapes encircled them once again. Slowly the shapes moved, this way and that, the circle ever tightening.

One of the encircling shapes was smaller than the rest, and the warrior took it to be a cub, but when it broke away from the line and dashed to the centre of the circle it became revealed as a jackal. It yelped and growled and teased at the warrior and the young woman until he landed a kick and it ran off.

In the midst of such danger, the warrior still had time to wonder at the bizarre discovery of a jackal running with a wolf pack. In a surprising world, perhaps everything was possible, given the right conditions. Perhaps this mist had changed the usual order for beasts as well as people.

Now the wolves were close enough for the misty veils to part. The beasts became visible in all their sharp-fanged, yellow-eyed malevolence. No kick would deter any one of these huge beasts when they decided to attack. One in particular, which the warrior took it to be the leader of the pack, was the biggest wolf he had ever seen. It had a great mane of silver and black hair and its eyes shone with intelligence where its three companions lacked any such noble attribute. The smaller wolves were the most fearsome in aspect and the smallest was pure venom in an ill-kempt and flea-ridden coat.

'Sir,' the young woman said with trembling voice. 'Please kill me. Break my neck and give me swift release, for it should be preferable to being torn apart while I yet live.'

'Don't let them see your fear. There is hope for us yet, and we should not hasten the end in the face of these beasts.'

It was then that the smallest and cruellest of wolves launched itself to the encouragement of the yapping jackal, fury and ravenous hunger all encapsulated in one body, and it was then that a huge bulk bowled from the concealing air, with a voice of thunder.

With its breath on the warrior's face, the wolf was taken from the side and smashed to the ground by a mighty dog. Its jaws clamped around the wolf's midriff, and there came a sound that was the cracking of ribs. Two of the other wolves rushed to the aid of their pack-mate and two more dogs charged in from the mist. The jackal ran away.

The warrior waded in kicking at the wolves, and the young woman found her staff and aimed blows. In a flurry of fang and claw and a desperate flailing of foot and staff, the battle was over in seconds rather than minutes. The wolves ran into the mist pursued by the dogs, and once again the warrior and the young woman were left alone as the howling and the baying lost their sharp edges and diminished into silence.

The warrior and the young woman took a moment to come to themselves and then they established with great relief that they had endured the encounter without hurt, other than to their oppressed spirits, and even they in the light of survival against all odds, were beginning to soar.

'Devil-monsters and wolves,' the young woman said. 'Whatever next?'

'I hate to imagine … but wait!' The warrior put his nose in the air. 'Well, well! What do you think of that?'

The young woman was still, and then she smiled. 'I can hear it! Sweet music, though mournful, at the very edge of hearing.'

The warrior frowned. 'I hear no music. No, but can't you smell the delicious aromas of cooking? Someone nearby is preparing a meal.'

The young woman could not smell the food, nor the warrior hear the music, but as it is hard for a man to follow a scent, the warrior followed the young woman who followed the sound. In time the warrior did indeed hear the music, and the young woman could eventually smell the cooking.

They came at last upon a young man who sat on a rock draped with a simple plaid of white and black that appeared to be both his blanket and only garment. His back was to them so that he was unaware of their approach, and he played a pair of pipes. Beyond him there burned a hearty fire so that a halo of orange seemed to light the air about him. He did not appear to be well equipped, the only gear visible from where the warrior stood being a small leather bag and a shepherd's crook.

'Hail, shepherd! Have a care and see to your raiment. I travel in company with an innocent young woman.'

The shepherd put down his pipes and quickly gathered the plaid around him. With a few deft folds and twists, his blanket covered him as well as any clothing. 'Forgive me friend, but I believed I was the last man in the world and that there were no people left to see my nakedness. I meant no offence.'

'And you gave none, at least not to me,' the warrior said.

'Nor I,' said the young woman. 'I am more pleased to see another human being than you can imagine, and after the frights we have endured, your nakedness is almost a delight.' The young woman's hand flew to her mouth, too late to hold back the words that she had not planned. 'That is, if you understand my meaning, master shepherd.'

The shepherd smiled, gave a slight bow and then invited the travellers to share his fire and such food as he had bubbling in the pot. 'Help yourselves,' the shepherd said. 'I hope you will forgive me if I continue to play, for the tune is not ended, and I do not like to start a thing and then not

146

take it to its conclusion.' He resumed his seat upon the rock and began to play.

While the shepherd played, the warrior and the young woman sat on the ground by the fire.

'It is sweet to hear such music when the cloying mist has deprived us for so long of all but base sounds,' the young woman said.

'And such a relief to the eyes to have those veils of white and grey pushed back so that we might see other colours. The yellows and oranges and reds of this fire are soothing to my eyes and a boon to my spirit. I missed these things more than I missed food, but now I have it before me ...'

The warrior and the young woman ate of the sustaining meal, nourishing their hungry, tired bodies. While the shepherd played, they spoke in hushed tones of the time they had endured since the storm, and they could not guess at the passing of the hours, only that it was not more than a day, because the darkness had not yet returned. The warrior relived his encounter with the wolves. He embellished the story for some future audience, and then the shepherd stopped playing on an ascending note that was obviously not the end of the melody. He lowered his pipes and peered into the mist where the light of the fire could not reach. The warrior followed his eyes in time to see two people emerge, like wraiths taking on form as they came within the compass of the warming light.

There was a woman of outstanding beauty and fine raiment and a well-made youth of about the same age as the club-footed young woman. The uncertainty that clouded their features fled as they saw the fire and the people gathered about it, and the warrior guessed that these were two others who had been isolated in the soundless, sightless void of cloud that he had so recently quit.

The warrior rose to greet them and welcomed them to the fire, and then, wondering if he might be usurping the prerogative of the shepherd, cast an eye in his direction. The shepherd smiled and dipped his head, then continued playing. Feeling that he had the shepherd's cheerful acquiescence, he continued.

The beautiful woman was a poet whose plays were enjoyed and whose poetry was beginning to receive attention. The black-haired youth was an apprentice who had been separated from his master during the storm. The warrior had scarce helped them to a serving of stew when another man came in from the void. Heavily bearded as was not the fashion in this land, and with unusual attire, the man was obviously a foreigner, but he was welcomed to the growing circle about the fire, while the shepherd kept playing.

Somewhat diffident and uncertain of his welcome, the foreigner had just begun to settle when another man and a woman came from the now darkening mists. The man was known to the warrior as an important court official and holder of state-office. His long white hair fell about his shoulders and his clothing was of the finest cloth. Try as he may, he could not maintain his look of imperious distain, and the smile of relief in coming to this oasis of light in a dark world was not lost upon the warrior.

The woman with him was of middle age and her clothes were simple as was the style of her hair. The warrior marked her for a servant.

As soon as this last couple stepped into the warm circle, the shepherd finished his tune with a simple flourish. 'Now,' he said, 'my fluting is done.' He looked at every face in the circle around the fire and smiled with great satisfaction. 'And I believe we are all here.'

II

The seven strangers fell to talking while the shepherd slipped away from the fire and into the darkness. Neither the warrior nor anybody else noticed him go.

At first neither wealth, health nor station in life separated the people, so glad were they to have found each other.

The warrior was not surprised to hear that all of them, every one, had been on the road between the town and the city when the storm overcame them. Their stories were all very similar and it was only when the initial happy and excited conversations died down, and the realisation came that they were all still isolated from the world, that they began to speak of their lives, which were all very different.

Used to taking stock and observing, the warrior sat back, his cloak for a rug, and watched as divisions began to make themselves known, and a hierarchy was established, not by negotiation or mutual agreement, but by subtleties of dress and dominance of character.

It was only when the Senator took the shepherd's rocky seat as his own that the warrior noticed the shepherd's absence. He also noticed there was no food left in the pot. They had eaten all, leaving nothing for the shepherd. The warrior felt a pang of shame, for he had eaten as heartily as the others, and it was not right that their benefactor should go hungry.

The Senator called for the warrior to join him by the rock where the fire was warmest and the ground underfoot most smooth. The others sat at positions ever further from the fire and less comfortable, and the warrior was sorry to see that the young woman with whom he had gone though so much sat at the furthest reach.

The Senator began to give orders for the furtherance of everybody's comfort, but chiefly his own.

'Listen!' the warrior called out. He was the captain of a company. He was used to giving orders. The people listened. 'I would like to make a suggestion and it is this. We have been in the cold grip of this weather for a night and a day, and night comes on once more. Soon the only cheer will be that which springs from this fire.

'We have found each other, and no two of us are from the same station in life. Unnatural forces continue to pluck at the strings of our fate, and here we all are, sharing this tiny circle of light in a world that may as well not exist except in eternal darkness.

'What say you all, that for the duration of our fellowship, we forget station and wealth and any other thing that may in our previous lives have come between us?'

The people exchanged glances, some hopeful, some with a little disdain.

'Will the rain wet the Senator less than the foreigner, or the wolf prefer the flesh of you boy, the apprentice, or of the poet?'

The poet pulled her robe about her neck and eyed the shadows fearfully.

'While we are captives of the night and the mists, shall we not be brothers and sisters and endure what comes, all together?'

The servant stood up. 'Yes!' she said. 'Surely it is our best hope to overcome this adversity.'

'I agree,' the poet said.

'I'm for it,' the apprentice said.

The foreigner assented with a nod and a smile and at length the Senator agreed although showed no sign of giving up his throne. 'The more I think upon it, the more I believe you have hit upon a good idea. Let us begin by introducing ourselves properly, by name and station, and then we shall see what may come of it.'

'Let's not bother,' the warrior said. 'I am a warrior, so call me Warrior. There may come a time when the order of the world is restored, and it may be awkward for us if we remember what has been spoken of under our own names.'

The apprentice laughed and bowed low. 'I am Apprentice, and pleased I am to meet with you all.'

The others all introduced themselves with mirth or diffidence as was their nature until only the warrior's first companion remained unnamed. She sat, downcast, and looking into the flame. 'And shall I be Cripple, or Ugly?' she whispered.

The warrior felt her pain. 'You shall be Young Woman, and the equal of us all.'

'Indeed you shall,' Philosopher said.

For some minutes the people spoke with each other, trying out their new names. The warrior noticed that even Senator appeared to relax and relish the novelty of equality, although none moved to change their place in the circle.

Just then, Warrior noticed four figures at the borders between darkness and light and as they advance he saw they were the shepherd and three great hounds. He recognised the dogs and was glad to see them again. Young Woman also let out a cry of happy recognition, but some of the others were afraid.

The shepherd told them not to fear, and that they were his trusty sheepdogs and he named them as Focus, Drive and Direction. He was carrying a bundle of sticks and a dead lamb.

'I am sorry to see your dogs were too late to save that little one. Did the wolves kill it?' Warrior said. The lamb's wool was red with blood.

'No, not that,' the shepherd said. 'I slit this one's throat.'

Young Woman gasped and Poet commented upon the ugliness of the spectacle of a shepherd killing a lamb too young for the slaughter.

'I understand your motives,' Senator said. 'There are too many of us for too little meat in the pot, and you mean to replenish it. I wonder though, perhaps you should have taken something a little bigger.'

The shepherd shook his head. 'This lamb is poison, both to he that nurtures it and those who eat of its meat.' So saying, he threw the carcase into the fire.'

'What wicked waste!' Senator said. 'I could have made good use of that and made it grow into something more formidable. Now it will be consumed in the flame.'

'It is the kind of lamb that would have grown all too easily,' the shepherd said. 'There will be sweater meat for us, but ...' he looked all around and sniffed the air; 'I believe the world will be restored come tomorrow. We shall easily endure a single night without meat.'

Warrior acquainted the shepherd with details of the conversation the people held while he was away, and the young man appeared overjoyed. 'Then I will be Shepherd,' he said, and so they all had a fireside name.

Focus, a wide-headed animal of lean muscle and great power, nuzzled Warrior as he took a place by the fire. Shepherd sat nearby. Warrior told the gathering about his last encounter with the dogs, and how they had saved him and Young Woman from a jackal and a pack of four wolves.

Shepherd chuckled. 'I know them all well. That jackal I call Mockery. And the wolf with the black and silver mane is Opposition ...'

'Oh spare me!' Senator called out. 'Dogs called Focus and Drive? Beasts called Mockery and Opposition? Don't think to regale us with a tale full of schoolboy imagery and the rhetoric of fools.'

Shepherd rocked back on his haunches and laughed into the dark sky. 'No schoolboy imagery,' he promised, 'for I never went to school and I have never before heard the word "rhetoric"!'

Warrior thought this was funny and laughed into his cuff so as not to embarrass Senator.

'Leave him alone, Senator,' Poet said. 'One never knows where pearls lay hid, and those that lustre from the dusty earth sometimes shine more brightly then those set in gold.'

Senator flapped his hand in the air as if to dispel Poet's words.

'Shepherd, may I ask?' Foreigner said. 'Do the other evil wolves have names?' He had not spoken before, except to answer questions.

'Opposition is the leader of the pack,' Shepherd said. 'He is not evil and I carry for him a certain respect, although I will never give in to him. He is often wise, but those that run with him show no wisdom. Their names are Intolerance, Oppression and Cruelty and there is not a scrap of wisdom between the three of them.'

Foreigner nodded sagely. 'I thought as much. I believe I have met them before, many times.'

Senator huffed impatiently and mumbled something about fools and simpletons until Poet slapped his knee. Warrior chuckled to himself. He enjoyed watching interactions between people who would never ordinarily move in the same circles. Senator stared at Poet in utter disbelief that his dignity had been assailed, and she stared back until at last his disdain was overcome by her persistence. Senator shook his head and the Warrior saw the glimmer of a smile.

'Tell me Shepherd,' Senator said. 'Why do you name the beast so?'

'I name them thus because they are impediments in my work and so I name them for the greater impediments I have experienced in the world.'

Senator shook his head and frowned. Shepherd fed the fire from his bundle of sticks and the others fell once again into quiet conversations between themselves. They spoke of their experiences since entering the void of darkness and mist, all the more hushed when the distant howling of wolves caressed the night air. Shepherd sent his dogs out to watch over the flock.

After a spell, the gathering fell to silent contemplation and Warrior studied each face. There would be no sleep this night, but at least they had the warmth of the fire and the comfort of fellowship.

'Why don't we each tell a story?' Apprentice said. 'We could take it in turns, and it would help to while away the dark hours.'

Poet was inspired. 'A fine idea, Apprentice. Perhaps you would all allow me to recite some poetry, or we could all take on the characters of one of my plays.'

'I think I would prefer stories of great deeds,' Warrior said.

'We could each follow our inspiration and that way the stories would be varied,' Foreigner said.

'I would like to sing a song instead,' Servant said. She looked towards Shepherd. 'And our host might play some more on his pipes.'

Senator stood up and raised a hand. 'We must indeed come to a way of lasting through the night, which will be long and tiresome, but why waste the opportunity on stories and songs? Instead we should speak of our faith and belief and how we might work to spread the word. What say you all?'

Nobody answered and Warrior felt uncomfortable. He looked from Foreigner to Shepherd, and could not help thinking that such discourse was unlikely to result in harmony. He was about to suggest that perhaps it was better to stick to stories when Shepherd saved him the need.

'Happiness!' Shepherd cried. 'We should all talk about happiness.'

'Frivolous nonsense!' Senator said but the others did not agree.

Warrior thought Senator on the verge of dissent, but the gathering appeared to be inspired by the subject and Senator, no doubt aware of the mood, showed restraint.

'I think we have our subject then,' Warrior said. 'Happiness it is!'

'You go first then, Shepherd,' Senator said. 'And I shall follow.'

'No, I'll go last.'

'And as for the order thereafter,' Warrior said, 'let us continue with the topsy-turvy imposition of the day. The furthest from the fire shall go first, and the warmest last.'

Senator took a deep breath and let it out in a sigh. 'Being so topsy-turvy, it is clear my word is least and will trail so far behind, nobody will care to even listen.'

'I'll listen,' Shepherd said cheerfully.

'And I!' Apprentice said and the gathering agreed and Warrior could tell that in spite of himself, Senator was gladdened.

'Me first then?' Young Woman asked.

Warrior stood close as Young Woman made her way to the stony seat which by silent agreement had become the speaker's dais.

'What to say about happiness?' she began. 'I am sometimes happy, but not very often. It is difficult to be happy when pain is a constant companion. It does not help that I cannot walk unaided or that my looks do not attract people.'

'We should all be thankful that a person's worth is not judged by their looks,' Apprentice chipped in, and then shrank back feeling that he had trespassed by speaking out of turn.

'It is easy to say that when you have good looks, as you do Apprentice. I am sorry to make you blush but you cannot know how the world treats those of us who are not so blessed. Sometimes I think people are indeed judged by their looks. I am not without intelligence, although my opinions are often ignored and my qualities such as they are, passed over, but all that is as nothing compared to my affliction. I am resolved that I shall never feel happy for long which is not to say I never feel the glimmer of happiness. The kindness of strangers can always kindle a small flame of happiness in my heart.'

Warrior felt Young Woman's eyes on him and he responded to her smile. She stumbled as she got up from the rock and he went to catch her, but she righted herself and held up a hand to stop him. Leaning heavily on her staff she shuffled back to her place by the fire.

Foreigner now stepped up to the rock and sat. 'Thank you for this moment,' he said, and then he composed himself. 'I am very fortunate. My health is good, I have employment and I have the love of a good family. My children make me happy … in small measure. I enjoy times of happiness with my wife so I cannot say that I am never happy but it is a happiness always marred by the reality of our lives. I am different from my neighbours and my neighbours judge me upon these differences knowing nothing of the man I am. I am shunned for no other reason than the differences. I am treated less favourably by merchants and the laws often conspire against me. The church holds me to be of little worth because I do not hold to all of its beliefs. Consequently, ignorant people, feeling that the powers care nothing about me, subject me to tyranny and assault and neither the law nor the church nor my neighbours stand up for me. How can a man be happy when he is without acceptance or equality?'

'You are welcome among us,' Warrior said, and the others showed their agreement in nods and low murmurs, one or two of them feeling a pang of guilt.

Next to the rock was Servant. 'I work hard. Thank goodness my master is a good and kind overseer, even if he pays little. Never mind, my family gets by. But it is a constant struggle to make ends meet. I am bound to a tedious employ and I need more money that I earn. I wish I could be free. I wish I might have enough money so that I could afford the things that I need and want. These things, freedom and money, they would make me happy and I strive for them knowing one day I will achieve them.'

Apprentice then bounded up with youthful energy and sat cross-legged on the temporary dais. 'I love to sport and swim and wrestle with my friends. It makes me happy to overcome my friends in games and when my team wins at sport. Like Servant, my master is also a good employer and he pays more than enough for my needs, considering that he gives me board and lodging too. Like Foreigner I am blessed with good health but unlike him there is nobody in my life with whom to share precious times. I ... erm ...' His energy appeared to ebb.

'Come on, spit it out!' Senator said. 'You are among friends, so there is no need to be shy.'

Warrior looked at Senator and wondered at the transformation in so short a time.

'Well, I blush to say it but I long for the warmth of a woman. I am inexperienced in the ways of love and often my blood burns so hot ...'

'That your ears go red!' Senator said good-naturedly. He laughed and the others did too but it was not meant in mockery and nor was it taken so.

Apprentice smiled sheepishly. 'So you see, there is a powerful need on me and it keeps happiness at bay. I am at a man's age but still lack a man's experience and it shames me and magnifies my loneliness. When I take a wife, I shall be happy.'

'Don't be too sure of that,' Warrior said and the men laughed and after a heartbeat the woman did too.

As Apprentice left the seat, Poet sat and arranged her costly gown about her. Warrior wondered if she was about to strike a pose, but she did not. 'My plays bring me plenty of money and even if they did not, my husband is a wealthy man. I do not lack for anything that money can buy not do I lack for love, for my husband is modelled upon Adonis himself and he has such energies that … well, never mind. My children are healthy and my house is in a fashionable part of the city. But let me ask you all. Who knows me? We all know Warrior, but who knows me?'

The people exchanged looks, shrugged their shoulders or mumbled in the negative.

'Just as I thought, and yet my plays are renowned and my poems recited throughout the land. But you see, it is actors who speak my lines, and orators who recite my poems. Nobody knows the woman behind the words and it is so galling. Actors are lauded in our land if not in others, yes even worshipped almost, but I am as anonymous as the crushing throng. Would that people knew my face and recognised me as I passed, so that they might love me. When all is said and done, my skills have done nothing to elevate me and how can happiness flourish in my anonymous heart.'

Warrior thought the arm across the eyes was a little too theatrical as Poet quit the seat, and was surprised when the people applauded. Poet seemed pleased out of all proportion. Warrior was pushed from his revelry when nobody made towards the seat and he realised it was his turn.

What had appeared easy while he was a mere observer now felt difficult as he sat on the cold stone facing the other seven people, and at first he was at a loss for words. 'Many of you knew of me before we met today.'

'All of us, I'd say,' Apprentice said.

'Not me,' Shepherd said.

Warrior laughed. 'Thank you for that, Shepherd. It was a slap my ego rightly deserved. Nevertheless my fame is widespread, not for the least reason that Poet has dedicated a ballad to the more illustrious of my deeds. My skills have brought me station and wealth. I have a small farm with staff and my sons are strong and my daughters beautiful. I am good at what I do and for the most part the men under my command respect me. And yet, I command no more than a company of warriors. My word has no influence at court lest I be reporting upon the numbers and dispositions of our enemies. Present company excepted, I see those that govern us leading us ever closer to disaster, but I am powerless to stop them. I do not think about happiness. Perhaps it is a compensation for those who have little else. Am I happy? No, but I am often content. Now, if I should somehow manage to gain the power necessary to make changes, then I think I might be happy. And now Senator, it is your turn.'

Senator did not sit down but wandered about the stone with his chin in his hand. 'What you said about happiness Warrior. It has a ring of truth. Happiness is not for the likes of us, but it is a thing for simpler people who do not carry the hopes and fears of their nation upon their backs. As I have listened to you all, I have noticed that I have all the things you lack. Each one of you has what he or she sees as a barrier to their happiness. Each one of you thinks they will be happy if only they can achieve that one missing element. And yet, I have it all and I am not happy. And do you know why? Happiness is not a thing to be pursued. It is base albeit enjoyable, but it is the least thing of importance. We are not meant to be happy in this world, because happiness is for the life that follows when we may be blessed in the presence of the Maker. To pursue happiness is to be a fool. Rather try to catch the wind or harness the clouds, for these may be achieved before securing happiness.' Senator emphasised the importance and finality of his words by sweeping his robes in a majestic arc and then sitting squarely upon the shepherd's rock, claiming it once again for his own.

'My turn!' Shepherd cried and he skipped up to the rock like an excited child.

'I'm so sorry,' Senator said rising. 'I had quite forgotten.' He proffered the seat with an elaborate bow and Shepherd sprang up, more like a frolicking lamb than a young man. He beamed at the gathering with such infectious joy that it kindled a smile in each of the others. They waited upon his words, expectantly.

At last he began. 'I have air to breathe. I have clean water to drink and food to fill my belly. I have clothes and a shelter to keep me warm. I am happy!'

A distant wolf howled but nobody heard it. The dogs bayed far outside the circle but nobody paid any attention. The fire snapped and crackled and the darkness drew in. The shepherd sat smiling and those gathered around waited for more.

'Is that it?' Apprentice said at length.

'It is,' Shepherd said.

'Well,' Poet said. 'That was worth waiting for.'

'Any fool who has nothing and wants nothing can be happy,' Senator said. 'Just as I implied before, happiness is compensation for simple folk without higher ideals.'

'And yet,' Warrior said, 'Shepherd is the fool that made the fire that saved the rest of us.'

Senator imposed his superiority. 'He made the fire for himself. It was only that we were led to him by the Lord that saved us.'

'Surely we were led here by Shepherd's pipe-playing?' Young Woman said.

'That was the Lord's work,' Senator said.

'Funny,' Shepherd said. 'I could have sworn it was mine.'

Warrior was astounded to see the group break down instantly into a cacophony of argument and counter-argument until Shepherd jumped up and stood on the rock. He blew a shrill note from his pipes and everyone came to their senses.

'Is it that my story was too short?' Shepherd said from his vantage point. He did not wait for an answer. 'Then why not be seated once again, and I shall tell you more, and then maybe you will understand.'

Good cheer was restored and everybody sat down.

'Are you comfortable? Good, then let me tell you all about my flock ...'

III

When everybody had settled, Shepherd brought his feet up and sat cross-legged on the rock. Warrior noticed that all looked expectant, even the Senator. It was not so surprising that they all wanted an answer to help them see beyond their respective problems, but he found it exceedingly strange that they should expect the answer to come from Shepherd who could not have been much past his seventeenth year. Surely Senator should be the one to help, but then, he was not happy and Shepherd was. Warrior shook his head and prepared to listen.

'There are many sheep in the flock I watch,' Shepherd began. 'But I wish to speak about only seven of them. The first of these I call Ambition.'

Senator held up his hand, like a command for a traveller to stop and listen. 'Shepherd, once again I feel your story is going to stray into puerile analogy. Let me tell you, I have studied at the most learned cities in the world and at the feet of the great ones. I have immersed myself in logic, and oratory. I have seen the course of the stars and planets and am well-versed in mathematics and in the ancient languages of our ancestors. Without wishing to be rude, I do not think there is much I can learn from a shepherd.'

'Except for my story,' Shepherd said. 'I am the only man who can tell my story, and I intend to tell it to the best of my ability. I am not learned and I cannot read, but for all your great wisdom, you cannot tell my story for me.'

Senator said 'Granted, but why not just tell it as it is, without attempting to tap into a level of learning that you do not possess?'

'Oh do shut up!' Apprentice said, and then added 'sir' and shuffled nervously as he became the centre of unwanted attention. 'I mean to say, sir, that we all like stories. Let Shepherd tell us one.'

The others agreed. Senator bowed. 'Then proceed, and right glad I am that you have ambition, be it only in the name of one of your sheep.'

'Come now master shepherd. Let us hear about Ambition,' Poet said.

Shepherd took the crook and laid it across his knees. 'Ambition came to me early. She was one of my first sheep and remains with me still, though others come and go. Eventually she was got with lamb by the great ram, Strength, and her lambs were Purpose and Excitement.

'The next to join my flock was …'

'Hold! Shepherd, we now know you have ambition, but you have not named it,' Senator said. 'What is your ambition?'

'You're not listening,' Shepherd said, grinning. 'Ambition is a sheep!'

Apprentice laughed, a little too loudly and somewhat at Senator's expense. Poet covered her mouth as her shoulders showed her mirth by their shaking, and the others hid or showed their appreciation of the jest as was their nature.

'Touché, master shepherd. I shall not interrupt again.'

Warrior hoped Senator would be as good as his word. He had certainly taken Shepherd's mild rebuke with good cheer, but it was as if he had appointed himself as devil's advocate, and spoke out against Shepherd in spite of himself.

'Well said, Senator,' Warrior said. 'I am sure you will credit each of us with the sense to interpret Shepherd's words according to our own learning and experience.'

Shepherd smiled guilelessly and continued. 'Obsession came next, and although she was very amenable to the directions of my dogs, whose names were … Who can tell me?'

Young Woman answered. 'How can I forget those who saved my life from the wolves? Your dogs are Focus, Drive and Direction.'

'Indeed they are, and Obsession needed hardly any help from them. But she was single-minded to the exclusion of some of the necessities of life. She did not eat properly and neither did she take any time to bond with the others in the flock. Ambition tried to get close to her, but I had to work hard not to allow Obsession to dominate.

'Fear was next, a timid little thing she was, for ever turning to look for the wolf at her heels.'

'You should put her out of the flock,' Servant said. 'I have known her like, and there is no place for her.'

'Ah, but she is a healthy sheep and I regard her well. One of her lambs is Caution, and that one has served me to great advantage. But if she is got with lamb by my second ram, Anger, her offspring are Insecurity, Jealousy and another whom you saw me throw into the fire. That one is called Hatred, and I have no use for her. Of all my flock, only Hatred will I slay at birth. If left to thrive she will grow to a massive size in the shortest of times and devour everything that is good.' Shepherd paused and looked at the faces gathered around. This time he invited comment, and Senator put up his hand. Shepherd cocked an ear.

'Warrior must surely affirm that there is a place for Hatred. Surely on the field of battle, Hatred must be given leave to roam among the warriors, for without it, who could slay an enemy.'

Warrior shook his head. 'That I cannot affirm, sir. The warrior who hates is useless and flawed. We must face our enemies with respect and apply our skills, such as they are, with cold calculation. Why, I have more in common with the man I face in battle than he who sent me to war in the first place. And once the battle is won, our enemies are warriors overcome who are our brothers in adversity, and to treat such a man with hatred or cruelty is wickedness. No, I too will join Shepherd in slaying that pernicious lamb wherever I encounter it.'

'Yes, but surely you face enemies who hate you,' Senator said. 'And if you are captured and treated with barbarity springing from their hatred, surely that will make you hate in return.'

'We often meet enemies who are filled with hatred. Let me say this. They fight two enemies and they are the foes that stand before them with weapons and the foe in their hearts that will conquer them even if they prevail against us.'

'You have it, friend!' Shepherd said. 'Hatred is infectious and one has to guard against allowing a single fibre from her fleece to lodge within you. She must be utterly destroyed, to the last fibre, wherever she is born.'

Senator stroked his chin and shifted from one foot to the other. 'If we encounter Hatred within an enemy then, we must slay the enemy to end Hatred.'

'No, she will simply gambol from one heart to another. You must make sure she has no contact with her mother, and while exercising her sister, Caution, you must assist your enemy while Hatred withers and dies within him. Hatred, once grown, cannot be eradicated by imposition or force.'

'Very well,' Warrior said. 'I think we have roasted Hatred into a cinder and crumbled the remains to dust. What of your fourth sheep, Shepherd? I hope she is a prettier one than the last two.'

Shepherd shrugged. 'Not so that anyone would notice. My fourth sheep was Doubt. She often stood in the way of Ambition but she came together with her sister, Optimism. These sisters often vied for attention hopping up onto the high rocks to be king of the castle. Neither of them was inherently bad or good, for each had their qualities. Doubt at her best gave birth to Reassessment, at her worst to Resignation and Depression. Optimism was a pretty little thing but quite useless without the intercession of my trusty friend, Direction. It was the same with the next sheep to the flock, whose name is Acceptance. At her worst she suckled Inaction but at her very best she was one of my most valuable sheep. Without Acceptance, the flock often railed and fought against factors that could never be changed. They would run here and there fruitlessly, losing condition and adding mightily to their pain. Acceptance came at last and the flock became almost serene.

'So you see, apart from Hatred, those that make up my flock all have good and bad within their nature, and it is up to me, together with my dogs, to keep them all in check and deal with them according to their natures so that I might encourage the best within them and keep the worst suppressed. But just as there is Hatred, the one potential part of my flock that is thoroughly bad and without the slightest saving grace, there is also one who is all good, without a blemish. Her name is Happiness, and although I knew her early in my life, she did not come to my flock until last.

'She came to me unbidden and at times I could not predict, but she never tarried for long. I tried to encourage her with tasty morsels or kind words, but she could never be coaxed or beguiled. I began to think that she would come once my flock was large, or my house was built, or my work complete, but the more I thought about her the less she came. She was the last of my sheep and so I reasoned, all the others must be seen to first and then afterwards, there would be time for Happiness. How wrong I was.

'One day while I was playing my pipes, she came to me and I was glad to see her. As I enjoyed her company, knowing that soon she would be put to flight by one of the other sheep, or scared away by the jackal or the wolves, the simple secret of her presence came to me. I had always put her last instead of first. I worked hard on the conditions I thought she would favour, so her presence by very virtue of my mistaken belief, was always conditional. Do such-and-such, achieve that, acquire this … and then Happiness will come. And then she will tarry a while and be off so that I must do and achieve and acquire more before she comes again.

'The secret that came to me on that bright and sunny day was that the visitations of Happiness could never be dependant on conditions that were not within my control. I could not allow her to spend her days in that far distant field where I could glimpse her but not feel her presence. I wanted her to be with me always and not just on those rare days when I completed a task or achieved a goal. I wanted her to walk with me on my journey, and not simply wait for me at my destination, only to get up and gambol off after too short a time. And what if I never achieved my goal? Would it matter hugely, so long as Happiness was at my side?'

Warrior assumed the question to be rhetorical, but once again Senator took it to be an invitation to offer a counter-question.

'Shepherd, it is hard to listen to you, and to behold you in your good-humoured simplicity, without the heart responding with gladness. But surely happiness is the goal that spurs us on through hardship. If happiness was with us at all times, would we not just lie back while the world passes us by and our goals, if ever we had them to begin with, stay fast-stuck to a future we will never know? You are a shepherd, almost the humblest of professions, and you are happy, so will you ever be anything more?'

A sheep walked in from the dark void and came into the light of the fire. Young Woman gasped and Apprentice beamed. The sheep walked up to Shepherd, who reached down from his perch and buried his hand deep into the luxuriant fleece. His face glowed.

'I am a shepherd, and I am happy. But I still have Ambition. There are things that I wish to achieve and I shall make my plans and work towards those things, but they will not bring me Happiness. She is here all the time and dependant on nothing but my acceptance of her, and my will that she should remain.'

The sheep bleated and walked towards those gathered by the fire, coming to rest by Young Woman. 'She has come to me, as I never thought she would. That Happiness can come to such as I who cannot walk ...' Young Woman embraced the sheep before it moved on, to each of the group in turn at last stopping before Senator. It looked up into his face and bleated softly and Warrior wondered at how the whiteness of her fleece matched that of the old man's hair.

'Be off with you, and back to your master. Though you be a pretty thing, I am not worthy, for my journey takes me to a reward beyond this life and there shall dwell my happiness.'

The sheep bleated again and nuzzled against the old man's legs. Warrior could tell that Senator wanted to reach out and touch it.

Shepherd jumped down from the rock and touched Senator's arm. 'This is my Happiness, but you are welcome to share until you come to your own.'

Senator reached out, but withdrew again before his fingertips had even brushed the gleaming wool. 'You are a good man, Shepherd, and I thank you, but I find I cannot. We are very different people, as are we all,' he said as he encompassed the gathering with a sweep of his arm. 'We cannot all share the same happiness.'

'That which we are shines through many filters imposed by our experiences and our station in life, so that each of us gives off a different hue, and yet our differences spring from the same pure light.'

Senator nodded. 'That light is God,' he said quietly and with the strength of faith.

'I cannot tell. It may well be,' Shepherd said, 'but I believe it is the light of humanity and humanity encompasses all beliefs and all the many faces of God.'

Warrior was not a religious man. He had met with wickedness wrapped up in the skin of religion. Elsewhere he had seen selflessness and sacrifice carried out in the name of the same religion and he had seen the same extremes of behaviour where there was no religion at all. 'Does it matter what we call it if we are all in agreement that we share the light? God or humanity, it matters little.'

'Of course it matters!' Senator cried.

'Then it matters to you, Senator, and I will not try to persuade you otherwise, but it matters to me not a whit and I would have you return the same considerations.' Warrior folded his arms to demonstrate the finality of his words.

'But ...'

Shepherd held up his hand and Senator held his tongue. 'If we concentrate on the light in our own way, the names become irrelevant. Let us all be strengthened by that which is greater than us and happy to be a part of it, be it deity or nature, and keep our own council as to its name.'

Senator regarded Shepherd sternly from under bushy eyebrows. But Shepherd's cheerful countenance did not falter, and when Happiness nuzzled the old man's knees once again, his face broke into a radiant smile. He bent down and ruffled the sheep's fleece. 'I think I can manage that, master shepherd, at least for the duration of our sojourn together.' And then he got down to his knees and fully embraced the sheep and buried his face into the wool and Warrior was of the impression that he wept. At length he stood up and straightened his garment, and drew a sleeve across his eyes. 'When in the world's history did seven such as we share the fire of a shepherd boy in harmony and equality?'

'Never before, and more is the pity and the likelihood, never again,' Foreigner said. 'For that reason I hope this night never ends, for here there is acceptance and ... and yes, love, but in the morning the world will be restored in all its glory and in all its injustice.'

The sheep walked to each of the people once more and then left the circle to be swallowed up by the night, and the people were crestfallen.'

'Never mind.' Shepherd's cheerfulness was undiminished. 'She is with me still and I am glad to have shared her with you all. Now you must find ways to tend to your own happiness and then, if you follow my creed, perhaps you can be instruments in nurturing the happiness of all those you meet. But first, let us sustain ourselves against this cold night.'

The others fell to talking among themselves while Shepherd tended the fire and set some water to boil. He declined the offers of help that many made. Soon he had made a thick broth which they took, one by one, drinking from the shepherd's cup.

It was past midnight now, by several hours if the Warrior's calculations were correct, and while he longed for the light, like Foreigner he wanted the fellowship of the fireside to continue, though he feared it could not. And yet, as he watched Shepherd, always cheerful, ever positive, he could not help but hope that there might be a way, and he grew impatient for what the young man might say next. He had enjoyed Shepherd's little tale with its simple truths, and he liked the thought that the shepherd stood for every man and woman, and that his flock stood for those characteristics that all people may experience. He had heard other stories that spoke of shepherds and flocks, but in those the shepherd represented a deity and the flock his followers. Either way, it was a powerful analogy, but Warrior preferred the think of himself as a shepherd, and not one of the sheep. His was the power to nurture and care and lead, and not just to follow meekly and without question.

When all had partaken of the sustaining broth, Shepherd forsook the rocky seat for a place in the circle with all the rest. 'Earlier, Senator asked if I had ambition, and I made a joke.'

Young Woman remembered and giggled. Senator smiled and chewed the side of his cheek at the same time, which made Apprentice laugh.

'Well, I do have an ambition, apart from my sheep, and it came about like this. Many hours I spend without human company and I have time to think. I thought upon the joy of the world, which I believe to be happiness, and I thought about the blight of the world, which ruins lives and brings nations low. That blight, perhaps it is disagreement. But no, for disagreement can be cordial, and no man or nation can hope to have all the answers to life's questions. Disagreement leads to discussion and discussion to solutions that neither side of an argument may have reached alone. No, as I hope we have all learnt, Hatred is the blight of the world, and it is the favoured meat of those ravenous wolves, Oppression, Intolerance and Cruelty.'

'Come the day when I might fight the beasts that tear men apart instead of the men who my masters name enemy,' Warrior said.

A murmur of assent touched the lips of all gathered, and then the shepherd continued.

'So having after a while got my own flock in order, I thought it was time that I should do whatever I might, be it a tiny thing or a great, to spread the word. I have a creed and it is this.' And Shepherd spoke his creed.

All people deserve and are worthy of respect, compassion and equality. This is the immutable truth, and I will do whatever is reasonable and within my power to realise this truth by my actions, words and behaviour, especially where respect, compassion and equality are lacking.

'That's it,' Shepherd said, 'and though it could not be simpler, nor could it be truer.'

Senator clapped once and smiled. 'So that is the Shepherd's Creed! I find it sits well with my own. But who in the world will listen to you, a simple man and unschooled?'

'Anybody who listens properly,' Warrior said. 'And if you have to be of the same status as the storyteller to understand his words, then this night I am a shepherd.'

'I declare that this night we are all shepherds,' Poet said. 'For I can hardly believe that any of us here gathered could attest that in their hearts there is not a snug place for those words.

'We are a veritable Fellowship of Shepherds, and you my friend, who might otherwise be thought the least of us, are the greatest and Chief of Shepherds.'

Senator stood and held up his arms, a look of wonder on his face. 'Why let the Fellowship die with the coming of day?' he said. 'Let us become a true Fellowship and appoint a hierarchy, with our friend here as the Arch-Shepherd and ourselves as his First Disciples. We could ...' He broke off because Shepherd was laughing so much.

Warrior guessed the reason why. 'Let us indeed be a Fellowship, but let there be no division or hierarchy among us. Let the least in learning and age and station be the equal of the most learned and honoured in the land. As long as a person holds the Shepherd's Creed to be the cornerstone of their philosophy let them be full and equal members of the Fellowship, without any other consideration.'

Everyone rose as one, Young Woman with the help of Apprentice who lent his arm, and they were all glad and they all spoke together of how they might spread the immutable truth which was the Shepherd's Creed.

The first glimmer of daylight touched the distant hills when they all sat down again and in hushed voices, so as not to scare away the rest of the night, they discussed how they might make the Fellowship a lasting reality.

'If there should ever come a time when the Fellowship has spread widely upon the face of the earth, how might we know one another?' Apprentice asked. 'Should we have a secret sign, or perhaps a handshake like those ancients who built the pyramids?'

'There is no need for secrecy,' Warrior said. 'Let us simply ask "Are you a Shepherd?" and let the proud answer be "I am a Shepherd" and in that way we will learn more about a person than with any other statement.'

'So say you,' Foreigner said. 'But I have been to lands where the very thoughts of a man and his deepest beliefs are prescribed by law. How should they say "I am a Shepherd" and not put their lives at risk?'

Servant suggested that certain masters might be equally disapproving. 'Perhaps we must make take our own council in such matters, and do such as we can without incurring the wrath of our masters.'

'I think the clue is in the Shepherd's Creed. "I will do whatever is reasonable and within my power to spread this truth." And yes, Servant, you are correct. We must take our own council in these matters.'

"We need a symbol!' Apprentice cried excitedly. 'What say you all? I say a lion, for strength.'

'Or an owl for wisdom!' Poet said.

Foreigner laughed. 'In my land an owl stands for stupidity.'

'Oh dear,' Poet replied, crestfallen.

'You choose animals to represent noble human qualities while ignoring innocent blood on claw and beak. I say the only symbol to represent man is man,' Warrior said.

'Or woman!' Poet said.

'Then it is simple. Why not choose a shepherd for our symbol.'

'Male of female?'

Warrior laughed and so did Poet, who continued. 'Instead of a person, sir, let us choose the instrument of shepherd-hood and have for our symbol the shepherd's crook. What say you, Shepherd?' But when she looked, the shepherd was gone.

As the sun rose and the land came back into focus, without a covering of mist so that its beauty was undiminished, the newly formed Fellowship spied no sign of Shepherd or his sheep, except for his crook that rested

171

against the rock, and for a moment all were silent and bemused by his absence.

At last, Warrior approached the rock and took up the crook. 'I think he has set his seal to your idea, Poet. We shall know each other by the simple question aforementioned, and if we feel the need, by the sign of the shepherd's crook.'

The sun rose higher, changing from a heavy red globe to full effulgence. Warrior's page ran from the road and begged his master's forgiveness. Poet recognised the distant cart as her missing transport, and Young Woman's friends came to her and were glad to be reunited.

Warrior told his page to build up the fire and much to the page's surprise, Warrior helped prepare a simple breakfast. The Fellowship parted with sadness and promises to remember each other and the night and to spread the Shepherd's Creed. Warrior sent his page ahead and told him to wait by the way-stone that marked the city limits until he came, and so Warrior was alone again just as he had been when the storm first came.

He sat on the rock and ran his fingers over the surface, wondering if the shepherd had ever really been there, and then he heard the merry chimes of distant laughter. There, atop a far hill, he thought he could see a figure, and if he stood on the rock, screwed up his eyes and shielded them against the sun with his hand, he thought he could see the tiny silhouette of a man and some sheep. Again the laughter drifted to him across the distance and lodged in his heart. He waved and smiled and said to himself, I am a Shepherd.

Blinking away tears brought by the brightness, he looked again, and the shepherd was gone. But not entirely: they might never meet again, but the shepherd would be with him always.

The End of the Story

PART TWO

Considerations & Controversies

With the exception of the part of Chapter One below, which clarifies The Shepherd's Creed, *Considerations & Controversies* discusses ideas and thoughts that are likely to be of interest to a Shepherd. It is not dogma. Agreeing with every part won't make you a better Shepherd any more than disagreeing will make you a bad Shepherd or no Shepherd at all. Just to reiterate, and at the risk of sounding like a parrot, the only qualification required to be a Shepherd is the open-hearted acceptance of The Shepherd's Creed.

Why include the rest then? Well, without the rest, this would be a very short book indeed, and secondly, Shepherds are questioning people who probably have legitimate concerns that need to be considered before they feel ready to state "I am a Shepherd" and here is where I hope some of those concerns will be acknowledged, if not answered fully.

CHAPTER ONE

Considering "The Shepherd"

The trouble with parables is that they are open to misinterpretation, and as simple as it is, it would be naïve to believe that parts of The Shepherd, whether because of obscure imagery or omission, might not suffer the same fate. For the most part, that's fine, except as it applies to the Shepherd's Creed.

> All people deserve and are worthy of respect, compassion and equality.

It sounds simple enough, and it is, but let's put it into something a little more akin to legalese, just so there is no wriggle-room, no doubt as to its scope or meaning.

> All people deserve and are worthy of respect, compassion and equality *irrespective of age, race, ethnicity, nationality, physicality, physical or mental ability, sexual orientation, belief, faith or lack thereof, marital status, class or social standing, or any other defining characteristic.*

The bad news? It includes that group of people you have always had certain reservation about. Stop wriggling! You know exactly who I mean. The good news? It also includes you.

That is the Shepherd's Creed and that is the essence of a person who calls him or herself Shepherd. So, does that make a Shepherd a smiley, skippy, hug-the-trees and kiss-the-flowers resident of Fluffyville, Cotton-Wool County? I don't think so. We know the world is often a dangerous place and that the wolves and jackals (sorry for typecasting you guys, but you do play the parts so well) are always among us. Shepherds are a force for good in the world, but we would not be hugely effective if we allowed ourselves to be ground into the earth by the harsh realities of existence. Recognising the one immutable truth and accepting that all people deserve and are worthy of respect, compassion and equality is not the same as acquiescing divisive, immoral or anti-social behaviour, not to mention out-and-out criminality.

Alright then, what exactly is divisive, immoral or anti-social behaviour, you may well ask. What is immoral to me might be perfectly acceptable to someone else. Very true, and these definitions will be considered later in a chapter of their very own (Chapter Five: Considering Morality), but first a word on the "one immutable truth" part of the Creed.

All it takes to be a Shepherd is to fully embrace the Shepherd's Creed. It is the one immutable truth, and all the other considerations in this book are just that: considerations and not edicts cast in stone.

Does the one immutable truth apply to absolutely everyone though? Surely a person's action may be so appalling as to remove them from its scope. I am talking the cold-blooded murderer, the rapist and the predatory paedophile. Are these people really deserving and worthy of respect, compassion and equality?

Yes they are. Now, stay with me on this one for just a minute, and you will see what I mean.

Being deserving and worthy of respect, compassion and equality is not the same as saying people should be immune from the proper sanctions and punishments that attach to their proscribed actions. But once you start saying, this or that person falls outside the compass of the Creed, you leave the door ajar and unguarded, and that's just what hatred sees as an invitation to enter. Hatred, as the shepherd tells us in the parable, is as pernicious and poisonous to the hater as it is to the hated. More so, in fact.

It will be as difficult for a Shepherd as for any other person to hear news of, for example, an act of terrorism,

175

without feeling anger, but we must guard ourselves against allowing the anger to fester and warp into hatred, especially when considering terrorism, for then the terrorist has achieved a large part of his aim.

It can be seen from this that there is an element of selfishness in the Creed as applied to people who, through their heinous actions might be thought less worthy, because in one respect we are extending the Creed to them in order to keep hatred from our own door, as it were. So be it! We're Shepherds, not angels ... or Nobel Peace Prize winners for the atheists among us.

Is the all-encompassing Creed actually the inherent flaw within a Shepherd's thinking, for surely it would be possible for those who have perpetrated horrible acts to be Shepherds themselves, so long as they accept the Creed? Actually, no: as Shepherds we accept the Creed and we act upon it so far as we are able. Whereas we accept the Creed extends to all people, we do not accept that all people are Shepherds unless their actions support the Creed, and this cannot be said of perpetrators of victim-based crimes or any other action that involves treating a person with anything other than respect, compassion or equality.

I dare say a master criminal with a good lawyer could stretch and distort the definitions and endeavour to call him or herself Shepherd if they so wished, but the thing is, why would they want to?

Moving on to the last part of the Creed

> ... I will do whatever is reasonable and within
> my power to realise this truth by my actions,
> words and behaviour, especially where respect,
> compassion and equality are lacking.

To take a baseball bat to a person who opposes the Shepherd's Creed and beat them until they agree with us, is not reasonable. To give up all our money and possessions and spend all our time to the exclusion of everything else,

176

spreading the Creed, is not reasonable. To stand up for the guy in the group who is being picked on because he isn't quite as fast on the uptake as others may well be reasonable, and to defend your colleague in the office who has been side-lined because of gender issues seems reasonable as well. To campaign and demonstrate for human rights in those instances where they are lacking will also be reasonable in certain circumstances. In short, as long as an action is reasonable and within your power, nothing is too small, or too big. The smallest of actions might have life-changing effects far in excess of expectations, and the many seemingly insignificant actions of us all as individuals can add up to a considerable influence for good.

Moving on from the Shepherd's Creed: the people who make an appearance in the parable – the players, if you like – deserve a little consideration.

The aim of this book as stated in the introduction is to start a dialogue that may increase happiness and eradicate hatred in those people who choose to call themselves Shepherds and all others we can reach. The players in the parable address the first of these aims.

Specifically, the players' wants and needs represent various perceived barriers to happiness. Each character, in order of speaking, has what the previous speaker lacks and sees as the key to personal happiness, and yet subsequent speakers are not happy with their lot and see the key as something more, something in the future or otherwise out of reach.

It is the young shepherd's contention that they are all putting the cart before the horse, and that happiness should be the goal of every person and that happiness should not be dependant on any factor outside of a person's direct control. We'll return to this theme in a moment when we consider the sheep named in the story, but it should be pointed out that all the people in the story are assumed to have achieved all the basic needs for survival and general health. It would be difficult, but not impossible, to worry too much about happiness, or anything else, if every day was a struggle to find enough food to eat.

Lack of description in the parable is quite deliberate, both in terms of the people involved and the landscape. I see the people as being based in some Celtic or Anglo-Saxon long distant past living in a land of forests and grass, because that is the ancestry of my culture. But I wanted the story to be accessible to all, and so it is equally valid to see them as Mongolian, Masai Mara, Indian, Lebanese … it really does not matter. It doesn't even matter that the Masai Mara generally keep cattle rather than sheep. There are few cultures that cannot respond to the image of the lone herdsman doing his best to keep his charges safe against everything the world has to throw at him.

It hardly needs stating that the sheep represent some of the qualities we all find ourselves imbued with at one time or another, both the positive and the negative, but why do they appear so prominently in the parable? It comes from the premise that a Shepherd is likely to be far more effective in spreading happiness and eradicating hatred, if he or she has first achieved these aims in their own lives and within their own being. In other words, if I may borrow a reference from the New Testament of the Christians and then give it a Shepherdian slant: "Shepherd, first see to your own flock." We are not shepherds of other people, but shepherds of our own thoughts and impulses.

The imagery and import of each of the named sheep is, I believe, clear enough within the confines of the parable not to need repetition here, all except for Happiness, and she demands her own consideration in a chapter to follow, for you will recall that the shepherd talks about Happiness and declares his belief that it should not be dependant on factors outside a person's control, but that he gives very little information of how to realise his belief. The chapter on happiness goes some way to redressing his omission.

Skip it if you prefer. Personally, it's a chapter I need to look at once in a while.

The jackal and the wolves represent the external impediments that Shepherds are likely to encounter. We will all run into Opposition from time to time, but reasoned opposition is not inherently bad. There are bound to be many good people, who through previous teachings or lack of engagement seek to exclude one or other or several groups of people from under the umbrella of the Creed. It is right that a Shepherd should engage with them and try to persuade them that none are deserving of exclusion. If we can't, then they will remain Opposition although in other respects they may be our friends.

I am willing to bet that Mockery might put in an appearance or two, snapping at a Shepherd's heels, and sadly so may the other wolves, Intolerance, Oppression and Cruelty. Mockery? Big deal: let it bounce off our backs. The last three wolves though, must be given no quarter. They are behaviours that must not be allowed to thrive unchecked. I am of course, talking about the behaviours, and not the people who display them. The two can be separated.

The dogs, Focus, Drive and Direction represent those traits that should be under a Shepherd's own control, and will be with a little practice. The sheep may well drift in or out, seemingly of their own will, but the dogs must be under a Shepherd's control and are his most loyal allies in keeping the flock in order and fending off the beasts. They do not need their own paragraphs here as they pretty much fit in with the next chapter, Considering Happiness.

CHAPTER TWO

Considering Happiness

Shepherds' Health Warning: nothing you will find written here … or anywhere else … will make you a hundred percent happy a hundred percent of the time. And before we move on it is very important to remind ourselves that there is a kind of deep, unremitting and all-consuming unhappiness that amounts to clinical depression. It is a condition that will not respond to reasoning and it imperative to seek the proper medical assistance and to maintain the prescribed regimes.

As a general rule, Shepherds are happy people. We have conquered hatred in our lives; totally eradicated it, and so we are more effective at spreading happiness where it is needed and eradicating hatred wherever we encounter it. We are not immune to the knocks of life and we cannot dodge all the slings and arrows, but like that popular toddlers' toy of the 1980's, we might wobble but we don't fall down.

The shepherd in the parable states quite clearly that people must not put the cart before the horse. Instead of attaching the prospect of happiness upon escaping negative conditions they do not enjoy, or achieving a goal or dream that they see as key to their happiness, they should make happiness itself their aim. At first this view seems to fly in the face of generations of professed wisdom. Surely happiness is a by-product of reaching a goal, or of being accepted for the person you are. Happiness cannot be harnessed, so what sense does it make for such an ephemeral and flighty condition your aim? The shepherd did not tell us, hence this chapter for consideration. The shepherd was not the first person to elevate the importance of happiness to the very pinnacle of objectives. Nor is this the first book to promote the idea. There are several and I acknowledge the importance of my predecessors in influencing the following thoughts.

Before defining happiness and setting down the sure-fired, tried and tested methods to achieve it, here are a few impostors that often slip in wearing a happiness-wig and false moustache when they're actually another kind of emotion altogether. The following feelings, welcome visitors though they may be, are not happiness.

The feeling that accompanies

- a nice surprise, such as winning the lotto;
- achieving a goal towards which you have worked long and hard;
- receiving kudos for your work;
- finding that one special person;
- coming first;
- being famous.

But surely this feeling is happiness! If these things make us feel good, they must be forms of happiness. I don't think so. This is pleasure, not happiness, and whereas that pleasant rush is desirable, it can also become a false beacon, because like lust, a person who sets their compass towards pleasure can never get enough of it. The pursuit of pleasure can become all-consuming and a person who craves pleasure becomes addicted to it and suffers the consequence in its absence.

Pleasure equates to feeling good, therefore lack of pleasure must be the cause of feeling bad. Name your pleasure. It could be nights out with your friends at the rave, or the opera. It might be tied up with the adrenalin rush that comes with extreme sports, or being best in your particular field. So name your pleasure and enjoy it when it comes, but do not make it your over-riding goal.

Okay, so if all these things make us feel good, and happiness makes us feel good, what is the difference? The difference is you have *to do* to feel pleasure, whereas you only have *to be*, to feel happiness.

Happiness is that feeling that it is great to be alive and to be an equal part of the amazing adventure that is humanity. What am I saying? Humanity? The adventure is greater than that, for we are all part universal existence and ... whoa ... don't go yet. If this sounds all hippy twaddle or new-age cop-out and you're fixing to leave, stay with me a minute more. You want to know what happiness is and how to achieve it without signing up to a crystal-healing or aroma-therapy class. I understand that, and from now on I'll keep my feet grounded on the good earth ... until we get to Chapter Four that is. Meanwhile, here are the nine steps to deep, lasting happiness.

1. Define Happiness

Happiness is a self-contained emotion. Despite what the world may chuck at us, being happy means that the simple act of being and of having life feels good. So if you have not already realised that and found a way of living in happiness, read on. It won't make you become rich or famous, but in that happiness is a very stable base from which to launch into any given project, it might just help you reach your goals, and even if it doesn't, you will love the ride.

Happiness is the quality of feeling a peace with oneself and of feeling the joy of being.

2. Prepare the Ground

Now we know what happiness is and what it isn't how do we till the fields of our personalities to make it a fertile environment for the growth of happiness? Begin by taking the time to realise what a truly one-off you actually are. A one-time, one-off never to be repeated person that will interface with the Universe for the span of only a few-score years ... if you're lucky. You might share the basic body-type of several hundred thousand people, have similar beliefs and live a similar lifestyle, but of all the millions of people that are, have been, or ever will be, you will never be repeated. Final offer, hurry while stocks last. You are one rare, nay unique, person … but then so am I, so don't get too carried away.

The point is, there is nothing to be gained by looking at the lives of others, other than to learn from those that inspire you. You can learn, but you cannot change places, and nor should you want to. How do you know how they really feel, for all their appearances of happiness?

As unique as each one of us is, there is a very basic condition we all share, and that is, try as we might, we will only ever have one perspective, one window onto the world. Being the only person you will ever see from the inside-out can be a little isolating, until you consider it is the same for every one of us. I'll sum it up in a rhyme, and before the critics seize up their pens in righteous indignation, I said "rhyme", not "poem". I know my limitations even if I don't know my dactyls from my pentameters.

Before the Battle

When you are outside looking in,
The face you see is flesh and skin.
Flesh is good at hiding feeling;
A wax mask over fear congealing?

When you are inside looking out,
The face you feel is fear and doubt.
Fear is good at isolating;
All good feeling doubt's deflating.

If you were me and I were thee
We'd likely see the same.
We'd both spy a brave 'un
While each feeling craven.
The old appearance game.

You might not have the stunning good looks or natural athletic ability of Mr Perfect from the other office, or the sharp intellect of Ms Genius: in terms of the raw materials, you are what you are and it's up to you to make the best of them. Life or nature may have dealt you a measly plot of land with a dry and meagre soil, but happiness is a resilient seed. So long as you are alive, it has a chance. The poorest soil or the richest, happiness grows best with good husbandry and knowing without the least shadow of a doubt that happiness is attainable and independent of conditions outside your control, is the best fertiliser there is.

Now, we know what happiness is and we are satisfied that the soil will nurture it, we're ready to sew.

Killed it? I supposed so. No more agricultural analogies then, I promise. Or rather, I promise I'll try.

3. Set Goals

If you were a shark, you would have to keep swimming to keep the oxygenated water flowing through your gills. Stop and you'd suffocate. So it is with people that we must have goals, otherwise we have no direction, no purpose, and happiness will not take root. The goals do not have to be on a heroic scale. We cannot all reach the summit of Everest. I'd be hard-pushed to make it to Base Camp. My mountaineering goals are far more modest. Goals can be set far into the future, and depend on working slowly towards them, or they could be more immediate affairs that can be achieved in a few days. The scale is not important, although there should be at least some element of challenge.

I recently saw the most moving documentary. It was about a young soldier who had lost both legs above the knee and one arm above the elbow. Most of us could not even begin to imagine the challenge of maintaining our optimism under such circumstances, but this remarkable young man had a goal, and his goal was to be able to walk at the medal ceremony. His love of life, his cheerfulness and positive attitude in the face of such pain was humbling and a lesson for us all. He had accepted his lot, in that he knew that no matter how bitterly he might rail against the world, he would never fully regain his losses. He had accepted his condition, but had not accepted them as limitations on his happiness. Life is about moving on. He was optimistic and, of immense value to his determination to recover, he had a goal. Yes, achieving the goal was important, but having the goal was even more so.

The important fact to remember in setting goals is that they must be achievable. They might be hugely difficult but they must be possible or at least there must be the perception of possibility. Remember we are talking of the importance of having goals here, rather than achieving them, but there must at least be reality peeking over the horizon. If your goal is to think yourself to the moon, it is unlikely to take you anywhere very far away from men with white coats.

You might consider a goal that is achievable, although with several stages that are outside your direct control. One of my current goals, for example, is to complete this little book. I am spurred on by the hope that its simple message may kindle a flame in its readers and that The Shepherd's Creed may become a cornerstone in the lives of many people. I cannot let my happiness be conditional upon success, for many of the stages between writing and achieving the goal are outside my control. First the spark has to ignite the imagination of other people, and that is only the first hurdle. But I am enjoying the process; having the goal and having the vision, is an important part of preparing the field for happiness.

Despite the seemingly impossible odds in the short time available, that young soldier mastered the control of prosthetic limbs, stood and walked on the day of the medal ceremony. He achieved his goal, and the man's the gold, for all that, but then what? Why, he set a new goal, of course. A goal reached is not a cue to rest on your laurels, but to set the next goal. Remember the shark.

4. Don't Worry, Be Optimistic

It gets you out of bed in the morning. It launches many a project. It is the golden fringed guidon that flutters high on the lance of vision. It is the quality that makes me wax a little too lyrical for my own good. Lances and guidons indeed! "Guidons" doesn't even pass the spell-checker although I know it is a word and I can't think of any other way to spell it.

Optimism is the antithesis of gloom and doom. There is a whole industry dedicated to gloom and doom, so leave it to certain sections of the media, those unsurpassed experts at spreading – and in some cases engendering – negativity. Optimism is seeing hope for the world and for oneself in the future, and knowing that there is a real possibility of it all coming to fruition. It isn't about wearing rose-coloured spectacles, but about seeing past the obstacles and recognising there is a way.

5. Pick Yourself Up, Dust Yourself Down

The time will come when you have given it your best shot and not hit target. Within reach of that pinnacle, a thundercloud bursts and down you slide, right to the bottom. When that happens, you really only have two choices: you can stay down, or come up fighting ... or at the least, come up planning the next fight.

Writers have a lot of practice with this one. That wonderful manuscript, so witty and erudite, such storytelling and what masterly use of analogy and imagery ... and so swiftly back upon the hall carpet together with a rejection letter. It can feel like rejection of an altogether more personal kind and it can take a lot of self-convincing that it is an opportunity for improvement. It is also a pretty poor example to use in the face of people who suffer real and devastating setbacks.

Whether a minor or major goal needs reassessing, whether the setback is trivial or life-changing, it really is a case of *dum spiro spero* … with a little less of the "dum" if you don't mind: while I breathe I hope.

6. Don't be a Perfect Fool

We are fallible. It's a deliberate fault and a function without which evolution would not have been possible. Fallibility is built into you. If you were a fallible and fault-ridden bug back before the ancestors of the dinosaurs, evolution may well have snuffed you out. Nowadays the worst you can reasonably expect is a chewing out from the boss.

Actually, there is something far worse that a bad boss, and that is being too hard and too unforgiving on yourself. You try, you fail; you beat yourself up: who needs evolution to take you out of the running when you can do such an efficient elimination job on yourself? Let's try another paradigm (whatever that means): you try, you fail, you learn, you fail, and you learn some more … you succeed.

Perfection is rare in nature, but "perfectly as it should be" is all around us. If nature cannot achieve perfection in the life-span of the planet, why should you not accept yourself perfectly as you should be? A slip here, a regression there; all are opportunities for continued improvement, but just as it is more important to have a goal than to achieve it, trying is more important than being.

7. You've got to Laugh

Sometimes life is just too absurd. Sometimes we take ourselves far too seriously. Remember that TV advert for instant mashed potatoes, where the little robot-aliens look down on us, and collapse in a scrapheap of gyrating, giggling, side-splitting hilarity at what they see? It isn't at all difficult to empathise with them, for we are a pretty hilarious lot. If we really are all poor players who strut and fret our hour upon the stage, a lot of us must have obtained our Equity cards from the Ministry of Silly Walks. The point is, we must avoid taking ourselves too seriously. That is not to say we have to move through our allotted time like clowns. We have objective to achieve and goals to attain, but in achieving and attaining we would do well to keep our self-importance in check with a good laugh at our own expense … just once in a while.

8. Hitting the Reset Button

At some stage we are all going to be hit by the big one, the event which is so cataclysmal in our lives that point 5 above just won't hack it. It would not seem appropriate just to pick yourself up and dust yourself down in the face of bereavement or news of a serious medical condition. We would be lucky indeed if grief never paid a call.

Elisabeth Kubler-Ross established a model for grief. Applying it to people who were terminally ill, she found the five stages of grief held true for all kinds of major loss. The stages are:-

- Denial
- Anger
- Bargaining
- Depression
- Acceptance

It was never envisaged that these stages would always be experienced in the stated order, or that everyone would experience all stages. Observation also showed that some people got stuck in one stage or another, and herein lay the most danger.

Shepherds will recognise the importance of Acceptance, and the faster we can move to that stage the more readily we can leave grief behind. It is doubtful that many of us can pass through with all our goals intact and Happiness is bound to wobble or disappear altogether. This is what is meant by "hitting the reset button". Once the initial, raw-edged grief is past, it will be time to re-evaluate and start again.

9. Maintaining the Machine

Even if you are a dualist who believes the soul or spirit is separable from the body, you have to admit, the two of you are stuck together, at least for your ride through life. You might feel that your mind is the driver, and your body the vehicle. If that's the case, how are you going to look after it? Fill it with diesel instead of petrol? Never get it serviced? Do nothing to maintain it? You will break down despite the best planned and most meticulously mapped out route. It's a no-brainer really: the better you maintain the vehicle, the further it will go and the less hassle it will give you.

Looking after your body is another subject too large for the scope of this little book, but you could fall over with all the advice that is available out there and it is easy to obtain.

Just two thoughts:

1. No need to be obsessive about it.

2. If your BMI height-to-weight chart indicates your healthy weight is up to a maximum of 12 stone (168lbs/76.2kg) and you are actually 13 stone (182lbs/82.5kg), don't weight … oops what a slip … don't wait until you are 15 stone (210lbs/95.2kg) before you do anything about it. Of course, you could laugh it off, but when your knees give out, it won't be quite so funny.

And that's it! The Nine Steps, all done and dusted. What do you mean, this chapter has told you about happiness and how to go about achieving it, but it doesn't actually tell you in any detail what you have to do? You're kidding, right? You want a book that tells you everything? Where is the control and self-determination in that? It has been said that people are happiest at work if they have control. If they have no control than the next best thing to have is stability and routine. Are you going to settle for stability and routine, paint your life by numbers, or are you going to seize control? If you can't have control at work, than at least you can have it in other aspects of your life, starting with [*fill in as appropriate*].

CHAPTER THREE

Considering Faith & Belief

I am a Shepherd. The statement tells you I follow the Shepherd's Creed, and that is about all it tells you. Am I a Hindu Shepherd, or a Buddhists Shepherd, a Jewish, Christian or Muslim one? Does it even matter? To a Shepherd, I would suggest it doesn't matter very much, but as we are about to consider faith and belief, I will begin by nailing my colours to the mast.

I am a Humanist. I do not believe there is a God, or gods, or any form of higher intelligence or deity that rules over us. That is my belief, which I hold with as much conviction as the most religious among us do for their particular brand of faith. Empirical evidence tends to support my belief very strongly, and I hold it without any realistic doubt. What I do not do, is wish to impose my belief upon any other person. Persuade by use of logical argument, maybe, but never impose or force for that would merely be the reverse of an ugly coin we have seen far too often throughout history, and even now blights the lives of untold thousands. Be that as it may, this chapter is not an excuse for proselytizing; rather it is a musing upon faith and belief and how it pertains to Shepherds with religion and Shepherds with none.

Unfortunately, my own condition forms a filter that colours my light. I cannot get away from it, although I try. I apologise for that and I reiterate: Shepherds are united only in acceptance of the Creed and may be proud of all other differences without fear of recrimination or patronisation.

It is not within the scope of this chapter, nor of the entire book, to attempt a comparative study of the many different religions and beliefs that exist. Here we consider religion as a whole and to come to a conclusion as to the efficacy of religion as a means of improving the lot of mankind and to answer the question "Does religion help or hinder the Shepherd?"

Some might say it is not the purpose of religion to improve the experience of being human, and that its purpose is to worship the deity to whom the religion is dedicated in order to make us fit for a life to come. If that is the case, we might consider whether or not the elevation of the human condition is a by-product of religion.

It can be very difficult for a person who places their faith in science and the natural order of the Universe to see anything of value in religion. In one respect, most atheists, at least in the generations of baby-boomers or older, have one advantage over those with religious belief. Most of us were not born atheist and neither did we drift towards atheism. Most of us have, at one time or another, held religious beliefs or at least been brought up within a religious environment, whether devout or of the sort that pays lip-service. We have sought answers, and studied, and evaluated; in the end we have let go of the last remnant of religion. Following our personal epiphanies, some of us become like former smokers who find they cannot bear to be within a hundred yards of the smallest puff of smoke, and we find the merest whiff of religion anathema. We find ourselves thinking "Nothing good ever came of religion". Is that so? Well then, take Tenzin Gyatso, (the 14th Dali Lama) or Archbishop Desmond Tutu. These are individuals who radiate loving kindness. Highly spiritual men with personalities and philosophies of life strongly rooted in their faith, they represent the best interface between religion and mankind. Clearly much good can and does come from religion.

Having stated my beliefs above and throwing my lot in with science, nature and empirical evidence, I cannot evade the fact that evidence suggests that a need for religion is almost part of our evolutionary make-up. All the world's cultures and societies are associated with religion in one way or another. If it is true that the capacity to believe in a deity is in-built, I am led to wonder how and why.

Whether our remote ancestors were apes, or we were placed upon the face of the earth as fully formed human beings, there must have been a time when an individual or group of individuals stood up and pre-empted René Descartes by several hundred thousand years by pronouncing the caveman version of "I think, therefore I am." Being a thinking being, fairly new to the process, what is a chap to think about, once the necessities and comforts of life have been secured? What is that fiery globe up in the sky, and the other one that comes at night? Why do these flames dance so, and what makes them warm? Why is it so hot on some days, and on others water falls from the sky?

Just as there must have been a time when our ancestors developed the capacity to think in terms of questions, there must have followed a time when they sought, not merely to ask the questions, but to provide the answers. "I rolled this round and heavy rock that I use as a seat. I moved it from there to here, so someone must live up in the sky and it is they who roll the great sun from sunrise to sunset!" Eureka! I wonder if that is; the big-bang of religious thought. Over the years the story became embellished. "To move such a great and fiery object, the mover must be that much greater than I and possibly as fiery as the sun, and as the task must be wearisome we must give thanks to the great sun-mover, for without him we would be forever in the dark."

It appears quite logical to me that the need for explanation came close on the heels of our ability to think, and so it is hardly surprising that religion sometimes feels so ingrained. A need to know and a need to understand is surely part of the human condition, and when knowledge is lacking, we must speculate and philosophise. In our infancy as a race, the gods must have come to us. And in that we were comforted and given solace against the harsh world, the gods were good.

As mankind developed, religion walked beside us, and rules were made to tame the beastliness within us. God – or gods – spoke to our condition and we heard with out hearts, and in that the gods made us better people, the gods were good.

Then came a time when people met in adversity and their tribes believed in different gods and held different customs, and for the sake of their beliefs or using their beliefs to justify their actions, there was war. In that the gods led to suffering, the gods were bad.

By the time the great religions came to us and were established, religion in one form or another, and many forms at the same time, was already thousands of years old. In quoting a time-span, I make no apologies to the literalists here because after all, they won't be reading this book and they certainly would not respect the Shepherd's Creed.

When the new religions began to arrive, and I am talking new 2,000 years ago, they came to a pre-existing framework of priests and dogma. The new priests stepped into the shoes of the old and merely changed the colour of their garments, just as established religions adopted the feast days of pagans and nature worshippers.

It makes sense to suppose that the prophets of the new religions were moved to speak out for the salvation of mankind by a feeling of spirituality or revelation within them that they identified as the voice of their deity. It could be that they really did hear the voice of God, and that events unfolded much as it written down in the holy books. I doubt this very much, but my doubt does not make a fact. There will be those Shepherds who believe in the metaphysical truth of their god rather than the allegorical. It does not matter that much to me. I have my belief and other Shepherds have theirs. We are brothers and sister in the Shepherd's Creed.

Agreeing to disagree on the genesis of gods and refusing to allow our differences to come between us, let us consider religion as it is today, and here I mean religion, and not the causes to which it is attached by fanatics. Islam is no more Al-Qaeda or suicide bombers than Christianity is abusing human rights. Shakespeare summed it up in *The*

Merchant of Venice, Scene III: "The devil can cite Scripture for his purpose. An evil soul producing holy witness is like a villain with a smiling cheek." I want to look at the benefits of religion and not the perversions of it at the hands of hateful or deluded people.

On the plus side, religion provides focus on something that is greater than us as individuals or as a society. It formalises the natural morality of human beings. It helps adherents make sense of a confusing and often cruel world. It provides a sense of belonging and brings people together in harmonious society. It leads people to selfless, often courageous acts. It leads us to see the best in each other. It comforts people in time of distress. Even though I believe all these things are possible without religion, I say "Bravo religion!"

On the negative side, religion can make the kindest and most innocent of people feel guilty. It can add to the burden of the bereaved by making them wonder why and for what purpose. It is all too easily hijacked for reasons never intended.

Religion insofar as it engenders unity and provides its followers with support and a moral framework is good. Where it provides a platform for bigotry and hides hatred behind the name of a deity, it is nothing short of reprehensible. In truth, few religions provide such a platform willingly, although sometimes they are constructed in the name of religion but without its proper leave. For example, a putative Christian who waves a derogatory placard and demeans gay people by quoting Leviticus 18:22 (King James Version: "Thou shalt not lie with mankind, as with womankind: it is abomination") and chooses to ignore the next paragraph that says sex with animals is merely a confusion, and to let Deuteronomy 21:18-21 (the edict to stone your disobedient son to death) slide by with ne'er a sideways glance, is not saying much about either the spiritual message of the Bible or the god of the Christians, so much as he is exposing his own hatred and bigotry. Such a person might be considered a ridiculous and dangerous fool, but as Shepherds we must remember the Creed and instead consider him deluded, and perhaps a little lacking in reason. If he is consistent in espousing the Old Testament as literal fact, he might as well wave a placard stating "GOD HATES VEGETARIANS: Leviticus 11:3"

The shepherd tells us that Intolerance, Oppression and Cruelty are the names of the wolves. How should a Shepherd deal with a wolf? Should the Shepherd hate the wolf? Absolutely not! Fancy even asking, for by now we all know to where hatred leads. We must try to understand. A person who peddles hatred has almost certainly suffered hatred or the kind of fear that gives birth to hatred. Understanding will often be a hard task to manage when we see the Shepherd's Creed so foully assaulted, but a person so possessed of negativity is to be pitied rather than hated and in that pity is the extinguishment of self destructive anger.

I am a Shepherd who is also a non-theist, but I am thankful that the vast majority who follow beliefs which are Pagan, Hindu, Jainist, Jewish, Buddhist, Shinto, Christian, Muslim, Sikh, Baha'i, Wiccan, Jedi, or any of the many others, have faith that brings them closer to a greater something that enriches their lives and in turn those of the people with whom they have contact.

It is doubtful there will ever be consensus on the topic of faith and belief, so what is a Shepherd to do? Carry on being a theist Shepherd or a non-theist Shepherd and keep being true to the Shepherd's Creed, for it bridges the divides, unites us all and imbues us with the same spirit.

'Spirit? What is that?' says the non-theist Shepherd. It certainly does appear that the whole dimension of spirituality, so central to most religious beliefs, is of God or gods and must therefore exclude non-theists. But I believe there is an ethereal yet sustaining counterpart to that spirituality which is open to the non-theist. That is the subject of the next Consideration.

CHAPTER FOUR

Considering Spirituality

Define spirituality. The dictionary tells us the word refers to spiritual quality, and "spiritual" means "of spirit as opposed to matter, of the soul especially as acted on by God; of or proceeding from God, holy divine, inspired, concerned with sacred or religious things."

Hold on a minute. Part of the subtitle of this book mentions secular spirituality. Having just read the Oxford Dictionary definition of spirituality above, isn't that the same as saying "wet dryness", or "opaque transparency" or any other two completely incompatible states of being you care to imagine? In short, isn't the term "secular spirituality" an oxymoron? How can spirituality exist without the spiritual? Let me bring the question to a very personal level: how can I, a non-theist, experience spirituality when that quality is so manifestly synonymous with the soul? As I do feel an indefinable something that I equate with spirituality, am I really an atheist at all? Try as we may to loose the bonds of religion, are we still touched by the deity, so that the spirit of God or gods moves within us whether we like it or not? Is it this feeling, I wonder, that holds otherwise non-religious people to a remnant of belief?

It can be seen that spirituality is easier to explain for those who are theists because the very language used to define it is inseparable from religion and matters of the soul. As a non-theist who accepts the reality of spirituality then, I am in the position that I must try to redefine spirituality in non-theist terms, or I have to redefine the terms that are already used. Redefine God? Redefine soul? Oh yes! What a challenge. I think I will opt for the latter.

Traditionally, and attempting to be non-denominational, God is seen as a supernatural being who has power over all things. God is alpha and omega. God is everywhere and everything. Under my definition, God has power over all things. God is alpha and omega. God is everywhere and everything. So apart from the "supernatural being" part, there has not been a lot of redefinition, but I have redefined God in a way that non-theist can believe in, for God to me is nature and the physical workings of the Universe. God joins all things because God is all things and all beings, completely connected and interrelated. By my definition, God is not an intelligent being, although God is the sum of all intelligence. Without God there is nothing, for all is God. The thought can be very humbling: in this entire vast Universe I am less than a speck. Or the thought that can be the opposite: I am part of this unbounded greatness.

If that is the Darwinists and Dawkinists I can hear, throwing down the Shepherd's crook in disgust, hold fast! It's all, or almost all, semantics. If I define God in this way, it makes sense of the dictionary's definition of spirituality. I can give the term "soul" the same treatment. I believe I have a soul, and it is that combination of life and thought that animates me and makes me a vital human being, far more than the sum of the chemical constituents that make up my body or the physiological processes that keep me alive. It is the combination of all I have ever been and it is as real as it is difficult to define. Unlike my theist friends I do not believe it is viable as an entity in and of itself or that after the death of my body it will move on either to reside in a new body by way of rebirth or in a metaphysical abode there to hold together the characteristics that make me unique, like some kind of a software program, ready to be uploaded to a new kind of reality. If my soul – my spirit if you like – lives on at all, it will because its resonance has set up reverberations in other souls, or to put it another way, I have had an influence upon other people, and I will live on in their memories and perhaps some essential element of my spirit will live on in them too.

It is desirable; maybe even necessary, to have that inner sense of being a part of something much bigger. If that something encompasses the whole Universe there is nothing bigger. My team isn't bigger than your team, because my team is your team and all the others in existence put together: it can't help but lead Shepherds to a feeling of empathy with all other people, irrespective of their nature.

But what if you are a Shepherd and you feel none of this sense of spirituality? Perhaps you are a non-theist and you wish to have no truck with this ridiculous talk of spirit and soul. You have made a decision, based on the only empirical evidence that exists, that there is no God; therefore spirituality is the Emperor's new suit, just as invisible and impossible. If that is the case, I can't help feeling you have thrown out the baby with the bathwater. But we are talking about your inner life. If it works for you, I am not the one, nor is anybody else, to impose another way upon you. You are a Shepherd, and so am I, and vivre la difference. Nevertheless, I ask you to read on.

For me, my spirituality and happiness are linked. Like happiness, spirituality has nothing to do with worldly success. It doesn't have to do with religion or personal relationships. It rewrites the definition of success: with it a person is successful for they have attained the highest of goals. Without it they are the poorer despite the all the worldly attributes of wealth and status they may have accumulated. For you, it might be quite different.

Spirituality adds another dimension to happiness as it comes from a sense of wonder at the beauty, vastness and complication of the Universe and a feeling that humanity, for all its faults, still has the potential to overcome that which is base and selfish. In that one person is able to, then so may we all. As we move in the Universe, so the Universe moves in us.

Most theist Shepherds perhaps, and many non-theist ones, will already feel this sense of spirituality, but what if you are one of those who do not, but wish to? Accepting the existence of the quality may be enough to let it in, because in reality it just calls for an adjustment in the way you think. Really, all it takes is a change in thinking and that is a process that can happen almost instantaneously … as quickly as it takes a penny to drop.   If not, then like Siddhartha or George Fox, you are a seeker of the truth, and will find your way there by your own road, for my road may not suit you.

CHAPTER FIVE

Considering Morality

The many ills of society, as it exists at present, have been blamed on the lack of common morality, which in turn has been blamed on the decline in religious belief. Anti-social behaviour is the bane of existence for many and the use of knives is seen as an indication that things are getting worse. Consider then, why in 1953 the Prevention of Offences Act was passed in England and Wales. Essentially, it was, and still is, an act of Parliament passed into law to regulate the criminal use of offensive weapons and it was instigated in response to the increase in the carrying of flick-knives and cut-throat razors by Mods and Rockers. Not such a terribly new phenomenon then, this apparent lack of morals.

It's almost as if there has always been a period in the lives of many young men or women, somewhere between childhood's end and the beginning of true adult life, that the moral compass is assailed by forces so strong that it no longer shows the way. While others are slowly taking control of their own lives by roads well trod and sanctioned – higher education, taking the first steps towards a career – other take control in the only way they can, by perpetrating anti-social acts.

I find it most probable that a misplaced sense of gaining control fuels most anti-social crime and is at the core of much long-term criminality. Luckily, the vast majority of the youth who stray for a time do find their way back and learn how to control their lives and direct their energies in positive and productive ways. Others of a different nature conform without finding control, and that is the scenario that I believe leads to unhappiness. Even if we cannot all be bosses or at the top of our chosen field it is imperative that we have control of our lives at other levels.

But having control is not synonymous with having good morals, and moral standards do not always fit in with what is or is not legal. Nor does everybody agree that the various religions are the prime sources of moral guidance, let alone the varying viewpoints of what does or does not equate to moral behaviour in the first place. Taken to its basic meaning, most of us will agree that moral principles have to do with what is right or wrong, the ability to tell between the two and the capacity to be virtuous in our general conduct. And then we come to the question, what is right and what is wrong? How does a Shepherd decide?

I believe that the Shepherd's Creed provides the only moral guidance that any of us really needs. It does not say "Don't steal," or "Don't murder," but as neither of those activities would be treating the victim with respect, compassion or equality, it doesn't really need to. The Creed is a kind of moral well-head from which all others flow. Know the source and you automatically know the distributaries.

Is The Shepherd's Creed just another way of expressing the ethic of reciprocity that some Christians call the Golden Rule? The Rule is expressed many times in both the Old and the New Testaments, perhaps most famously, here.

And as ye would that men should do to you, do you also unto them. Luke 6:31

The ethic of reciprocity is certainly not exclusive to Christianity. It is to be found in the holy books of all the major religions, as the following few examples show.

Never impose on others what you would not choose for yourself. Confucius, Analects XV.24

One should never do that to another which one regards as injurious to one's own self. This, in brief, is the rule of dharma. Other behaviour is due to selfish desires. Hinduism: The Mahabharata, Anusasana Parva, Section CXIII, Verse 8

Hurt no one so that no one may hurt you. Islam: Muhammad, The Farewell Sermon

And finally, one I particularly like.

That which is hateful to you, do not do to your fellow. That is the whole Torah; the rest is the explanation; go and learn. Judaism: Talmud, Shabbat 31a, the "Great Principle"

On the face of it, The Shepherd's Creed appears to be another manifestation of the ethic, but for all its good intention, the Golden Rule is flawed and in that the Creed does not share the same fault, it might be thought of as the Platinum Rule.

Where is the flaw in the Golden Rule? It is perfectly valid among people who all share the same lifestyles and the same cultural backgrounds, but what if somebody does not want to be treated in the same way that you would like to be treated? In this modern age of multiculturalism, it is highly likely that what is acceptable or even desirable for one person might make another extremely uncomfortable. The Creed is perfectly compatible with diversity because it does not call for a Shepherd to see personal needs and expectations as universal, only to recognise themselves and others as people who deserve and are worthy of respect, compassion and equality and then to put that observation into action.

In that nothing is new under the sun, it can come as no surprise that the message of The Shepherd's Creed is neither unique nor new. The seven principles that the Unitarian Universalists (UU) hold dear come very close. The seven principles and the Creed are a hundred percent compatible. The UU affirm and promote:-

- The inherent worth and dignity of every person;
- Justice, equity and compassion in human relations;

- Acceptance of one another and encouragement to spiritual growth in our congregations;
- A free and responsible search for truth and meaning;
- The right of conscience and the use of the democratic process within our congregations and in society at large;
- The goal of world community with peace, liberty, and justice for all;
- Respect for the interdependent web of all existence of which we are a part.

Spoken like a true Shepherd. The UU principles and the Shepherd's Creed are wholly compatible. But then, they would be, for the Shepherd's Creed is the mother tincture of morality, the basic common denominator of, if not all then most, of the varied moral codes that exist. Whereas in pluralist societies we can never hope to draft a moral code that suits everyone, we can submit the varied codes to the crucible and recognise the resulting gold as valid currency for us all.

To change the analogy, one size can never fit all. This is the reason why it is impossible to establish a detailed moral code upon which we can all agree, but we can provide the basic cloth out of which a finished garment can be made. That material is The Shepherd's Creed. You may not like the cut of my cloth, but if you recognise the weave and accept it as valid, we can agree to disagree. Maintaining the weave of the cloth also makes the Creed immune to the moirés of future fashion; morals change with the times but the heart of morality is an unchanging constant.

What of sin? According to some religions, we are born into sin and of sin. We are encouraged to think of ourselves as sinners who need to be saved, and the only way to be saved is through religion. For some, morality is concerned with sin and sin is almost exclusively concerned with sexual conduct. Sexuality has a section of its own in the chapter following, but having raised the subject of sin we should look at it with the Shepherd's eye. The word "sin", as opposed to "evil" or "unlawful", is generally applied to offences against the will of a deity. Few will disagree when the deity says, "Do not murder," but we will be less willing to agree to certain edicts concerning the food we eat or the people we love. It is further complicated that different deities have different and sometimes opposing lists of sins, so when trying to formulate a recipe for good morals that crosses personal, cultural and religious divides, sin is an ingredient that is impossible to blend into the mix so that it is palatable to all.

From a Shepherd's point of view, it is better to leave it out altogether. That might appear to be a difficult option if you are a theist Shepherd who is guided by a particular faith as to what does or does not amount to a sin. Luckily, "difficult" does not mean "impossible". If your faith tells you certain sins amount to immoral behaviour, and you agree, remember you are agreeing to a belief that is held by you and your fellow worshipers. It is not necessarily a universal truth.

To a Shepherd, whether theist or non-theist, immorality is anything that affronts the Shepherd's Creed. A theist Shepherd may subscribe to further advice on morality as supported by their religion, but they are no less a Shepherd, provided they still uphold The Shepherd's Creed. There are few religions that will call upon their members to do anything less, and those that appear to do so are probably being misinterpreted.

CHAPTER SIX

Controversies

There exists the potential that one day membership of the Fellowship of Shepherds will be as diverse as humanity itself, where Shepherds treat each other, and everybody else, according to the Shepherd's Creed irrespective of widely varying backgrounds, beliefs and points of view. No difference of opinion will be so strong that it can overcome the immutable truth. This is in spite of highly emotive subjects that cause such polarisation of opinion that it might be thought no two guardians of those opposite poles could stand to be in the same room.

The original purpose of this chapter was to look at some of those subjects, and act as guidance, never rules, as to a Shepherd's thoughts. It soon became clear that there is no way to fit such a discourse into a book meant for your pocket. You would need one of those suitcases, with wheels, even to cover the introductions. Furthermore, for any one person to think they have all the answers to all the problems would indicate a certain degree of arrogance. So instead of trying to cover all the bases of all the topics, I will list a few headings that may, one day, become topics of discussion among Shepherds, and then choose one to discuss in detail, that one acting as an example for all. What we are aiming at here is how the Shepherd's Creed can be compatible with all disagreements whilst still maintaining the one immutable truth.

So, here are a few of the biggies in no particular order, with one of them saved for discussion at the end.

- The State of Society
- Threats to humanity
- Privilege v Deprivation
- Crime and Punishment

- War
- Abortion

And now, the subject up for immediate discussion. None of the topics above have featured anywhere near as often in religious works as the one that follows. Some come close, others never get a mention, but you may be assured that religious teachings rarely, if ever, leave out sexuality as a trait that needs regulating and subjecting to various laws and punishments.

Let's get to it then.

Sexuality
The need for sexual intimacy in the emerging adult of the species is a physiological need that endures until old age or death. Its primary object is the propagation of the species. In humans, most other mammals and some other classes of animal, there is the very important secondary function of bonding, a feature that no doubt adds to the chance that the species thrives and becomes more robust in the face of the challenges and dangers of the world. In humans, serious mental conditions are less common in people with strong bonds of this kind. I have as yet said nothing very controversial. In fact, it is pretty much stating the obvious and few Shepherds would find much with which to disagree ... so far. We wouldn't have to get a lot further into the discussion before Shepherds from different backgrounds would have very different and very strong views on a wide range of topics that come under the heading "Sexuality", and probably non stronger than on the subject of homosexuality.

Oi! Come out from behind that pillow. It won't bite you. These days few in the secular world worry about it. People have moved on a great deal. The same may be said of the majority in religious circles too, but there is a very strong and verbose minority who are only too eager to cast stones. To this minority, gay people are sinners. I am not going to try and persuade them otherwise. My purpose here is to explore how Shepherds of diametrically opposed views can still live true to the Shepherd's Creed. Oh very well then: I will try to persuade them, just a little.

Each person born free from serious disability has the capability of falling in love. Controversially, I do not care whether or not a person's sexuality is directly governed by genes, whether it is the product of nature or nurture. Science is not conclusive on the matter. However, I believe this is wholly irrelevant, because a person has absolutely no control or choice in the matter of sexuality, and nor do their parents. Although I think it is unlikely that there is a straight or a gay gene, our personalities are the product of hundreds of thousands of impressions and impulses, so it is vain to even hope to control them. And why should we want to?

I believe that once a person's sexuality is formed it is set for life and that it cannot be changed or manipulated. When the parties involved are fully informed and consenting adults it is an infringement of human rights to attempt to control or proscribe sexual intimacy. When encountering the argument that homosexuality is unnatural, it is as well to realise that same-sex bonding involving sexual contact has been observed in nearly all mammalian species.

As to my views on sexual morality especially as it pertains to homosexuality, I could not do better than quote a large chunk from the Society of Friends (Quakers) book of Faith & Practice.

'It is the nature and quality of a relationship that matters: one must not judge it by its outward appearance but by its inner worth. Homosexual affection can be as selfless as heterosexual affection, and therefore we cannot see that it is in some way morally worse.

'Homosexual affection may of course be an emotion which some find aesthetically disgusting, but one cannot base Christian morality on a capacity for such disgust.

207

Neither are we happy with the thought that all homosexual behaviour is sinful: motive and circumstance degrade or ennoble any act.

'We see no reason why the physical nature of a sexual act should be the criterion by which the question whether or not it is moral should be decided. An act which (for example) expresses true affection between two individuals and gives pleasure to them both does not seem to us to be sinful by reason alone of the fact that it is homosexual. The same criteria seem to us to apply whether a relationship is heterosexual or homosexual.'

22:15. Quaker Faith & Practice

Due to the teachings of many religions, homosexuality or homosexual intimacies are seen as sinful. Often, a religious lead has caused the secular authorities of the land to reflect this view and back it up with laws. In a few countries, homosexual acts are punishable by death. The perpetrators of homophobic hate crimes often feel justified in their actions because the church has given them firm ground to stand upon.

As difficult as it is for me, I shall now try to see all this from a religious person's point of view, but first let me say that far from all churches and religions are in agreement with the view that homosexuality is some form of an abomination, even those whose holy texts seem to suggest they are. The majority of religious people know that the spirit of their respective gods are not governed or fully encapsulated in ancient words from a bygone world, but for the purpose of this section, let us assume that homosexuality is a sin. Let us assume that I am a Shepherd who believes this. How can I reconcile my religion with the Shepherd's Creed, which in all other respects I accept whole-heartedly? Here is another person who calls him or herself Shepherd, and yet he or she is gay and has a same-sex partner. That person is therefore, per se, a sinner. What can I do?

You can refer to the Shepherd's Creed. Does it say "All people, except sinners, deserve and are worthy of respect, compassion and equality"? Of course not! So, it really is as simple as that. You treat the person without rancour, accusation or dearth of compassion.

Okay, let's change the perspective. Now I am a gay Shepherd. How do I treat the Shepherd who I know belongs to a church that publicly attests that homosexuality is a sin, or the non-Shepherd member of the same church for that matter? There is only one Shepherd's Creed and it works both ways.

Ah, but what if the church is actively campaigning against the rights of gay people? They might be lobbying to bring in new or maintain old laws that are unfair to gay people or divisive to the community. Perhaps they are trying to promote doctrine above the law of the land. In cases like this it is perfectly correct to counter-campaign, and for the Shepherd who belongs to that church, gay or not, some tough choices may be in order. You might choose to remain within the church, and remembering the Creed, do whatever is reasonable to moderate and even change the views of your congregational colleagues. On the other hand, you might find the doctrines of your church and of the Shepherd's Creed irreconcilable and decide to leave the church or renounce your fellowship.

The thoughts that have been brought to the subject of sexuality can be applied to all other controversies. As Shepherds, we will often disagree, but we will never step outside the requirement of the Shepherd's Creed. That's what it means to be a Shepherd. As to what else it may mean, that is the subject of the next chapter.

CHAPTER SEVEN

Considering Fellowship

Why a Fellowship of Shepherds?

The Shepherd's Creed is such a simple, and to the vast majority of the world's people, self-evident statement, that one may wonder why it needs to be supported by a fellowship. It is one of those statements that in our quiet moments, most of us will know to be true, even if we do not admit it in our day-to-day lives. Unfortunately it is one of those truths that is not voiced often enough or with enough enthusiasm. It is a nice idea that is given lip-service or is stated to be true but with certain qualification or exemptions. Having reached this far in the book, you are probably a person who has by now accepted the Shepherd's Creed and are keen to find out more about Fellowship. But what if you are a critic who, with notebook in hand, seek out more ammunition so that you can mock like the jackal or rend like the wolf? Be thankful I have made your job easy, for like the shepherd in the parable, I am naked before your fangs and vulnerable to your attacks. I am no philosopher and not much of a warrior. I am the least of people to imbue my words with knowledge or artistry. Your howls would easily drown out my voice, but will they drown out the voices of a thousand Shepherds? This is why we need to come together in Fellowship.

Before moving on to the reason that make Fellowship desirable, let us first consider what it means to be able to say "I am a Shepherd". The answer is much in little. You could say "I am a Christian" and a person may be left wondering much about you. What kind of a Christian? Are you the kind who believes you can be nasty, superior and judgemental all week long, so long as you listen to the sermon and sing the hymns on Sunday? Are you the kind who has been flooded with the spirit of Jesus Christ and who treats people with loving kindness? Are you of this, that or the other denomination? Do you believe I will burn in Hell? Will you stand on a soapbox and demand that I do? You get the idea. It can be applied to all religions. But if you say "I am a Shepherd" it establishes something very fundamental and communicates an assurance that despite all other beliefs and allegiances, you are a person who accepts other people with good cheer and that you relish diversity.

Hark, I hear the baying of jackals: "If you tell people you are a shepherd they will wonder where your sheep are." Well, perhaps if we were in a farmyard environment or we hadn't already established the topic of conversation as being about ideology rather than animal husbandry, you might be correct, but let's not be too obtuse. In the early days of Fellowship, which is now as I write, the more likely question is going to be "What do you mean by "Shepherd", and what does it entail?" What an opening to spread the word and to speak the Shepherd's Creed.

So, here we have the first good reason for establishing a Fellowship of Shepherds. Membership makes a very clear, albeit simple statement. With four words – I am a Shepherd – it is a statement that speaks volumes. If committing to the Shepherd's Creed establishes that you have accepted a fundamental belief as the cornerstone of your life and indicates what you stand for, then confirming that you are a Shepherd says a lot.

The next reason is belonging. It is sometimes difficult to be a lone-voice, and our message is so simple that in isolation it might sound naïve in the extreme. But the immutable truth does not need to be complicated. Why dress it up in frills and attach bells? *It* stands well enough alone, but *we* stand better together. It is natural to want to belong, to show our allegiance, to have a metaphorical flag to wave. It is such a natural desire that nations, politicians and any number of other establishments, official or otherwise, have drawn upon it since the beginning of humanity. It could be that a new Shepherd needs no more than this sense of belonging from Fellowship, and that they

211

prefer to live to the Shepherd's Creed in their own way and without formal contact with other members. On the other hand, clubbable Shepherds may enjoy meeting and interacting, whether within the cosy confines of cyberspace or out in the real world.

Finally, Fellowship helps like-minded people come together in order to keep ourselves informed, increase our effectiveness and to coordinate our actions.

This brings us from "Why a Fellowship of Shepherds?" to the practicalities of how or what the Fellowship is, and thus to the next section.

What is The Fellowship of Shepherds?

You have accepted the Shepherd's Creed and therefore, without having to apply for membership, send a dollar, buy the pin or take an oath upon the shepherd's crook, you are already a full member of The Fellowship of Shepherds. Stand up and take a bow. But where is the Fellowship? It's a fat lot of good if it is a fellowship of one. Let me just say that even as I write the first draft, I am not the only Shepherd. There are a few of us about, but if you read at a time close to the publication date, feel proud that you are among the pioneers. If not, I hope the Fellowship may now be speaking for itself and this paragraph might be redundant. Feel proud anyway and feel very welcome.

The loosest definition is that The Fellowship of Shepherds is made up of every person who has accepted the Shepherd's Creed. Full stop ... oh very well then, colon: membership does not require a person to apply to any authority other than their own consciousness and heart. Remember the Shepherd's Creed is in two parts and those parts are accepting the immutable truth and pledging to do whatever is reasonable and in your power to promulgate the immutable truth. That is all.

There is already an online presence of Shepherds. There is to be a website and various groups on social networks. If you live in an area that lacks a local focus for Shepherds, you might consider starting one. But will your group be "official"? Why not? The Fellowship of Shepherds has the very great potential of being too big for any one site. And what's to be official about it? You might just as well have an official membership of the human race.

How to be a Good Shepherd?

Start by applying the Shepherd's Creed to yourself. Treat yourself as a person who deserves respect, compassion and equality. Remember some of the considerations we covered in Chapter Two: *Considering Happiness*, and try to avoid treating yourself with disrespect. Disrespect might apply to overindulgence or being too self-critical. We try, we fail, we move on: we do not wallow in self-blame. We try, we succeed: we do not deceive ourselves by overfeeding our egos, or resting on our laurels. We do not deny ourselves the pleasures of life, but we do not make pleasure our aim. The Buddhists call this philosophy of life the Middle Way, and I recommend it for all Shepherds.

Next, apply the Shepherd's Creed to your immediate environment, your home and place of work. You might simply support it by your own conduct, and if that is what circumstances dictate, then that is enough. On the other hand, you may feel it is reasonable in your circumstances to carry it into your daily life more overtly. Shepherds are not preachers or self-righteous nags; if we adopted the latter approach we would hardly be treating our fellows with respect, but we can and should be open about supporting the Shepherd's Creed and invoking it when a person or any group of people are being maligned.

As the Fellowship grows, there may be occasion for Shepherds to cooperate in tackling issues that threaten the immutable truth. A single voice might be lost on the wind. Several hundred will be heard. So, keep a keen interest in local, national and international affairs, and insofar as you can, be ready to add your voice when the issue is too great for one alone.

Be careful not to take any wooden nickels or to leap into the saddles of high horses. By this I caution people to check their sources. It is only too easy to read or hear of an issue on any number of emotive subjects that make the blood boil, only to find out later that they have been misreported. Avoid becoming part of any ill-informed band-wagon. I wonder if this paragraph takes the prize for the highest number of clichés in the smallest number of words? Who cares, so long as the message is put across?

Shepherds beware!
Any group or organisation stands the risk of being hijacked by people with less than noble aims. Here are a few cautionary points to protect FoS.

FoS is not a charity. It does not solicit, gather, or accept any funds. For people who wish to support the aims of the Fellowship financially, there are numerous well established charities to choose from whose aims are completely compatible with the Shepherd's Creed.

There is no hierarchy within FoS. All are equal.

The only essence of FoS is the Shepherd's Creed. There is no other canon, dogma or doctrine, not even this little book, which is nothing more than the musings of one Shepherd and an invitation to pitch in with your own ideas.

There now remains only one thing to say.

GO SHEPHERD!

An Unofficial Sequel

(God Damn a Potato)

Author's Note

This story, though stand-alone, may be seen as the sequel to an unnamed film. The story itself is original. The characters' names have been changed and there is no reference at all to the film. If you've seen the film, then within a couple of pages, you will register a flash of recognition. Recognise or not, read on and have a nice day.

I

Sergeant Nathan Seven-Elks had a rage on him so hot it was likely to pop the blue and red lights on the roof of his patrol car. His hand hovered over the parking brake as he considered doing a skid-turn. But no; these roads through wild, sagebrush Idaho carried so much grit the tyres would probably bite and he'd end up on his roof.

He watched the beat up old truck recede in his rear view mirror and swore through his teeth. 'Those Williams boy sons of. Get what's coming to 'em one day.'

Nathan's guts twisted inside him as he imagined Billy and Jimmy Williams laughing at him, but then, cresting one of the many humps in the road ahead was Johnny Rivas's big old sedan - straight out of the sixties with never a new paint job since.

The anger began to subside. Johnny as a good kid. Got drunk once in a while, rowed with his Ma, but kept himself out of the heavy stuff.

Johnny flashed his headlights, sounded his horn and steered over the double-yellows. 'The Hell's going on today?' Nathan wondered. 'They all taking lessons in cop-baiting?'

Perhaps not. Johnny was leaning out his window waving him down. He looked almost white, and he a full blooded Blackfoot. Nathan flipped a switch which set the roof lights strobing. The cruiser and the sedan pulled up door to door, a manoeuvre Nathan wouldn't even consider with someone he didn't know very well.

'What up, Johnny!' Nathan's voice was calm - almost flat. 'What's biting your tail?'

'I got a kid in here. Found him on the road a ways back. I think he's dying.'

'Hit by a car?' Nathan craned his neck to get a look in the back of Johnny's sedan.

'No. I don't think so. He's not all mashed up or anything - just kinda twitching and snorting. And he got no shoes. Been robbed I reckon.'

An image shot through Nathan's mind, of the Williams boys bushwhacking the kid and swiping his shoes. Them no good Williams sons of a bitch. 'You turn that heap around quick and follow me.'

'Okay, Bear. The County hospital?'

'Nope! Too far. We'll take him to Doc Wilbur.'

By the time Johnny turned his car, Nathan's cruiser was just a set of flashing lights and a cloud of dust. Johnny put the pedal to the metal. The kid slumped on the back seat and breathed deep and heavy - out for the count.

'His name's Mark Walker.' Nathan held out a dog-eared social security card. Johnny looked on from the doorway, a little embarrassed, as Hettie Wilbur shone a light in the kid's eye. He and Nathan had stripped him to his shorts and put him to bed, and now Hettie was doing doctor stuff.

'Hettie, you should take a look at this. It's from a doctor in Portland.' Nathan held out a letter.

Hettie drew up the sheet and tucked it around the young man - tenderly - as if he was one of her own. She took the letter and her eyes fell immediately to one word. The word was 'narcolepsy'. She smiled. 'Thank you, Nathan. Yes, this is what we need to know.'

'Is he . . .is he going to die, ma'am?' Johnny asked.

'Yes, Johnny, he is. But probably no sooner than any of the rest of us. The condition he has - well, it's like epilepsy. It can be controlled. Is there any medication in his pockets, Nathan?'

'No, Mam. Just the papers. No billfold, no cash - not even a cent. And no shoes.'

'What now?' asked Johnny.

'Well, I'm a little rusty, but I guess for now we just roll him into the recovery position and let him sleep it off. I'll have to speak with his doctor of course, but all that can come later.'

It seemed the next move was Nathan's. Both Hettie and Johnny turned to him. Here he was again - on the spot. Luckily, like most cops, he was a past-master at winging it.

He thought out loud: 'I got his name. I'll give him a 1973 date of birth and run him through N.C.I.C.'

Hettie raised an inquisitive eyebrow.

'It's a computer.' Nathan said in answer to the unspoken question. 'It'll show me if he's known. You sure you going to be okay, just him and you in the house? He could be dangerous.'

Hettie looked at the sleeping boy. 'I feel safe enough thanks, Nathan. And Dan will be home soon.'

Nathan smiled. He was a big man, but it would take two of him to make up one Dan. He nodded a by-your-leave and descended to the cruiser. Hettie escorted Johnny to the door, thanked him for his public spirited actions and bid him farewell. He smiled sheepishly and turned for his sedan, treating Hettie to a full view of the painted hawk on his brown leather flying jacket.

While Nathan sat half in the cruiser tapping keys on the terminal, Hettie closed the screen door and crossed to the book shelf with a certain medical reference book in mind.

Aha! Here it is she thought, reaching for the book as a gentle tap-tapping floated across from the screen door. Nathan peered in. 'He's known. No warrants outstanding but . . .'

'STOP!'

'Hettie?'

'I don't want to know.'

Mark came to, little by little - as usual. First, the deeply indrawn breath that always came with the realisation he was awake. Groggy, but awake. The eyes remained closed. It had become a kind of game with him. On waking from an attack, Mark had no recollection of the hours leading up to it, and he'd found it useful to feign sleep for a little longer while he got his head together.

He was in bed, naked. No, he still had on his shorts. He was in bed alone - no client getting his dollar's worth. Mark moved his hands slowly outwards until they found the mattress sides. Single bed, crisp, clean sheets. His nostrils flared to the smell of their freshness and then for an instant, his heart raced. Maybe he was at Ste's. Stephen would have a well laundered bed like this.

Mark had never been inside Stephen's house, let alone his bedroom, but as the grogginess left him he tried to shape reality with the strength of his desire. Let me be at Stephen's - God let me be at Stephen's.

Idaho - came an echo from pre-sleep events. A shitty old stone-strewn, black-tar road in Nowheresville, Idaho.

Mark exhaled disappointment in another volumous breath. Ste was gone, living in another world. Mark would probably never see him again, or if he did, maybe Stephen would cut him dead - look right through him - deny ever having met him.

He let his eyes open - shut them again; bright sunshine on white sheets - too much of a shock for misty eyes. He sat up drawing his palms from temple to chin, then shook his head before trying out his eyes again.

Mark Walker was a connoisseur of roads. He'd been tasting roads all his life and he always knew where he was by the way a road looked. His attacks didn't always start on a road, but they sure as hell had a way of finishing on one. Like a piece of trash, he'd wake up in the gutter amongst the lip-stick stained cigarette butts and Hershey wrappers. Like a human condom, filled up and thrown away, a few bucks tucked in his shorts if he was lucky.

Occasionally he'd come round in a room - a sleazy eight by twelve or a twenty dollar a night flea pit. More rarely still, to the urgent shaking of a bell-boy in an entirely more salubrious joint, eager to clean up room for the next guest.

This though, was very different. It was someone's home. Again, thoughts of Stephen Fulton surged up, but this time they were more ephemeral, dying quickly in the light of full consciousness.

Mark was surrounded by ancient wood; the polished floorboards, the carved bed-posts, a sturdy looking bedside table. A ceramic washbowl and jug, white with a blue motif of dragons and odd looking dogs graced the table. And there were pictures on the walls, mostly mountain scenes but in one corner a cardinal bird painted on a polished slice of tree trunk, bark intact and serving as a frame.

The floor felt icy on the soles of his feet as Mark slipped out of bed triggering a chill shiver up his back. A window mounted air conditioning unit was the only visible evidence that he hadn't slipped through a time warp back to the Civil War or earlier, and the chill it produced reminded him of the need to dress.

Where were his clothes? Not on the carved trunk at the foot of the bed or hanging on the door's single coat-hook. Not on the delicate-looking yet strong oak chair. Perhaps in the wardrobe. Look at that thing! A dozen men couldn't lift it. As he drew near he got a strong whiff of bee's wax polish. Mark grasped the gun-metal catch and turned, half expecting to find a minuteman's uniform in pristine condition complete with tricorn hat, but before he had finished turning, a knock on the door slapped his hand down as surely as a swipe from a grizzly. He felt like a burglar sticking his nose in where it didn't belong.

'Hello.' The voice female, gentle. A mature woman.

'Eh. Hi!' from Mark, uncertain, a phlegmy catch in the throat.

'Are you decent, Mark?'

'No, ma'am. I … I don't see my clothes anywhere.'

'No. You'll find a robe in the wardrobe. I hope you don't mind, but I took the liberty of washing your clothes. It seems you'd been lying in the road a while.'

'Eh. Yes Mam. Thanks. But if I could just have my bag. I've got clean stuff an' all.'

'I'm afraid there was no bag. Just you.'

Mark tried to dredge up the missing information. Where was his bag? Stolen? What had happened to him during his last spell of down-time? The grapple came up empty.

'It seems you may have been robbed, Mark. And whoever took your things stole your shoes too.'

Mark darted a glance at his bare feet, curled up his toes and started to laugh.

He had fallen asleep in some bad company and woken to any amount of horrors. Once he was face down in a Seattle alley amongst shattered beer bottles and broken hypodermics with his pants around his ankles. Once, for God's sake, he'd woken to feel a pill bug crawling up his nose. He'd had his pockets picked, his lunch stolen and fat old Walt, a regular customer, had on one occasion, finished off what he'd paid for despite Mark's attack. But he had never, ever, had his shoes stolen.

Nathan stuck a finger down his shoe to scratch an itchy heel. Wouldn't reach, so he stamped his foot down on the floor of the pick-up a couple of times to relieve the irritation. His regulation black leather shoes were locked away with the rest of his uniform and his point four-four engine-block buster. He felt more human in T-shirt and chinos' even if regulations did make him pack a snub-nose thirty-eight. He didn't like carrying a piece off duty, but then again, he didn't like having to tote the badge either.

Nathan had been a cop for fourteen years, but he still felt guilty if a black and white came up behind him, automatically easing off the gas and checking his speedo. To him, off duty was off duty - leave it all behind until it's time once again to drag on the badged shirt. Nathan Seven-Elks didn't much like being a cop.

But work was over for another day. He was homeward bound, and for a change he was bringing home a good feeling. He liked it when he could help someone out - those 'little-old-Granny's-cat-up-a-tree' jobs which many of his colleagues denigrated. Most of the time Nathan had to force himself to paddle upstream to do his job. His job was one you couldn't do being Mr Nice Guy all the time, so on those rare occasions when he could, the sun shone for him.

It was shining now. Nathan had been worried about Medicine Dove. He'd left that kid in her house and her all alone and the house so far out and all, so he'd decided to call in on the way home. If Dan's truck was in the yard, why he'd just pass on by, and no harm done.

No truck, so Nathan filled its usual place with his pick-up - next to the pump house. Hettie was in the back room ironing a pair of black jeans. The kid, swamped in Dan's robe, was in the kitchen tucking in to ham and eggs. Hettie called out introductions omitting Nathan's occupation.

'Hi, Mark. How you doing?' Nathan helped himself to a coffee from the stove-top.

'What up, Chief? I'm fine thanks. An' the name's "Mark".'

Nathan nodded slowly as he watched the young man shovelling in victuals like they were his last. 'It so happens I am a chief. But the name's "Nathan".' Firm, but without menace.

Mark stopped mid-mouthful. 'Yeah, right. Nathan. I'm sorry.' Mark blushed deeply and went back to his eating. His manner, his way of talking - it was like a junky after a speed trip - bunged up and sniffy, like someone recovering from a severe bout of flu. Nathan was surprised; knowing what he did for a living, he figured there couldn't be a blush left in him. The blush is what did it. Nathan had visited the Wilbur's place to read this kid the riot act, but the blush made him seem vulnerable. Nathan was a man with a stubborn streak. No amount of pleading or reasoning would have achieved as much as that one blush.

Nathan always had a soft spot for the vulnerable. Once, while on patrol, he'd come by a coyote cub near dried out in the desert and close to death. He'd taken it home - much to Jay's delight and mother's horror - and father and son had enjoyed bringing it back to health. Jay was just a little boy then and he cried when the time came to let it go' and Annette had too, despite her constant cussing of the beast.

The blush receded to a faint pink. He was a good looking kid in a scruffy kind of way. Short - about five-eight - with blond hair that had a way of flopping over his dark eyes, and thick wide brows across a similarly wide forehead. From high cheekbones his face narrowed to a small, boyish but stubble-strewn chin. If it were not for the narrow, slightly turned up nose, Nathan thought, this kid would have a face which spoke of Indian blood somewhere in the family.

'How d'you come to be in the desert, miles out from town? Nathan asked. Mark shrugged. 'Where you headed? You got folks hereabouts?'

'I got a brother. He lives in a trailer north of Pocatello.'

'So you come to pay a visit with your brother?'

'No way man! He hates my friggin' guts. Freaks out whenever I show up.'

'Nice brother, huh? Nathan watched as Mark wiped his plate with a biscuit. He coughed, dry and throaty, then sniffed. Nathan had seen plenty of coke-heads sniffing like that.

'Well, let me do some guessing.' Nathan said. 'You hopped on an eastbound freight at Portland and came along the Union-Pacific jumping train at Burley. And then you hit the trail - see the mountains, maybe pick up a little work. How'm I doing?'

'Near enough.' Mark said, smiling but at the same time shifting in his seat.

'Look Mark, I know what you do. Know how you get your money.'

'Oh yeah? Want some?' Mark's manner changed instantly - now alert, defiant, feral.

It was Nathan's turn to blush. 'No I don't want some. I'm a cop.'

'Jeez! An' all this time I thought you were Little Red Riding Hood. Get real man! I knew you were a cop the minute I saw you.'

'Well don't ask me do I want some. It disrespectful.'

'Come on! I got a discount rate for cops. D.A.'s and judges are the only ones who get me cheaper.' He was getting cockier by the second, and Nathan began to think he'd taken the wrong tack.

'Shut up about all that and listen for a while.' Nathan had an edge to his voice, an edge which cut, for Mark dropped his fork. 'If you like doing what you do, stay here till your belly's full and your shirt's dry and move on. But if you don't ...'

'Like it?' Mark said, voiced raised. 'Man I do what I have to do. Don't work, don't eat.'

'If - you - don't; if you want to change your life then kid, you've landed on your feet.'

'On my bare feet is what!' Mark went back to eating and feigned indifference, but Nathan had seen that a thousand times in a thousand kids - he could tell he caught the boy's interest.

'Hettie's a real good lady. She don't know about your life and she won't have me tell her. And if she did it would make no difference.'

'So I've landed in with Idaho's Mother Theresa.' mumbled Mark to his plate.

'You've landed in with a chance that don't come along too often. Now tell me. What do you want? Heavy stuff, no chicken-shit ambitions. What you crying out for?' Nathan surprised himself, but there was something about this kid, something deep down that needed the strength of truthful words to drag out.

Mark stared at the grease on his empty plate. Hell, thought Nathan. I've gone too far. Now he's feeling sorry for himself, and no kid opens up when he's gotten into that frame of mind.

Nathan was wrong again. 'I tell you what I don't want.' Mark said suddenly fired up and eyes locked into Nathan's. 'I don't want to be made no-one's pet project. I don't want no-one getting off on how they saved a no good thieving hustler. I don't want to be loved by someone who'd love any down and dirty dog that strayed into the county. I want …'

But then the spirit failed and the words clogged, like the brain. He knew what he wanted - what he really wanted - but they were sacred longings that couldn't be spoken, naked words that couldn't countenance the world's staring eyes. Nathan saw all this, felt he knew the shape of the unspoken desires. Something in him reached out for this kid, and for once the right words seemed to fall from his lips.

'Let me guess. You want a little love, a little respect. You want someone to make you feel a little special, because you're Mark Walker, not because you're down and dirty. But if you want all that, just like the mangy mutt, you got to take a little grooming first. Hettie and Dan - they mighty decent groomers. What d'you say?'

Nathan had come here to warn this kid off. This town ain't big enough. There's the state line - cross it and don't come back. Now he was persuading him to stay.

'Well? What d'you say?'

Mark looked up and grinned - another instant change. 'What I say is "woof woof".' He laughed an instant before his face spasmed and his body tensed up. 'Oh shit!' he whispered to himself.

As he lowered Mark's twitching body to the floor, Nathan called out for Hettie. She assured him, Mark would be alright. She had some medication on order. For the second time he put Mark to bed, but now he was more than a John Doe.

Nathan was nearly home. He had a good feeling about the kid, like maybe he could really help do some good. He turned in to his drive. A dog barked welcome home and Rivas's sedan was parked across the way. Rivas's little sisters were playing in the yard - one-a-side soccer. Home at last. Another day, another dollar. He looked forward to telling Annette about his day. Maybe Johnny Rivas had already told her about Mark and he'd be able to …

As he opened the street door, he heard Annette screaming in anger. Then her screaming was all mixed up with Jay's yelling.

God, why did it always have to be like this? 'Why don't you two quit rowing?' bellowed Nathan. He might as well have whispered for all the effect it had. Jay stormed from the kitchen, still yelling, a cuss word or two in there with all the rest.

Then Jay was sprawled on the floor - all six foot of him. 'Don't you dare speak to your mother like that!'

Then Annette screamed 'Don't you push my boy!'

'How about "Welcome home" for once? How about "Welcome-the-hell-home"?' yelled Nathan, his good feelings of a moment ago all dashed.

Mark thrust his hands deep into his jeans pockets. It felt good to be back in his own clothes, and he was glad of the trainers the Indian cop had brought by. He had a comfortable night and an attack free Sunday morning at the Wilbur's place and was now idling about, wondering if he should stay a day or two.

It was warming up rapidly, but earlier on there had been a bite in the air even though the sun shone bright enough to hurt your eyes. Mark's eyes always seemed to hurt. He kicked a stone absentmindedly which bounced off the white painted clapboard of the Wilbur's homestead. White painted clapboard, white painted picket fence. Hey man! Where was the faithful old 'coon hound that would make the scene complete? And the kid playing in the yard. Maybe Mark was the kid. No; too old: why in a couple of months Mark would be twenty, although he hid it well. You couldn't put out for money if you looked too far out from puberty. Santa Monica Boulevard was full of twenty-year-olds trying to pass themselves off as sixteen. No, if there ever had been a happy kid in this yard, he'd be a graduate by now and off somewhere getting good and famous.

First impressions were that the Wilbur's set-up came pretty close to an image of perfection, but Mark knew from experience, that kind of image was for the movies. They made movies to make rich people buy what they didn't need and poor people feel like shit.

Mark stepped up to the porch and flopped down onto the rocking chair. He could smell dinner cooking. These Wilburs were sure being good to him. He wondered when they would want the pay-off. People always wanted the pay-off sooner or later. Perhaps they got money from the state for taking in strays, or maybe Dan was a raging queen and the little lady did the procuring for him. Perhaps they were into porn films, ritual murders, snuff movies or - Mark's imagination ran off down the tracks, but he slammed on the brakes before he ran out of line. Maybe they were just nice people, pure and simple. Somehow, it seemed too much to hope for. And if they were, Mark thought, he would have to leave before they found out the truth about him. Leave so that when he left they waved him off, smiling. There goes a nice kid. Shame he couldn't stay a while. The alternative was Dan's boot up his rear-end and a tail-wind of unprintable maledictions. And don't come back you little son of a bitch.

Mark leapt from his chair and over the picket eager for a wider view of the place. It stood alone at the end of a small, tarred road with only the pump house and a small barn for company amidst a sea of sagebrush. It was well maintained and Mark figured a good deal of Dan's time was taken up painting and creasoting.

How old was Dan? Perhaps sixty or so - about four or five years older than Hettie. They didn't ask questions, apart from enquiries into his comfort. They didn't seem to require his background story, or knowledge of his folks, or anything at all. They told him he was welcome in their home and to help himself to this and that, and showed an interest when he wanted to talk. Apart from that, they left him alone.

Mark smiled - one of those smiles that starts in the heart and brings a moment of serenity and joy which all too quickly vanishes - the type of smile that very rarely came to Mark. It came, and it was gone, leaving Mark by himself and without comfort - but it had been real. Joy was a thing soon killed in Mark's heavy heart; nothing for it to take root in. People like him, they didn't deserve it. That's the way Mark saw it.

Mark began to wonder what Stephen was doing with his life. Stephen, the rich boy, had forgotten his life on the streets and taken up his inheritance. Hal had become King Henry and disowned all his old friends - another pain for Mark. He started to feel sorry for himself when the distant popping of tyres on grit turned his attention to the lava coloured road, made to look river-like by a rippling heat haze. An old but well-loved brown sedan sailed towards him.

It rounded the pump house in soft-sprung majesty and hove-to parallel with the porch, close enough to suggest the driver was on good terms with the Wilburs. This was soon confirmed as Dan, who had come out to investigate, smiled and waved as the driver climbed out.

'Hi, Johnny!' he called. 'And is that young Jay riding along with you?'

'Sure is, Mr Wilbur.' called the emerging passenger. 'How you doin'?"

'I'm just fine. Everything all right at home?

'Everything's okay Dan. We just come out to see how Mark's getting along.' Johnny looked over at Mark and snapping off a casual salute.

Mark frowned, not having the least clue who his visitors were, and half raised his hand to return Johnny's greeting.

'Well, just go ahead and ask him yourself. Hey Mark! Let me introduce you to Johnny Rivas. He's the one who picked you off the road and brought you here. Say, do you men want to eat?'

Dan could tell by exchange of glances and hesitation in response that the answer was 'yes' and he disappeared inside with a shout: 'Two more for dinner, Hettie.'

Mark's two unknown friends approached him: Johnny though shorter by several inches was obviously the elder. Mark felt a rush as he noticed how like Stephen he looked. He didn't move with the same, easy, pigeon-toed lope of Stephen's - the one that Mark could never tell was an affectation or for real. But in most other respects, he was Stephen. Same black hair, cut in the same collar-length style; the open, confident look; the wide crooked-toothed smile under cheek bones a little higher and broader than Stephen's - Stephen with a deep tan, that summed up his looks. He was dressed in denim pants and a sand coloured drill shirt over which he wore a brown leather flying jacket - probably an original from the Second World War by its condition. Like the car, it had seen better days.

The younger of the two was tall and lean, and dressed entirely in black. His black, shoulder length hair tied back at the neck and his full-faced appearance spoke far more of his ancestry than did his attire. And the round lensed, wire-rimmed glasses gave a heavy clue as to the style of music he preferred. Black shirt, black jacket, black jeans, black socks - only the trainers differed, and they were white.

'You're looking good, Mark. How you feeling?' said Johnny as if Mark was an old friend. 'Hettie told me you had this condition.'

'I'm doing okay. You know. You kinda get used to it. It's no big deal. Like . . .I mean, thanks. For taking the trouble and all.' Mark felt exposed and ill at ease. Just how much did these guys know about him? Did Johnny catch Mark's look? Had he given himself away?

'Hey, Mark. This here's Jay Seven-Elks. You know his pa - the cop!'

'Cut it out, Johnny!' Jay was rankled by Johnny's choice of introduction.

'Take no notice of him, Mark. He's pissed with his old man right now.'

'Sorry, Mark.' Jay held up for a high-five. 'You know how it is. They just won't get off your case.'

'He's pissed with his old lady too.'

'Your father. He's a nice guy - for a cop.' Mark said.

'You live with him for a while. He'd soon drive you crazy.'

Mark shrugged and the three of them gravitated towards the porch steps where they all sat.

'You going to be here for a while? asked Johnny. Mark had been on the verge of moving on, but the timely appearance of Johnny with his uncanny resemblance of Stephen had caused him to think again.

'If the Wilbur's let me.'

'They'll let you stay 'til you hair turns grey. They never put no-one out.' said Johnny.

'Not even little Stewie, and he burnt their barn down.' added Jay.

'What are they? Mormons?' asked Mark.

'Hell no! Hettie, she's a Quaker lady. And Dan, well he's just Dan, but I reckon he's more Quaker than he lets on.'

'Don't they eh … supposed to dress in black and wear funny wide brimmed hats?'

'When Quakers dressed like that, my people would have been in feathers and buckskin.'

'Yeah! Regular whooping shooting scalping Warner Brother's Indians,' Jay said. 'Some people, like my dippy old man, think we should still go round like that every month or so, so we don't forget our roots.' Jay clearly did not share his father's sentiment.

'So you should,' Johnny said. 'Maybe not so often as every month, but hell Jay, where's the harm?'

Mark's interest in the two visitors pushed his curiosity concerning the Wilbur's into second place. 'So, what tribe are you?' he asked diffidently, fearing the question might break some taboo or other.

'Me, I'm Blackfoot,' Johnny said. 'My folks came over from the buffalo country at the turn of the century. Now Jay, he's...'

'Don't even think about it, Johnny!'

Johnny went ahead anyway, his grin widening: 'He's Nez-shoni.' He laughed and raised an arm to deflect a swat from Jay.

'Hardi-har-har! Hey man, you're so original! Excuse me while I have a heart-attack laughing. Not!' Then to Mark: 'What he means is my old man's Nezperce and my mother's Shoshoni. Dad came down from Lewis County when he was a kid. My mother's people have been here generations.'

'On his mother's side he's descended from a famous chief.' Johnny was still fishing for a rise.

'Johnny, cut it out!' Jay provided one.

'This chief, he made a real famous speech.'

'Okay! That does it!' Jay picked up a stone and made as if to throw it at Johnny's car.

'Whoa!' Johnny jumped to his feet and put himself between Jay and his beloved wheels. 'Jay! My mouth's shut!'

Jay dropped the stone. 'Good. How about keeping it like that?' Johnny shrugged and Jay went on. 'I can't be doing with all that stuff. The past is gone - nothing to do with me, and I don't know why the hell you can't see that. If I was an

Italian would you want me to go around dressed like a Roman centurion?'

'Forget it, Jay. You do what you have to do. Just quit ramming it down your old man's throat. Different strokes for different folks.'

'That's what I say too. Try telling Dad!'

Johnny returned to his place on the step between Mark and Jay, and they sat quietly for a few moments. Mark tried to think of something to say, but the semi-angry exchange between the other two had put him at a loss. He feared that if the silence lasted much longer, Johnny and Jay would call it a day and move on. Mark needed their company.

For the first time in an age he was with some regular guys. What did regular guys talk about? When you lived your whole life on the seamy side, your conversation was shot through with seaminess. You ate, drank, breathed and slept it - seeped out through your pores. You only felt truly at ease flying with your own flock - you wanted out, but you felt at home. He wanted to fly with another flock but feared his feathers would show him up for what he believed himself to be.

'There was something else we came for, wasn't there Jay?'

Jay looked at his feet. 'Well, yeah. But it's kind of embarrassing.'

'Spit it out! Mark's an okay kind of guy. He ain't going to rip your heart out.'

'What is it, Jay?' Mark asked, lifted at Johnny's opinion of him.

'It's on account of Pop screwing up again. See, he said you had no shoes. I'd just bought a couple of pairs of trainers and said he could take the white ones and maybe buy me a replacement pair next weekend. But he ...'

'He took the black ones, right?' Mark guessed. 'No sweat, man. Well maybe a little foot-sweat, but I've only had them on an hour or so.' He leaned forward to undo the laces. 'I guess this will make us Sweat-Brothers.'

Jay chuckled. 'Thanks man! I'd have let it ride, but I've got a hot date and ... well look at me!'

'See what you mean. White don't go so well, huh?

As the two younger men exchanged footwear, Johnny stood and stretched. It seemed to him Mark might get the impression they had only come to swap the trainers. He needed to counter that, not wanting to leave Mark feeling let down. Somehow he felt responsible for Mark, who until a few short hours ago had been a total stranger. 'After we've eaten Mark, how about taking a drive. I'm meeting some of the guys later - split a couple of six-packs, take a dip in the creek - that kinda thing. You'd be welcome to come along.'

Mark tried to hide his enthusiasm. 'Sure, Johnny. Sound good. I don't swim though. Could be dangerous see. Sleeping men sink!'

'Oh right. No big deal. We'll put you in charge of the barbecue. Seriously though, what do we do if one of your attacks comes on?'

Mark shrugged. 'Lay me somewhere's a scorpion won't sting my ass.'

Mark had learned a long time ago that it often paid to keep your ears open and your mouth shut. There was much he wished to learn about the folk he'd fallen in with, and he certainly wished to keep the sordid secrets of his own existence to himself.

So dinner around the Wilbur's table became a fact finding mission. He found out that Hettie was a doctor and that for years she had devoted her services to the people of Fort Hall, and to the occasional wanderer whom fate washed up on her doorstep - usually teenagers in trouble. Mark did not count himself as such a fate-borne wanderer - the Wilbur's had the knack of making each one of their temporary charges feel like the only one ever.

Mark also learned that Jay was a freshman at Idaho State, and that he worked for U.P.S. between semesters so he could buy books and live more comfortably than he could on his allowance alone.

Dan? Well he had been a soldier in early life. And a cop. He had also seen action as a paramedic, a paralegal, a deep sea fisherman and a roughneck on a rig in the Gulf of Mexico. He'd lived in just about every state in the U.S. and said of himself that he had looked all over for answers that were within himself all the time. What he actually said was 'Hell, I'd been all around the pan looking for the handle, and I couldn't find it 'cause it was stuck up my butt!' He punctuated this revelation with an apology to Hettie who was long past being shocked by his unique turn of phrase.

Mark found himself wondering if old Dan was one of Hettie's wanderers. Maybe once, but since his mid thirties he had settled down and built himself a successful agricultural rig-hire company. Starting with a third-hand, decrepit tractor and trailer, he now owned a wide variety of farm machines and at harvest time he still enjoyed driving the big old combines and seeing the grain in for another season.

It was all very interesting, but Mark listened most intently to Johnny and to talk about Johnny. It had been the same with Stephen, and now it was happening again. He was - what? Falling in love? No; too early for that. Or was it? Was it that, wanting what someone had set up an inversion of jealousy: if you can't have what someone else has and you desperately need it, fall in love with them?

Mark had labelled himself as gay some months back. (Funnily enough it didn't automatically go with the job). He had always feared it. The feelings he had developed for Stephen endorsed it and how he had felt when Stephen left the Portland streets to live the high life confirmed it.

Then along came Nancy McAlister and the confirmation was shattered. Their brief affair left him confused, for while it lasted he felt on top of the world and great to be straight. But when she left it was, once again, Ste he really missed.

Now it was happening again, but he would never tell. He would work at being a good buddy. He'd go through agonies playing at being straight. Slap the shoulder but never let the hand linger too long, catch the eye but follow up with a high-five. Johnny would never guess. He made that fatal mistake with Stephen in the Idaho desert, just a few miles from here, when he had spoken his true feelings. Stephen only did it for money: 'You do it for free and you get wings - like a fairy. Isn't that right, Marky?'

Johnny Rivas had his own garage. He was a qualified mechanic, picking up his early skills from Dan. He worked hard Monday through Friday and cruised in his sedan on Sundays - that's if he wasn't working on her. Her bodywork wouldn't bring a second look, but lift the hood without your shades only if you had good medical insurance - eye doctors didn't come cheap. Suddenly, Mark felt very enthusiastic about cars.

Johnny had a few minor scrapes with the law, usually concerning alcohol. Nathan had once run him in for driving under the influence and he had only just passed the tests at the precinct house by the skin of his teeth. He still got drunk occasionally, but never again put his licence at risk. If he was driving, no pressure on earth would drag him away from his soda.

'What about you, Mark? How do you earn your bucks?' asked Jay. Mark was thrown, but Johnny stepped in and rescued him.

'I guess you're kinda restricted on account of your condition, huh?'

'Er - yeah. That's right. I get around. Take what's going. I'm not much good at anything in particular.' He felt transparent, like they all knew about his disgusting life. The game would be up and he'd be walking the streets again.'

'Say, Bob's looking for someone reliable,' Dan said. '"Bob's Gas Station", a-ways down the road towards Minidoka. Vinnie skipped with the takings a month back, so now he's out of pocket and out of help.'

'You really think Bob would take on someone recommended by you, after Vinnie?' Hettie said. 'Anyway, I'm sure Mark can do better than Bob's.'

'No, that's okay. I'll give it a try, if Bob'll take me.' Mark tried not to sound too eager. He couldn't remember his last regular job.

Dinner was finished and Hettie watched as the car with its compliment of three caught the breeze and sailed into the haze. She felt Johnny would be good for Mark: he certainly had an affectionate concern for him. Why, whilst helping Hettie with the dishes he had been most particular in grilling her on all aspects of Mark's condition. How to recognise …? What to do …? How to treat him if he 'flipped out'?

It reminded her of Little Stewie when he had found an injured owl - he needed to know everything. 'Keep him warm, Stewie.' she told him. How was she to know he would run a kerosene stove in the barn? These days, Hettie was more specific with her advice - if she was compelled to give any in the first place.

Mid-afternoon found Hettie finishing a letter to the Rogue Valley Friends when Dan brought her a cup of coffee. The album was tucked under his arm as he sank onto the sofa and Hettie, leaving the letter unsealed snuggled up next to him. She let her head fall to his broad shoulder, her hair silver against his of white-flecked grey.

'Guess we'll have to get a photo of young Mark,' Dan said. 'He's a gutsy kid. Seen a lot of sorrow, still manages to smile some.' He flipped open the album.

'Too early to put Mark's picture in. Remember, we always wait until after …'

'Yes, sure. Hey! Remember Suzie?'

Hettie nestled closer to Dan: 'Do you think I could forget Suzie? Do you think I could forget a single one of them?'

'I guess not. But there's been so many over the years.' Dan let out a long tired breath at the thought of all those young people and all the years gone by. 'Maybe it's time to lay it all down, Hettie. We're not so young these days. I don't know that I could cope with many more rides to the Sheriff's office, or burnt down barns and wrecked bedrooms, let alone rescuing kids from crazy cults.'

'Dan, you make it sound terrible. We only ever had one barn burnt down, and that was an accident. And only one tangle with a cult. Think of all the — rewards.' Hettie reached out and turned a page of the album to reveal an eight-by-ten of a young native American teenager. 'He had his share of tantrums, didn't he?' she said, running the back of her index finger along the image of the boy's chin.

Dan smiled. 'Reckon he had more than his share. What you saying? The worse the kid the better the man?'

'Not exactly. More like, let them vent their anger before it has time to fester. The greater the hurt and anger, the more important it is that we … put them to rest.'

'I guess. But haven't we done our share?'

'I'm not so sure. I have a feeling Mark needs us more than any of the others ever did. Let's just listen to the silence and see how we feel about it then.'

III

One real advantage to Johnny's sedan was the space. And the seats were comfortable - more like lounging on a sofa than sitting in a car. Which was just as well, for Johnny and Mark spent much of the afternoon 'in the saddle'.

First they rode into Pocatello to drop Jay off at 4th and Benton so he could meet his girl at the station. Jay would like to have joined Johnny and the others for the afternoon, but the duties of an I.S.U. freshman were calling - not to mention the pleasures of being with his girl again.

Then it was back to Fort Hall to pick up Cody. Finally, Danny and his girlfriend Summer were waiting for them at Blackfoot. His passengers comfortably seated, Johnny showed them there was still plenty of life in the old sedan as he pointed her north-west and put his toe down. Another hour's passing found them sliding in next to a tiny Nissan saloon a mile or two off the highway.

'We're late,' Johnny said.

'Not too late for the game,' Cody said. 'Just late for setting stuff up.'

'Yeah! Nice timing Johnny.' Summer giggled. 'Just in time to eat I'd say.' The smell of a well fired up barbecue hit the nostrils as soon as the car doors were opened.

What was the attraction of the place? Mark was beginning to wonder. Sure it was out of the way, but for all the scenery and points of interest they might just as well be on the moon. Mark turned slowly to see if he'd missed anything - scrubby plants, yellow grasses, black dirt - that was about it.

Mark began to feel a tingling in his fingers. His head started to clog up and sounds ran into one another. Not

243

now, please not now. The first signs of an attack crept up on him. There was never any getting away. Those little white pills used to help, but then you'd get hooked on them or they mix all up with the other junk you took and give you heavy trips. It was hard to say what was worse. The clouds moved up to double time and streaked across the sky like time-lapse photography. Won't be long now - must lie - must lie down.

'You okay, Mark?' Johnny slipped an arm about Mark's shoulders, sensing the imminent fall. Mark could have answered. He could have lowered himself gently to the ground before total lights-out. But through the fuzz and confusion of the attack's onset, Mark wanted drama, so he allowed himself to collapse into Johnny's arms, and he felt the corner of his mouth turn up in a smile as Johnny's words rolled through the rumble of sound. 'Don't worry, Marky. I won't let the scorpions get you.'

Eighty-odd miles away to the south, Nathan Seven-Elks tightened the knot that held the buckskin legging to the cord of his breach-clout. The air up here in the mountains chilled patches of exposed skin, but he knew that would soon wear off as soon as he got moving - just as he knew the self-consciousness and feeling of slight absurdity would fly as soon as his pick-up was out of sight. When he was surrounded only by nature and far away from the products of technology, then he would feel at peace, then he would feel happy and proud to be clothed even as his ancestors had been.

The afternoon sun glinted off his badge as he turned it over in his hand. A cop must always carry his badge. Well, he couldn't leave it in the pick-up. As remote as this mountain track was, and even though he had thrown a camo-net over the pick-up, crime's arm was at least as long as the law's and its eye was as keen. There would be hell to pay if someone stole his badge. He paced out a line to some rocks carrying the offending piece of tin and his .38 wrapped in a plastic bag. Buried! Out of the way! A great big load off his shoulders. Then he threw in the pick-up's keys for good measure. Carefully replacing the rock, he took one last look at his vehicle, slapped the tomahawk at his side, and set off along the trail that no wheels could follow.

For the first twenty minutes it was a hard slog up hill. Nathan leaned on a tree to get his breath and looked at his round belly. Out o' condition, he told himself. He always did at this stage. Get up, get in the car, pull my uniform on and cruise round 'til it's time to go home. No wonder I'm thickening round the middle. He would take up jogging again - if he could stand the boredom of it. Maybe he would swim every morning like he had before Jay left the family home. The same lines, every time. But then he would crest the ridge and head down into his own personal lost valley and all at once he would catch his second wind.

Nathan's breathing settled as he snapped a couple of squares off a Hershey bar - the one icon of modern living he allowed on his mountain retreats. He thought of Jay as a three-year-old, his face covered over with melted chocolate. Nathan missed that face. He missed the little boy who thought Daddy was King of the Universe. He also missed the face of the eighteen-year-old who constantly reminded his father that he was a fool with one foot in legends of the past who supported a 'corrupt government by serving with the executive arm . . .' and all that other sixties crap. The stand-up rows it had caused were numerous, but from a distance, Nathan could smile at all that.

In fact, everything that soured life back home was blown into perspective by the mountain breeze. Jay would grow out of his bloody-minded cantankerousness, Nathan would finish his term and leave the department, and Annette would cease her nagging. Who knows; a miracle might even descend to earth so that Annette and Jay would quit rowing.

Those two, when they got to it, blew his head apart. Bicker, bicker, snipe, snipe. You wouldn't think a mother and son could lock horns so bitterly. It came, or so Nathan believed, of Annette's short temper and Jay's stubborn streak and it started just about as soon as Jay leaned how to talk. Parent's must show a united front they all say, so in those early days he always sided with Mom. Sometimes he had to step in and quite often it was left to him to dish out the punishment. And when he was smacking Jay, he often thought he should be smacking Annette instead - for starting the whole row with her bad-tempered rebuke, for not being able to cope with a little boy, for dragging him into it all for Christ's sake!

The number of times he had finished a hard day's work and driven home, all the while looking forward to the peace of the family home, only to find World War Three raging when he got there was beyond count. When he got to thinking like this, he knew it was time to hit the hills.

He savoured a second chunk of chocolate. Guilt? Hell no; who invented the damn stuff, eh? The Aztecs is who. Even the word 'chocolate' was from the Aztec, and who were the Aztecs if not ancient brothers.

Poor Annette. Stuck at home, day after day performing chore after chore while a feisty little boy zipped around, constantly calling for attention and getting under her feet. No wonder her temper had worn thin. Perhaps, now that

Jay was grown and living away from home, things would ease up. No more living on a knife edge; take it easy; step back from the precipice.

Nathan breathed deep, drawing on the life giving substances that infused the air. Contentment filled him and a second breath changed the contentment into joy. The mountains healed. Next time, he'd bring Annette with him - there would be no excuse now, no chores that couldn't wait, couldn't be shared on their return.

He thought of his first time in these mountains, guided not by his father or an elder of the tribe, but by a simple down-to-earth white man who knew much but said little, giving credence to the premise 'The more you know the less you show'. And then, of their own, Nathan's thoughts turned to Mark Walker. A trip up here would do him good. Perhaps ... but no; Mark would get the wrong idea. But if Nathan couldn't bring him to the mountains, maybe Jay could, or Johnny. Somehow it didn't even cross his mind that his son could be in danger of corruption. He had confidence in Jay and Johnny. If influence was going to rub off, it would be *on* and not *from* Mark.

Mark sucked in air - outdoor air. He felt a breeze on his cheek and in his hair. He stretched out his hands; the right one encountered hard rock - he was on a blanket overlaying rocky ground. His left hand came against another material over something firm but yielding - someone's thigh felt through their pant-leg. He quickly withdrew his left hand. Ste?

'You coming to, Mark?' That wasn't Ste's voice, but then who ... Yes! It came to him and he opened his eyes, far more suddenly than his usual routine allowed. Johnny was there, shielding him from the sun with a battered straw

Stetson. Mark tried to speak - too soon, for the words came out slurred.

'Just take it easy. You didn't get scorpion-bit.' Johnny helped Mark sit up. 'Even managed to keep the ants out o' your pants.' Johnny shouted for a beer as he propped Mark against a rock. 'Keeping the ants out was one thing. But man! The fight I put up keeping Summer off your bones - well - that was something else.'

The giggling shout of protest from Summer was drowned out by laughter from the others. 'She thinks you're kind of cute,' Johnny added as a coup de grace. Mark hadn't had such a happy awakening in years - and the beer was ice-cold.

Mark was beginning to believe the cop - Jay's old man - was right after all. He had landed on his feet. Johnny's crowd accepted him as an old friend - without getting in his face and poking awkward questions at him.

Including himself, Mark counted seven folk all told. There was Danny and Summer, Cody who seemed to pair off with Lianne, then there was Kate who may or may not have been Johnny's girl. Apart from Kate and Mark, all were native Americans, but here at least, race appeared irrelevant.

After the introductions, Mark kept his head down whilst he invoked his tried and tested mouth-shut-eyes-open strategy. These were clearly people who knew each other well; Mark had no wish to shift the balance. Perhaps of them all, Kate was next newest member to himself.

She and Lianne had driven from town in the Nissan. He could tell those girls went back a long way together. Maybe Lianne had acted matchmaker, bringing Kate and Johnny together. Or had she? As he watched, he saw no clues which linked the two, so that he began to think of the group as being made up of two pairs and three singles. For some reason, he hoped he was right.

For an instant that feeling of joy returned to Mark, and it lasted almost long enough for him to grab a hold. He breathed deep and looked in turn at each of his companion's faces. Cody was treading water in a rock pool scooting great columns of water over Lianne who screamed on the bank before leaping up and bombing him for revenge. Danny and Johnny tended the barbecue - this time getting supper - while the two girls were atop a bluff giving their attention to what appeared to be a small box.

'Hey Johnny. Where'd this river come from? We parked in a scrub desert and I wake up to find a God damned river.'

'Comes out the mountains.' Johnny thumbed towards some distant ripples on the horizon. 'And a few miles downstream it just disappears. One minute there's a river - then there ain't. More beer?'

'Thanks man.'

Mark caught the can Johnny threw and pulled the ring. Then, curious as to what Kate and Summer were doing, he climbed the bluff. The box was a portable T.V. and the girls were watching an episode of Star Trek. Captain Picard and Wesley were stuck on a desert planet and poor old Cappy got knocked out by a rockfall.

'You a Trekker, Mark?' asked Kate, the wind wrapping her shoulder-length yellow hair around her neck.

'Sure. Isn't everyone? 'Cept I like the real thing - Bones, Spock and ole J.T. The bald Brit's okay but . . .'

Mistake Mark! Two mock-angry young Patrick Stewart fans dragged him to the ground demanding recantation. Lucky for Mark they dealt in tickles, not blows.

'Okay! Okay all right already. Cut it out. It makes me flip!' yelled Mark through laughter, writhing under the assault.

The three of them made an interesting show against the westering sun, like a battle of shadow-puppets. 'D'you think your buddy needs rescuing?' Danny asked as he tossed a chop, its juices sizzling on hot coals.

'Nah! Let him fight his own battles.'

Danny prodded and poked at the chicken legs. 'How come you never spoke about Mark? I mean, you two have got to have known each other a long time.'

'Two days is all.'

'Two days? What's he doing here then? I'd been running with you *two years* before I got to come along.'

Johnny didn't answer immediately - the silence started to make Danny uncomfortable.

'It's just that ... I kinda saved the guys life and. Well, now I feel sort of ...'

'Oh I get it! Like a Chinaman.'

'Like who?'

'If a Chinaman saves someone's life, he's responsible for that guy forever. He has to feed him, find somewhere for him to live - the whole works.'

'I guess,' Johnny said, his eyes distant. 'Used to be like that with some of our people too. Yeah! I do feel responsible for him.'

Danny forked a couple of hamburgers off the griddle. 'I guess it's only natural. You go to all the dern trouble of saving someone's ass, you don't want them to go get bust up or all your efforts were for nothing..'

'Yep. That's right. Then there's something else.' Johnny looked sidelong at Danny who immediately caught the drift of his thoughts.

'Whoa, Johnny! You ain't thinking about the ceremony?' But Johnny was, and Danny knew it. 'The hell you are!'

'Sometimes you get a feeling about it. I reckon he's a good candidate.'

'But Johnny, a white boy?'

'Danny. His blood's still red ain't it?'

'Sure Johnny, but I thought you liked the guy, and here you are talking about putting him through the ceremony.'

'Turn the chicken leg before it catches.'

Danny flipped the chicken from the grill and scraped at the blackened skin. There was something in Johnny's last command that held a clear warning. Further talk of the ceremony was off limits.

Would the afternoon and evening have passed so well for Mark had he known Johnny's plans for him? Definitely not. But then again, maybe they would. Mark enjoyed himself so much that events in the future - even the immediate future - may well have been blotted out. Here were people who liked him, or so it seemed. People who wanted no more from him than his company. Chew the fat, fool around, and splash about in the river. Yes, Mark even took the plunge, quite literally, and in the past he had avoided water like it was acid. Sure, he stuck to the shallows and was ever vigilant for early signs of an attack, but Johnny wouldn't let anything happen to him, so he felt safe. Safe. Good and safe - and happy.

Mark didn't feel all that comfortable with 'happy'. It was a sure sign disaster would soon strike. So let it strike, but let it wait at least a couple of weeks.

Warm evening drew its veil over the friends, but was held at bay by an ember-chucking camp fire. Danny and Summer held each other close - and Cody probably held Lianne closer and more intimately for they had taken to the privacy of the darkening shadows. But there was still no sign of intimacy between Kate and Johnny. In fact it seemed to Mark that she drew closer to himself in the loose circle about the fire while Johnny sat, elbows on knees and chin in hands, staring into the flame. Mark stared at Johnny staring into the flame until Johnny's face was like a disembodied globe glowing red against black. He felt someone at his side. Kate.

'A penny for them, Mark.' she whispered.

'Eh? What?' Mark snapped out of it.

'You seemed a million miles away just then. Floating out there somewhere with Jean-Luc.' she said, sweeping a hand toward the heavens.

'The bald Brit?' Mark chuckled. 'Yeah, or James T.'

'You know what the "T"' stands for? In "James T. Kirk"?'

'Nope. I mean ...wait a minute: it came up in the last movie. "Tiberius"!'

'You got it! We'll make a Trekker of you yet. Let's try you with another. What's the Enterprise's fleet number?

''s easy. "NCC 1701".'

'Okay. So what does "NCC" stand for?'

Mark looked up to the stars, checking out the Big E's medium for inspiration. 'Got it! "No Cruddy Cargo".'

They laughed softly, and then Kate giggled as the sound of Cody's and Lianne's lovemaking caressed the night. Mark looked over to Johnny who sat immobile, still lost in a swirling world of hot gasses.

'Kate. Are you and Johnny, like, going together?'

'No. Funny, but I was about to ask you the same thing.'

The reflected light of the fire coloured Mark's face red, so the deep blush was indistinguishable. He didn't try to speak - he knew confusion and embarrassment would twist his words into something less than coherent speech.

'It's alright if you are, Mark. I didn't just step out of the fifties. I don't believe in validating a relationship by the nature of the sexual acts by which it is expressed.'

'You what?'

'I said …'

'The answer is a big fat NO! Me and him ain't.'

'Okay already!' Kate wished she had kept her mouth shut. 'I wasn't prying. I was just curious.

They sat quietly for a while, looking in opposite directions, then Mark got up and walked into the gloom. Kate followed after a minute or two and stood close until they found a convenient boulder to share.

'I didn't mean to embarrass you.' Kate whispered.

'That's all right. I mean … I wasn't … embarrassed that is. Well, maybe a little.' Mark looked at his - Jay's - trainers and rearranged the dirt under his feet. 'Are you saying Johnny's gay?' Mark tossed the question away as if it were of no real concern.

'No. He's had girlfriends. Just doesn't seem to depend on them. I mean, if he ever took up with another guy I wouldn't exactly fall through the floor with shock. He's pretty much self-contained I suppose sums it up.'

'Self-contained as in lonely?'

'Could be. Waiting for the right one I guess.'

'Maybe he thinks she'll up and walk out of that fire.' Mark nodded towards Johnny's silhouette, maintaining his vigil. As Mark watched the watcher, thoughts of Stephen came again, like a cool breeze over the mountains. They were so alike, Stephen and Johnny. Maybe, Mark mused, Johnny would even get to quoting Shakespeare, and then the likeness would be sealed.

'So, eh. If Johnny's straight, why d'you ask about me an' him like that. Did you think I was …y' know. That way?'

Kate shrugged. 'Like I said, just curious. There's some nice looking girls here tonight, but you always seem to be looking at Johnny, so I just thought it might be possible.

Minutes passed. Johnny surfaced from his trance and snapped them a salute before grabbing another Pepsi. He shuffled in front of the fire for a while, restless, then took off over the bluff.

'Mark. Can I get close. It's kinda chilly.'

Before Mark could answer, Kate's arm slid around his waist. Mark lowered his voice a few octaves and put on his best British accent: 'Dr Crusher. Isn't this a little irregular?'

'Yes, Captain. But it's just what the doctor ordered.' Kate nestled her head into Mark's shoulder.

The scent of a perfumed shampoo flared Mark's nostrils as he swung an arm over her shoulder and, on impulse, pulled her close. Her hand dropped from his waist to the top of his thigh and sent a message which could mean only one thing.

Poor Mark! The tingle of arousal soon sublimated into that of an oncoming attack. Not now. Please not now. How many times the same plea, and how many times ignored.

Sometimes Mark's attacks passed like a little death during which time his soul drifted in an empty, less than black nothingness. Sometimes he dreamed: dreams so vivid it was hard to tell in those moments of groggy awakening what was real.

As Kate lowered his head to the ground and his mild spasms gave way to slack submission, his dream was, even then, under way.

He drifted through a pine forest, bare feet a few inches from the brown pine-needle carpet below. It was night, but there was a light up ahead sending shafts, laser-like, between the trees. Figures interrupted the beams every now and again, swaying to and fro between him and the incandescent light source. He drew nearer and the figures ceased their dance and turned to him calling out his name.

Close now, he could see that like him, the figures floated above ground. But at least he had legs and feet. These ghostlike creatures became smoky and ill-defined below waist level. They beckoned him into a clearing where burned a fire of unnatural brightness before which two human forms slept. As he looked they defined themselves into people he recognised: Stephen Fulton and Kate. They were more than asleep; not dead but as if awaiting the spark that would make them fully viable. They were both naked and lay with their feet pointing to Mark so that together their bodies formed a V-shape on lush, wet grass that was their bed.

One of the smoke creatures hovered between their heads as it sprouted true legs and took on human form. As the last wisps drew away, a red skinned woman stood, heavy limbed and round bellied and dressed not in clothes but in mosses, bracken and leaves. Her eyes bored holes into Mark's soul and her words implanted themselves into his head.

'Choose!' she said, her lips all the while immobile.

Mark looked at Johnny, who but an instant before had been Stephen. His eyes ran down from forehead past sharp-handsome features to strong chest, from flat belly to his sex, and trailed down smooth almost hairless legs to well-shaped feet. Then from Kate's feet, except now she had transfigured into Nancy MacAlister, up the slender calves and silken thighs, the wide hips and tapering waist past the generous, well rounded breasts to her elfin face framed with soft yellow hair.

'Choose!' urged the spirit-woman. Mark looked from Johnny to Kate and then back to Stephen and back again to Nancy. Why couldn't one of them help him decide? He wanted them both but he knew without asking this would not be allowed. If one of them would only show that they wanted him, that's who he'd choose.

The spirit-woman shouted, now angry and clapped her hands: Stephen/Johnny and Kate/Nancy vanished and at the same instant objects appeared in the woman's hands.

'Bring them back! I want them both!' he shouted, his voice falling away as his feet at last touched the ground. Now he was naked, and the woman stood before him holding out the objects in her hand. 'I want them both,' he whispered to the earth. 'I want her for love, and him for sex.'

The woman struck him - he felt the pain - and shook the objects. 'CHOOSE!' this time menacing. In her right hand she held a bow and arrows, in her left a beaded leather knapsack. Mark grabbed for the bow but before his hand made contact, the woman crossed arms. Mark recoiled from the knapsack, and tried again. Once more the woman crossed over and once again Mark pulled up short. Suddenly he was angry - more angry than afraid. The spirit-woman receded, her legs once more becoming smoke-like, but Mark surged forward in his fury and snatched both bow and knapsack.

The spirit-woman screamed and the others of smoke returned flying around and at and through Mark. He fell under the assault holding the trophies close to his body as the noise around him climbed to within a decibel of bursting his ears. Then - all was silent.

He was no longer naked, but dressed in worn-out jeans and his old, fringed suede coat. His ears throbbed rhythmically as he rocked the objects - but they were no longer objects. His arms were around a body, a body warm and smelling of leather and tobacco. The throbbing became a drumbeat, accompanied by the chanting of Native Americans - far off but distinct. A camp fire warmed his back.

'You all right, Marky?' Stephen held Mark a little closer. Mark smiled. This was his favourite dream; under the desert sky, just him and Stephen. No sex - that would spoil it all, diminish it. He wanted Stephen to hold him, to be his Dad, and his brother, and his best friend. He wanted to be accepted, totally and to the point of sex without sex actually happening. Yes, this was Mark's favourite dream, and all the more treasured because once, it had actually happened.

Once in four months, if he was lucky, he would enjoy this dream all the while knowing that reality would soon burst in. This time it came with vengeance. It struck him through the ribs like a knife, the pain taking his breath away.

IV

The sun melted away over the edge of the world leaving an orange-red stain. Nathan watched as the stain faded to blue-black. It would be a clear night and a cold one. The moon's borrowed light cast shadows and an eagle, somewhere far off, called its mate to roost.

'Brother-eagle, sister-sky.' Nathan, half remembered a tale he had been told as a boy, a story he'd heard again many years later from the same man who had first shown him these mountains.

The chill air brought Nathan back from dreams, and he set to lighting the fire. It caught quickly, giving light to the tiny interior of his wickiup - a simple affair of bent saplings and foliage, enough to keep off a frost and shade the flames from night-eyes.

Later, crouched at the opening to his wickiup, Nathan breathed in the steam from a mug of coffee held in both hands. He smiled as he realised he was beginning to think in the language of his ancestors. A good sign, because it meant his troubles were back under heel, where they belonged. The night was going to be perfect, and tomorrow he would go with the flow, follow the trail nature laid for him. The day after that? Well, of course he would be back in his badged shirt, but his batteries would be fully charged. Life would be a walkover.

Perhaps the night was not perfect. How much more heart-swelling it would be if Jay were here. Father and son; father imparting the ways of the Great Spirit, son teaching the father ...what? Something important anyway. But maybe Jay was a little too old for all that. Two men then, brothers, enjoying the freshness of life together.

Nathan laughed out loud. These trips of his washed away all pessimism. Maybe next time Annette would come along. They would make love under the moon. Before he could sink into the comfort of his thoughts, the fire at his back spat out a cinder and Nathan's gaze was drawn to its brightness. He watched the hypnotic, dancing flames, until his mind wandered and his eyes lost focus and the little wisps of smoke seemed to be people. They danced and gyrated, calling Nathan into the flame. Little people of smoke with no legs and fiery bodies, and looking at him from the depths of the flame was a face. Johnny Rivas was in the fire calling out for help. Nathan reached out, shaking the images away as the flame bit his fingers.

He stuck the over-warmed fingers into his mouth to suck away the pain. Silly, he thought, dismissing the fire-dream, but he was troubled for a while until he decided to turn in for the night.

His wickiup was warm and cosy, a luxury he would have done without as a younger man. He slept deep until a bear lumbered into his dreams, standing up on hind legs to draw a challenge. The roar trailed off and came again so loud that Nathan woke up. The sound of the bear's voice remained, so springing from his blanket, Nathan fumbled in the dark for his tomahawk, although now he began to wish he had brought his piece along after all. A .38 round would bounce off of a bear, but the noise might scare it away.

There was no bear. It was the distant gravelly purr of a four-wheel-drive picking its way along the trackless valley. Nathan watched as its headlights sent unsteady beams into the night, beams which would of a sudden plunge earthward and then soar again as the vehicle bounced along uneven ground. It came steadily onward, straight towards Nathan's camp, but he knew it would soon be brought to a halt. Unless the crew had a whole load of chain-saws, they would never get through the tree line.

Halt it did. Nathan could no longer see anything as it was too dark and the trees were in the way. But the night air brought sounds. Doors slammed, people spoke, a laugh, the cry of some night creature, called out in alarm. Nathan was curious. What would bring folk out in the middle of the night to this rarely visited spot unless it be deeds nefarious.

It wasn't the cop in him. Nothing like that. Just plain puzzlement that set Nathan to investigate. He moved down the valley through the trees, silently enjoying the game. He felt like he was out to count coup with the ghosts of his ancestors, on a night raid of an enemy camp. As he neared the tree line, the voices grew louder but he still couldn't make out the words. He heard the noise of stone on stone, like men building a wall, but then came the slamming doors and even as he broke the tree line, the sound of an engine being turned. It fired and in the next instant the headlights stabbed into the wood raking across Nathan as the truck swung round. Evidently he wasn't seen, for the truck - it looked like a Dodge - drove away back down the valley tail lights bucking furiously.

Nathan's world became one of total darkness, the moon's light blocked out by the forest. Whatever they had been up to, it would stay a mystery until morning. The illusion of the game faded as Nathan made back for camp. He became hopelessly lost and it was only by luck he stumbled into his camp after casting around in the dark for hours. So much for the inbred sense of direction, he thought as he drew himself close to the embers to enjoy what was left of the night.

Then came bright morning shouldering with it the consequences of a dark deed.

It wasn't the way things were supposed to happen. Cops were not supposed to find dead people direct. Look, this is the way of it: an old hobo say, out early to be first in the soup queue, would stumble over the corpse, and mindful of his civic duty he would phone it in (probably anonymously) or trot off to the nearest precinct house. A day shift cop, bleary eyed before his first coffee break would get the call 'John Doe between the trash cans in the alley between 4th and 5th half a block south of Where-ever Avenue.' The cop would have a good idea of what to expect - he would be ready, steeled for the worst.

Nathan was neither ready, nor steeled. He felt mildly sick and faintly ridiculous, dressed as he was. For once he wished he were in uniform. But all these feelings were blocked out by a mounting fury. This young man, this boy, lying twisted and broken below him had been murdered.

It was clear now why they had driven all the way into the wilderness in the middle of the night. They hadn't been burying treasure or stashing drugs. They had come to throw away this beaten boy, like an empty and worn out potato sack. Oh, they had been so clever, tipping him headlong into a stony gully and carefully placing a few boulders about him. And had the coyotes eaten a bit more of him, the whole thing may have passed off as an accident. They had even put a rucksack on him, but it cut no ice with Nathan.

The boy was thin, would have been about five-nine. One boot was off and wedged between two rocks. Under a fleece-lined denim coat he wore jeans and a heavy duty plaid shirt. The coyotes had ripped the shirt tails out and torn open the jeans at the top. They had made a good start on their meal, opening up the abdominal cavity and tugging out some of the guts. One boot was in place on a foot that pointed the wrong way on a leg smashed below the knee. The head bore a wound on the crown but the face was untouched. The fall had left it unscathed, and for some reason the coyotes hadn't even scratched it.

The partially opened eyes, dirty windows to an empty room, showed more than anything else that this thing, this body, was no longer an object of beauty; no longer an abode for part of the Great Spirit. The temple had been desecrated, the spirit evicted and all that remained was mouldering clay.

No cause, thought Nathan, could justify this. No insult, no offence, no wrong could be done that would allow the perpetrator to be used like this. Well, perhaps one: whoever had done this evil deserved no less themselves. There was no space on earth filthy enough for them to tread.

Nathan had risen before the sun and had breakfasted on raisons and water. Eager to solve the mystery of the night he jogged down the valley with the first light behind him. He found the scene almost immediately, its location marked by the patient group of buzzards who waited upon the pleasure of the coyotes. Nathan put them all to flight. He feared the worst before he came to the edge of the shallow gully, but the sight was still a shock.

A terrible, terrible accident. Somewhere this kid's folks would be thinking of their son, wondering if he was having a good time, and here he was all smashed up.

Then, as Nathan slid down gravelly sides, he saw the boy's face. There would be no worrying parents for this one. His death would inconvenience very few, if any. Perhaps the Wilbur's would be a little sad for a while, but they would cope - as they had in the past.

He had been dead maybe a day. Certainly not more, for the animals would have made a better job of him. And then Nathan remembered the visitors and their pick-up. The cop in him stirred, and in seconds he suspected. This was a set up.

The body lay on its side on a slope head downwards. There was a massive wound, but where was the blood? Then Nathan noticed the bootless foot, and how strange it was that the sock was all twisted with the heel uppermost. And then again, where the coyotes had laid the midriff open and torn the clothing, there was a label on a shredded and bloodstained flap of cotton; the shorts had been put on back to front.

Nathan was in full cop mode now. He checked the laces of the boot on the other, broken, foot. Yes, they had been tied from the front, unless the victim had been a sou' paw. Nathan thought back, saw in his mind this boy when he walked and breathed and cussed. Nope, he was pretty certain he'd been right handed.

Then came the clincher. Nathan carefully and reverently checked the corpse for signs of foul play and all too soon found them. Each wrist showed signs of having been tied up; marks and skin abrasions. Ankles too, while under the shirt was the mark of the cut of death. Small, neat and in line with the ribs, a half-inch cut above the heart. Here, steel had slipped in through young flesh and between sound ribs to rob away a life.

Nathan climbed to the gully's edge and looked down. How could anyone be so sick, so evil, so warped as to be blind to the sanctity of life? What was it that raged inside them? How did they feel afterwards? Oh, the clever bastards! In a day or so the animals would have destroyed any sign of . . .

263

Nathan was suddenly struck by a further horror. Ten months or so back, a couple of hikers found a skeleton, lying in a ravine just a few miles from here. It had never been identified, the file shut up and put away. Of course, the poor man had fallen, broken his leg, and died of exposure - probably. And what was he doing way out here? He had a back-pack, didn't he? Well, must have been a lone hiker. What a shame. Poor man. And according to the medical examiner he must have only been in his late teens or early twenties. Such a tragedy. But these people will insist on going it alone, against all the rules.

Serial killings!

Nathan hardly allowed himself to think it. Hell, some sick Hollywood shit would be screaming for the film rights before this boy was in his grave. Nathan had to sit down. On the edge of the gully with his legs crossed, he refused to look away from the horror. What the hell was the matter with people? Internal tears added weight to his heart.

He would bury the kid with rocks, then get back to civilisation and call it in. The detectives would give him hell for disturbing the scene of a crime and failing to preserve evidence, and he would say, 'What do you want? A slightly re-arranged corpse with all the marks in tact, or a coyote-chewed bag of rags and bones.' They would cuss rather than apologise and dig deeply into their ever open box of hindsight. He would give them the finger and tell them to piss up a rope.

Hours later, Nathan dug with blistered hands for his gun, badge and pick-up's keys. Weary to the bone he threw the camo-net off of the pick-up, dragged himself into the driver's seat and twisted the ignition key. He must have left the radio on for it blared into life as the key clicked to the first position. Eden someone-or-other was singing 'Boys Cry.' 'The hell they do,' Nathan whispered to himself. He punched the off button, switched on another set by its side and called a breaker on the emergency channel. In just a little while he'd meet with the county sheriff or a ranger, then he could get home to his wife and telephone Jay. Right now, he needed them more than anything.

The towel roll spilled from the dispenser and snaked dangerously close to the urinal. A faucet dripped and the light bulb was too dim for the room. In other words, business as usual at the station house.

'Snap out of it, Sarge! You've seen dead people before.' Officer Lee Cornell said. 'Hey, will you get this for me?'

Nathan pulled at the Velcro strap and pressed it into place.

'Thanks.' Lee pulled his uniform shirt over the Kevlar body armour. 'I don't understand why this is getting to you so much.'

'I knew him. He was just a kid.'

'He was a drifter. He died a drifter's death. Anyway, you didn't know him that well.'

'Enough to go on the sheet for the formal i.d. That's good enough I reckon. But Lee, it isn't so much that he's dead. It's the way of it. To think that some slime-ball is out there lining up another kid to ... to Hell knows what. You know they didn't kill him easy. He was tormented. And it wasn't just one off-the-wall psycho with a buck knife. There were at least two of them.' Nathan punched the side of his locker.

Lee cast a sidelong glance at it. 'That's a rare old dent you've just left on the Chief's property. How's your hand?'

265

Nathan didn't answer, but shrugged it off before setting his gun right on his belt. 'And on top of it all,' he mumbled, 'I've got to break the news to the Wilburs.'

The room was comfortably cool and the only sound was he gentle hum of the air conditioning unit. Dan had closed the blinds on hearing the news, so colours lost their edge. A few shafts of sunlight fell on a vase of cut flowers making the simple wooden table appear as a spot-lit stage where the flowers were playing the lead role. The soft furnishings, arm chairs and couch took on the role of silent and rapt audience. Hettie and Dan settled on the couch and offered Nathan the master's arm chair, then they fell into a contemplative silence, as was their way.

Neither Hettie nor Dan took much coffee, but the pot was always ready for visitors. This time though, they sat with Nathan, each cradling a steaming mug. Dan sniffed as a tear splashed into his. 'Hell of a time to get a fly in your eye.' he whispered. Hettie placed a comforting hand on his knee. This time, silence was not enough and after a few minutes Hettie was moved to speak. 'We none of us get out of here alive.'

Nathan looked up at her face and for the first time noticed how old she was getting. She went on. 'So this is how I'm going to deal with it. You can die in a car crash, or a house fire. A disease can carry you off. Or you can be murdered. Murder is just another way of passing on.'

Cop out! Nathan thought. When he needed a solid answer, all he got was a cop out. But then, as he thought about it, he saw the sense in Hettie's statement. Not so long ago, violent and untimely death had been the norm. More than that, some of his ancestors would have prayed to the Great Spirit for a glorious death on the battle-field.

Nathan returned in silence to communion with the elderly couple and reflected deeper on Hettie's words. He had just centred down when the door opened.

'Oh! I ... erm. Sorry. I didn't know anyone was ...'

'It's all right, Mark,' Hettie said. 'Come right on in.'

Mark stepped into the darkened room. 'Hi, officer.' He felt uneasy about calling the cop by his name despite the given leave. 'Is everything okay?'

'Yeah. Generally,' Nathan said.

Then Dan spoke, his voice a little tremulous. 'It's just that we've had some real sorry news about little Stewie. He lodged with us a while back, and now ...'

Mark knew by the way Dan's words trailed off and by sorrow in his eyes that whoever little Stewie had been, he was no more. A lump came to Mark's throat and he was seized by the desire to comfort the old man; put an arm over his big shoulders, tell him everything would be okay. People did that kind of thing in the movies; in real life you just stood there feeling stupid and helpless, so Mark followed the lessons of real life. But then, Hettie got up and followed the lessons of the movies. It was Mark though, not Dan, who received the benefit of a consoling hug. She sobbed silently, burying her head into his shoulder, and then Mark realised he was supposed to be giving and not receiving comfort. He closed his arms about Hettie as he too felt a stinging behind the eyes.

V

Mark didn't sleep easy that night. The murdered boy would creep into his room every time he began to doze, shocking him into frightened wakefulness. He got up and fixed himself coffee, padding around the kitchen and hall in bare feet; then into the living room to watch a little TV. Wrong move! But then what else could he expect in the early hours but a horror movie.

He poured another coffee and sat, small and huddled around the warm mug while the bloody face of the dead boy hovered at the edge of Mark's vision. Sometimes he cursed the strength of his imagination.

Little Stewie had lived in this house. Maybe he was a street kid just like Mark himself and maybe he too put out for money. Mark reminded himself, he was done with all that. That was in the past. Maybe Stewie had done what Mark *used* to do. Perhaps the Wilbur's had been as good to Stewie as they now were to him. And maybe ...the coffee wasn't hot enough to ward off the spine-chill - maybe Mark would end up just like Stewie.

Mark swore at the voice in his head - the one that was so damned pessimistic. It always came along, when things were going well; did its best to sour things. When he was little and it was nearing Christmas, it was this same voice that would tell him "Mommy might die before Santa gets here. Then how will you feel?"

He forced down a mouthful of coffee and with that swallow he felt the ghost of the previous evening's heartburn. The pain of it had dragged him into wakefulness and away from the cosiness of his favourite dream. But after all, it had been a good way to wake up, with the concerned faces of Johnny and Kate looking down at him. For an instant he thought he was still in the dream and he was about to reach out to one of them - about to make the choice. Then reality poked him in the chest with another flaring of pain.

'I'm okay. I guess it's just gas. Help me sit up.'

'You went out like a light,' Kate said. 'Does it always happen so fast?' He could smell her perfume as she leaned closer to get a steadying arm behind him. Then he smelt the musty leather of Johnny's jacket. He knew which he preferred.

Johnny's strong arms hoisted him to a sitting position. 'Who's "Stephen"? You kept saying the name. Over and over.'

Mark became instantly glad of the pain in his chest. He winced against a stab of pain that wasn't really there to cover the blush he felt rising. What else had he said in his sleep? He covered his blush - and avoided answering the question, in one go.

'Steady, man,' Johnny said. 'You're one hell of a mess. You were a horse it'd be cruel not to shoot you.'

'Thanks, pal!' Mark noticed Johnny's wry smile. 'Just having a bad day is all.'

Mark smiled at the memory and let his coffee cup rest against his arm, where Johnny had held him. But then bloody Stewie burst in again.

'Will you get the hell out of my head, you little shit!' He took a deep breath and ambled over to the window. The stars were bright. And the moon! It was a hunter's moon, but as Mark always felt hunted, it brought no cheer.

269

The hunter though, he felt fine and right on line to make a kill. In a diner on one of the seedier strips of downtown Pocatello, Rob Thacker felt close to acquiring his target. He didn't need to study the dog-eared six-by-four photo he carried in his wallet. He was a professional, and by now he knew every feature of that face like it was his own little brother. He was in no rush either, as he sipped sweet coffee and licked the sugar of his last doughnut from his fingers. Rob didn't look much like a hunter, and that helped. You walk wary of a man who in any way resembles your average TV hero. Rob though, you'd walk right by him and not give him a second look, unless it was to check out who the fat guy was. Familiarity – or an unwary attitude – breeds contempt. Then Rob would strike. Then Rob would bag his target. Rob's record was unsurpassed. Like a Canadian Mounty, he always got his man. Tonight his man was the other side of town and then some, hugging a cold mug of coffee to himself and having nightmares about another target who had been called 'Stewie'.

The hunter's moon also served well as a killer's moon. While Rob sipped his hot coffee, peering over the rim at the hustlers as they took time out to eat and hang with each other, a body grew chiller than the coffee in Mark's mug.

The killer's moon shone bright over the mountains. A coyote screamed and Billy Ray Williams nearly had an accident in his pants. What with that - that and the eyes. Vinnie's eyes were half-opened as if they could still see. Billy Ray kept out of their line of sight.

'Put his fuckin' shoes on, will ya'?' yelled brother Jimmy.

'You do it. I'm staying up this end where his eyes don't look.' said Billy Ray.

'His eyes - don't - look NOWHERE, you dumb shit! Now put the shoes on or I'll clip you, I swear I will.'

Billy Ray chewed on his bottom lip for a moment, then picked up the black trainers and walked to the foot-end of Vinnie's corpse. He kneeled in the dewy scrub and put the trainers down while he pulled Vinnie's socks up. Then, loosening the laces, his slipped the left trainer on, all the while taking care not to make eye contact with the dead boy. He started to giggle.

'Now what?' Jimmy said, close to the end of his tether with his brother.

'It's just that, well, these here trainers. Must be the unluckiest shoes in the State. We take 'em off a kid dead in the road and now we stick 'em on another dead kid. Dead man's shoes – get it.'

'Jeez, you cracked a funny. I'll send you a post card when I start laughing.'

Billy Ray finished trying the laces and stood. Jimmy pulled at Vinnie's cheek like he was teasing a living boy. 'There you go, Vinnie boy. Now you's all ready to be some critter's dinner.'

Jimmy stretched the soreness out of his lower back while Billy Ray rummaged in the flatbed of the old pick-up going through the clothes that Vinnie had worn on the day he was taken. He grabbed a Texaco gas-boy's shirt and read the name patch. 'This here says "Bill". He weren't called Bill. Hey, can I keep the shirt Jimmy?'

'Nope. Now get in the cab. We're out of here.'

Back at the Wilbur's place, Mark was again sitting in front of the TV. It was nearly three in the morning, and Mark still couldn't sleep. Why wouldn't his disorder flip him out when he was having a bad time? Only ever happened once, as far as he could remember. About a year ago, in Las Vegas. Mark had been cut by a bunch of muggers who wanted his bag. It was full of dirty socks and underwear, and a few other things, but he would not let go – even when the knife came out. They cut him deep on the hand and then he flipped. When he woke up Ste was there, and another guy they used to hang out with. That was the one time his condition had taken him away from anything really bad. Ste had cleaned and bandaged the wound and stayed by him, like he always did. Until he inherited all that money. Then he cut Mark, and it hurt worse than the knife. It still hurt. Mark felt a tingle in his nose and pricking at the back of his eyes.

'Shit! Haven't blubbed since that time at brother Richard's trailer.' Mark whispered. 'Not starting again now'.

'Maybe you should, Mark'

Mark jumped out of his skin, but kind of internally, so Dan didn't notice anything but Mark's head turn slowly as their eyes met.

'What's up, Dan? You can't sleep either?'

Dan pulled his robe tight round him and sat next to Mark. 'Hell, no. Feel kind of - rode hard and put up wet.' he said pushing a big hand through his mane of salt-and-pepper hair. 'Hettie though, she's up there with the angels. Smile on her sleeping face like a wave on a slop-bucket.'

Mark smiled. A warmth came off Dan, a warmth that scared the chill out of a man's bones. Dan nodded towards the congealing coffee. 'Fix you another? It's decaf so it won't keep you awake. Any more'n you are already.' Mark shook his head.

Dan looked at Mark who looked at the TV screen. A good-looking kid stuffed his face with Golden Grahams while the voice-over spouted on about how cool you'd be if you ate them. 'Sometimes,' Dan said 'you need to talk, best person to talk with is yourself. Like you was when I came in. Other times ...What I'm saying, is if you need anyone to listen, I'm right here.'

A long silence stretched between the ticking of the clock. Conflicting emotions flowed through Mark, back and forth, back and forth, like the waves on Dan's proverbial slop-bucket. Dan didn't fill the silence; he left it alone. A lesson Dan learned from his time as a cop, nature abhors a vacuum, and dammed up words hate silence even more. 'I appreciate that,' Mark mumbled. 'Like, I feel I can talk with you. And I'd like to.' Mark looked around the room lit only by a small table lamp and the flickering TV images. 'It's just that, some of the things I need to say – well, they're not in words yet. See, I don't know how to say them and make them sound the way they should.' Mark fixed on Dan looking for a sign. Dan sat, his green eyes soft and understanding.

'Whenever, Mark. If you find the words, and you want to let them out, you know'

'Yeah. Thanks.' Mark looked at the floor and curled his toes. 'You know, I haven't been a real good person. There are things in my life ...' Mark trailed off with a slow, long intake of breath and an even longer sigh. The time wasn't right, and Dan sensed it.

'Like I said, Mark. Whenever. Right now, I reckon maybe we should get some sleep.

'You're right. Thanks, Dan'. As Dan turned to go, Mark pulled him up short by calling out his name. He turned slowly, like his bones were tired and aching. 'What is it Quaker people believe in?'

Dan screwed up his face while he wiped cobwebs out the corners of his mind. 'They believe in peace, as best as I can sum it up.'

'Yeah, but, like do they believe Jesus was God's son and all?'

'Some do. Some don't.'

'And all that other stuff in the Bible.'

'Same answer as before. Reckon Quakers don't believe God stopped talking to us as soon as the Bible was writ. Those prophets and saints who wrote the Bible were listening to God's voice, and we can still do that listening today.'

Mark nodded as he thought over Dan's answers. 'What about, oh I don't know – things like – a queer faggot guy – stuff like that? Would he be damned all to Hell?' To Mark, this was the question that would test any religion. Would Quakers damn themselves by damning others, or would they pass Mark's test?

Dan yawned. 'Pretty ugly words, seems to me, for a man who just loves in a different way. Damn him to Hell for killing someone – maybe. Do the same if he rapes someone. Don't damn him for loving someone.'

'That what it says in the Quaker Bible?'

'That's what it says in *this* Quaker Bible.' Dan pointed to his heart. 'And end of the day, that's all any Quaker has as a Bible.'

Mark yawned as he nodded understanding, setting off another yawn in Dan. The talking seemed done. Dan left the room as Mark took one more look out of the window. The moon was high, and looked twice as big as Mark could ever remember seeing it before.

Out in the mountains, that big old moon threw the shadow of a coyote pack gathered replete from a meal they didn't have to kill. Vinnie's empty ribcage reflected the light like the picket fence he's once helped to paint for Dan Wilbur.

The heavy smell of gas fumes made Mark's stomach heave. Bob Forde had given him the lowdown on working the pumps and how to use the credit-card swipe-box. That was twenty minutes ago, and still no customers. Mark got to thinking this stretch of the road out of Minidoka was a road to nowhere.

He pulled at the thick cotton collar of his pump attendant's shirt and ran his fingers over the embroidered name patch. It labelled him as 'Bill'. Bob promised if he lasted longer than a three-month, he get him a shirt with his own name patch. Same he promised all his pump-boys. What happened was this: three months passed - if they lasted that long – and all the regulars became used to calling the pump-boy 'Bill'. Bob Forde would carry on about how it would be best not to confuse the customers, and so not a single one had themselves a shirt proclaiming their true name. Anyway, Mark was lucky to get a shirt at all. Bob thought he was out of shirts since Vinnie ran off. Stole the till cash and the Goddamned shirts. Mark's shirt turned up hanging on a hook in the men's room just that same morning.

'Here you go.' Bob sniffed at the armpit. 'Don't seem worn hardly at all.' He threw the shirt and Mark caught it back-handed. 'Think I'll call the Sheriff. Vinnie must've snuck it back since opening time. Maybe he's still toting some of my cash.'

Just as Mark was beginning to get really bored, a mid-sixties, black Cadillac pulled off the road and swung round by the main pump-set.

'Howdy, kid,' the driver said, a guy in his forties with a baseball cap and a walrus moustache. 'Fill her up. Check the windshield and kick the tyres.'

'Firefox!' Mark said, the man's words reminding him of a scene from a Clint Eastwood film.

'Say what?' from the guy, a suspicious frown on his face.

'Er, "Firefox". Just means, like, "Straight away".'

'Yeah? Really?'

'Yup!' Mark flipped the petrol cap.

'You kids. Speak a whole different language.' The guy leaning on the long wing of his car.

As Mark pumped gas, he became aware of the man's eyes on him. He looked up and as their eyes met, the corner of the man's mouth turned up and his eyes did that thing. Mark looked away. Then he turned to check out his reflection in the office window. Nope! As far as he could tell, there was no sign hovering above him with a great big arrow pointing down and saying 'HUSTLER'. Why did his old life follow him around no matter where he went? A small corner of his mind began to wonder how much he could get from this old fart, and just what he'd have to do to get it. He ground his teeth and thought he'd rather squirt the sonofabitch with gas and set him on fire.

The pump cut off. Mark checked the reading. 'That's fourteen dollars.'

'You filled up the trunk as well as the tank?'

Mark did not answer. He decided he hated this guy pretty much for reminding him of what he was.

'Fourteen dollars.'

The man took out his billfold as peeled off a twenty. 'You going to clean my 'shield? Check my tyres? Maybe sell me - a little something else?

Mark snatched the twenty, took it over to the office and rang the till. He returned and held out the six dollars change. 'My windshield! My tyres!' the man said with exaggerated exasperation.

'Firefox!' Mark said.

The man smiled. 'That's more like it!'

Mark didn't make a move. 'It don't mean what I said it did, mister.'

'What then?'

'It means "Screw you!". And you know why.'

The man looked at his feet, embarrassed, and swung open his car door. 'Yeah. Well. Sorry. Maybe I read the signs wrong.' Climbing in, he slammed the door, reconstructing his glass and metal fort about himself. 'Keep the change.'

Mark threw the six dollars in through the open window. 'Stick your change up where the sun don't shine.' Mark turned his back on the Cadillac and smiled to himself. As the engine fired up, he felt that he had somehow prevailed. Against whom, or what, he was unsure. He only knew he'd turned a bad feeling into a good one.

From then on, the day's work began. He worked hard and only flipped once. Dan had briefed Bill on his condition, and when Mark woke up he was in an armchair at the back of the office with a blanket over him. He got his head together in double-time and got back to the pumps. Time flew, and soon the auto sailing in was Johnny's. Mark felt his heart lift. Johnny saw him casually throw a wave in his direction.

As Johnny drew up, Bob came hurrying from the office. He congratulated Mark on a good day's work and handed him another two uniform shirts. 'These here are my own. You'll need more than just the one I gave you already.' He grinned. 'Some days you can be "Bill", others you can be "Bob". That'll really get the customers confused.'

'How'd it go?' asked Johnny as he opened the throttle.

Mark yawned. 'Cool.'

'You flip?'

'Once.'

'Soft landing?'

'Soft as they get.'

Johnny smiled. They'd struck a deal, him and Mark. He'd run Mark into work every morning. Pick him up each evening. Mark would pay for the gas.

'How about you, Johnny. You have a good day?'

'Sure. Got one more oil change then that's me for the day.'

'Need any help? I mean – I can't hardly tell a gear from a gasket but you tell me which nuts to twist and I'll twist 'em.'

Johnny shook his head and chuckled. 'Okay, but I'd better be careful which nuts I'm pointing to, huh?'

Mark flushed deep red, but then laughed in spite of himself. Then, in the guise of a joke, he put out a probe. 'Whatever nuts you want twisting man, you got it,' he said through laughter.

Johnny chuckled at that, but not in any way that Mark could read.

'When the oil's done, I could drop you back at the Wilbur's, or you can eat with me. I'll just get a take-away or something. And after that, I've got a favour to ask of old Bear.'

'Bear?'

'Jay's old man.'

'The cop? Nathan?'

'Yeah.' A jack rabbit ran across the road and Johnny swerved. 'Look. Try and keep Saturday after next free, Mark, will you?'

'Well, yeah. So long as I don't get invited to the Governor's house for dinner or such like.'

'I'm planning something, see. Kind of special. And to do with my people, you know?'

Mark nodded understanding that Johnny's 'my people' meant Indians and not his folks. He was intrigued but asked no questions.

'It's something I want you to be part of Mark. You got Indian blood?'

Mark shrugged. 'Maybe. I don't know a lot about my relations.'

'You're a quarter Indian, Mark. Tell me you're a quarter Indian. It's important.'

'But ...'

'Just tell me, Mark. Trust me.'

Mark was thoroughly puzzled, but he couldn't see the harm. 'Okay, Johnny. I am one quarter Indian.'

'Hey, Marky! That's really cool! What tribe?'

'Johnny?'

'Come on! What tribe?'

'Oh, for crying out loud. I don't know. Kiowa?'

Johnny took his eyes off the road and beamed a huge grin at Mark. 'Kiowa's cool. That'll play.'

Mark was one hundred percent bemused. He knew Johnny wasn't playing him for a fool, but he couldn't fathom the reason behind the last few minute's conversation.

Nathan Seven-Elks was feeling pretty good with himself. The chief had pulled him in for an appraisal and spent a good forty minutes singing his praises. Said he should go for lieutenant. It made Nathan smile. Hell if he even half-way liked the job, he figured he'd be at least captain by now. He had no intention of going for lieutenant. Couldn't hack the politics. And anyway, the job already stood in the way enough. He would have to commit to be lieutenant, and even more home life would slide away. Still, there was the good feeling that despite it all, he was seen to be doing a good job.

Now, there were certain things that Nathan believed were his God-given right, and one of them was to drink Bud from the bottle after a hard shift. Annette told him he was uncouth, and would always bring a glass. Nathan would use the glass – by turning it upside down and making it a stand for his bottle. Nathan sat in his favourite chair reading about the Oklahoma State Cowboy's last game. He'd no particular love for football, but he'd had a friend who played for them some years back, and since then he kept up a loyal interest.

Annette came in leading Johnny Rivas. 'Visitor for you.'

'Hey, Johnny! What up?' he said folding his paper.

'Like a beer, Johnny?' Annette asked.

'Sure, thanks. I'm done driving for the day.'

Nathan motioned for Johnny to take a seat. 'You in trouble of some kind, Johnny?'

'No, sir!'

Nathan nodded, slow and knowingly. 'Must be buttons then.'

Johnny smiled and nodded affirmation. 'Yeah. Buttons. Just two Nathan. Proper use, I swear.'

Nathan shook his head and screwed up his brow. 'They're getting rare now, y'know? I've a mind to send you down to scrubby old southern Texas and pick your own.'

Annette came in with a bottle of Budweiser, the cap off and beads of water forming on the bottle. 'Here you go, Johnny. One beer, and one glass.' she said, looking side-long at her husband as she emphasised the last word. Nathan winked at her. As she left, Johnny took a swig from the bottle, then up-ending the glass, put it to the same use as Nathan's. The two men exchanged conspiratorial smiles.

'So. What kind of ceremony you planning?' asked Nathan.

'Initiation. Double-initiation, as a matter of fact.'

'You can handle a double? Who?'

'Jay,' Johnny said, to Nathan's obvious pleasure. 'And Mark Walker.' Nathan's face immediately fell.

'Uh-uh! No buttons. It would be illegal. He's a white boy.'

'He's a quarter Kiowa!'

Nathan quit gulping, mid-swig, and held the beer in his mouth for a moment before swallowing. 'You don't say?'

'It's true, Nathan. Told me just tonight. His family name used to be "Eagle-Walker"'.

Nathan's face lightened, and then beamed. 'You know, I thought there was Indian blood in him first time I laid eyes!'

'So, do I get the buttons?'

Nathan dragged it out, slowly drinking a little more beer. 'I guess you do. But I'll check with Hettie, see if peyote can have any bad effect on him – him and his condition.'

It was a pack of Pebble-Pups found Vinnie's remains, out on a field trip from I.S.U., all with their hammers and collection bags, their notebooks, maps and compasses. Instead of finding notable rock formations, the young geologists stumbled across Vinnie's chewed bones. A few days later and there would have been a debate about how long they'd lain in the gully, but as it was there were signs all about that screamed 'recent'. Two of the girls dashed back to the transport to make use of the CB. The other girl and two guys waited by the remains – not too close though.

Serial killers, thought Jay, his mind following the exact same path his father's had a fortnight ago. Jay kept it from the others that his Pa' had made an equally grisly discovery within three miles of here. Stewie's murder hadn't reached the nationals, and only rated a four-line filler in the local rag. Jay leaned against an outcrop, his legs apart and his upper body angled forward. His head lolled and he chipped aimlessly at the rock between his legs letting gravity and the weight of his geologist's hammer work together to find a rhythm. He wished for once that Dad was close by. His friends sat each wrapped in his or her own thoughts. Mark was close to tears and Terri slipped an arm about his shoulders, comforting herself as much as Mark.

Within an hour a State Trooper's helicopter landed a hundred yards away chucking up a hill of dust. Jay knew this place was way out of his old man's jurisdiction, but he still hoped against hope that somehow it would be Sergeant Nathan Seven-Elks who stepped out the chopper. The door opened and out stepped the county sheriff.

'Idiot!' said Jay under his breath. 'God only knows what evidence that bird just trashed.' As the dust settled, the elderly lawman strode purposefully across to the gully, inadvertently kicking over the last trace of the tyre-track left by the Williams boys' pick-up.

Technology was a wonderful machine, and money a fine lubricant. Put the two together and there was almost nothing that wouldn't run smooth. Rob Thacker knew just how to run things smooth. His target had now stepped a little closer to Rob's sights. Soon he'd be at the edge of the scope, then right in the cross-hairs. One of Rob's contacts in public service had furnished him with a very valuable set of targeting co-ordinates. His quarry's social security number had cropped up – on the Texaco payroll. It didn't take a genius to work out he wasn't likely to be drawing an executive's salary. No, he'd be pumping gas somewhere. Rob's contact was frustratingly non-specific about the exact gas station, but Rob enjoyed the chase, especially when the smell of blood was in his nostrils.

Mark's social diary was pretty well empty, but it didn't matter. Days were good. Mark spent most of his free time with Johnny, and he wouldn't have wanted it any other way, except maybe one, and that way was long past realisation. Still, Johnny looked a hell of a lot like Stephen, and Mark wasn't complaining.

'You ever read Shakespeare, Johnny?' asked Mark as they sat in a Pocatello department store's coffee room. Mark was surrounded by purchases – mostly clothes – and he still had sixty-five bucks in his jeans pocket. His first pay packet in an age. Gave some to the Wilbur's for his keep and spent the rest on replacing his stolen wardrobe.

'Shakespeare? Sure not for fun.'

'Well no, sure not for fun. But I mean, like, ever?'

Johnny wiped pastry from his lips. 'Did "Titus Andronicus" my last year in high school. This guy eats a bunch of pies with his family cooked in 'em.'

'Cool!'

'And "Hamlet"'

'Yeah!' Mark said tucking into a Danish.

'And "King Lear"'

'Jeez! How much stuff did the old fart write anyhow?'

'Beats me. Why d'you want to know?'

284

'Just used to know someone. Always speaking Shakespeare. I kinda got to like the sound of it. Can you remember any of the lines?'

Johnny leaned back into his chair, furrowed his brow and sucked the sugar off of his teeth. 'Well, here goes. Look at that cloud and don't it look like a camel.' He struck a pose and gestured to the ceiling with one arm.

'That Shakespeare?' Mark laughed out a spray of crumbs.

'Sure is! Here's some more. Give me thy arm – Poor Tom shall lead thee.'

'Now *that's* Shakespeare! Or rather, it ain't.'

Johnny pulled a what-the-Hell-you-talking-about face.

'See, this guy I knew loved Shakespeare. He studied it an' all and he would tell anyone who'd care to listen that Shakespeare never wrote all that stuff. He said it was some other English Lord-type guy with a French name. Edward de Something-or-Other.' Mark noticed the quizzical look Johnny was aiming at him. He took another bite of his pastry and washed it down with a mouthful of coffee. 'Guess I'm full o' shit, huh?'

Johnny nodded thoughtfully. 'Kind I can listen to though.' It was Johnny's turn to gulp down some coffee. 'This guy you knew. Wasn't called "Ste", was he?' He waited for an answer that didn't come. Thought maybe he'd hit on a raw nerve, and he was just about to change the subject when he noticed Mark's eyes had lost their focus, and his fingers were twitching spasmodically 'Oh, man. You flipping?'

'Yeah, I'm tripping out. Help me to the floor.' He grabbed Johnny's arm as he helped him down. 'Give me thy arm, poor Johnny.'

Johnny took the bag that held Mark's new underwear and socks, then propped it under his head for a pillow 'Have a good sleep, Mark,' Johnny whispered. 'Flights of angels, and all that shit.'

The store management was only too glad to supply three assistants to help Johnny with Mark. It didn't look good for them, a young guy unconscious in the middle of the floor, and helping him out of the building was quicker than sending for the paramedics. Reputations were at stake. Two helped Johnny get Mark into his sedan and the other followed behind carrying the bags.

Driving back towards home Johnny tried to put himself in Mark's head. He didn't want his friend to wake up and wonder what happened to the missing hours, and he didn't want Mark to get the story second hand – say, from the Wilburs. He checked his watch. Coming up for eight. He figured Mark would surface around ten. He took his eyes off the road for a second and looked at Mark's sleeping form. 'You're coming home with me, little bro. I'll phone the Wilburs and let 'em know.'

By way of a reply, Mark snorted and jerked his head.

Mark woke up on a couch, head propped on one of the arms. It was not an uncommon awakening as far as the furniture went, but when he opened his eyes, two identical little girls were staring at him. He stretched as he got his head together and took in his surroundings. He was in a small room with dark walls and little furniture. Just the couch he was on, two worn-out easy chairs, and four wooden chairs arranged untidily about a battered table. A large TV dominated the corner left of an open fireplace. There were pictures on the walls; a large oil of a forest scene with two deer peering from the undergrowth, a much smaller one of Jesus calming the storm and framed in ornate, gold-painted wood, and several other of mountain scenes.

'Mom's out,' one of the girls said.

'Johnny's fixing us supper,' said the other.

'Er, right. That's good,' Mark managed.

'Johnny's strong. He hefted you in here all by hisself.'

Mark sat up and drew his hands down his forehead and across his eyes.

'Are you a damn junky?' Nicola asked.

'No, I am not. Just get, kinda sleepy is all.'

'Because Johnny hefted in another boy once and he was a damned junky and he died right where you're sitting.'

The kitchen door opened and Nicola shut up quick, as if she was treading on sacred territory.

'You okay, Mark?' Johnny said, pan in one hand.

'Sure. Just talking with your sisters.'

Nicola came in, her voice a little higher than before. 'We were just telling Mark about Toby.'

'He died here?' Mark looked a mite spooked.

Johnny nodded. 'I couldn't do anything for him. Story for another time.'

'Bad junk?'

Johnny nodded slowly and he took on a distant look. 'Like I said, story for another time.'

After supper the girls went to bed, then Mark and Johnny watched some TV while that swapped stories about the day's work. Johnny made up a bedroll on his floor, and they turned in a little after midnight.

Mark awoke next morning to the sound of screaming. Nicola and her sister Kim were fighting over whose turn it was to have the free toy out of the cereal packet.

Sitting next to Johnny, Mark looked out at the passing scrub as the sedan sped towards Minidoka. Johnny checked his mirror for cops, then edged it up past seventy-five.

'She goes some for an old model.'

'Shit!' Johnny yelled as he braked hard. 'Damn jack rabbit!'

Mark saw the creature scuttle off into the scrub with a dust cloud behind it. 'D'you think he's out to get us, that rabbit?'

'I reckon it's Nathan, shape-shifted. I'll get back home to find me a speeding citation.'

The sun shone in through the windshield and warmed Mark as he enjoyed the ride, thinking about how his wake-ups just got better and better. He contemplated faking a flip after the day's work, if it meant waking up in Johnny's bedroom again. So, the floor was a bit hard – but that was the only minus. Mark liked that room, sparse and untidy, piles of books everywhere there was a place to stack them. He liked the pyramid of washed but un-ironed clothing behind the door, the PC and printer tucked away in the corner with more books piled on that, and the Idaho State flag tacked on the ceiling above it. He liked the postcard sized pictures of classic motorcycles, and especially the pair of crumpled boxers lying at the side of Johnny's bed, right next to Johnny's hand where it had flopped out from under the duvet. He like the thought of Johnny sleeping naked just a couple of feet away.

Mark snapped out of his sun-induced revelry. 'Hey, Johnny. How come you got no Injun stuff in your room?'

'That would be on account of my tomahawk being all bloodied-up from the last scalping.' Johnny swatted Mark's thigh with the back of his hand. 'Seriously, who I am is about what's on the inside. I don't have any ceremonial threads. My Indian stuff is these jeans, this jacket – or any other damn thing I happen to have on at the time.'

Mark got close to get a better look at one of the motorcycle shots. 'You and Jay are alike in that respect.'

'Uh-uh. He wears white-man clothes. Wait till Saturday. I think maybe some of your questions will be answered.'

The gas station hove into view, a little too soon for Mark's liking. He was enjoying the conversation.

'Here you go then, Marky. Another day, another dollar.' Johnny reached over to the back and grabbed Mark's jacket. 'Reckon you could call Dan and Hettie? Let 'em know you're sleeping over at mine Friday?'

Mark's heart tripped a fandango. 'Well, yeah. I suppose. I didn't know I was.'

'It would be best. There's a lot of preparation to be doing. Sleep over and we can make an early start.'

Mark screwed up his face, like he was thinking about it, then, as casual and as unexcited as you like, 'Sure. I'll tell 'em. See you after work then.'

Johnny winked, pulled the door shut behind Mark and got started on another day in the garage.

The day passed quickly. Mark was by now an expert pump-boy. He did his work cheerfully and the customers seemed to like him. Half-way through the morning and his pockets were already bulging with tips. He used his hustler's charm, but not as a hook for action. Just because it made the customers happy, and it felt good doing that. Generous tips were good too, but they were the dessert and not the main course.

Mark was filling up a sleek, graphite-grey Jaguar XJS and passing the time swapping jokes with the owner when a junk-tip on wheels pulled off of the road. Billy Ray slammed on the brakes – a futile action, for the ill-maintained old pick-up ignored the urgency of the command and ground to a lazy halt. Jimmy wasn't even thrown forward.

'Jesus Jimmy lookit!' Billy Ray said.

'What the hell's wrong with you? It looks like yo' ass is knittin' button holes!'

'The kid at the pumps. He's that dead kid off the road!'

Jimmy leaned forward so he could see better through the fly-splattered windshield.

'Him all right! Guess he couldn't a been dead after all.'

'No Jimmy. He was dead as dead as dead. I felt his pulse!'

Jimmy thought for a while, watching Mark as he laughed and chewed the fat with the pretty blond lady owner. Then he stuck his arm out towards his brother. 'Feel my pulse.'

Billy Ray stretched his fingers and did like his brother asked. His face fell. 'Jesus Christ in Heaven, Jimmy Williams. You's dead too!'

Jimmy let his head fall into his hands and refrained from saying what was on his mind.

'So what we going to do? Maybe we should use him for . . .' Billy Ray recoiled from Jimmy's punch and put a hand up to his now bloody nose.

'We don't do the findin'. We don't do the killin'. We only do the dumpin'.'

'And the dressing!' Billy Ray said through his hands, one finger and thumb pinching his nose to stop the flow of blood. 'Don't forget it's us that put the clothes on 'em and burns their own stuff, and we ...'

'Come on,' Jimmy snapped. 'Let's get out o' here. Get our gas someplace else - then make a phone call.'

Mark noticed the pick-up pull off onto the road, but paid less than a little attention to it. The sun was high in Mark's sky, and he didn't see the gathering of the clouds.

Late in the afternoon, just when he was beginning to look forward to the sight of Johnny's big old sedan growing from a dot on the horizon, a Dodge pick-up pulled in. The driver was overweight, but he had a kind look that Mark took to, and a cheerful smiling face. He wore a baseball cap and Mark recognised the Star Ball logo. 'Mariners!' Mark said pointing to the hat.

'Yes, son, it certainly is. Say, are you from Seattle?' asked the guy.

'I've been around. Lived in Seattle for a while. But you've got Idaho plates. How come you cheer for the Mariners?'

The man smiled as his eyes drifted to another time. 'Oh I was raised in Washington State, just outside of Seattle. Right up until I got my call up papers.'

'Vietnam?'

'Yes, sir. Vietnam. But I got lucky. The "policing action", ended before I was shipped out.'

They chatted on for a minute or so, then the guy paid by Visa card asking Mark to be sure and provide a receipt.

As he eased to a halt, waiting for a truck to pass before pulling back onto the road, Rob Thacker looked at Mark in his mirror. Cross-hairs on target. BANG!

VI

By the time Friday night came, plans had been laid and wheels were turning, and they all zeroed in on Mark like it was one of the unwritten laws of the universe that every now and then, his world had to be turned upside down.

Over at Fort Hall Jay carefully placed a change of clothes into a rucksack. He was curious about the events of the following day, and keen to try some new junk. But the prospect of staying in the mountains overnight, not so very far from where the bodies of guys about his own age had started turning up thicker than ticks on a coyote, gave him an eerie feeling. 'Dad!' he shouted.

'Don't yell!' yelled Nathan from the porch.

'Can I pack your piece?' he shouted louder.

Nathan's slow footfall grew louder until his large frame filled the doorway to Jay's bedroom.

'Worried about the murders?'

'Kinda.'

'You can take my hunting rifle. But don't be worrying. The bodies are dumped in the desert. They're killed somewheres else.'

Nathan returned to the porch and watched the sun settling down. He chewed on a toothpick and tried to dislodge a fibre of beef stuck between his molars. At least, that's how it started. The meat particle had long since gone, but his mind was in the mountains, so he kept picking. Those murders. Just as he'd thought, the FBI had taken over the investigation. Special Agent Richard Marshetta headed the team. Nathan knew a little about him from an article the agent had written in a recent issue of the FBI Law Enforcement Bulletin. Wrote like a hotshot with a dozen law degrees flying out of his ass; acted like a regular guy. Nathan liked him. He never did have to tell him to piss up a rope.

Those murders. They worried Nathan real bad. There was one fact he knew, that nobody else seemed to. There was Stewie. There was Vinnie – they identified him from dental records. And then there was the skeleton of a few months back. The court gave an order of exhumation and once again, dental records proved to be a winner. Those bones, when they stood, had carried the flesh of twenty-two year old Juan Mendoza. Drifter. Lived local for a while. Disappeared. No fuss, no panic, no Federal case. At least not until now. Stewie, Vinnie and Juan shared various aspects of height, build and lifestyle, they were all the same age within four years. And. And. Nathan hated to think about the 'And'. He was burdened by it, as if he was the only one who possessed the knowledge. And. And at one stage or another, they had all lived with the Wilburs.

Jay turned in early. He wanted to write up an assignment before heading off to the mountain to meet Johnny and the others, but it would have to wait.

Johnny and Mark drank some beer and watched a little TV, but they too were mindful of events to come. Mark felt a sense of expectation as he got undressed. He heard Johnny's zip snick and the jeans sliding down. He dare not look over his shoulder, so his imagination worked a double shift. He felt the tingle of arousal as he let his own pants hit the floor. Stepping out of them, and frightened his feelings would give out a signal in the form of the obvious activity in his boxers, he held himself down and quickly slipped under the blankets. Looking over he caught the length of Johnny's thigh in the moonlight an instant before it was covered by duvet.

Johnny settled, and when his breathing became regular and heavy, Mark stretched out his arm in the darkness where the moon couldn't see. He silently sought, and found, Johnny's boxers – still warm. Mark suddenly wished he were sleeping on the moon, or at least a thousand miles from Johnny. He grabbed his jeans and wriggled into them not bothering to put any strain on the stitching by doing up the zip. Johnny turned to face him and Mark hoped he was going to lift a corner of that duvet and say hop in.

'You okay, Mark?'

'Sure. Just need to use the can.'

It was a two-and-a-half hour drive to the place where Johnny had planned to hold the event, the last forty minutes or so along a steep, bumpy dirt road. And there was a lot of work to do to get things ready. First, the two men set up a tent. Not a tipi or anything like that, just a six-foot high dome tent. The tent would have no part in the ceremony, but out of place as it was, it had its role to play and it was the best Johnny could do.

Then they set about preparing the sweathouse. The dug a two-foot deep, six-foot wide hole and constructed a wickiup of supple canes and animal-skins over the top. In the centre, they put together a raised fireplace of flat rocks.

Johnny called their first break when the sweathouse was done. He and Mark sat shirtless, sharing a boulder and an ice-cold beer. Mark flicked perspiration from his chest and belly using the edge of his hand. The leather of Johnny's belt was dark with it.

'Nothing compared to the sweating we'll be doing in there.' Johnny pointed to the low dome of the sweathouse.

Mark reached over and slicked the sweat off Johnny's back, running his hand from just below his neck to about level with his kidneys. Johnny didn't say anything, or react in any way, and as he wiped Johnny's sweat off onto his jeans-leg, Mark wondered if it had really happened.

'We'll set up a camp-fire over there.' Johnny chucked a glance towards an outcrop that formed a half-circle about a flat, sandy piece of land. 'Then we'll eat. After that, we'll clear any sharp stones lying between the rock-pool and the sweathouse – it'll be dark when we start the ceremony.'

'When are the others gonna be here?' Mark hoped the answer was never, and that the others had all cancelled.

'Jay, any time after noon. Cody and Danny, late afternoon or early evening. Before dark anyhow.'

As it was, Jay turned up early evening and Cody arrived alone just as the sun was setting. Danny didn't show at all. Mark sensed that Johnny was annoyed. They chowed down into the food Mark and Johnny prepared on the barbecue, and sat around the campfire, all sharing a feeling of anticipation. Nobody spoke of the ceremony – Johnny would know when the time was right, and he would give the signal. Until then, they were all happy to hang loose.

The four young men encircled the small fire - stared deep into the flames. A small fire in an Idaho desert; it triggered a feeling of deja vu in Mark. It had all happened before and Mark was warmed by the memory. An old saying came to him linked closely to the memory. It was appropriate to his present situation, but would it upset the guys? No, how could it? What the hell, Marky, go for it.

'You guys have probably heard it before.'

'Heard what, Mark?' Johnny asked.

Mark hesitated for a few moments. 'Red man make small fire - keep warm. White man make big fire - keep warm running around for firewood.'

Johnny smiled. So did Jay. Cody laughed so as you could see his shoulders move, but there was no sound. The main thing was, Mark's comment amused and was accepted generously by the others.

Mark's mind drifted back to that other time when he and Stephen Fulton had been alone in the desert - just them and their thoughts sharing the comfort of a small fire. They spoke quietly, Stephen gentle and with confidence; Mark stilted, choked up with emotion. He told Stephen what he really wanted, and, after a time, Stephen acquiesced, put an arm around Mark and slowly lay down.

The two young men lay together on the dusty ground the warmth from their bodies hotter than anything that came from the fire. Mark's head spun - it was hard for him to tell if the Indian drums were still beating out a rhythm in the distance, or if it was just his heart. This was all he had ever wanted for nearly two years, and now here it was - or here it so imminently was.

Or was it? Ste had only agreed to hold him - maybe that's all it would ever amount to. Maybe he would have an attack at the crucial moment to rob him of his love. Mark could smell the leather and tobacco smell of Stephen, feel his hand at the back of his head, the caress of his breath against his cheek. No; it couldn't just stop here.

'Please Ste. Let's do it. Please. I love you.' whispered Mark, but to speak those words took a mammoth effort.

Stephen pulled him a little closer.

'Okay, Marky. But this is it. Just this once and never again. You know it's not my scene.' Stephen spoke in a gentle, reasoning tone, and then in a whispered aside to himself, 'Jeez, I'm going to grow wings.'

Stephen led; didn't rush things but moved on slowly; undressing Mark like he was unwrapping a precious gift. That mattered to Mark, mattered that Stephen made the effort, mattered that he at least acted like he enjoyed it too. Stephen stripped, then finished helping Mark out of his clothes. It was too cold under the night sky to stay naked for long, so they made out under the blankets.

Stephen made love with his hands and his mouth, and the moment came quickly for Mark. To hold off the climax for as long as he could, Mark used the old tried and tested mind-trick he employed with clients. He imagined a house, floating up in the sky held aloft by the power of his thought. He concentrated on keeping it airborne, diverted all his will power until pleasure surged past all control and burst out from his loins into every part of his body. The house came crashing to earth and shattered into a million fragments, one piece for each of Mark's bared and fire-scorched nerve-endings.

And that was just the beginning. Stephen led a to and fro of lovemaking covering all the bases of frenetic, tender, inventive and vigorous. The giving and taking, the holding and the stroking; they made a path of pleasure that pierced deep into the night.

After, the chill set in and they pulled the blankets close about them. Stephen lit a cigarette, took a long, deep drag and passed it to Mark.

'Thanks, Ste. I know you don't want to hear it man, but I love you.'

'Marky, Marky, Marky. I knew in the end you'd grow wings,' Stephen said, not unkindly.

'I've always had 'em Ste.'

'So, you get your buck and enjoy your work into the bargain, eh?'

'I hate my work!'

Another coyote - or the same one - yowled to the moon, and at the same instant the drums stopped. Suddenly it felt very chilly. Stephen threw the blankets off and sat up grabbing his shirt. Mark shivered from the cold and from the beauty of Stephen's body.

'Don't get dressed yet.'

'I have to, or I'll freeze my butt off.'

'No. There's more blankets - and I'll feed the fire.' Mark said, the blanket slipping off as he rose to get brushwood. Stephen watched as Mark's naked form darted about, arms enfolding his chest against the chill. He soon had the fire revitalised - sending up quite a flame.

'Red man make small fire, keep warm. White man make big fire, keep warm running around for wood.'

'Where d'you get that from? Yo' mama?'

Stephen bounced a small pebble off of Mark's butt. 'Heard it some place, I guess.' Ste rearranged the blankets around himself. Mark placed a few sticks deep into the flames. 'Come on in.' Ste wore a blanket like a cloak and held the corner up for Mark to join him. Mark smiled like a kid being offered a candy bar, trusting and kind of shy; it pulled a little at Stephen's heart. He scurried into the hollow Stephen made for him and a spasm of joy went through him as Stephen's arm folded around him. They sat, facing the fire. He felt better than he ever had before. The sex and the physical closeness represented total acceptance of all he was.

'So, you hate your work, and you have wings? Whereas I like my work and don't have wings.'

'You're calling me a fairy, Ste. Cut it out. I ain't no limp wristed, hip-wiggling faggot. I'm just a guy.'

'Who likes doing it, with other guys.'

'Whatever I have to do for sex, I'm still just a guy. Can't blame me for how my Goddamned dick works. I didn't get in the queue and ask for one that stood up for other guys.'

'But it helps. In our line of work, I mean.'

Mark shivered a little and let his head fall on Stephen's shoulder.

'So Marky, who-ain't-no-fairy-but-likes-boys, what do you think of - when you're working?'

Mark breathed deeply before answering in a whisper. 'You Ste. I mostly think of you.'

Stephen caught his breath, then let it out, slow and easy. He felt a little twinge of something: guilt? Pity? Mark was an okay guy. Not too bright, but attentive and loyal; sometimes a little goofy; off the wall when he'd had a few beers or a snort. Stephen kept Mark around, like a pet dog; wore him like a favoured jacket. Loved him even, but not the kind of love Mark was speaking about. For the first time, Stephen put himself in Mark's shoes. Mark loved him, and soon Mark would have to do without him. The empathy vanished quickly, but prompted him to another love session - call it payment for loyalties rendered - then he could sleep sound when he was next in bed alone. He ruffled Mark's hair, ran the backs of his fingers down Mark's forehead, let his fingertips brush down his neck.

'You got any vinegar left in you, because I'm about ready again!' Stephen's fingers brushed down Mark's chest, lightly skimmed over his stomach and moved on down through the coarse hair. Mark took his hand and moved it back up to his stomach.

'Just hold me, Ste. Through till morning. Just hold me.' He stared into the fire, the flames drawing his mind in as he felt Stephen's embrace tighten.

Mark snapped back to the here and now, snatching a glance at each of his three companions. He felt bared, transparent - he felt that maybe they could read his mind and would soon disown the gay sonofabitch. But each was deep in his own contemplation of the flames and Mark's feeling of insecurity passed. He thought back to the other time, not recalling the sex. The sex had been good, but in memory, and in dreams, the holding was enough.

After some time away from the others, Johnny returned from preparations in the sweathouse. 'Okay. Everyone up for it?' Time's now.'

Cody wimped out. No other explanation than he didn't feel like it. Johnny raised an eyebrow and said adios, and Cody took his leave. As Cody's car was heading down the valley, Johnny slipped his shirt off over his head, then unbuckling his belt, he stepped out of his jeans. 'Keep your drawers on if you feel shy.' he said, pulling off his trainers and socks. 'But I'm going for traditional.'

'You what?' Jay said. 'What is this? Some kind of a faggot's convention.'

Johnny gave him a sidelong stare. 'Like I said, you feel shy, keep 'em on.' Then he kicked his own off and turned for the sweathouse. Mark closed his eyes and breathed deep. Then he started to undress. In the end, Jay gave in to peer-pressure and went naked like the other two.

As you would expect, it was as hot as Hell in that little wickiup, a fire crackling away in the centre. Johnny lifted the flap and slid in, dropping to the floor two feet below ground level, and took his place by the ceremonial paraphernalia – a small drum, a rattle, a tortoise-shell vessel, a medicine bag and another smaller bag made of goatskin.

'Yeah, right,' Jay said as he took a place opposite Johnny, eying the artefacts with suspicion. Then Mark slipped in feet first, and hunkered down to complete the three-man circle. The fire was hot but small, and it threw a flickering dance of shadows all around the men and up onto the skins that formed the roof. Johnny poured a little water over the rocks about the fire and the small enclosure became hotter still with the steam.

Jay and Mark exchanged glances. Jay shrugged at the question evident in Mark's face. Johnny sat still. Johnny sat quiet. Johnny breathed slowly, leaving the others' expectations unanswered.

At last, Jay broke the silence. 'So, when do we get a chew of the buttons?'

'Not yet,' Johnny said.

'What then? What do we do now?'

'We sit here. And we sweat a lot.'

Jay shook his head and rolled his eyes to the ceiling. He stuck his hands over the fire and made a flying bird shape, so its shadow was thrown up onto the pale skins that formed the roof. He made an eagle noise. Johnny took no notice. Mark felt uncomfortable and wished Jay would quit fooling around. Then Jay did something with his hands and the flying eagle on the roof changed into something obscene.

Johnny let his eyes drift up to take in the show. 'Of course, you prefer, I can drag your sorry ass outside and kick two or three shades of shit out o' you.'

Jay froze, and then decided he would play the game.

After an hour of sweating, when they felt good and cooked, Johnny led a dash to the rock pool where they plunged into icy water.

They towelled off quickly and returned to the sweathouse which had been allowed to cool. Now it was pleasantly warm, pushing the ice-water chill out of invigorated bodies. The second part of the ceremony began. Johnny picked up the rattle. 'We'll start to get the feel for this by trying to empty our minds. Concentrate on the sound of this rattle, and nothing else.'

'Jesus, Johnny,' Jay protested. 'What's with the rattle? I'm sitting here buck naked an' as if that's not enough you're gonna start shaking some rattle? What's with the Goddamned rattle?'

Johnny stayed calm, much to Mark's relief. 'This rattle helps make the ceremony. Just flow with it. No rattle and we're just a bunch of junkies getting spaced.'

'But ...'

'But nothing, Jay. No one's making you stay. You feel uncomfortable with all this, off you go an' no worries.'

Jay shifted his weight as if about to turn and leave.

'No, Jay.' Mark said. 'Don't go. I mean, I can see why you might want to, all this old Indian stuff and being naked and all. But like Johnny says, relax into it. I can do it, and I'm white. It's cool.'

Jay settled down again, crossing his arms over his lap. 'Yeah, well okay. But Johnny, you start dancing an' hollering like a dog soldier, I'm gone, slicker an' quicker than a goose goes to shit.'

'Fine. You comfortable now?'

'Oh, I'm comfortable alright. As comfortable as you can be with ants tickling your nuts.'

'So, we'll go for it again.' Johnny started to shake the rattle, once hard, once soft then back again. SHUSH-shush, SHUSH-shush, SHUSH-shush. Mark half-closed his eyes and concentrated only on the rattle. He, and Jay,

302

concentrated to the extent that that did not notice Johnny. He kept up the rhythm with his left hand, while with his right he began to prepare the peyote – the little button-shaped cactus plants that would help to open the eyes of the participants. He dropped them into a tin cup, poured on a little water and held it over the fire. Then he began to chant, slipping the words in with the rattle-sounds, then expanding them so that eventually they replaced the rattle altogether.

He stopped, not abruptly, but trailing off until the only sound was the crackling of the fire.

Mark became aware that Johnny was holding out the tortoise-shell towards him. Mark took it, and reading Johnny's gesture, he drank the liquid it contained. Tasted like peppered puke, but he managed to swallow it without gagging. He handed the shell back and Johnny refilled it for Jay.

Then it happened. Right on cue, as always, to rob Mark of another experience. The shadows began to dance in triple time, sounds thickened and echoed and distorted. Mark could feel his fingers start to shake. Not now. Please, not now. How many times the same plea? How many times ignored?

And then, miracle of miracles, the sounds regained their clarity, and the shadows started to behave themselves. Mark was a little confused, as it had never happened before, but he had actually beaten an attack. That the peyote had many of the same active ingredients as the medication he had once used to control his condition was a fact unknown to Mark, so to him it was as if his plea had actually been answered – for once.

Neither Johnny nor Jay had noticed Mark as he went through the early stages of an attack, and so the ceremony moved on. Ancient secrets played their part; secrets that have no business appearing in any account. The peyote played its. Then the time came when the initiates were to lay their souls as bare as their bodies.

'The truth? Okay. That's cool. But have we got all day? I mean some of us might have a whole lot more guilt crap to unload.'

Johnny nodded. 'If it's on the edge, Mark, tip it over. Get rid of it. We got as long as it takes.'

Mark breathed in deep, his eyes closed, then snapped open and he locked on, eyeball to eyeball with Johnny. His face set hard, as if to throw up a shield against any response his imminent revelations would cause. 'Until I came here, I made money selling my ass. My father and brother is the same person. I'm gay. And Johnny.' Mark's racing heart went into overdrive. 'Johnny, I'm in love with you.'

In the silence that followed Mark forgot to breathe and as he waited for a response, the moments wove a black web about the periphery of his vision and his ears began to buzz.

Jay was transfixed, his jaw agape. He didn't know what to think. Would Johnny explode and swing for Mark? Would Mark crack up and say it was all a big joke? The moments stretched to fill a span of years.

'Phew! That took some guts,' Johnny said. The tension eased for Jay, but still Mark didn't breathe and the wreath of black constricted.

'Look, Mark. We're telling the truth here. And I feel kind of weird saying this, but hearing as how someone loves me, it makes me smile in my heart. Hell, it would be smiling a lot more if you were Julia Roberts. I'd know what to do with that. But Mark, I ...'

'It's okay, Johnny. It's cool.' Mark said, remembering to breathe at last. And suddenly Mark's heart was smiling too - in an instant his feelings for Johnny had changed. There remained love, but somehow Mark no longer felt gay. It was a word that confined him, sought to mould him. The seed that was to take root later in the ceremony put out its first tender shoots.

The feeling in Mark's heart spread. He was no longer outside looking in at the candy-store window. He was part of something; he belonged. A smile sparked in his heart, blossomed and burst out transfiguring his face, spreading from mouth to eyes. And then, as he saw the same reflected in Johnny, it bounced back to his heart setting up a feedback-loop of joy. Then the two men were laughing, a deep song of happiness that reached the stars and made them shine more brightly.

Jay smiled too despite his confusion. In its own unhurried time, the laughing subsided; Mark and Johnny became joyfully solemn.

'What about you, Jay?' said Johnny. 'It's your turn, if us two haven't destroyed the mood.'

'God damn a potato!' Jay said, drawing quizzical looks from his friends. 'Hell, no!' he continued. 'It just makes what I've got to say easier. Jeez, Mark. Like Johnny said, that took guts.' It was Jay's turn to breathe deep. 'Well, you know that great ancestor of mine - the Shoshone chief? His big speech?'

Johnny and Mark nodded.

'God damn a potato!' Jay said.

'Huh?' from Mark.

'That was it. The whole speech from start to finish. God damn a potato!'

'And that's what you're ashamed of?' Johnny said. 'That's your big secret? We all know about the speech. That old Shoshone couldn't have dealt a better blow if he'd jaw-flapped for a whole day.'

'No, brother. I'm ashamed of being ashamed of it. I'm pissed at myself for cutting off my past. God knows what's in this cactus junk but I'm feeling things I never felt before. Like maybe my old man's right after all.'

'Like the great philosopher once said, we are what we are and that's all what we are,' Johnny said.

'That's Popeye!' Mark said.

'Got him in one!'

The solemnity re-established itself, and Johnny shook the rattle. 'We're ready. We move on. Now we wait for our hearts to see.'

'What about you, Johnny?' asked Jay. 'What's your hang up?'

Johnny gave a lop-sided grin. 'You're the initiates here. I'm exempt.'

Johnny Rivas had good cause to be proud of himself that night as he lay in the dome tent listening to the snores of his two brothers. He had successfully carried the ceremony to its conclusion, and each initiate had ridden on the wings of dream to a place where they realised a deep, personal truth.

Next morning, they bathed in the rock-pool before breakfast, one last nod in the direction of ceremony, before breaking camp. At least, Jay and Johnny did. Mark used the excuse of his condition not to join them. In reality, he didn't want to risk embarrassment. After all, they knew about him now.

Later, Johnny and Mark waved Jay off as he pointed his car down the track and as Jay's arm rose out to wave back, his unbuttoned shirt-sleeve flapped in the wind. It hooked into Mark's mind and teased out an unanswered question.

'Johnny. You have on jeans, and a shirt and that old leather jacket. And it's Indian stuff. Jay's over there in jeans and a shirt and a leather jacket, and you say it's white man's clothes. How come?'

Johnny shook his head. 'Jay's wearing Indian clothes too.'

'But yesterday, you said . . .'

'That was yesterday. Different man in them clothes yesterday.'

Mark was on the verge on saying he didn't understand, when suddenly, he did. After all, there was a different man in his own clothes on this fine, new day. Mark understood perfectly.

But at least they were his own clothes. As the sun approached its zenith, Billy Ray Williams was gathering together a set of clothes, some old, some new - but all very unidentifiable. He aimed to be dressing Mark Walker in these clothes within the next day or two.

Mark knelt, his knees pinning down one end of the folded tent while Johnny rolled it up tight from the other end. So, he thought, Jay's a different man today. Mark was too. He felt powerful. He felt optimistic. He felt just happy to be himself – with one or two nagging reservations. Johnny rolled up his end of the tent until it met Mark's, and Mark squeezed out the last pockets of air before Johnny tied the whole thing into a roll and slipped the nylon cover over it.

'Kinda like putting a condom on an elephant.' Johnny said.

'Elephant-shmeliphant! Check me out next time we're in the showers!' Mark's mood dropped a level almost immediately. 'Except now you know what I am, you'd rather go shower with a bucket of pit-vipers.' He grinned unconvincingly and turned his attention to stowing the tent poles; one huge dent already dealt to his feelings of only moments before.

Johnny grabbed the same pole Mark picked up and held it firm. Mark didn't want to meet Johnny's eyes, but Johnny forced the issue taking Mark's chin in his hand and turning his head with a gentle firmness of a caring father.

'You think the things you said last night makes me think less of you?

Mark shrugged.

'You're wrong man. Here's what I think. I've had some good friends in my life, but until last night I never felt I had a brother.'

Without warning Mark threw his arms around Johnny, and Johnny returned the tight embrace.

'You okay, brother?' Johnny felt Mark's head nod against his shoulder. 'That's good, man. But, stick your tongue in my ear, and you're a dead brother!' Now Johnny felt the laughter rising in Mark, and he joined in.

They worked well together - a good team – and soon there was little trace of the camp or the sweathouse. Just a few ashes and a mysterious hole in the ground, already filling up with sand. As Johnny's sedan sailed out of camp, a jack-rabbit raised on its haunches to see them off.

The miles slipped by all too swiftly for Mark. He was going over the weekend's events in his head as the Wilbur's place came into view.

'One thing, Johnny. What's the story? Jay's Shoshone chief ancestor and the God damned potato?' Mark asked just before bailing out of Johnny's sedan into the Wilbur's yard.

'Kind of a legend with his people, how that old chief bested a bunch of white people intent on stealing the land. They wanted the Shoshone people to give up hunting and start planting stuff. Corn. Wheat. Potatoes an' all. They sent a passel of commissioners and soldiers, and they spent hours speechifying as to the advantages of growing crops. Then it was the chief's turn to reply. An' you know what he said.'

'I like that. A lot.'

'Yeah. It's cool. Tomorrow then, brother?'

'Yeah. See ya!'

Meanwhile at the station house, Sergeant Seven Elk was bent over the computer keyboard working on a hunch. He still had not told Special Agent Marshetta about the Wilbur connection even though the two men got on well together. Marshetta would rib Nathan about his round gut, and Nathan would retaliate with a comment about the agent's freaky hairstyle. Each made disparaging remarks about the parentage of the other.

Yes, they got on well – like brothers almost. But certain facts you kept to yourself. Facts that might hurt the two people who took you in as a kid and treated you like a son. Facts that might make them look like prime suspects, when you knew that was so much bull. He wanted to protect Hettie and Dan Wilbur, because he knew they were innocent of any crime. He also knew that Richard Marshetta would want to run them in for questioning – probably search their house, dig up the yard. He figured

Marshetta had enough cop in him to soon see the obvious, and let them both go. But they were getting on in years, and people say no smoke without fire. It would be a bad trip for two people who deserved better, and Nathan was doing his level best to make sure "better" is what they got.

Nathan's mind drifted back to the mountains again. This time he saw them through his own fourteen-year-old eyes, and the man guiding him was Dan. And it was all the proof he needed. If Dan got off on killing kids, Nathan knew he would have been bones these last twenty-six years.

Dan melted away in Nathan's mind to be replaced by the blood-stained and broken Stewie. Nathan's lip curled in an expression of hate for the monster who had killed him.

As those thoughts went through Nathan's head, the monster finished a bowl of cornflakes and placed the bowl in the dishwasher. Leaning over the kitchen sink, Harry Bixby saw the sun bouncing off the windshield of his old Cadillac – not so much 'bouncing' really, more like 'glancing'. All the fault of that damned pump-boy who wouldn't clean his windshield or sell him a piece of tail even though it was so damned obvious he was out for rent. Never mind, thought Harry. He'd learn. It would be his last lesson on earth, but would he learn it good!

Harry Bixby had a mission in life, given to him by God. The whys and the wherefores had all got kind of mixed up in his head, but he trusted in the Lord – and anyhow, he got a kick from the work. His mission was to rid the world of evil, and evil was found aplenty inside the scum-drifter-trailer-trash boys that seemed to fill the world. Now, Harry knew he couldn't rid the world of every one of them, but he at least could do his bit.

Hettie Wilbur would have called Harry a damaged soul who needed love and understanding to lead him from the brink. Harry knew most everyone else would agree what he really needed was an ounce of lead and a suitable means of delivering it into the centre of his brain – that's if they knew of his mission. But nobody did, except Jimmy and Billy Ray Williams and one or two other very trusted servants of The Church.

Yes, Hettie would try to help him, even if she knew how much Harry Bixby hated her. She and her stupid ox-head husband had dried up a ready supply of – shall we call them sacrificial offerings – when they'd steamed in and closed down The Church. "Crazy Cult Busters", the press had called them. They had only wanted to rescue one of their filthy brood. Nobody suspected murder, but The Church shrivelled and died in the light that was caste upon it. Unconstitutional. Quasi-religious conditioning. The Church was labelled thus, and much else – but nobody ever suspected the true mission of its acolytes.

Well, revenge is a dish best served cold, and it had taken Harry a long while to cool down. Now he was like an iceberg. Now his altar-boys all came to him by way of the Wilbur's – and he wasn't nearly so careful with the bodies. He did not want to make it too obvious, but he wanted them found. He wanted the Wilbur's to suffer.

Harry decided to check out his garage, except now it was known as The Temple. Hadn't been a car inside of it for eight years. Inside, it was dark. There were candle holders, some affixed to the walls, and some on the table where Harry had arranged various instruments of 'release'. At the heart of The Temple was the altar, and here Harry Bixby carried out the Lord's work in that special way he alone had been ordained to serve.

VII

Monday morning, early, and Mark stood in front of the bathroom mirror and looked at the reflection of his newly shaved face. He took a towel and mopped up the left-over foam that had avoided the razor but hiding in his long sideburns, then leaned forward to look deeply into his own eyes. He was looking for a difference on the outside that fitted the changes he felt within. And yes, maybe he did look more relaxed, more confident – happier. A little twinge of fear shot through him. He never felt at ease with happy. The little twisting worm of fear died as Dan shouted up the stairs, saying that breakfast was ready. Mark pulled his shirt on as he descended the stairs three at a time.

This time though, that little blighting fear was more premonition than pessimism, for by lunchtime, Mark's short experience of a life worth living was to be snatched away.

Bob called Mark into the office. Mark had a busy morning; must have shifted several hundred gallons of gas. Trucks, pick-ups, a convoy of four-by-fours driven by old guys with white hair and towing silver, bullet-shaped trailers. One little compact full of luggage and kids and the biggest Pink Panther ever stuffed with kapok.

Mark had fun with that Pink Panther, pulling it out the car and making like it was the Panther pumping the gas, much to the amusement of the six-year-old boy who was its Daddy. Made it dance, walk along the hood. The kid's dad gave him one healthy tip!

Mark figured Bob was going to tell him he could take an early lunch. As he walked in though, a knot twisted in his gut as soon as he saw Bob's face – and the guy who was standing next to him.

'Mr Bixby here claims you may have some of his property,' Bob said. Bixby stood behind a pace and sneered.

Almost resigned to the worst case scenario from bitter experience, Mark answered unconvincingly. 'I don't have anything that belongs to this guy.'

'Try looking in his jacket pocket. He was wearing his jacket when I saw him in my car.'

'That's not true,' Mark said. I've never have been in his car. Haven't even seen it since the first day I worked here.'

'That's gold-plated bullshit, Mr Forde,' Bixby yelled. 'I stopped off to put air in my tyres. Went to use the men's room and when I came back, this little shit was inside.'

'That's a lie!' from Mark, his anger beginning to bite.

'Now don't be insulting the customer's Mark. Mr Bixby's been a regular here for as long as I can remember. What possible reason could he have for . . .'

'Because he tried to hit on me is the reason, an' I told him "Screw you!"'

Bixby moved to take a swing at Mark, making a good act at appearing wronged and indignant. Bob caught hold of him and held him back. Mark squared up ready to defend himself.

'You watch your mouth, Mark! And you, Bixby. Hold back.' Bob was small, but his size hid a wiry strength. He shook Bixby until he dropped the attack. He pointed a warning finger at Mark, and he also eased up. 'Do you mind if I look in your coat, Mark?' he said, pointing to where it lay over a chair-back.

'Go right ahead, Mr Forde'.

313

And you've guessed it. Plumping out the inside pocket of Mark's jacket was a billfold full of twenties and fifties, and credit cards in the name of Bixby.'

'It's a God damned plant!' Mark protested, but quietly, knowing already what the upshot of all this would be.

Bob spoke quietly and looked on Mark with betrayed eyes. 'I'll call the Sheriff.'

Bixby shrugged as he took his wallet. 'Nah! I don't want to get the kid into too much trouble. Just sack the little sonofabitch. That'll be punishment enough.'

Bob nodded. 'I'll have to let you go, Mark.'

He did not bother protesting his innocence. After all, he was just a nobody, who thought he'd try a stab at life off the streets. He was next to worthless, and the last few weeks hadn't happened at all. He took his jacket and walked out.

Out onto the road. At least he hadn't forgotten the art of hitching. At home, the Wilburs were out. He packed quietly, left a scribbled note of thanks, pulled a loose-fitting wool hat on to ward off the cold of a night in the desert. And left. He didn't look back. It would have hurt too much.

Mid-afternoon found Mark on the desert road. Home territory. Mark knew roads, and if his sack was a little heavier than usual, his heart was heavier still. Five miles of undulating black tar stretched away behind him, separating him from the turn-off to the Wilbur's place. Twice that ahead to the nearest town. He covered the ground slowly all the while thinking of what he was leaving behind, and what he was returning to.

The further he walked, the more he wondered what was in store for him, and the more he realised that in his heart, he knew. Maybe tonight, maybe tomorrow – he'd be turning a trick. Some old John would be bumping and grinding into him, and he'd have to act like he was enjoying it. His stomach turned and he stopped, turning slowly to look back the way he'd come. Maybe if he went back – but no! He let his head fall and for the first time noticed he still had on his uniform shirt. When they find me on the road, they'll think I'm called Bob.

And they would find him on the road. He started walking again, straight down the centre-line, so it would be harder for a truck to miss him. Mark decided that when he flipped, and that would be anytime soon, he would stay in the middle of the road so he had the best chance of never waking up again.

Something about the road made him take a second look, away into the distance where the black tar merged with the horizon. It had to do with the skyline, and how it blended in with the mountains. The scene called out to a memory that wouldn't form properly in his head.

I just know that I've been here before, thought Mark, just one fucking time before. He dropped his bag and tried framing the horizon like an artist does, with his hands. Then he took out his pocket watch and using that old boy scout trick, used it and the position of the sun to work out which way was north. Snapping it shut, he put the watch away, now knowing where north was, for all the good it did. There's not one road looks like this one. Not exactly like this road. One kind of place. One of a kind. Like someone's face. Like a fucked up face. He walked a few more paces and froze as something moved in the brush. It was that old jack-rabbit. He knew it was the same one that had been out to get him and Johnny.

Mark howled like a wolf and the rabbit scooted. 'Where d'you think you're running, man?' he shouted to the bobbing scutt. 'We're stuck here together, you shit!'

Whoah, now, Marky. Let it all out, one last time. Here it comes. His body drained of energy. The downtime express was on its way. Mark half smiled as he knew he was going to hit that tar road dead in the middle. He'd wake up good and squashed and dead. He sat for a moment, taking in the clouds and the sky. He would be part of them soon. He sure had filled up on living. As he closed his eyes and gave up the fight, he knew this was final curtain.

Back at The Temple, Harry admired the altar, all his own design. He ran his fingers along the bar that ran across the slab, positioned so it would thrust the sacrifice's hips high. He checked the back-strap and the shoulder constraints. Checking his watch, he felt a shiver of anticipation run through him. Time to light the incense burner. Harry was wearing his robes – he felt all-powerful. Life and death were at his command. He was sure this afternoon was going to be special – and so that the moments would be captured for posterity – and for his own occasional entertainment – the video camera was ready on its tripod and pointing in the right direction.

And then he wondered. Could he trust those Williams boys? All they had to do was pick the kid up. He toyed with the idea of supervising them, rather enjoying the idea of being there during all the key stages; pick up, ceremony, sacrifice and relocating. Maybe he'd go for it, just this once.

Harry Bixby had done his homework. The boy would collapse. He'd just be walking along, then zammo! Lights out. They had been following at a distance, hovering like buzzards, and now it was time to swoop. Billy Ray brought the pick-up to a grinding halt twenty feet past Mark's sleeping body. Jimmy jumped out and ran the short distance back to him. 'I don' like this one bit, Jimmy. We just never do the pickin' up!'

'Look at him, Billy Ray. He ain't goin' to be giving us no hard time. Let's get him loaded. Get out here now, an' hep.'

Billy Ray stretched his neck, turtle-like, to see a little further over the horizon. 'No way. Jimmy Williams. There's a car coming.'

Jimmy checked the rise. Yes, there was a car coming. So what! Looked like a big black limousine. Jimmy couldn't have cared less as he hauled Mark up and over his shoulder. He threw Mark's dead-weight into the flatbed without even bothering to drop the tailgate. As he turned, it was only of mild interest to him that the car appeared to be pulling up.

Mark endured a little death. He floated in the dark without dreams or thoughts of any kind. It could have been an hour, it could have been a whole day. His mind slowly surfaced up through layer upon layer of cloying blackness until he became aware of his first conscious thought. He felt pressure at the base of his spine, across his upper back and tight in on his left shoulder. Maybe he'd been hit by a truck and he was all mushed up. In a moment or two, perhaps the pain would kick in. He felt disorientated and tried to remember where he was, but as he surfaced through another thermal, he knew that whatever had happened during downtime, he hadn't got himself killed.

He breathed deep, and caught the smell of something that ached for the associations that would attach it to a specific memory. Someone ran their fingers through his hair, and he felt the rise and fall of a chest closely in contact with his own. Then, absurdly all the clues tied themselves together. Mark felt that if he opened his eyes, he would be on Stephen's lap - in Portland, under a huge grey statue of an Indian boy sitting astride a stag with a full set of antlers, the plinth bearing the legend "The Coming of the White Man".

Mark knew it couldn't be true, so he kept his eyes shut enjoying the lie for just a little longer. Then Mark placed that smell. It was Stephen's favourite after-shave. Tears welled up behind his closed lids. His heart began to rally, and to lead an attack against all logical thought. Mark still kept his eyes tight shut while he ran a list of possibilities through his head. One: he was dead and gone to heaven, and for all his pain and suffering, God had made him an angel in the image of Stephen Fulton. Two: he'd finally flipped into cuckoo land. Three: he was still asleep and dreaming.

Then through it all came the sound of the voice he loved. 'Marky. Come on, man. Wake up Mark.'

Stephen Fulton cradled Mark across his lap in the back of a chauffeur-driven Lincoln. It had taken a while, but private investigator Rob Thacker always got his man, and Stephen had been on cloud nine when the call came in that he'd been traced. He knew, at last, he would see Mark again, but he had no idea the reunion would be so dramatic. Stephen's right hand still ached from the knock-out jab he'd dealt to the guy trying to load Mark onto a pick-up like he was a sack of potatoes. The other guy, in the driver's seat, just took off – obviously in no mood for fighting.

'Marky. Come on, wake up.' he called gently. Mark began to tremble. Then he opened his eyes and closed them again letting out something between a wail and a sigh. He started to breathe irregularly, and broke up when he tried to speak.

'This ... isn't ... happening, man. This for sure is not happening.'

'It's happening, Mark. Now get sat up.' Stephen helped him sit. Mark opened his eyes again, reached out and touched Stephen's face, and collapsed onto his shoulder as uncontrollable sobs erupted from deep inside. He cried like a kid for his mother. He cried for lost times. He cried up all the evil all the slights, all the bad trips, all the ill-usage and pain that had been his lot for most of his life. And all the time Stephen held him.

Joe Parsons kept his eyes on the road – mostly. His eyes did stray, maybe a couple of times, to the scene playing out on the back seat. He didn't have much time for queers, but what he saw in the mirror felt kind of right. Like two brothers – more than brothers – parted long ago, meeting up again for the first time in a decade. He decided there and then, he didn't have much against queers either.

Eventually the crying stopped, and Mark sat up straight throwing Stephen's arm off with some force. Stephen was puzzled.

'So, how are you Mark?'

'What the fuck do you care?'

Stephen recoiled, like he'd been slapped. 'I care, man. I'm here. I came for you.'

Mark looked out at the passing desert. 'You came for me?'

'Sure.'

'Great! The magnificent Stephen Fulton came for poor little Marky Walker. Put a fucking collar on me, why don't you? So, when you gonna leave me at the dog pound again? Tomorrow? Next week?'

Ste shook his head, confused and saddened. 'Never, Mark. Never.'

'Hell you say, never! You have decided, for whatever reason, that you, the great Stephen Fulton, needs me, the low-life Mark Walker. As it is written and so it shall be!'

Stephen swallowed hard. 'It's not like that Mark. I missed you. Look!' he said, chucking a thumb over his back. 'I went and grew wings for you.' He found it hard to countenance Mark's cold stare. 'I'm gay, Mark. All that stuff I used to say. I thought it was true, but I was kidding myself. I'm like you.'

'Bullshit! There's no such thing as gay. Or straight.'

Stephen's preconception of how this would all go was wildly off kilter, and he was stuck for a direction. 'I don't buy that. When I at last admitted to myself, what I was, I felt good. It made sense of all the problems in my life. I missed you so much. You can't say there's no such thing.'

'Is that so? Well, I can, see! I had a vision. I'm not straight or gay – or even bi before you can chuck that one at me. I'm Mark Walker, I am a man, and I can fall in love with people. Same as every last person on the whole planet. They all don't know though, so they let themselves stay in their little box and they're never free.'

'No, it's not true. I do not accept that.'

'Stay in your box then.'

'You're saying we're all the same? What about those guys who hate us so much they beat up on us – even kill us.'

'They're trying to beat it out of themselves. They're killing on the outside what they themselves have on the inside, but they are so fucked up they won't even look in that direction. I'm telling you. I know what I'm talking about.'

'I'm ...'

'You are Stephen Fulton, and you're in love with you. Stephen wants it, Stephen gets it. Well, fuck you! I love you, but I don't trust you and I'm not going to let you do to me what you did before.'

Now it was Stephen's turn. Stephen had not shed a single tear since he was twelve years old. Mark reached out and caught one on his finger tip. Rubbing it between finger and thumb, he felt on the verge of comforting his old friend. He swayed on the edge for a while, but having once before experienced the fall, he stepped back. 'Best get your man to stop the car. Drop me here. I'm used to long lonely roads.'

Stephen cried silently turning his face away. Mark would not be diverted from his course. 'Hey, man!' he shouted to Joe Parsons. 'Stop the car. I'm getting out.'

'No.' Stephen said quietly, unsteadily. 'Please. You hear me out first.'

It was some speech that Stephen laid out for Mark. Covered just about his whole life, but heavily loaded in all those areas that involved Mark. He spoke of his unhappiness after taking up his inheritance, of how every day his thoughts would turn to Mark, and how he'd force those thoughts down. He spoke of his shame for the times he'd cut Mark – outside that Portland restaurant, at Bob Crow's funeral – at the empty life he was leading. He was thorough, eloquent, and if a word or two of Shakespeare crept in it was because those words ran through Stephen's blood and not from a deliberate sense of the dramatic. Mark paid the closest of attention to each word and he could see that Stephen meant every one.

From his first word to his last, Joe Parsons covered forty-two miles, and Joe wasn't a man prone to speeding. Stephen completed his monologue with another declaration of his love, another promise that he would never deal Mark so cruelly ever again. The two men held one another's gaze in the silent moments that followed. Mark could see in Stephen a vulnerability never before apparent. Stephen saw in Mark a strength he'd never suspected.

Stephen took in a full, quivering lung-load and let it out. 'That was one hell of a long speech, Mark. I guess it's your turn.'

The corners of Mark's mouth turned up into that embryo of a smile that Stephen remembered and loved. 'God – damn a potato!' he said, and began to chuckle. Stephen didn't know what the hell he meant, but he started to chuckle too.

Joe saw the two young men in his mirror and heard their laughter build. Usually a paragon of driving precision, he let one hand drop from the wheel and punched the air. 'All right!' he said, and then he too joined in with their laughter.

Like three ships at anchor in a friendly port, Nathan's cruiser, Johnny's sedan and Dan's pick-up formed up line abreast outside the Wilbur's porch.

Inside, Hettie, and the captains of all those vessels sat around the kitchen table. Dan had the album opened in front of him, and Nathan leaned over to get a better look. It was opened at the photo of the Indian boy. 'Good looking kid, weren't I?'

Johnny nodded. 'Looking at you then, and now, makes me feel I should give up chocolate.'

Dan turned a few pages until he found the one with Vinnie and Stewie. Dan let out a big sigh. 'I wonder where that Bixby bastard would have stopped. Would he have gone for Mark next? Or you, maybe?'

'Reckon I'm too old and fat for his tastes,' Nathan said. 'Anyway, he'd planned all this real careful over the years.

Get off on killing young guys and build up one hell of a case against you into the bargain.'

Hettie shivered. 'And all because we rescued a child from an evil cult, so many years ago.'

'That was just his excuse, Hettie. He'd have found another, and likely the same victims.'

They all returned their attention to the album. 'We never did get one of Mark,' Dan said. 'Do you think he'll be okay?'

'Sure I do,' Nathan said. 'I got Lee looking for him and the Troopers are helping. And Bob Forde is out searching with all his family. He says he feels kind of responsible, taking Bixby's word about the theft like he did.'

'How d'you nail the – excuse me Hettie – the shit?' Johnny asked.

Nathan explained, the only fact that linked the dead boys, apart from them being brought (at least part of the way) up by the Wilburs, was that they had all worked for Bob Forde. He eliminated Bob from the enquiry early on, and started to work on the regular customers.

It had been the right track, but in the end, the solution came by chance. Billy Ray came storming into the station house claiming some young dude had upped on out of a big black Lincoln and killed his brother with a single punch. Nathan put Billy Ray in the cruiser and drove out to the location, during which time Billy Ray made a lot of unguarded comments.

It did not take a Columbo to form a suspicion and trip him up with questions about the murdered young men. Before long he was singing like a bird in between crying like a baby. Jimmy was of course, not dead. He did however, have a broken jaw. Nathan handed it all over to Agent Marshetta, and the truth came tumbling out.

Hettie spoke after another pause during which time everyone took it in turn to shake their head solemnly, or to suck in a care-laden breath. 'You know, it's like I said once before. We all die, and death is rarely pleasant. When it's murder, it appears to many that the death has blighted the life.' She looked at the others and felt that she wasn't getting through. 'Imagine the worst death possible, oh I don't know. Maybe, to be dragged to a lonely place, crucified on a barbed-wire fence and tortured and battered with hammers. Then left in the cold for days to slowly die.'

'You sure have got an evil imagination, hun.' said Dan.

'Well yes, it is about as horrible as you can get. But as wicked and as horrible as it is, it doesn't take one iota from the life that went before. We should remember people for the way they lived. That's how I'm going to cope with Vinnie, Stewie and Juan.'

'I know just what you mean, Hettie,' Johnny said. 'I knew a guy, he killed himself trying to lose something in drugs. People said another junky dead, big deal. But I knew him. Toby was a beautiful person. The way he died doesn't matter a f ... . Doesn't matter at all, unless it serves to warn other people like him.'

The smooth purr of an auto-engine growing from a whisper, and the popping of grit under tyres went almost unnoticed. But at the sound of the doors slamming Dan asked Hettie if they were expecting visitors. Apparently they were not.

There was no knock. The door swung in and there stood Mark. Mark and another guy maybe a year or two older and looking remarkably like Johnny. Mark and the other guy were standing close, and Johnny noticed something in the way the backs of their hands touched.

324

It seemed everybody at once greeted Mark and bid him come in. Then Johnny stepped forward and extended his hand towards the stranger. 'I reckon you must be Ste.' he said as they shook. He saw Nathan approaching from the corner of his eye. 'You Kiowa too?' said Johnny. Stephen couldn't help but notice Johnny's big theatrical wink, and cottoning on quick he confirmed that he was indeed of the Kiowa tribe.

Nathan leaned over and whispered into Johnny's ear. 'You think I floated down the Snake River on a pancake, don't ya? Him an' Mark's got as much Kiowa in 'em as I've got Chinaman.' Nathan turned on Stephen and they shook hands. 'Got an eye for faces, Stephen. We've met before.' Nathan tried to get a fix on the time and the place.

'Yes, me too,' Stephen answered, remembering both. 'You turned a motorcycle for me once. Out in the desert.'

The penny dropped, and he snapped his fingers. 'Got it! And there was this other guy, didn't like cops, who ran head-long and hid in the brush.'

Stephen chucked his eyes towards Mark. And for Nathan, a second penny slid down the ramp. 'That was Mark?'

'Yes, it was.'

'That'll be two more for dinner, Hettie,' Dan called.

Mark held up a hand, then disappeared outside. He darted back in, to be followed by yet another stranger, this one wearing a grey uniform. 'This here's Joe.' Mark said.

'I, er, drive,' Joe said.

'That's three more for dinner,' Dan said.

Later, around the dinner table, Mark sat back and took himself out of the loop, so he could see it all as an observer. He looked at the faces about him, all glad to see him, all glad to be with each other. Big Dan, his laughter loud and unbridled and his turn of phrase as salty as ever. Nathan, quiet unassuming but still a powerful part of this family. Johnny, the life-saver, passing food, and sharing jokes. Hettie, who was undoubtedly the source of all this, or at least the main channel for the source.

Sharing sorrow too, but ultimately each one caring about each of the others. Even Joe the driver slid right into the space made for him as snug as you like. And each time Mark turned his head and caught a glimpse of Ste across the table, Ste would be looking at him and smiling with his eyes.

This had to be pretty near the happy ending. Turn up the soundtrack. Fade to black.

And that, as they say, is that. But what about after 'run credits'? What about those little inset pictures of the main players with a sentence or two telling you how they wound up ten years after the film ended? Did Johnny marry Kate? Did Sergeant Seven-Elks make Captain for busting the sorry ass of that murdering nut Bixby? Did Jay get his geology degree and land a job with a big oil company? Did me and Ste move to England and take up carpentry? Did we live happily ever after? Does anyone?

Well, it's not over, is it? Me and him are still together. He's still queer and won't be persuaded there's no such thing. I'm still Mark Walker and I can love people. Happens I love Stephen Fulton. Sometimes things aren't so great. Sometimes they are. Plans work out. Or they bomb. Sun shines. Or it pisses a river. Whatever. Whenever.

But more often than not, we manage to have a nice day.

Acknowledgements
For Tallahatchie Timebomb

In chronological order: thanks to Bobbie Gentry: her song *Ode to Billie Joe* provided me with the puzzle of the missing back-story and the impetus for this book. Thanks to Herman Raucher for his film, *Ode to Billy Joe*, for his book of the same name but mostly for his time and for the generous advice that sent this story in a completely different, and I believe better, direction. Thanks to Robby Benson for providing the image of Billy Joe that stayed with me throughout the writing process. Finally thanks to Lewis Nordan: his writing has opened this English boy's ears to the music of the swamp.

~o~

Sadly, since the above acknowledgements were first penned, we have lost Lewis Nordan, who passed away 13th April 2012.

We have not lost his words:-

- Welcome to the Arrow-Catcher Fair (1983)
- The All-Girl Football Team (1986)
- Music of the Swamp (1991)
- Wolf Whistle (1993)
- The Sharpshooter Blues (1995)
- Lightning Song (1997)
- Boy With Loaded Gun (2000)

www.ingramcontent.com/pod-product-compliance
Lightning Source LLC
Chambersburg PA
CBHW062027170626
46813CB00001B/322

* 9 7 8 0 9 9 2 9 0 4 5 8 6 *